MESSENGERS OF ILBEOR

LEGENDS OF ILBEOR
BOOK ONE

T.J. KLAPPRODT

This book is a work of fiction. Names, characters, businesses, events, and incidents are the products of the author's imagination. Any resemblance to actual persons, living or dead, or actual events is purely coincidental.

Copyright 2024 T.J. Klapprodt

All rights reserved. No part of this book may be reproduced or used in any manner without the prior written permission of the copyright owner, except for the use of brief quotations in a book review.

To request permissions, contact the author at tj@tjklapprodt.com

Hardcover: 979-8-9898905-2-1
Paperback: 979-8-9898905-0-7
eBook: 979-8-9898905-1-4

First Edition: February 2024

Edited by Alan M. Rogers
Cover Art by GetCovers.com

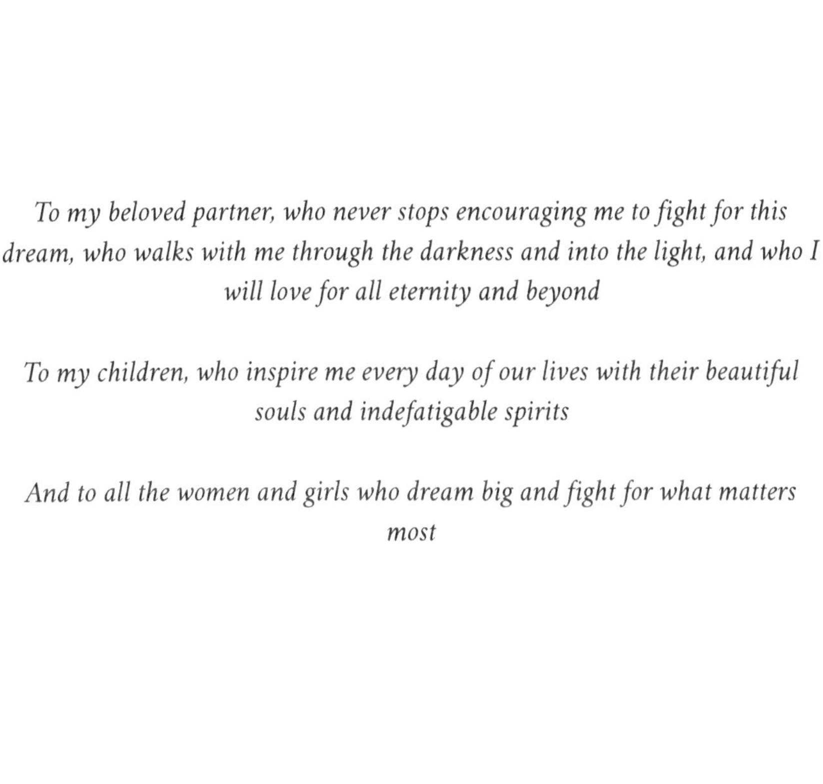

To my beloved partner, who never stops encouraging me to fight for this dream, who walks with me through the darkness and into the light, and who I will love for all eternity and beyond

To my children, who inspire me every day of our lives with their beautiful souls and indefatigable spirits

And to all the women and girls who dream big and fight for what matters most

PROLOGUE

*S*ounds of distant, soft thunder echoed in her head, and she stared down at him. Her soft gaze, that of a sated bedfellow, belied the utter contempt in which she held him; she would not let him see how she felt. Her breathing, practiced and almost as natural as a land-bound being, punctuated the otherwise silent room in time to the rumbles of the thunder, her white-clad breast rising and falling as she stood.

He gazed up at her from the silken blankets of the rich feather mattress, his dark eyes pools of desire and repletion, soft and almond-shaped in his preternaturally pale face. His long hair, a darker black than his eyes and without a hint of aged color despite the millennia since his birth, spread out in a smooth fan across the cushions.

She wanted to sneer, but as her mind encompassed the possibilities and guarantees of the moment, she was reminded that letting him see the lovely face of her chosen form marred with such an expression would endanger her plans. She had toiled too arduously to let her effort be wasted by impropriety of expression. Her face remained smooth in its apparent adoration of him.

A soft whistle sounded, whispering across the vast reaches of her consciousness. The language of the elves, indecipherable to any unfamiliar with it, reminded her who she was impersonating, who she was supposed to be. It warned her against any movement that would reveal her true nature, any sound that would belie the form she had taken. The creature, soon to be formed into the puppet she needed, smiled up at her in satisfaction. A hint of his desire for her touched his expression, but the shudder of distaste flitting through her mind did not show itself.

Rwisa kyamando eki bnabra kai.

The words, an echo of the language of the last land-bound form she had taken, took her by surprise as they entered her mind. She could not deny the truth of them; to reveal herself to him would be to leave him whole. She had no use for him as a whole being, for only broken and bound to her would he be pliant to the purpose she intended.

Still unmoving and standing at the foot of the bed they had so recently shared, she studied the sharp planes of his chiseled face, unlined by the long expanse of his existence, smooth of any wrinkles and untouched by the rays of the sun. He was not attractive to her; of all the land-bounds she took possession of, elves were least appealing. Their bodies, lithe and tall and untouched by time, spoke to her of a lack of the change she craved. Though not timeless as she, their nearly unbreakable immortality irritated her; land-bounds were meant to be disposed of when their usefulness had abated. Elves were only a reminder of her brother's power, of the immutable song of his creation, of the stability she wanted so badly to upset.

L'ulmi paxiam aqaes.

Certainty rolled through her in waves as the result of the long game she had played with this being came to fruition. This one was more powerful than almost all other land-bounds; this one was driven by a grief and rage even deeper than she had intended when she had ended the lives of his partner, his family, and his friends nearly two hundred years before. This one had the potential to create the upset she needed.

Balance. This one could bring the balance to the world that had been missing since its creation; this one could create change beyond petty chaos, beyond wanton destruction. This one, sculpted by her talented hands and driven by her rage and hatred of all that was claimed by the Nine, could be the last one.

She smiled grimly, and she only caught the barest hint of his confusion at her change of expression before she blinked slowly at him, and he fell into a deep, unassailable sleep.

FREED from the need to guard her countenance while he slept, she allowed the fleshly form she had taken to relax into the cold, inexorable irritation she felt at having to achieve her purposes by manipulating the land-bound rather than acting directly upon the lands herself. She looked away from him in disgust, taking in the room she had carefully appointed.

Designed with every comfort and luxury the elf could have ever dreamed of, the room was situated in a small castle she had shaped from the rock of the Gray Hills. Created expressly for seducing her conquests, the castle was changed every time she chose a new land-bound, furnished with the adornments desired by her victim. Fulfilling desires was an important part of making them pliant and moldable; land-bounds were nearly always motivated by comfort and wish-fulfillment.

The bed, as soft as any in the land and richly laid with silken linens and thick furs, stood large in the middle of the stone room. Tapestries of the past works and triumphs of the elves lined the walls, bringing extravagant color into the room with their threads of reds and blues, golds and greens, brilliant whites, and darkest blacks. Though unused, the gleam of the highly polished and intricately carved wooden tables and chairs added an air of wealth, making it seem the living area of the greatest lord of the land.

The lamps were the most significant decor, for they would aid her in achieving her desire. Light was the greatest agent of binding she had, a tool whose use had only been touched in the smallest of increments by even the most powerful land-bound magicians. Her lamps gleamed beautifully, even to her eyes. Sculpted in silver accented by gold, light was encased in smooth glass globes decorated with dazzling dwarven gemstones.

Arim.

The single word floated into her consciousness on flapping wings like a large, hunting bird, insistent, breaking through the stormy background of her subliminal thoughts. The word, a form of an ancient language that had changed over centuries of rough use by inarticulate humans, reminded her that immediacy was vital. It was time to begin the change in the creature before her; it was time to bind him to her. When he woke, even his rich surroundings would fade from his mind compared to the longing she would place in him.

She did not have to raise her hands or even turn her head; she did not have to make use of the lilting, genteel voice she had adopted as part of the form she inhabited. All she had to do was move her eyes to the first of the lamps, and the work was begun.

At her silent command, light flowed smoothly through the glass globes, changing colors as it broke the physical boundaries encompassing it. Bright purples, blues, reds, golds, greens, and pinks streaked towards the inert creature on the bed, at first bathing him in their rays and then surrounding him with light, swaddling his body until he lay in a rainbow cocoon. Pulsing, the light entered him until his very skin seemed to glow.

She raised one pale-skinned hand, gesturing with one finger as though summoning him to come to her and then opening her palm. He did not see the gesture, of course, but the lights obeyed the summons, sending a cord of each color to her outstretched hand. When all the cords had reached her, she closed her hand, slowly turning her fist until she held them as she would the reigns of a stallion. The warmth of the thousand suns she had touched suffused her, and she drank in the power of it, drank in the million flavors of warmth and sunlight and fiery destruction they held.

The thunder crashed in her mind as she was filled with the power that only came from complete possession of the object of her desires. The creature on the bed, the powerful elf she had selected and carefully molded to meet her every need, lay still as she infused her will into his very being, ensuring that when he woke nothing would be as important to him as obeying even her unspoken commands.

Meahn.

She knew he was hers before the light began to fade; she could feel his will melding with hers, could feel the bonds she was forming take shape in the very fiber of the world. The pulsing lights dulled, his skin dulling with them, as she drank in the sovereignty of the control she was taking of him, drank in the mastery of his free will, the desecration of the most sacred of her brother's edicts over the land-bound beings he had created and brought into the land.

The light faded completely, not returning to the lamps but disappearing into the inky darkness of the moonless night, and she lowered her arm. Carefully setting her face into the loving expression she had worn before, she glided to the side of the bed nearest his face, still in its repose.

Bending over him, she tenderly brushed the smooth black hair from the side of his face and began to whisper in his ear.

PART I

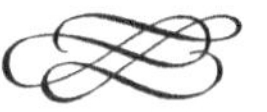

FROM THE PROPHECY OF BEIANARIAN AND THE MAGUS

From distant realms in waning summer heat
Born of purest snow in midnight's embrace
Cloaked with a child's ambition, a woman
Seeking destined fate on new roads from home,
Ignited by the very fires of day
Falls low and tastes the permanence of death.
Raised up by hands foreign with life's pure touch
Magic suffuses, quenching the deadly fire.

Giv'n the bounty of magic not her own
She thrives, thrumming with the life of the stars
And the light of the brightest day gleaming
Though she knows not from whence it came to her.
Speaking in tongues fluent with foreign song
She becomes one with those who lent her aid
And is known to the walker of knowledge
For the one she will become yet is not.

Tracing a path from magic to heartache
Footsteps fall to songs of wakened longing.

Harbor found in the gaze of the stranger
Sunlight and moon blaze with long fated dreams.

from The Prophecy of Beianarian and the Magus
set forth by Algernon of House Agelon
Second Age, 246

MESSENGER

Uht, the time between the first lightening of the sky in the morning and the glorious colors of the sunrise, sat upon the small house in the valley, placid and still. The late summer sky, cloudless and clear, held promises of a beautiful day. The human family inside the house took little notice of it other than to anxiously watch for the coming of the first rays of color that would signify the true dawning of the day.

Alanda had been ready to leave since the night before; her pack, large enough to dwarf her slight form but well-balanced and carefully arranged, sat propped against the front wall, seeming to call to her. *Uht* was the time of departure for those in traveling professions; no daylight could afford to be wasted in the busy lives of the working villagers. As a messenger about to embark on her first solo journey after her apprenticeship, Alanda was keenly aware of the passage of time and eager to leave the confines of her home and set out across the valley.

She waited only for her father, Jondolan. She had not expected him to see her off; he had spent the previous evening at the inn, and he did not prefer to wake at *uht* after such excursions. He had surprised her by being at the table with her mother when she emerged from the sleeping room. He had smiled broadly at her with clear and excited eyes before asking her to wait and hurrying through the house's only door, she knew she would obey even if it meant a late start.

Alanda's mother, Dandelion, carefully braided her own long, golden hair, working through touch. After Jondolan had left the house, she had bustled about preparing Alanda a hot breakfast of porridge laced with honey, a treat usually reserved for Celebration days. Now, breakfast eaten, and the small bowls scoured with sand and water, she waited with Alanda, smiling at her daughter's anxious foot-tapping and entreating her to be patient.

"What will happen if the sun rises, and you're not gone yet?" Kitz, Alanda's younger brother, was nearing the age of apprenticeship and was acutely aware of Alanda's responsibilities. He watched the window, certain there would be dire consequences if his sister did not leave the house before the sun rose.

Alanda smiled despite her own impatience. "Nothing really." She reached over to rustle his hair fondly. "Now that I'm traveling alone, no one else will be inconvenienced or concerned with when I set out, though I do hope Papa hurries back. I need all the daylight I can get to make the journey to Basendale in two days."

"You don't travel alone," Kitz reminded her.

"Well, no." Alanda leaned to her left side to scratch her dog behind the ears. "But Alis doesn't concern herself with time until we stop for the evening and have our dinner."

Alis, a medium-sized fluffy white dog, perked up and pawed at the floor, seeming to notice Alanda's eagerness.

"Calm, Alis," Alanda said automatically, her voice carrying the sure sound of her authority but with no hint of reproof. She and Alis had been paired when she began her apprenticeship at thirteen and Alis had been a newly weaned puppy, and they had learned the job together over three years. Alanda stopped her own foot from tapping as she realized the dog was reacting to her movements, and she looked at her mother. "Where *is* Papa?"

"I believe he had something to finish in his workshop this morning," Dandelion replied, her voice melodic and sweet. "Patience, daughter. He doesn't want to miss seeing you off on your first journey, and I'm sure he won't be much longer."

The leatherworking shop where Jondolan spent his days was a short distance from the house, half a mile to the east. Its placement outside the confines of the village of Blackwell was hardly surprising, given the stink of the tannery next to it. Alanda often wondered why they had to live so close. She knew they had once lived in the village in a larger middie dwelling just outside the village square, but she could not remember it. They had moved to the poor dwelling on the outskirts north of the village when she was little more than a baby.

The front door opened and Jondolan came in, his hands full of a stained, unworked leather burden. Alanda wondered what it could be; her father rarely brought his work into the house. He strode to Alanda's seat at the table, his long legs making the journey in just four steps, and held the bundle out to her. "For you," he said, his voice serious but laced with an emotion she couldn't identify.

"For me?" Alanda asked in surprise. She could only remember her father giving her a gift on one other occasion; her family could rarely afford gifts for one another, even during Celebrations.

"Open it!" Kitz said excitedly, getting up from his place on the sanded wooden floor to stand next to his sister.

Alanda untied the leather bundle. When the wrapping fell open, she wasn't sure what she was seeing at first. The folded black leather looked like nothing she had ever seen before. Setting the package on the table, she lifted the topmost item to reveal a black leather jerkin held together by tight, small stitches and leather lacing running up the front. Alanda gasped; she knew the jerkin must be for her, but she could not imagine where her father had found the time or coin to make it for her.

Under the jerkin, a pair of black leather pants, a black linen shirt, and a pair of traveling gloves lay similarly folded atop a brand-new pair of black leather boots. Alanda's eyes filled with tears. "Papa... how?"

"I've been working with Theldan for weeks," Jondolan told her proudly. "I worked on it in the evenings when I might normally have gone to the inn; I had my ale while I worked. I thought you might like it to protect you from the sun."

The sun was a particular danger to Alanda, who had a sensitivity to it no one in the village could explain. Her skin, preternaturally pale and matching her white-blonde hair, was almost translucent and entirely without color. Even short exposures to sunlight could cause dangerous burns and illness. After Alanda had almost died as a toddler because of her condition, her parents and the healer had concluded that she must be covered at all times when out of doors in daylight, and she used a sun salve created by Deena, the village healer, on all parts of her skin that couldn't be covered with clothing.

"Go put it on," Dandelion urged. "You'll want to hurry. The sun will rise before much longer!"

Alanda, not knowing what to say to her father for the magnificent gift, gathered the black leathers and linen shirt and hurried into the sleeping room, drawing the wool curtain closed over the doorway for privacy. In the semi-darkness of the room, which only had one small, glassless window, she replaced her worn linen clothing with the black leathers, drawing the laces tight on the pants, shirt, and jerkin before pulling on the sturdy boots. The leather was smooth, soft, and fine, the kind usually reserved for the wealthiest of the village folk or even the nobles living in the castle on the hill above Blackwell.

How could Papa afford something like this?

Jondolan, though a kind and caring father and husband, spent many of his evenings and most of his money at the Seaside Inn, drinking until the innkeeper sent him home, usually stumbling drunk. It was only through the industry of Alanda's mother, who made perfumed soaps and oils and did exquisite needlework, that the family survived at all. A gift like this was unheard of and overwhelming.

Alanda knew she couldn't question her father about the leathers; he was proud of what he had given her, and she wouldn't spoil it. She drew the curtain back and stepped back into the main room, noting that she didn't feel even a hint of the early morning chill as she had in her linens.

Her mother, her father, and Kitz all grinned at the sight of her. "You look wonderful!" Dandelion cried. "And that will certainly protect you from the sun."

Alanda crossed to her father. "Thank you, Papa," she said softly, rising on tiptoe to kiss his cheek. "It's beautiful."

As she grabbed her pack, Alanda noticed Kitz picking at a loose thread in his dark green tunic. It was too big for him, as were his pants, and he was barefoot. His clothes, like most of what the family wore, had been donated by middies in the village. She knew he was happy for her, but she also knew he must have felt at least slightly envious. She promised herself that once she had made some money she would buy new linen and make him an outfit that fit properly.

"The sky's changing," Kitz said, not noticing his sister's expression.

"Right." Alanda hefted her pack, securing it on her back. "I'm going to Basendale and then to Kilynelle in the mountains; it'll likely be nearly a month before I come back." She tied her worn linen headscarf securely under her chin so it covered her head and neck.

"We know," Dandelion said with a small laugh. "Go! And travel well."

"See you soon!" Alanda clicked her fingers at Alis. "Heel, Alis," she said, and the dog happily trotted to her left side and followed her out the door.

As THE SUN ROSE, turning the wide valley sky first into a burst of pink and orange in the east and then to the vibrant, cloudless blue of late summer, Alanda traveled happily along the southern valley road with Alis. The journey between Blackwell and Basendale, its closest neighbor, was well-traveled and safe. The road, a dirt track long bereft of traces of the high valley grass, stretched out in a long, unbroken line before her, completely deserted. Alanda knew she was likely to see others on the road during her journey, but for the moment, she rejoiced in the solitude.

Padding beside her, her footfalls creating a familiar rhythm that both soothed and invigorated Alanda, Alis kept her pace even and her path straight even as her head swerved back and forth, looking for wildlife in the surrounding grasses. About knee high to most adults, the valley grass was home to many small animals and some larger ones, and though she had been trained not to give chase, Alis still enjoyed watching them and searching for their scents.

"It's quiet this morning," Alanda commented, once again touching her brown leather message bag as she walked at a steady pace. Though she had performed messenger duties as an apprentice for three years, she felt very aware of the importance of her journey. No longer did she have Alicia, her trainer, to make corrections and remind her of her duty; no longer did she have the lighter responsibility of an apprentice. The messages she carried were now hers alone, and she was responsible for bringing them safely to their recipients. Though she did not know what the messages contained, she knew the people who used messengers depended on their speed and reliability.

Alis barked once in reply, seeming to agree with her. Just then, two small rabbits hopped onto the road from their left, stood on their hind legs to look at Alanda and Alis, and then bounced back into the grasses. "You're safe," Alanda called after them, laughing as she continued her steady pace along the road. "We're not hungry right now!"

Alanda and Alis traveled through the day, only once seeing another human, a farmer with a cart heading back to Blackwell after selling some of his summer harvest to the northern villages. They greeted one another politely and exchanged what news there was, though there wasn't much to tell. They only stopped briefly to drink from a stream that gurgled to the right of the road for a few miles and to eat a meager lunch of cheese, berries, and bread.

Alanda knew exactly when to stop; she measured the sun's distance from the mountainous horizon with two fingers and immediately veered off the road to find a place to camp. Though she had her short bow and arrows, she decided not to hunt that night. She had been well provisioned by her mother, and she would reach Basendale in only another day.

Knowing the area, Alanda walked perhaps a mile to the west of the road to the banks of the Innislin River, a quiet, meandering waterway running from Nipadern Lake to the north all the way to the Pasling Sea, many miles south of Blackwell. She could bathe in the warm summer afternoon, and she and Alis would have plenty of water.

Alanda enjoyed her bath, using a small chunk of scented soap left over from one of her mother's orders. She enjoyed being clean, and one of her favorite parts about summer travel was warm enough weather to bathe nearly every night.

After she had dried and redressed, she set about taking food for dinner out of her pack: several strips of dried meat, a cake of hard-tack, and a lump of cheese from the general store in Blackwell. Paired with water from the clear, cool Innislin, she felt it was a good meal for their first night alone in the valley, and Alis seemed to agree, snapping up her portion with alacrity.

When she had put away their dinner things, she called Alis to her in the dimming light of early evening for her nightly combing. With her long fur, Alis picked up debris easily, though there had been little to pick up on the road. Still, Alanda combed her until her fur was silky smooth, petting her softly for a while after she was finished.

Since she had opted against a campfire, Alanda had little time for her evening hobby before it grew dark. Customary among messengers and some of the other traveling professions, the evening hobby was how they occupied themselves between stopping their work for the day and when they went to sleep. Alanda pulled out a small whittling knife, the only other gift she had ever received from her father, and took a piece of soft, lightly colored wood from her pack. With what light she had left, Alanda hummed to herself and Alis and drew the knife across the wood with practiced strokes; she was making a gift for Kitz's upcoming thirteenth birth celebration. The carving of a small dragon would be the first gift she had ever been able to give him, and she wanted to get it just right.

Working from the pictures of dragons she had seen in the town hall, fanciful things full of color and nearly all breathing fire, she carefully worked the wood, crafting the points of expanded wings before the fading light meant she had to stop. In the nearly silent expanse of the sleeping valley with only Alis for company, Alanda laid out her sleeping blanket and fell asleep, her hand on Alis as the dog curled up next to her.

~

AFTER TRAVELING STEADILY throughout the next day, Alanda camped just outside the outskirts of Basendale, as she had been taught to do if she neared a destination at the end of working hours. Eager to deliver her first messages, she slept more lightly than usual and woke before Alis whined with the coming of *uht*. Packing up, she drank from her waterskin and ate the last of her hardtack to break her fast; she would have to provision herself with her earnings for the journey to Kilynelle.

Soon after sunrise, Alanda, her pack secure on her back and her message bag across her chest, walked at a slightly faster pace than usual into the village square of Basendale. Knowing she was still early for delivering her messages to the recipients' places of business, she took some time to acquaint herself with the town. Though she had been there several times during her apprenticeship, she wanted to make certain she knew where to go.

Like Blackwell, Basendale was centered on a village square. Surrounding a large, empty area with a large oak tree and a boulder that had probably been there since time forgotten were several faded wooden buildings. Alanda saw the general store, the bakery, the butcher's shop, and a small store boasting various colors of linen along with several finished dresses in styles for well-to-do middie wives. Across from the shops was the village hall, and on the north end stood Basendale's sanctum.

Aware that she was not alone in the center of Basendale, Alanda decided it was time enough to deliver her messages. She approached the bakery first, riffling through her message bag until she found the message addressed to Herve, the town baker.

Despite the obvious nature of her business, the heavyset, balding man did not look happy to see her, glancing up from a ball of dough he was kneading on his wooden countertop to scowl as she came through the door. Alanda, having never met him before, carefully kept her face neutral as she stood straight in the doorway, her head slightly raised and her arms outstretched. The tradition signaled vulnerability and the lack of weapons when entering another person's dwelling, but most people simply did it by habit.

Herve grunted as she dropped her arms and stepped into his shop. "Message?" he asked gruffly. "Who's it from, eh?"

His cinnamon skin was flecked with flour from the dough he was working, but he didn't seem to notice as he continued with his work.

"Renfred in Blackwell," Alanda answered promptly, her voice calm and businesslike as she named the baker in her home village.

"What's he want?"

"I'm sure I don't know, sir," Alanda said, stepping forward to hand Herve the message.

"Wait," he said, his voice nearly a growl. Giving the dough on the counter a final thump, he turned his back on her and washed his hands in the basin of water behind him. She noticed he took his time and dried them thoroughly with a rough cloth.

"Barnaby!" he shouted suddenly, making Alanda jump. "Get that first run in the oven and be quick. I haven't got all day to wait for you."

A muffled voice from the back room shouted back that it was already in, and Herve finally turned back to Alanda, holding his hand out for the message. She handed it to him, and he broke the wax seal and scanned the contents.

"Always wanting something," he grumbled. He looked up at Alanda. "Suppose I ought to pay you for the carrying," he grumbled. "Wait here." He disappeared into the back of the shop.

Though she didn't show it, Alanda was excited. Throughout her apprenticeship, Alicia had been paid for deliveries, doling out only tiny amounts to Alanda at the end of each journey. This would be the first time Alanda had been paid directly, and the thought of holding the coin in her own small purse made her happy. She knew her family would appreciate her contribution, and she was glad to have a way to help.

Herve came back, his fist closed as he offered it to Alanda. Holding her hand out, she smiled as several small copper coins clinked into it. Three or four copper was the traditional payment for message delivery, and she could see that despite his sour attitude, the baker had not skimped on her payment.

"Thank you," she said, and turned to leave. At the door, she stopped and turned slowly on the spot, again with her arms outstretched, to show goodwill and that she had taken nothing that did not belong to her.

Alanda waited until she was back in the village square to glance at the coins. Five coppers! Two more than she had expected for her first delivery. She placed the coins in the small purse at her waist with a slightly shaking hand.

After the bakery, Alanda made her way to Mawde, the healer, who she had delivered to with Alicia. Mawde and Deena kept up a lively correspondence. Stunningly beautiful, Mawde was also painfully shy and said little to Alanda as she accepted the message and paid Alanda four coppers, though she smiled kindly.

After Mawde, Alanda quickly delivered to Tomkin, the innkeeper, and Davi, the horsemaster's apprentice, who accepted the message on behalf of his master. Having completed her Basendale deliveries, Alanda sat down in the village square with Alis to decide when she would set off for Kilynelle, over a week's journey high into the Guilnora Mountains.

Alanda poured the contents of her purse into her hand and counted it. Seventeen copper coins glinted in the sunlight, small and round in her hand, and she felt a heady pleasure at the weight of them. *Provisions for the journey to Kilynelle will cost four or five*, she calculated, placing five coins back in her purse. She quickly added another three, accounting for the fees she would have to pay the Messenger's Guild. Nine coins remained in her hand. Nine. She had never held so much coin in her life.

Her gaze wandered to the inn's sign, reading The Mellow Thicket over a faded painting of the travelers' glyph. *Five coins would get me a proper bed, a hot meal, and a warm bath.* Alicia had only treated them to a room at an inn when they had been away from home for many days, if not weeks, but Alanda wondered if it might be worth it to prepare for her journey up the mountains.

She looked at the coins. Five would buy her and Alis a night off the road, a full belly, and a warm bath in a private tub. She would still have four to give her family, and she would receive more when she delivered her messages to the elves of Kilynelle.

Shaking her head resolutely, Alanda placed all nine coins into her purse and secured it to her belt. Her family needed her to bring home coin, not spend it at inns when the weather was fine and warm. She could sleep perfectly well on the trails. Shaking her head at herself for what she had been tempted to do, Alanda got up, made sure her pack was secure, and called Alis. Without another glance at the inn, she headed for the row of shops to get what she needed for her journey to Kilynelle.

SUMMER STORM

Alanda traveled across the valley for three days, eschewing the road that would have taken her out of her way as she headed for the foothills of the Guilnora Mountains. The grasses brushed the knees and calves of the leathers her father had given her, and it only took part of a day before the swishing sound of the contact became part of the background noise of her trek.

On the second day, she spotted several rabbits in the tall grasses and decided to shoot one for their dinner. Taking her short bow off her back and nocking an arrow, she assumed the stance she had been taught and aimed for the fattest one of the group, a plump one that would provide ample food for her and Alis for the evening and, perhaps, the midday meal the next day. Her arrow caught the rabbit in its side, and her heart broke as she imagined the pain she must have caused. As the rest of the rabbits scattered into the anonymity of the grass, she put the injured one out of its misery with a quick slash of her hunting knife to its throat.

That night, Alanda built a fire at their camp near a gurgling stream, clearing enough grass to avoid setting the valley ablaze. Striking her flint and steel to small bits of kindling, she expertly started the fire and enjoyed the warmth as tongues of flame danced through the larger branches she had taken from under a copse of trees.

She constructed a small spit and, as the fire heated, expertly skinned and cleaned her kill. As she turned the rabbit on the spit, she anticipated the meal she and Alis would share under the darkening twilight; hot meals were always better than the cold, preserved meats and breads she carried. She was glad her apprenticeship training had included campfire cooking and hunting; wilderness survival was one of a messenger's most vital skills.

On the afternoon of the third day, Alanda and Alis reached the foothills, the land rising in sharp relief against the flat valley behind her. The Guilnora Mountains, though not the most severe of the ranges in Ilbeor, still posed significant challenges to travelers, including steep trails and the untamed wilderness outside the elven and tselq settlements.

Alanda did not worry about the trails as she climbed through the foothills and into the mountain range itself. The messenger trails in the Guilnora were old and well-established, she had her maps in case of any uncertainty, and she had traveled there many times during her apprenticeship. The journey to the elven settlement of Kilynelle northeast of Blackwell would not be overly difficult.

She loved the smell of the trees and greenery of the mountain forest. It was a fresh, enlivening scent that made her want to move, to be a part of the landscape surrounding her. She realized with some regret, however, that the sunlight was fading, and she would have to camp for the night before setting off up the mountain towards the elven settlement.

Alanda heaved a sigh and unstrapped her pack, letting it drop beside her. The trailhead was a common campsite and she could see where many campfires had been. She supposed this was as good a place as any to spend the night.

After collecting wood for her fire, Alanda shared a cold dinner with Alis and worked on the dragon figurine she was making for Kitz. She felt proud of it; the shape that was emerging after hours of careful work was well-carved and lifelike. She would finish it in a few days if she kept going at her current rate, and she was excited to give it to him at his birth celebration soon after she returned home.

By the time she stretched out to sleep, the embers of her campfire glowing in the darkness, she was content in the knowledge that she would reach her destination on or even before she had intended to, and that the next day's travel would take her well into the mountains she loved.

ALANDA AND ALIS traveled happily up the steep earthen paths of the Guilnora Mountains. As she had been trained, Alanda followed the established trails, consulting her maps when she was unsure. Between her training, her maps, and her compass, she traveled confidently, Alis always at her side. She hunted small game along the way, and most nights, they ate a hot meal.

Her days began at *uht*, but as they began early, so they ended. While there was still plenty of daylight left, Alanda and Alis left the trail. The first task was always to build a campfire and eat; during the day, all they ate was dried meat or cheese, and they drank from the abundant rivers, lakes, and streams running down the mountain. Though she didn't stray from the trails, if she found any fresh fruit or safe berries along the way, she ate them happily, though Alis showed little interest.

After supper, Alanda worked on the small dragon she was carving for Kitz, carving out details on the finished product. Alis explored the area, making her mark and amusing Alanda by attempting to catch a flying squirrel as it soared several feet over their heads. Alanda gave her a pat on the head when she came back seemingly dejected, and Alis submitted to her nightly combing with good spirits. The weather had been fine and nothing about the journey had given either of them cause for concern.

The pleasant weather didn't last. That night, after they had gone to sleep, a harsh wind roared through the small clearing. Alanda, who slept deeply, did not wake at first, but Alis began barking almost immediately.

Alanda sprang to her feet to find their neatly arranged belongings being scattered by the strong wind. She rushed around, gathering her things and ensuring the remains of her fire would not start a larger one. Just after she found everything and stuffed it pell-mell back into her pack, the skies opened, and rain poured down.

Alanda didn't become frantic; sudden weather changes were common in the mountains. Shouting above the noise for Alis to follow, she found the best cover she could - a particularly lush evergreen - and huddled with Alis until the rain abated. As soon as they were settled, Alanda carefully evaluated the storm. Was it a rock-eater, a dangerous storm that could uproot trees and tumble boulders from their long-held places, or was it simply a summer storm?

She listened carefully to discern the telltale noises beneath the roar of thunder and wind. Rock-eaters always came with crashes from the wildlife and even buildings they destroyed in addition to the other storm noises, and their winds were strong enough to knock a fully grown person to the ground if they were not braced. It only took Alanda moments to ascertain that this was simply a summer thunderstorm. Sitting on the wet ground, she relaxed against the tree's trunk, ignoring the patter of raindrops on her skin and hair as they filtered through needles and branches, her hand restraining Alis, who became nervous during storms.

"Well," she said nearly an hour later when the rain had slowed to a sprinkle, "we've seen worse, haven't we, girl?" She patted Alis's sodden head. "Unfortunately, this means I'll have to comb you again."

Alis whimpered. Alanda knew it wasn't because of the promised combing; she was sure Alis knew the word, but she had never seemed worried about it. Alis hated wind, rain, and storms, and she barely tolerated being wet.

It was only the next morning, after a sleepless night, that Alanda discovered the real cost of the storm: her linen head covering was gone. She cursed loudly after searching the area. She was going to have to use her sun salve on her head and neck as well as her face, and she had little left since Deena had run out of one of the ingredients required to make it. Her mother had given her a bottle of perfume to trade to the elves for enough salve for her return journey.

Alanda knew she was still at least four days from Kilynelle. Despite the rainstorm, the skies were clear and bright. She didn't have enough experience to stray from the trails and stay under the cover of the trees, and any amount of sun would burn her.

I'll really have to be careful with the salve. She knew using it on her head and neck was going to deplete it before she reached the elven settlement.

THE SALVE LASTED a day and a half.

Alanda felt the effects of the sun as soon as it wore off mid-afternoon of the fifth day. She stopped immediately, digging the wooden container out of her pack and desperately taking off her traveling gloves and scraping her thin, pale fingers against the sides and in the cracks of the wood. There was simply nothing left.

"Alis, hunt," she said, her usually melodic voice toneless and shaky. Alis looked at her, clearly confused at the lack of the usual strength and authority in her mistress's voice.

"Alis, *hunt*," Alanda ordered firmly, knowing she had to get under cover quickly and decide what to do.

The dog trotted off, not looking back again. Alanda knew Alis would find her own dinner, and if she was lucky, there would be enough for them both. She dashed for the cover of the trees hours before she would have usually stopped for the night, closer to a genuine panic than she had ever been.

Nearly two hours later, Alis returned to Alanda, a dead rabbit dangling from her jaw. She seemed proud of her kill, and Alanda praised her generously as she took the animal and cleaned it. Having had time to think, Alanda felt calmer, and she had considered what she might do to mitigate the effects of the sun.

❧

ALANDA MADE it another day before her situation became unbearable. Alis, understanding her mistress was in trouble, hunted for them both. Instead of finding a clearing, Alanda set up camp at the base of a large tree, hoping for some relief before nightfall.

As a stopgap measure, Alanda had smeared thick mud on her head, neck, and face to protect her from the sun, and though it provided some relief, it was not nearly enough protection for her sensitive, white skin. The first night, she was sunburned, but by the end of the next day, she was in agony. The following day not only were Alanda's head, neck, and face severely burnt, but her limbs were showing signs of resistance to movement even though they had been protected from the sun by her leathers.

"Alis, hunt," she ordered once again as she settled down under the trees for what she hoped was the last night before she reached Kilynelle and the aid of the elf healers. She knew this would be a blow to her family because the money she would have made from the deliveries was going to be bartered for healing and a new head covering. Her return would be delayed, which would also decrease her earnings; it would be that much longer before she could take another job.

Alanda's head felt like it was on fire. Though only mildly burned where her hair covered her scalp, the part in her hair hurt so badly she wondered whether she would have any skin left, or only a blackened line where her part had been.

Her face had fared even worse. Once the sun went down and she could remove her gloves, she touched it gingerly. She felt bumps everywhere from her hairline down to the neckline of her jerkin that she knew were going to become painful blisters. The skin around her eyes had swelled, but not so much that she could not see. Her throat felt dry and blistered, even though it had not been exposed to the sun.

She checked again; there was still no trace of salve in the container. She had known there wouldn't be, but somehow feeling the bare wooden sides of the jar was almost more than she could take.

When she woke before *uht* on the fourth day, Alanda knew she was in real trouble. At least if she reached Kilynelle, the elf healers could help her much more quickly than Deena would have been able to. Though she had never been healed by an elf, she knew they used a combination of sophisticated herbalism and magic in their art and were sought after by the very rich, who could afford to bypass the village healers and send for the elves.

It would hard be to get there. Overnight, Alanda's eyes had swollen into small slits, making it almost impossible for her to see anything, trapping her tears of pain and fear.

Alis nudged her. "I don't know what we're going to do, girl," she croaked, realizing her throat was almost swollen shut. "Damn the messages; we've got to get to a settlement for our own survival."

She didn't mean it. A messenger's prime duty was to deliver their parcels and letters regardless of what they faced on the trails. Alanda knew that and believed it; it had been repeated and emphasized through her apprenticeship, and she knew she would deliver her messages no matter what.

Alanda also knew she would not be able to see her map or her compass.

I know this trail fairly well. They chose this mission for my first because I've been to Kilynelle several times. She also knew Alis, who had been with her from the first day, knew the way.

Alanda felt around in her pack for Alis's leash, which hadn't been used since she was a puppy in training. She had it now only for emergencies and had thought she'd never need it again. Now, it was her only hope.

She felt along Alis's neck until she found the leather collar her father had made, with a tag containing Alanda's rune as well as Blackwell's. Alanda fumbled but attached the leash to Alis's collar. She could feel Alis stiffen as the now-unfamiliar leash pulled at her neck.

"We've got to get to Kilynelle." Alanda shouldered her pack and her message bag with difficulty; the back of her neck hurt so much that the pull of the straps was almost more than she could bear. "Alis, lead."

The command came only as a whisper, but the dog knew it was now her responsibility to get them along the steep trails safely. She started forward confidently, keeping to the trail they were on without deviating.

Alanda stumbled along while Alis pulled at her leash. She had no choice but to hope that, if not Kilynelle, Alis was taking her somewhere she could get help. She thought of the tselqs, the earthy-green, horned race that bred the dogs for the messengers and hunters. Was there a tselq settlement nearby? Alanda couldn't remember, and she had no hope of consulting her maps.

With growing terror, Alanda thought of even worse dangers than exposure to the sunlight. What if a predator spotted them and thought of them as an easy kill? What if she ran into the Urothu, the dark-gray race that seemed to glory only in killing and destruction? She would be defenseless.

With difficulty, Alanda mastered herself, reminding herself that the Urothu had not been seen in the Guilnora Mountains for years and that she was still bigger than most predators in the forest. It was unlikely they would be bothered, but the fear stayed strong even as she tried to refocus on the sound of hers and Alis's footfalls on the trail, on the obstacles she had to climb over, and on the pull of the leash.

Can I even do this? Can I even be a messenger? It's only my first journey, and -

She stubbed her toe on a protruding tree root and fell, cursing croakily and dropping the leash. Alis stopped and trotted back to her, whining quietly and licking her face.

"I'm all right Alis," Alanda whispered, reassuring the dog with a few soft strokes on her head. "Thank you."

She stood up, ignored the pain in her right knee where she had landed hardest, and picked up the leash. "Alis, lead."

Alanda continued to stumble, her face and head growing ever more painful, her eyes almost completely swollen shut, and her joints growing weak. She thought of the other career possibility offered to her when she was searching for an apprenticeship. Deena, the herbalist and healer, had offered to train her, but there was a catch. Deena was not old enough to consider retiring, but an herbalist several towns northwest, Claudia from Hardfelden, was. Alanda would have to move away from everything she had ever known if she wanted that job.

Her breath came in gasps as Alis led her *somewhere*.

Alanda fought just to stay upright. *I should have been a healer. How could anyone have ever thought that I, of all people, could take on a profession involving wandering through the wilderness in daylight?*

The messenger apprenticeship had seemed so glamorous; trekking through the wilderness with her dog, meeting the different races, and exploring in her spare time. She had been ecstatic to learn a spot had opened for a female messenger in her area and had jumped at the chance. *Glamorous! Ha!* Her thoughts grew more bitter as her pain and weakness increased.

All thought ceased about five minutes later when she felt her stomach roil.

"Alis, halt!" she gasped before turning to the side and vomiting violently, dry heaving for several minutes before the retching finally stopped. By the time she could stand again, her stomach ached, and her throat was so swollen that her voice was entirely gone. She wouldn't be able to give Alis any more commands; she would have to trust the dog to figure out where to go.

An excruciating hour later, Alanda stopped. Just ahead, she could hear what sounded like a lively aviary. Deena kept a room full of birds attached to her house; slightly eccentric and loving the colors of the various plumages, the healer was well known for her collection and her house was always noisy with birdsong.

The sound was accompanied by a smell so fresh, floral, and lovely that Alanda nearly wept. Her eyes did tear up as she realized Alis had done it. Alis had led her to Kilynelle.

Aside from the common tongue spoken by all five of the civilized races, elves spoke their own language. Called Yrui in the common tongue, the language was why walking into an elven settlement was like walking into an aviary for those who could not distinguish the sounds and intonations. Yrui was whistled instead of spoken, and it allowed elves to speak with each other over greater distances without shouting. Just like voices, each elf had a signature timbre of whistle, and just like a spoken language, the whistled language was complex enough to hold entire, involved conversations.

The whistling got louder as Alis led Alanda closer to Kilynelle. Soon, the sound of Yrui was joined by a burbling stream and rustling wind in the leaves of the purple elven trees. The three distinct sounds were familiar to Alanda; they spoke of civilization beyond even Blackwell; they spoke of harmony, and they spoke of the magic that was always in the air around elves. Elven settlements like Kilynelle were bastions of tranquility, for rare was the person who had heard an elf speak in anger or frustration. Their centuries of immortal age seemed to have imbued a preternatural calm in them.

Alis let out a single bark, loud but distinctly non-threatening. The whistling died down in a wave, first from the elves closest to them, until all that could be heard was the stream and the wind in the leaves.

After what seemed like forever to Alanda, a voice rang out in the common tongue. "Fair nature. What has happened to this child?"

As if these merciful words were a catalyst, Alanda's knees gave out, and she collapsed to the forest floor.

GIVING AND RECEIVING

The first thing Alanda became aware of was the searing pain she had tried to push aside on her journey. Her body felt as if it was on fire, and for a moment she was consumed by the tiny, blistering tongues of flame dancing over her face and head and the throbbing soreness of her throat. A croaked, whispery moan escaped her lips as she tried and failed to open her eyes.

"I am sorry, child," a soft, musical voice murmured. "This may hurt initially, but the pain will ebb, and you will feel much better when the herbs and magic take effect."

When she heard the word "magic," Alanda remembered where she was.

I made it to Kilynelle, she thought wonderingly. *Alis did it; she got me here.* The female voice reassuring her had to belong to Myrine, the settlement's healer. Alanda had delivered messages to her from the elven settlement in the valley, but she had never needed her services before. She remembered Myrine: a honey blonde, rosy-complected elf who robed herself in bright colors and had a more gregarious personality than many of the others.

She moaned again as Myrine gently applied a sweet-smelling salve to Alanda's face, her fingers soft and her touch gentler than a mother with a newborn babe.

"Hush, now," Myrine crooned. She whistled, the pitch lower than her speaking voice, the timbre somber. Alanda felt her face tingle and knew it was from more than the salve; Myrine was using magic to heal her. A relieved breath escaped her swollen, blistered lips, and she relaxed. Thankfully, the pain in the part of her hair and in her throat diminished as well.

"Where - " she whispered, having to force even the smallest sound.

"You are in Kilynelle, child, but you probably already knew that. I have brought you to my home and placed you in a small bed reserved for those I am healing. Could you try to tell me your name?"

"Ah…ahhhhhh…"

"Hush. We will find out later. I know I have seen you before, but never alone. You must only have just finished your apprenticeship; you are quite young, even by human standards."

Alanda, although no longer in acute pain, found even nodding in agreement was not possible.

"I am going to dribble some liquid into your mouth," Myrine continued. "It will taste foreign to you, but it should not be unpleasant."

Alanda heard Myrine break a wax seal, and a tiny vial was held to her lips. Alanda did find the taste foreign, but not entirely so. The concoction tasted of honey and herbs she could not identify, and there was a slight taste of spirits that repelled her. Because of her father's frequent intoxication and the toll it had taken on their family, Alanda had vowed from an early age never to let any ale, wine, or liquor pass her lips, even refusing the watered ale often drunk by village children.

"Is that any better, child? Could you tell me your name now?" Myrine coaxed.

"Alanda, from - "

"Blackwell! I remember you. You are the pale child always covered in linens from head to foot," Myrine exclaimed. "I did not recognize the new clothes and, pardon me for saying so, but your hair and skin are so dirty I cannot discern the color."

Before Alanda could reply or defend herself, Myrine began to whistle again, the same low-pitched, somber sound. Alanda's lips throbbed, and again, the pain ebbed.

"My parents - " she croaked before Myrine interrupted her again.

"You will require several days to recover," Myrine told her seriously. "Perhaps more. We will send a messenger on horseback to inform your parents you will be late returning home. They will not be worried. What are their names?"

"Jondolan and Dandelion," Alanda answered. "They live on the outskirts of Blackwell." She thought of another immediate concern and came very near to the panic she had experienced in the forest. "Where's Alis?"

"Oh, my dear, do not worry. She is being carefully cared for. Just now, she is being bathed in the spring and she will be dried and combed before she returns here. I have no doubt you will have her soon, and I will see to it a meal is brought for her."

Though she hadn't been able to see for the last part of her journey, she had been aware of Alis's deteriorating state. Alanda had combed her as best she could the first two nights, but everything had been flecked with the mud Alanda had used to protect herself.

"My messages – " Alanda began, remembering her duty as her mind cleared.

"They are safe in your message bag, and I am certain you will make the deliveries soon," Myrine soothed her. "At present, you must put all your energies into your healing, child, but we will not forget your duty."

Alanda nodded very slightly, the movement causing spasms of pain along the back of her neck.

"Sleep, now," Myrine commanded softly. Instead of whistling, she hummed a low melody, almost melancholy, but soothing. Alanda fell asleep almost at once, certain she could feel the latent magic of the elf's home thrumming through her.

~

A CONCERNED WHINE WOKE ALANDA, and she automatically reached out and found Alis's soft, furry head. Alanda tried to open her eyes but couldn't. Despite Myrine's ministrations, they were still too swollen, and Alanda found the blindness disconcerting. Though she trusted the Kilynelle elves and knew she was safe in Myrine's house, being in an unknown house among a foreign people made her instinctively defensive.

"Hi, Alis," Alanda whispered, her voice again failing her. She soothed herself by continuing to stroke the dog's head. "Thank you for bringing me here. You're such a good girl."

"Good morning," a pleasant but unfamiliar voice said in the common tongue. The voice was deep, the kind of voice Alanda associated with a large man, and she started with a bit of fright. Knowing a stranger was in the room with her when she could neither see nor move felt wrong. She soon realized Alis wasn't growling or barking, however, and she relaxed as heavy footsteps announced the approach of the stranger.

"I am Garratt," the voice announced gently. "I am Myrine's father, and we live in this roundhouse with her mother. Myrine will return shortly. She had to tend to a minor injury on one of the elf-children."

"Hello," Alanda whispered. "I'm - "

"Alanda from Blackwell," Garratt interrupted with a short laugh. "Yes, my daughter told me. She also told me you were uninjured other than the skin on your face and head and that I should help you sit up and take a potion and some water." The wooden floor creaked as he stepped to the side of Alanda's bed, and she fought to keep her face composed. She tried to open her eyes again, but it was like trying to wring water from a dry cloth. Her eyelids just wouldn't budge.

Could she sit up? Would she throw up if she tried to eat or drink?

"Hold out your hand."

Alanda complied with outward obedience and inward turmoil. His hand, when he placed it in hers, was rougher than she expected, callused like a working man's. Somehow, Alanda didn't associate elves with the kind of manual labor that would cause such coarse skin, though she knew they grew and hunted much of their own food. She wondered what Garratt's profession was.

Alanda tried to pull herself up with Garratt's support, but she ended up needing him to bear most of her weight. Once she was sitting upright with her bare feet flat on the smooth wood floor, Garratt handed her a tiny, uncorked vial of what Alanda guessed to be the potion Myrine had given her the previous day. Remembering the slight taste of spirits, Alanda wrinkled her nose and then gasped in pain as tiny blisters burst with the motion. Arranging her face into a stoic nonchalance almost immediately, she drank the contents of the vial without further complaint.

"Good." Myrine's voice sounded as though she had just entered the roundhouse, and the sound of her footsteps as she crossed the room confirmed it. "You will talk again in no time, as the swelling in your throat subsides."

"She does not like the potion," Garratt informed his daughter.

"Inconsequential," Marin replied in a businesslike tone. "It is my job to heal this child, and she will do just as I say."

"Yes," Alanda agreed, her voice once again just above a whisper. "My eyes?"

"I will treat your face and eyes again soon," Myrine assured her. "*Apa*, is there food and water?"

"Yes, there is water and a soft wheat mush with honey and blackberry juice, just as you asked."

Much to Alanda's discomfort, the two began whistling in Yrui while Alanda sat awkwardly on the healer's cot, trying to discern any sort of pattern in the musical language. It might as well have been the melody of a nightingale or dove for all she could discern. She wondered what they were discussing.

"Let us eat breakfast," Garratt finally announced after speaking for some minutes with Myrine. "Alanda, may I assist you to the table?"

Before she could reply, he began whistling again, his timbre low but somehow jovial all the same. Alanda felt her muscles, tight from stress and illness, loosen, and she stood hesitantly, grasping his brawny arm for support. Even though she couldn't open her eyes, she swung her head around, able to see a bright redness in one direction; that must have been the open door.

"Just step slowly," Myrine said soothingly, sensing Alanda's unease. "The floor is smooth and there are no obstacles in your path. *Apa* will guide you well."

Alanda made it across the room without trouble. As Garratt helped her sit at the table, Alanda heard another elf enter the round-house, knocking three times on the wood of the open door.

"Hello, child," he said, his tenor voice smooth and pleasant even compared to the other elves. "I am Julen, and I came to see if you would like company while you convalesce."

"Hello," Alanda whispered awkwardly. Extra company was the last thing she wanted, but she would never have been rude enough to say so.

"Julen is the songmaster of Kilynelle," Myrine explained. "Most of the clan is busy, but Julen's principal work takes place in the evening, so he has the leisure to see you during the day."

"Garratt and Myrine have many demands on their time, and I did not want you to be left alone," Julen explained.

"Thank you," Myrine said, her tone slightly amused. "But the child will not be left alone often. Her recovery is my greatest priority."

"Even so," Julen answered. "Surely variety will be helpful."

"Her name is Alanda," Garratt interjected.

"Alanda, well met," Julen said smoothly, slowly taking her hand in a warm gesture similar to humans' traditional handshake. His skin was almost perfectly smooth, and his fingers seemed to be long and thin as they wrapped around her small hand.

"Well met," Alanda whispered.

"Just now she must break her fast." Myrine placed a wooden spoon into Alanda's right hand as Julen released her left.

Alanda found the wheat mush delicious and sweet. Though the

texture was different, she was reminded of the porridge her mother had laced with honey on Celebration days. As she ate, Julen surprised her by beginning to hum. Though he used no words, she felt herself relax even further, and even the flavor of her breakfast seemed enhanced.

"Enough for now," Myrine told Julen when Alanda had finished the last bite of her breakfast and drunk from a cut crystal goblet of water. "She must rest."

Julen touched Alanda lightly on the shoulder, and she was as surprised as anyone when the contact did not make her flinch. "I will see you again soon," he promised.

As the first few days passed, Alanda's skin improved but did not heal entirely. Despite Myrine's best attempts, her eyes remained swollen closed, and her throat remained tight. She still could not speak above a whisper, and she felt completely out of sorts and uncomfortable.

"Child, you have a problem with the sunlight I have never seen before," Myrine commented concernedly on Alanda's third day in Kilynelle. "Even elves are apt to burn if they spend too much time unprotected in the sun; I must often treat the back of my father's neck after he has been working in the wheat field, and I send him with sun salve when the sun is at its highest. You are different. It makes sense your skin would burn badly given its pale coloring and thin appearance, but your body seems to have reacted to the burn in a way I cannot explain."

"It's happened before," Alanda croaked, "when I was very young, before my parents knew how badly the sun hurts me. Deena, our healer, couldn't fix it either. We just had to wait."

"Then we shall wait," Myrine said calmly. "In the meantime, I have concocted more potion for you. It differs slightly from what we have been using, but I think it may help your throat."

The small pop of the cork was a familiar sound to Alanda, and she waited expectantly, wishing she could see what Myrine was doing. A few moments later, she felt the familiar press of the small bottle into her hand. She immediately raised it to her cracked lips and drank, noticing that the taste of liquor was absent, but the taste of honey and herbs was stronger. The potion was sweet and thick, almost cloying.

"Thank you," she said a bit more clearly. She noted her throat already seemed less swollen and she wondered what had been put into the potion.

"You are most welcome," Myrine responded. "Where is Alis?"

Alanda smiled at the note of concern in the elf healer's voice. "I sent her out to hunt," she said, her voice yet stronger. "I know you're feeding her well, but she needed something to do." Alanda had been taught that messenger dogs were working animals and needed to be kept busy in the rare days of idleness.

"I have a gift for you," Myrine told her unexpectedly. "It is a rather unusual thing for a human, but I believe you will find it meets your needs." Alanda heard a rustling sound, and Myrine placed a piece of cloth, smoother than anything Alanda had ever felt, into her hands. As she ran her fingertips along the surface of it, it seemed to flow like a liquid, moving slightly under her touch. It didn't feel like fabric at all, but something completely outside of her experience.

"Water-cloth," Alanda said wonderingly.

Water-cloth, as humans called it, was an elven invention and was prohibitively expensive. Only the wealthiest humans could afford it. Smoother than silk, the fabric was finer than anything made by human hands and virtually indestructible. It had earned its name by the very quality Alanda had first noticed: rather than feeling solid, it seemed to flow like water.

"Yes," Myrine confirmed. "I know you cannot see; would you like for me to describe what you are holding and why I believe it will help you?"

"Please," Alanda responded, stroking the fabric with wonder.

"The water-cloth has been fashioned into a cloak made specifically for you. I hope you will forgive the intrusion, but I took your measurements while you were unconscious, for I knew immediately what you needed to keep you safer. It is body-length and will be only an inch above the ground while you are traveling. The hood, however, is the important part. It will cover your entire head and most of your forehead, leaving much less of you exposed to the dangers of the sunlight."

Alanda sat silently, amazed at the thoughtfulness and expense of the gift.

"It is black on the outside to match your leathers but lined with forest green. I felt that would add some color to your ensemble without making you stand out in the forest. Will you accept this gift?"

It took Alanda a moment to find her voice. "Yes," she whispered, "but only if you accept mine in return."

It was Myrine's turn to be surprised. "You have a gift for me?"

Alanda carefully laid the cloak on the bed beside her. "Will you please hand me my pack?" She hated having to ask for it rather than getting it herself.

Alanda soon felt the bulky heaviness of her pack on her lap where the light, smooth water-cloth cloak had been. She opened it and felt around inside, knowing where the bottle of perfume her mother had made was. As she shifted her belongings, however, she felt the tip of one wing of Katz's dragon across her palm, and she stopped rummaging.

The small carved dragon was her finest carving she had ever made, but she had made it for her brother. Should she give it to Myrine instead as thanks for saving her life? There would not be time to make another figurine before Kitz's birth celebration, but she knew her family would not begrudge her the single coin it would cost to get Kitz some sweets. The gift would not mean as much, but she had a strong feeling that the dragon belonged here, in Kilynelle. Her mind made up, she took hold of the small wooden object, rummaged further in her pack for the bottle of perfume, and pulled them both out. She handed the carved dragon to Myrine first.

"For me?" Myrine asked, surprising Alanda with the wonder in her voice.

"Yes," Alanda said simply. "I carved the dragon from wood I found on a previous journey. Though I've never seen a live dragon, I used the pictures they have in the town hall."

"It is perfect," Myrine breathed, and Alanda wondered whether the elf had ever seen a dragon. "It is so smooth and detailed; even the ribs on the wings are visible. Who taught you to do this?"

"My father," Alanda answered. "He also loves to carve figurines and things out of wood.

"There's something else." She handed Myrine the bottle of perfume. "My mother made this. I was to trade it for more sun salve, but it seems appropriate to give to the elf who saved my life."

Alanda heard Myrine uncork the bottle and her intake of breath as she smelled the contents. "How lovely," she said appreciatively. "I can smell starflowers and summer roses in this. Your mother is very talented. Of course, I was already planning to send you with as much sun salve as you can carry - you did not have to do this. Elf healers are bound by honor and oath to heal those in need of treatment, regardless of reward or cost."

That surprised Alanda; she had thought, because only the wealthiest of humans called upon the valley elves for treatment, that their services would be prohibitively expensive. Their settlement was north and east of Blackwell, and the odd valley-dwelling elves were often the only ones most humans saw. The elves living in the forest comprised most of the elven population, but they rarely came into the valley.

"Most of the expense of elven healing in the valley comes from a combination of travel and messaging costs and the freely given gifts many humans bestow upon them for their services," Myrine told her, correctly interpreting Alanda's confused expression. "In truth, any one of us would treat any one of you if asked, even taking on the costs of travel and materials if necessary.

"Now," she continued, returning to business, "may I take your pack so I can treat your eyes?"

Alanda nodded, tying the strings of her pack tightly. Myrine took it, and she heard it being set aside at the head of the bed. The foul smell of the ointment Myrine had been using on her eyes filled her nostrils, and she hurriedly pushed aside the cloak, lest anything drip onto it.

"Do not worry. It will not take on stains or water, though humans call it water-cloth. Dirt will brush off easily as well."

Alanda kept the cloak beside her to show she trusted Myrine, but she still worried; it had already become one of her most prized possessions.

"Try to open your eyes," Myrine instructed after she had whistled in Yrui for several minutes.

Alanda concentrated on her eyes more than she ever had. To her great surprise, she could open them with only slight pain, but she was still not able to see well. The roundhouse was mostly dark, with blurry flecks of light around the top.

"I can't see!" Alanda exclaimed, panicking. She felt Myrine kneel at her side.

"Child, your eyes are as red as your skin was when you arrived, but do not be distressed," Myrine said soothingly. "It seems they burned along with your skin or are suffering the same reaction as your throat. Part of the reason for the darkness is that it is nighttime, and the only light comes from our small beacons at the junction of wall and roof."

"But my eyes - " Alanda began.

"I have a treatment for your eyes we will begin tomorrow," Myrine told her. "For tonight, simply focus on keeping them open until it is time for sleep."

From the table across the room, Garratt suddenly whistled in what Alanda was starting to recognize as the form of Yrui used in Kilynelle, and it no longer sounded like birdsong to her. Without her sight, she had paid more attention to the surrounding sounds, and she had started recognizing some of the patterns. She thought she could pick out the most common greetings, a light doublet that started out low and was quickly followed by a trilling higher note, and she was almost certain she knew the sounds of Garratt's and Myrine's names.

As she had many times since beginning her convalescence, Alanda felt her muscles relax at what seemed to be Garratt's whistled command, but she wasn't yet sleepy.

"Have you heard the story of the fisherman who met a mermaid?" Garratt asked in the common tongue.

Alanda shook her head, noting that the motion was much less painful than it had been even the day before. The back of her neck must have finally begun to heal.

"Then listen now and heed my words." Not waiting for a response, Garratt began the tale.

ALANDA WOKE EARLY the next morning to a melodic whistled song she faintly recognized rather than to Garratt and Myrine's conversations in Yrui. She thought it might have been the melody of a tune played at Summer Celebration, but the notes were slightly different. Somehow, the whistled tune sounded more fanciful, though Alanda knew she wouldn't be able to explain exactly how.

Remembering Myrine's admonition to keep her eyes open as much as possible, Alanda opened them to slits and then fully. The whistled music stopped abruptly.

"Best of the morning wishes to you, Alanda from Blackwell," an unfamiliar but preternaturally pleasant male voice said. For a moment, she thought it might be Julen, but remembered Julen's voice was lower.

Alanda looked around, her eyes no longer showing her a dark haze but a bright one. She found the speaker, his form blurry but clearly light-toned with darker hair. She wished she could see him more clearly, but Alis's contented breathing told her that this man wasn't a threat.

"Hello," she croaked. "Who are you?"

"You may call me Grayson," the man replied, as if stifling a laugh. "It's as good a name as any." His voice had a lilting quality to it, as though he were a bard telling a story. The words flowed naturally, yet with a kind of understated rhythm, a mix of poetry and prose. "I was traveling and heard of your ailment, so I came to find out what happened. My child, you have the sun-sickness."

"I know," Alanda replied a little defiantly.

"You do not know," Grayson answered. "It is a sickness in which the sunlight affects the internal body as much as or more than the external body. I have told Myrine as much, and she now knows how best to treat you. Sun-sickness is unique to humankind; the elves are not known to suffer it. I myself have only known two others, even among the humans."

"You're not an elf?" Alanda asked curiously. Though his speech didn't sound particularly elven, neither did it sound exactly human. It was too smooth, too rhythmic. She couldn't see him well enough to discern his facial features, nor whether he had pointed ears.

"I am human, much like yourself," Grayson told her. "I have the same frailties, though I must admit my skin and hair are not as pale as your own." He said these words with a sort of wistful longing, as though he would like nothing better than to have Alanda's complexion. "I have a gift for you. I was told you have a talent for crafting small objects from wood."

"It's my evening hobby," Alanda explained.

Grayson placed something in her hands, and for a moment she thought he might be more akin to the elves than to the humans, after all. His skin was smoother than that of any human she had ever touched, so soft it seemed he must never have worked a day in his life.

The object he gave her was nearly cylindrical, and with her eyesight still blurry, all she could see was that it was a pale brown color. She ran her hands up and down it, trying to discern its purpose. "Wood?" she asked uncertainly.

"Yes. It is something I found on my travels and kept, despite not knowing what its destiny would be. It became obvious when I saw the dragon you gave Myrine that it belongs to you. I have rarely seen work so fine."

"It feels…different."

"I found it on the shore of the Unresting Sea," Grayson explained. "It didn't to seem to be normal driftwood, so I picked it up. I have carried it for years." He laughed lightly. "As you can see, it is quite lightweight."

Alanda continued to run her hand over the wood. It was smoother than any she had ever felt before, but her sensitive fingers could feel the slight grain. "It's beautiful," she marveled, wondering how she could possibly improve it by carving it.

Alanda noticed the room grow dimmer as someone blocked the light from the doorway. To her surprise, Grayson greeted whomever it was in fluent, sweet-sounding Yrui. She recognized the dialect as the one belonging to Kilynelle, but somehow coming from Grayson it sounded even smoother and more melodic than from the others, except perhaps Julen.

A human who knows Yrui, Alanda realized in amazement. *How did he ever get the elves to teach him?*

When the elf in the doorway answered Grayson in kind, she recognized the timbre of the whistle as belonging to Myrine. It seemed she was not at all surprised to find Grayson by Alanda's bedside, for her intonations were calm and slow, an everyday conversation as opposed to an urgent one.

After a few moments, Grayson greeted her again in the common tongue. "Myrine has told me it is time for your treatment to recommence. Until we meet again, Alanda from Blackwell. You are in excellent hands and will resume your own journey soon." He stood and gracefully ambled toward the door, his feet barely making a sound on the wooden floor.

"Now," Myrine said in a businesslike tone when he had left and she had taken his place beside the bed, "it is time to see what we can do about your eyes. Lie back, please, with your head on the cushion."

Moments after she had done so, Alanda felt Myrine's cool fingers holding her left eye open. Alanda tried to control her breathing like she had been taught to do when she was anxious, but she barely had the chance before a cool liquid was dripped into her open eye. To her surprise, it was not painful in the slightest; it felt refreshing. As soon as Myrine released her eyelid, she blinked several times in quick succession. The vision in her left eye had cleared considerably.

"What was that?" she asked.

"A bit of this and a bit of that," Myrine answered. "Grayson assisted me with the mix; he is quite the herbalist. Let us treat your other eye now, and I will speed the healing with a minor spell." As she dripped potion into Alanda's right eye, she whistled softly, her tone low and somber.

As Alanda's eyes became less painful and her vision cleared somewhat, she had an idea.

FRIEND

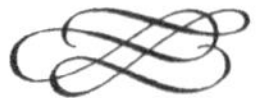

*A*landa asked Garratt to portion out several inches of the wood Grayson had given her; she did not want to mar the whole for what would be a small carving. Once she got used to the texture, she found the wood a joy to work with: soft enough for her whittling knife to carve with ease, but hard enough to rigidly hold the shape she was creating. Shavings and small chunks of wood soon littered the floor around her chair, but as her eyesight improved, she found cleaning them up to be simple.

Day by day, under Myrine's treatment and magic, Alanda was healing. She had finally been allowed to bathe, and the magically warmed water of Myrine's bathtub felt wonderful as she scrubbed off the grime of both her travels and her attempts to soothe her burned skin. Having given over her leathers for cleaning and repair, she was dressed in one of Myrine's sets of robes in a dark plum color she rather liked.

To Alanda's delight, once she was able to see the names on each of her messages, intended recipients were invited to Myrine's roundhouse; Myrine would not yet allow her to venture into the sun. Despite her protestations, each of the elves paid her several coins, and when she offered the coins to Myrine to pay for her healing, the elf kindly refused. Alanda added them to her belt purse, feeling very fortunate she would be able to take them to her family, despite the delay in her journey.

Alanda finished the small flute she had begun carving before her vision fully returned; she carved as much by sensation as sight. She could discern enough by daylight to recognize Myrine and Garratt, and Julen's visits were frequent enough that she recognized his tall, dark-haired form easily. As she whittled the flute, however, she noticed something that had escaped her: Myrine's mother, Kataryna, was nowhere to be found. Keeping up her rhythm, shaping and carving the unusual wood Grayson had brought her, she asked Myrine about it.

"Child, I would have thought you might have known the answer," Myrine said more sharply than usual. She tossed her honey-blonde curls and scoffed. "My mother does not like humans or, in fact, any of the other races. She dislikes humans so particularly, she refuses to sleep in the roundhouse whilst you are present. She is spending nights at the barn with the horses she raises."

At the time, Alanda had felt guilty that Kataryna was spending her nights in a barn, but as she finished the flute, she reflected it was probably better if Kataryna was not present as she tried her experiment.

Alanda placed her fingers over the six small holes in the instrument and brought it to her lips. The wood felt smoother against her mouth than any she had carved before or even any her father had carved for her when she was smaller. It was almost as though the flute was made of glass. She blew softly into it. A pleasant, medium-pitch tone sounded, and Alanda smiled. She knew she had carved the flute correctly. Alone but for Alis snoozing beside her bed, she practiced.

When Julen arrived at the roundhouse that afternoon, Alanda was ready. After taking a deep, steadying breath, she put her flute to her lips and played the best approximation she could of a greeting in Yrui.

Julen stopped in his tracks, and Alanda could see the pointed ends of his ears rising against his dark hair. For a moment, neither of them made a sound. Then, slowly and deliberately, he whistled a doublet that sounded very similar to what Alanda had played on the flute.

Alanda grinned so widely she had trouble reforming her lips around the flute. Taking another deep breath, she played back what Julen had whistled to her.

"Almost," he told her. "Listen, now." He whistled the doublet again very slowly, paying particular attention to the inflection of the trilled higher note at the end. Thus, Alanda's education in Yrui began.

Julen returned to the roundhouse often after their first lesson to continue teaching her, so often that Alanda wondered if he was neglecting other duties to do so. She enjoyed his company; the olive-complected elf had a ready smile and a patient manner of teaching that allowed her to learn quickly.

Of course, she could not keep her lessons secret from Garratt and Myrine. As she healed, Myrine had begun to leave the roundhouse more often, but with as much practice as Julen expected Alanda had to play when she was home, and Myrine couldn't fail to notice. To her delight, Garratt and Myrine added to her tutelage, increasing the number of words and phrases she could recognize and play.

After a week of lessons, Myrine informed Alanda that it was to be her last night in the roundhouse; she was fully healed and would continue her journey at *uht* the next morning. Alanda knew her family would not be worried; she had received a reassuring message from her mother when the first messenger had returned from Blackwell. Still, she was ready to see them again, to share her earnings with them, and to resume her duties.

"Are you ready to journey again, Alis?" Alanda murmured. "Just you and me?"

Alis barked in what seemed to be joy; at least, Alanda took it that way and thought it to be a good omen. She was tired of confinement, even with all she was learning.

"Tonight, you will join the rest of the clan in a celebration of your recovery," Myrine told her with a smile. "It will be held at the circle, and almost every elf in the settlement will be there to express our joy at your return to health."

Julen had told Alanda she would join in the final circle of her stay in Kilynelle, and she looked forward to it. In the evenings, Alanda could hear his song and the discussions of the elves from her cot in Myrine's roundhouse, and she thought it would be nice to join in. Myrine had never allowed it, however, insisting Alanda needed to stay indoors and out of even the evening sunlight while she recovered.

Myrine whistled in simple Yrui and Alanda, picking up on her cue, brought the flute to her lips for some extra practice before the festivities.

~

Though Yrui no longer sounded like birdsong to Alanda, she could not understand much of what was said as she took a seat next to Myrine on the stone benches around the central circle.

"They are simply discussing their days and tonight's festivities," Myrine told Alanda, correctly assuming Alanda could not discern the individual phrases of Yrui among so many. "Nothing of particular import."

Alanda nodded, continuing to strain her ears for familiar words or phrases. She caught some greetings as different elves, mostly clad in robes of various colors, sat around the edge of the circle. She could understand some random bits of the conversations closest to her. Still, she had her own ability to share when it was time; she only hoped she could do what she needed to in front of so many.

A low, monotone whistle, not words, but a wordless call for silence, rang through the crowd with immediate effect. Julen was wearing dark blue robes and looked especially nice, his almond-shaped brown eyes sparkling, and his long brown hair tied back with a leather thong. He smiled at the crowd as he seemed to meet each pair of eyes directly, moving around the circle to gaze at each of the elves. Occasionally, he would stop and converse for a moment, always in a beautifully intoned form of Yrui that Alanda could barely comprehend.

"Julen enjoys conversing with us before the beginning of each evening's circle," Myrine whispered.

Just then, Julen met Alanda's eyes and smiled, speaking for the first time in the common tongue. "Alanda from Blackwell," he said formally in a smooth, low voice. "You are most welcome here tonight."

"Thank you, Julen," Alanda replied, bowing her head and touching two fingers to her forehead in the elves' sign of respect.

Julen bowed his own head, touching his fingers lightly to it before moving his gaze onto the elves sitting next to Alanda and Myrine.

After Julen had quietly gazed at each member of the circle, he made his way back to the center. The elves and Alanda sat silently. To Alanda, the silence felt sacred, as though it were part of one of the rituals of the sanctum in Blackwell, though she knew the elves held no spiritual beliefs and that this was the norm for their evening ceremonies. She had overheard it enough times that she was familiar with the ritual.

Soon, Julen opened his mouth and sang, his voice low, intense, and soothing.

Though Alanda had heard echoes of Julen's song in the evenings from Garratt and Myrine's roundhouse, she did not expect the feeling of awe that washed over her as his voice rang into the softly lit dusk. His song was not formed in language. He sang a simple "ah," but his intonation was anything but unsophisticated. Alanda's heart flew when he reached the highs of his song, and she felt a sense of foreboding when his melody became slow and deep.

How can he tell a story without using words?

Alanda shivered even in the warmth of the summer night. Julen, though handsome, was not distinctive in looks from the other elves, but as he sang, he seemed imbued with a power, his own form of light and wind, as his robes gently swayed around him and his voice soared.

The song was long, and yet somehow it ended too soon. Alanda felt smaller when the last note faded into the night. "How - " she began in a whisper, but Myrine shushed her gently.

Julen began whistling in Yrui, and his whistle was lower and more intense than what he had used when instructing Alanda. Alanda, with a practiced ear, caught the notes that named her and understood enough of what he was saying to know she was next to be called to the center of the circle. Despite her outwardly calm demeanor, she felt as though her insides had turned to jelly.

"Alanda," Julen called in the common tongue, his long arms outstretched in welcome. "Come and show us what you have learned."

Grasping her small wooden flute, Alanda walked to the center of the circle. Julen smiled, and she was surprised to see his eyes twinkling as though in happiness or even amusement instead of the seriousness she had come to expect from the elves. He whistled something low and soft in Yrui, and Alanda felt herself relax.

Had he just used magic on her? The notes differed from what Garratt had used to relax her during her early days in the roundhouse, but somehow, she thought he had.

As Julen had instructed the day before, Alanda did not speak in the common tongue prior to bringing her flute to her lips. Ever so carefully, she began to play, her eyes downcast and her fingers working mostly from memory. First, she played a greeting and then a simple phrase of gratitude. She could sense more than see the surprise among the elves that she was using their language.

What happened next surprised Alanda because it was not something they had rehearsed. As Alanda switched from Yrui to a haunting melody she had created over the past week, Julen hummed from behind her. She paused momentarily, startled into silence, but as she met Garratt's eyes and he nodded his encouragement, she played once again.

As Alanda's melody rose and fell, so did Julen's humming, and what they created was magical both for them and for the enthralled elves. A frisson of energy seemed to emanate from the human and the elf as they harmonized.

During the song, darkness fell across the circle. Though Alanda knew it was going to happen, it still startled her when the tiny, magical lights of the elves came to life on the outsides of the houses and around the circle as she played. From an ethereal twilight at the beginning of her music to the light-dappled darkness at the end, it seemed even the light of the evening was reacting to their tune.

As she finished with a long, low note and Julen hummed in harmony, Alanda lowered her flute and finally raised her eyes. Most still seemed enthralled, but out of the corner of her eye, she saw someone she wasn't expecting to see: Kataryna, who Alanda recognized from the distinctive clothing Myrine had described, half-hiding behind the trunk of a large evergreen. Kataryna, clad in an unbleached linen shirt and a brown leather jerkin and pants, met Alanda's eyes for the most fleeting moment, but when Alanda blinked, she had disappeared into the darkness behind the trees.

Alanda felt Julen's hands lift from her shoulders, and he leaned down and whispered into her ear: "Stay." The word was more a plea than a command, and she wondered why he didn't want her to rejoin the circle.

Alanda barely felt herself nod, and she found herself almost paralyzed with all the elves' eyes looking at her expectantly. Was she supposed to play again? She had only prepared the one song and didn't know what they would expect from her. Singing was out of the question; she had been told often enough that she had a pleasant speaking voice, but she couldn't carry a tune.

What am I supposed to do?

Just as Alanda had decided to quietly walk back to her place beside Myrine, a group of elves with Garratt at the head appeared from around the circle. They moved silently on their bare feet, each garbed in robes of white that swished a bit on the forest floor. With a gentle nudge, Julen prompted her to step forward before he circled around her and joined the group. His dark blue robes contrasted starkly with the rest of the group, but Alanda felt he still looked as though he belonged there, his serious gaze mirroring the others. She felt almost as though she were stripped naked by those stares, and she hoped someone would speak soon.

Garratt finally smiled at her, his smooth face suddenly looking more like the familiar elf she had talked to so often. He whistled a formal greeting in Yrui. Alanda, glad for something to do, made the elves' traditional sign of respect and then played the greeting back. Though most of the elves in the group remained serious, Julen and one other, a raven-haired female Alanda had never seen before, joined Garratt in smiling at her.

To Alanda's relief, Garratt switched to the common tongue. "Alanda from Blackwell," he began, startling her with his use of the formal greeting. "You have lived among us for thirteen days, and in that time, you have not only recovered, but learned much about our clan and our customs. You have even shown yourself able and willing to learn our language, which you have done with great alacrity and attention to detail. You have been highly commended by Grayson, long a friend of this clan. It is for these reasons the Council of Kilynelle has decided to name you, Alanda from Blackwell, elf-friend."

Alanda felt her mouth drop open but immediately closed it because she did not want the elves to think her uncouth. She had heard of elf-friends, people of other races who were honorary members of the clan who had befriended them, but she had never met one. None of the other messengers from Blackwell or the surrounding villages held the title, nor had she even heard of one among the other traveling professions. She stammered a bit as she responded, "I am honored, Garratt of Kilynelle, to be chosen for such a privilege."

"Hold out your right hand," Garratt instructed, and she held her hand out palm up. Garratt gently turned it, so her palm faced the forest floor. Alanda held her position a little awkwardly, feeling foolish, while Garratt unwrapped the strings from a soft fabric pouch of a material Alanda didn't recognize. When he pulled a small object out of the pouch, Alanda could not help but gasp at the beauty of what he held in his hand.

She could see it was a ring, but it was like no other ring she had ever seen. Humans did not have many skilled metalworkers among them; the dwarves usually did such work. Most wore simple silver bands for weddings made by such silversmiths as there were among humans, and the only more intricate work she had ever seen had been when the traveling merchants came through Blackwell.

The circlet of the ring was silver, but the incredible part of the ring was not the metalwork. The gemstones of the centerpiece were arranged in a long diamond shape edged with multifaceted green gemstones with a clear stone at each corner. The middle was an ornate design of clear and green stones with a large clear stone in the very center. The piece glittered in the twinkling light of the elf-lamps, making it look almost as if it moved even though Garratt held it still.

Alanda had seen many wonderful things on her journeys: unusual flowers, trees in the vibrant colors of the fall, and springs bubbling joyously between banks of vivid green moss. Her soul had delighted in these things, but none of them compared to the beauty of the ring Garratt was sliding onto her middle finger; it shone as though it had a light of its own.

"This is Moonshield," Garratt told her.

"It's beautiful," Alanda breathed, unable to stop herself from gazing down at her hand.

"Wear it in remembrance of us and in remembrance that you are one of us. It will remain hidden by day unless you wish it to be seen, but it will protect you by night with wards imbued in the very stones of the centerpiece. You may sleep without trepidation wherever you may be, and your friends in Kilynelle will rest easier knowing you are safe from many of the dangers both of the wild and of civilized places."

Alanda somehow knew exactly what to do when he had finished speaking. She brought her flute to her lips and played a series of tones, speaking of gratitude. She had insisted Garratt teach her this because she wanted to properly thank Myrine for healing her; she had never imagined she would use her flute to thank the Council of Kilynelle for making her an elf-friend. This time, all the elves in the Council smiled at her as she played, well pleased.

As one, the entire circle of elves stood, faced Alanda, and bowed their heads, touching their foreheads with two fingers.

~

ALANDA SLEPT BLISSFULLY and well that night, Moonshield firmly in place on her right hand. She woke the next morning at *uht* to Alis's light whine and cool, wet nose on her cheek. She opened her eyes to the now-familiar sight of Myrine's roundhouse, still gloomy in the pre-dawn light. She sat up quickly. Myrine had released her to leave Kilynelle.

"Good morning," Myrine greeted her. She was up before everyone else, as always, and already dressed in pink elven robes, her hair loose and flowing in curls down to the center of her back. Alanda wondered if she ever rested. "I have something for you."

Alanda, feeling the weight of Moonshield on the middle finger of her right hand, wondered what else the elves could possibly give her. They had given her back her life and health, they had given her a water-cloth cloak, they had given her their rarely bestowed friendship, and they had given her the beautiful ring she would never take off. What else could there be?

Myrine laid something on the bed next to her, and Alanda immediately looked at it. It was her black leathers, but there was something slightly different about the outfit that she couldn't quite place.

"We cleaned and repaired your clothing while you were wearing the lighter robes of the elves. Forgive me, for I know your father crafted this for you, but I put some enchantments on the leather to protect you from both sunlight and rain."

"No forgiveness is needed. Thank you, Myrine, for everything."

Alis barked softly. Alanda reminded herself that her prepared pack and message bag, not empty but laden with messages for the elven village in the valley, had alerted the dog they were leaving that morning. Myrine left the roundhouse to give Alanda privacy to change from her simple shift into her traveling clothes, and before long Alanda was clad in the black leathers and the flowing water-cloth cloak Myrine had given her.

She was spreading sun salve on her face when Myrine re-entered. "I have put several pots of sun salve in your pack. I know they will add weight, but you should have enough to last you some time, and you should not use it sparingly. It is not, I am sure, the same concoction your village herbalist makes, but Grayson and I came up with the mix, and it should do nicely. Let us not have you fell into the same condition in which you came to us," Myrine told her. "Now, return home and bring your people the same joy you have brought to us, elf-friend." She smiled, performed the elves' symbol of respect, and stood aside. Alanda returned the gesture, smiling back warmly.

"Heel, Alis," Alanda said after she had shouldered her pack and her message bag. She smiled at Myrine in thanks and set off back into the woods.

MISSIVE FROM KILYNELLE

Though the carvings on the richly oiled wood panels in Altoneir's study suggested all manner of life, their trees seeming to shade the many animals and flora of the forest, it was usually silent and still. Altoneir preferred it that way; this place, with its walls carved by human artisans over a millennium ago, was his refuge from the constant activity of the castle. No one was allowed to enter without his explicit invitation; interruptions were to be kept to urgent matters.

The tall elf, garbed in his usual sweeping water-cloth robes, darkest black to match his straight, waist-length hair and beard, stroked a long finger along the carved wood of the arm of his chair. He held an open scroll in his other hand, small for easy concealment, and packed with tiny elven script of the kind rarely used in this age. He could not decide what he thought of the news it held: it seemed Kilynelle had named a new elf-friend, their first since naming Grayson over a thousand years before.

The news disturbed him perhaps more than it should have. Why should he care if Kilynelle had chosen a strange human girl to be an elf-friend? How would it have any effect on his plans? Still, there were several issues at the heart of the matter that did not let him rest.

Grayson, the strange immortal human who wandered Ilbeor at will, settling nowhere, had seemed an odd choice for an elf-friend but as the years had gone by, it seemed Kilynelle and the other clans who had befriended him had made a good choice. In his wanderings, Grayson came into contact with all six races and always had news to share. The idea, however, that Grayson had commended this *one* human to the Council of Kilynelle concerned him. Grayson rarely seemed to take notice of any particular individual of any race, even among elvenkind. What was special about this girl?

That she was pale with white-blonde hair and that she had come to the elves so badly burned she had almost died but for the ministrations of the settlement's healer made him wonder as well. What kind of messenger could not be exposed to the sun? Where had her coloring come from? Something grated at the back of his mind about her coloring, but as he couldn't identify it, he rejected it as simply an overabundance of fancy brought upon by this unusual news.

No, this is not of consequence. Still, the girl had an audience with the Kilynelle elves whenever she wished now. They had long been one of the clans most resistant to his mission, and perhaps this girl could help change that.

He considered the machinations he had available. He could send the travelers to explain his vision and convince her to carry it to the Council of Kilynelle once she believed. But would she be convinced? Humans had often been the hardest to convince that the seat of human power should be disrupted. *No*, he thought, *that is a waste of the travelers' time and energies when I may need them elsewhere.*

He thought of the Urothu. Those gray-skinned killers would level her village at his command. They would kill anyone and everyone there, destroy the habitations, and leave a ruin where the village once had been. *Blackwell.* He had never been there, but it was marked on his map as the southernmost village in the Claresea Valley. It would take the Urothu some time to reach it, but he had an affinity with them no one else could claim. That could backfire, however. If the girl was killed or even if she brought news of the attack to Kilynelle, they might see his hand behind it, though none yet knew he commanded the Urothu. He wanted that kept secret for as long as possible.

Perhaps a village near hers, a village not emotionally tied to her but known to her. Danger close to home, but not at home.

He stood abruptly and strode around the desk, his long legs making quick work of the distance between his table and the map table in the middle of the room. He stood over the map of Ilbeor, tracing a pale finger along the southern valley.

Basendale. The closest village to hers. He could send the Urothu there, and easily plant the idea among the villagers of Blackwell, who were sure to hear about the attack after it happened, that the king should have protected the villagers, even as far south as they were. He would have to write to his emissary there before it happened to begin spreading the seeds among the people. He would have to do it carefully and not appear he knew what was about to happen.

Steps upon steps, intrigues inside intrigues. Altoneir knew he would have to tread carefully with Kilynelle. They were a well-connected clan with familial connections to the elven city of Caalenor. It could be a great opportunity, but if he made the wrong move, it could also set him back. Though he did not have many followers in or from Kilynelle, to have them suspect him of controlling the Urothu would be dangerous. The elves would feel duty-bound to act in a way that they had not in the past if they knew of it, and he did not want a war with the elves.

Basendale would be perfect. The elf-friend would hear of its destruction and would surely bring the news back to Kilynelle, hopefully with a fairly large dose of doubt about the human King Florian. It was a small step, one among hundreds, but any seeds he might plant could bear fruit in their own ways.

He went back to his writing table and took out a long quill, some ink, and some thick parchment he reserved for communications sent by crow.

To My Esteemed Emissary,

It has come to my attention that the Urothu have been moving in larger numbers than usual along the southern foothills of the Guilnora Mountains. I wonder if your king has heard the same and if he is taking measures to keep you and the others in the valley unscathed. I am concerned about your continued safety in light of this news and wish you to do all you can to protect yourself and your people. Please keep me apprised and call for me should you need aid.

Your continued work on this mission is and shall remain much appreciated. Know that, though my intentions are as clear as they have ever been, the humans of the valley are not only safe, but under my protection. I would not see harm come to the innocent.

As ever, I remain true to my calling and mission. I trust you to do the same.

HE DID NOT SIGN the note; he never did lest it were to fall into the wrong hands. It was imperative that his human followers, few as they were, remain convinced of his good intent towards their race as a whole. It was not exactly a lie; he did not intend for human innocents to be harmed any more than he intended for the innocents of any race to be harmed.

He wrinkled his nose in disdain. He was uncertain that there truly were any human innocents. They all seemed mired in the same greed and hubris as their ruler, and they all seemed determined to strive for their own ends over the needs of the other races.

No matter.

Carrying the note to the crows' nest in the western tower of his castle on Sundersar Island, he sent it with all haste, knowing even as the crow flew, it would take several days to reach his target. The first part of his plan in motion, he moved back across the castle to his bedchamber to prepare for a journey of his own.

The Urothu would take orders from none other than him.

❧

ALTONEIR DID NOT HAVE to leave his island to communicate with the Urothu, but he had to go a considerable distance from the castle. Cloaked in a sweeping black wool garment more suited for late fall than the warmth of summer, he refused all offers of company or help as he swept through the castle on the way to one of the back entrances.

Servants, those new to the island or those who were generational members of lower ability, gawked as he passed. Though Altoneir sometimes enjoyed a stroll among the verdant gardens and courtyards of the castle, he rarely came this way, and he rarely moved with such an expression of combined hatred and determination on his finely chiseled face. The servants didn't dare to stop in their duties as he passed, but many looks of confusion and wonder passed between them as they bustled through the halls.

Once he had left the castle grounds behind, Altoneir slowed his pace slightly. He wasn't in as much of a hurry as he had seemed to be, but he thought it best to appear to be in a hurry and even in a rage to deter onlookers, both servants and advisors alike, from following him or questioning him. No one must know what he was about to do. Continuing northwest from the castle, the elf soon entered the woods that had always grown on this side of the island.

Trees grew here that didn't seem to grow anywhere else. Iantris, who had first suggested this place to him, had told him the trees were the offspring of forest life that had been grown and mutated by the arcane attentions of the old witch queens of Ilbeor, humans who possessed magic long before the Sashu existed to train them in its use. Most of the trees had bark so dark it was almost black; it seemed unnatural to Altoneir, who had always associated life and growing with the earthier shades of greens and browns. Still, after three centuries on Sundersar, he had grown accustomed to and even fond of the strange trees with their dark bark and transparent green leaves.

The flora of late summer was contrastingly vibrant and beautiful, matching its counterparts in the forests of the Guilnora Mountains and the Claresea Valley. Altoneir saw the usual foxfoil and blue aidrow, two aiyonia plants in full bloom, and - he smiled when he saw it - a perfectly bloomed nellatia plant. He had not seen one of those in the wild in ages, and he made a careful note of its location. Nellatia killed any living creature quickly and without a trace; it could be useful in the future, though he didn't have any particular need of it now. For the most part, he was scornful of healers who used herbs in addition to, or even instead of, magic. But nellatia was actually useful.

The walk to his destination took nearly two hours, even at the quick pace he set, and he arrived at the sending stone in twilight. He was glad he had; he appreciated beauty, and the reflective slivers of rare minerals in the stone glinted pink in the reflected sunset.

Looking around to ensure he had not been followed, even though he knew he had not been, Altoneir approached the large stone. It stood alone in the exact center of a small clearing surrounded by flowering brush and the strange island trees, and he knew Iantris had placed it there on purpose, to keep it away from those who should not see it.

He smiled softly at the thought of Iantris. His bedfellow and some-times-partner for centuries, she was a powerful and ancient elf - not as ancient as he, but formidable in her own right. She had been his closest advisor and the only one he counted friend since his partner-for-life, Aenwyn, had died along with most of his clan. It had been at her suggestion that he had formed the uncomfortable alliance with the Urothu.

Altoneir stepped closer to the stone, considering. It was not the first time he had used it, but he approached each occasion with considerable care. He had been one of the small group of elves who had captured three of the creatures and studied them for over a century, looking for a way to break the psychopathic streak and allow them to become functioning members of society. In the end, they had not been able to do so, and it was with little regret that they had ended all three lives. Urothu were to be handled with the utmost care, and no one knew that better than Altoneir.

After working out how to approach the matter, Altoneir placed one long-fingered hand on the stone, fingers splayed to cover as much area as he could. Despite the warmth of the summer day and of his own hand, the stone was cool to the touch and seemed as smooth as glass, though the glittering variety of crystal and mineral belied that smoothness.

It was some minutes before Altoneir sensed that the stone on the other end of the connection, a stone given to a band of Urothu living in the higher reaches of the Gray Hills, was being touched by another being. There were no words; the Urothu spoke not a word to anyone not of their race, and when they spoke to one another, the sounds were unrecognizable as language.

Altoneir did not speak aloud. There was no need, for the connection between sending stones was not a physical one. Speaking aloud would accomplish nothing; the creature in the Gray Hills would not hear him. Instead, he sent his thoughts with a force that spoke of the great power he wielded.

Humans need killing.

The answering thought came as emotion. He sensed the excitement from the Urothu as palpably as if the creature had loudly cheered five feet from him. He thought hard of the map of the Claresea Valley. He knew the creature would see what he saw, and he knew it was intelligent enough to understand. Though many saw the Urothu as nothing more than mindless, magical killers, he knew the race was as intelligent as any other.

A question floated across the connection.

Basendale. In his mind's eye, the dot representing the tiny southern village glowed. *Bring many of your kind. Spread fear among the humans. Fear of your power.*

The thoughts connected with his quivered with excitement again, but he also discerned something else, the something that made the Urothu the most feared creatures in Ilbeor: hatred. The Urothu hated all living beings so strongly that they often had trouble even living with one another. Those of other races, once seen by a band of Urothu, were marked for death without deviation or fail.

Soon. See it done.

Feeling slightly ill at the palpable elation the Urothu felt at the destruction of so many other living beings, Altoneir drew his hand up sharply, severing the connection. In truth, though he found his control of the creatures useful, he did not relish it.

They are a tool, nothing more, he reminded himself as he turned away from the sending stone. *When Ilbeor falls to me, I will destroy them.*

Feeling slightly less sick at the promise he had made himself, Altoneir quickened his stride and left the clearing.

TRYST

The beauty of the forested mountain trails in summertime never failed to stun Alanda. As she left Kilynelle behind her and angled southwest down the mountain, she drank in the smells of the green trees and moss, the sight of butterflies, flowers, and colorful lichen, and the sounds of the breeze riffling through the leaves and the birds calling to one another. Though she had enjoyed Kilynelle, the forest was what she loved most of all, and she reveled in the solitude of making her way back down to the valley, Alis at her side.

Alanda felt in no particular hurry and kept a steady pace alongside her dog. She had messages to deliver to the valley elves, and she was looking forward to being home again. She knew her family was not worried and would appreciate the coin she would earn when she delivered the messages to the valley elves.

The cloak Myrine had given her added almost no weight to her ensemble, and Alanda found it pleasant to have the silky hood covering her head down to her eyebrows. The way the fabric brushed her face and neck felt cool and nice, and she was thankful for the additional protection.

At midday, Alanda stopped and sat alongside the trail itself.

Offering a strip of dried meat to Alis, she crossed her legs and leaned against the trunk of a lush oak rising high into the forest canopy.

A noise from above her startled her, the crackling of leaves warning her she was not alone. Slowly, she looked up and was alarmed to see a small mountain lion stalking along one of the thick branches above her.

She kept her breathing steady, reminding herself that if the mountain lion was hunting her, it would not be moving away from her as it was. Alicia had told her what to do when she saw a predator in the forest. Unfolding her legs, Alanda slowly got up, gesturing to Alis to follow her. She could feel her heart beating in her chest, but when the big cat didn't make any movement towards her, she knew it was not a threat; it was simply time to move on.

Alanda headed slowly back down the trail again, listening intently for any change in the mountain lion's movements. Thankfully, there was none. It was not hunting her or Alis. It was a full hour, however, before Alanda felt safe enough to increase her pace, and her breath came in sharp gasps as she realized she was well away. She stopped, feeling her heart pounding a fast, staccato rhythm in her chest. Her hands were clenched into fists at her sides, and as she released them, she realized they were shaking with fright and the urge she had felt to run as fast as she could away from the danger.

Alis whined softly, the first sound she had made since their encounter, and Alanda reached down to pet her as she continued shakily down the trail. It was unusual to see large animal life that close to the trails; forest creatures usually kept well away from places the two-legged beings frequented. For the first time, Alanda wondered if the mountain lion had been hunting something else when she came upon it. She hadn't seen any large game, but she hadn't been looking for any either.

Her stomach growled; she had not eaten her midday meal. Slowing a bit, she pulled her pack back off and reached in to see what she could find. Her searching hand found a pouch full of dried berries, and she decided that would do. Stopping for only a moment to remove the pouch and fasten her pack securely, she ate the berries slowly as she continued.

When it came time to stop for the day, Alanda knew she was too hungry to eat from her pack; she wanted hot food, and she wanted lots of it. Taking her short bow from her back and stringing it, she veered off the trail and toward the sound of a mountain spring not far from her. She had seen several rabbits and flying squirrels as she had traveled, and she hoped she could shoot one for her evening meal.

Just as she had hoped, she found several gray rabbits near the banks of the stream, though they scattered when they saw her. She stalked them back into the trees and took the first shot she could, catching a fat one just behind one of its ears. Taking her kill, Alanda set off to find a nice clearing where she could build a fire and camp.

ALANDA DIDN'T NEED Alis's whine at *uht* to wake her; she was so glad to be back in the forest and on her way home that she had woken before first light. Knowing she couldn't travel in the dark, she stayed in her blankets until Alis alerted her.

Alanda sat up, pulling the blankets close as she let her eyes adjust to the predawn light. The remains of her fire were only glowing embers now; she would have to extinguish it before she resumed her travels. Once her eyes had adjusted, she threw the blankets off and prepared a cold breakfast of leftover rabbit and some hardtack the elves had sent.

As she gathered her belongings, she was pleased to find the elven cloak, though it had been folded in her pack while she slept, was not creased in the slightest. Remembering the dread of the stormy night when she had lost her head covering, she was grateful to find the cloak where it was supposed to be, along with the rest of her things.

Her second day of travel promised to be pleasant; the sky between the trees was cloudless and the weather would be late summer warm and not too hot. After she had bathed her face and refilled her water-skin in the stream, she made her way back to the trails. This part of the mountain was so familiar to her she didn't need to consult her maps; she knew which paths to take.

It was nearly time for midday meal when Alanda realized she was not alone; behind her, she could hear the unmistakable footsteps of one of the bipedal races, and whoever it was walked faster than she did and would soon catch up.

Her breath caught. Though it was not unusual to meet others of the traveling professions on the trails, she never felt comfortable when she could not see who was coming up on her. What if it was an Urothu?

Don't be stupid, she thought fiercely. *Urothu don't travel alone, and besides, if one of them had found you, you'd be dead by now.*

There was too much truth in the thought to ignore. Urothu, a gray-skinned, small-bodied race scattered throughout the wild places of Ilbeor, were the fiercest creatures in the land. Powerfully magical, they seemed to like nothing more than death and destruction, and no one had ever gotten close enough to find out more and lived to tell of it.

Alanda shook off the unpleasant thought and focused her listening even as she kept walking. Yes, a two-legged being, but there was something else. Alanda fully relaxed when she heard the unmistakable sound of soft dog paws treading the ground next to the stranger; this was surely just another messenger. She was not a tracker and couldn't tell what race the messenger was, but she would have recognized the footfalls of a messenger dog anywhere.

She stopped and stepped to the side of the trail to wait, thinking it would be pleasant to exchange news with another messenger before continuing on her way. Perhaps it would even be one she knew; she had become acquainted with several during her apprenticeship. Her thoughts went immediately to Alicia, her trainer, who often ran messages in the same part of the Guilnora Mountain range.

A few moments later, a human messenger accompanied by a fluffy black messenger dog rounded the corner behind her and stopped as soon as he saw her, his face splitting into a wide grin. He wore a tunic of bright red linen, the kind of color that was hard to find in the valley, and brown britches tucked into high leather traveling boots. Like her, he wore a brown leather messenger bag across his chest and a large pack on his back accompanied by a bow much longer than her own, a quiver of arrows, and a large hunting knife in a sheath at his belt.

"I thought I heard someone ahead of me." He greeted her cheerfully enough, but she noticed his eyes taking in her black leathers and the elven cloak. She realized she must look quite foreign.

She stepped back onto the trails to face him. "I heard you and stopped to see who I might meet today," she said. "I'm Alanda, from the village of Blackwell in the valley."

"Blackwell?" He seemed confused. "You're human?"

Alanda smiled. She supposed she might have looked something like an elf with her cloak pulled up, and she quickly swept the hood from her head to show him her rounded ears and white-blonde braid. "I am, though I suppose my cloak must seem strange. It was a gift from the elves of Kilynelle."

The young man blinked in surprise, and she took his momentary silence as an opportunity to study him just as he had studied her. His face, weatherworn and ruddy, was not unpleasant to look at, though an overgrowth of whiskers suggested he had been on the trails a while. His brown, tousled hair fell almost to his shoulders, and when he had smiled, she had noticed teeth almost unnaturally white and perfect.

"I'm Tostig, from Lakeland," the young man said finally, smiling again. "It's nice to meet you."

"It's nice to meet you, too," she replied, suddenly not sure what else to say. Something was washing over her, a feeling she wasn't familiar with, like a warm waft of air coming straight from him and into her.

"Are you traveling back down to the valley?" Tostig asked, cutting into her uncertainty. "I would love some company."

Alanda mentally shook herself. "I am," she answered, trying not to stare at features that suddenly seemed perfect to her.

"You feel it too, don't you?" Tostig asked softly, surprising her.

Not knowing how to politely deny him, she nodded quietly.

"Walk with me," he invited. "Tell me of the things and peoples you have seen, and we will pass the time getting to know one another."

Alanda glanced down at Alis for confirmation before agreeing to accompany this stranger down the mountain. Alis and Tostig's dog were sniffing one another, seemingly content to travel together. "What's your dog's name?" she asked.

"Ziva," he told her. "And it seems she and your dog - "

"Alis," Alanda interrupted.

"It seems she and Alis have no objections to spending time with one another, either. Shall we go?"

"Let's," said Alanda, making up her mind.

THE INEXPLICABLE WARMTH Alanda had felt upon meeting Tostig never faded as they traveled down the mountain together, and she knew, based on how he kept brushing against her as they walked, that he still felt it too. She wondered what it was and if it meant anything, but she was certain of one thing: she was enjoying traveling with Tostig very much.

They traveled together well, exchanging stories of places they had been in the course of their shared profession. Tostig was seventeen years old to her sixteen and had been a messenger for a year longer. He had a penchant for exploration beyond that of a normal messenger, and as he described the wonders he had seen, Alanda vowed she would spend more time off the trails on her future journeys.

"Just after I finished my apprenticeship, I was on one of the high trails between Eagle's Nest and Tichon - closer to Tichon, I think - and I heard the sound of water, lots of water, so I left the trail. I found a waterfall, but it was a waterfall like I've never seen before. It towered over the water below, and it was full, so full I imagined how fast it would cover my village with water. That wasn't the most amazing thing, though. While I was looking at it, I saw a rainbow form inside of it - a rainbow! I ask you, what kind of waterfall makes its own rainbows?"

Alanda shook her head at the wonder of it. She had seen many waterfalls on her journeys. The mountains were full of streams, ponds, and even larger lakes, and it was only natural that waterfalls would be a part of that. She had never seen one like he was describing, though, and she wished she had. "Between Eagle's Nest and Tichon?" she clarified.

Tostig nodded.

"I'll have to look for it next time I'm up there. Alicia and I spent most of our time in the southern Guilnora, since that's closest to Blackwell, but we went up that way a couple times. I never saw the waterfall, though."

"It was about an hour's hike off the trail," Tostig said. "We'd just had a lot of rain, which is probably why it was loud enough to hear it so far away."

Alanda thought about it for a moment. She wanted to contribute to the conversation, too, but she hadn't explored as much as Tostig had. Suddenly, she remembered the one truly wondrous thing Alicia had shown her. The trails had been difficult to traverse, even requiring them to make some short climbs, and Alicia had told her she had something to show her as a reward for her tenacity.

"Alicia showed me a strange pond, almost big enough to be called a lake, when we were traveling farther north than usual. It wasn't blue or green, but rather, the areas of water closest to the shores were bright colors, oranges and yellows and teals. She said the water was hot and dangerous, so we didn't get too close, but it was beautiful."

"Hursar told me about something like that!" Tostig exclaimed. "But I've never actually seen one."

"Hursar?" Alanda asked.

"A dwarf messenger I traveled a span with a while back," Tostig explained. "I know they rarely leave the Gray Hills, but this one had a long-distance message to a tselq settlement in the Guilnoras, and he was looking for company."

"I've never met a dwarf," Alanda said wistfully. "I've always wanted to. Alicia told me they're funny and they curse a lot. Is that true?"

"It was in his case, at least," Tostig laughed. "He was even shorter than I expected, only a little more than half my height, and broad. His face was red all the time, and it seemed like every other word was some kind of curse, or else some kind of joke I didn't quite understand. He was rough around the edges, but I enjoyed traveling with him. It was so different from traveling with a human or even an elf."

Tostig suddenly stopped and glanced to his left through what appeared to be a completely normal stand of trees and forest brush. "I have somewhere I want to take you," he told her. "It's only about an hour off the trail if we leave it right here, and we can spend the night there."

Alanda frowned. It wasn't time to stop yet, and it wouldn't be in an hour, either. She usually held firmly to the established traveling schedule for messengers, and she had messages to deliver and wanted to get home. She very much wanted to keep traveling with this man, though. She couldn't remember when she had enjoyed herself so much, and that warm feeling still lingered between them. "What is it?"

"It's a surprise. Something I think you might enjoy seeing. The hike's not so hard, even if it is through the trees."

"I'm not worried about it being hard," Alanda retorted, slightly insulted. "It's just that I haven't been home in weeks, and I have messages for the valley elves."

Tostig nodded in understanding. "This won't set you back more than a few hours," he pointed out, "and I can show you a shortcut to a lower part of the trail when we leave."

Alanda thought about it. A few hours wasn't much of a difference, and she had to admit she was curious. Another part of her, a small part of her of that seemed to have awakened only in the last few hours, relished the idea of spending the night with Tostig somewhere more special than the usual clearing. Deciding the few hours' difference wouldn't be a problem, she nodded silently.

Tostig grinned, flashing his perfect white teeth. "On to another adventure, then," he said cheerfully, and led the way into the forest.

ALANDA LOOKED up in awe at the crumbling tower in the middle of the clearing. She had never seen anything like it. It towered over the surrounding forest, so high Alanda wasn't sure how tall it actually was. Though the wildlife was taking it over with vines and lichen crawling up the stone walls, it was still impressive.

"Tostig," she breathed. "What is this place?"

"An old elf tower, maybe?" Tostig shrugged. "I'm not sure. My trainer and I found it when I was an apprentice, and I visit it almost every time I'm on this part of the trails. It's strange because the tower seems to be the only structure - if there had been a larger castle or building, the stones would still be there even if they had come down. There's nothing other than the tower."

"It's unbelievable."

It really was. The top of the tower, where it still stood solid, had slits where guards could fit a bow and arrow. The stone walls were of a dark gray rock Alanda didn't recognize, weathered from what appeared to be centuries in the forest. The northern side of the round structure was crumbled in on itself at the top, and Alanda could see what remained of a staircase encircling the inner walls. It looked like a tower built with defense in mind, but defense of what? There were no cities or even villages near.

Tostig strode forward and brushed aside some hanging vines, exposing an arched doorway standing two or three feet above his head and wide enough for two humans to enter abreast. "Come look inside!"

Alanda and Alis followed his lead. A large, circular room at the bottom of the staircase was littered with years of leaves and other forest detritus the wind must have blown in. The light was dim, as there were no windows at ground level, though there were some small openings further up the staircase. It looked like a perfect place to hide, and Alanda blushed as she thought of spending time alone there with Tostig. She didn't know why, but she wanted to be close to him – wanted it so much she was a little afraid of impropriety.

Mastering herself, she backed out of the space, followed closely by

Alis, who did not seem to appreciate the room in the same way her mistress had.

"Do you like it?" Tostig asked, leaning down to pet Ziva. "It's very comfortable on the inside, and though there's not much of a ceiling left, the walls protect you pretty well from the elements."

"It looks like it would be a wonderful place to camp," Alanda admitted. She took off her pack, indicating she was willing to stay.

Tostig suddenly became very businesslike, though the pink tinge in his cheeks made Alanda wonder if he had thought of some of the same things she had. "I'll hunt us up something for the evening meal," he said brusquely, removing his own pack and stringing his longbow.

"I can hunt," Alanda objected. She did not want to feel beholden to the man, no matter what the feelings she had were telling her.

"I nearly apprenticed to one of the hunters in Lakeland; my father, actually," Tostig bragged. "I'll be quick. Why don't you set up the campsite for us?"

Alanda, not sure what to say, only nodded. She still felt slightly uneasy accepting food from Tostig when she could hunt perfectly well and had plenty of rations stowed in her pack.

Tostig read her indecision. "Ziva, stay," he said when his dog made to follow him. "You stay, too." He had a teasing glint in his blue eyes. Without another word, he turned and strode out of the clearing, not even giving Alanda the chance to retrieve and string her bow.

Alanda sighed and set to work, building a small campfire in front of the tower and fashioning a spit out of some young, live branches she cut from the low-hanging trees.

Tostig returned less than an hour later, two fat rabbits dangling from his belt. Alanda, who had expected him to be gone longer, had to admit she was impressed. It was often hard to shoot a second rabbit; killing the first usually caused the others to hastily scatter.

"We'll sup well tonight," Tostig bragged. He held up his free hand, showing her the bunch of green herbs he had picked.

"I have some salt in my pack, besides," Alanda told him, rummaging for it. "The elves always include it in their supplies for messengers."

"I delivered to the tselqs at my last stop," Tostig told her. "And while they supply messengers generously, the rations aren't as satisfying as what you might get from the other races." He was referring to tselqs being strictly vegetarian. Committed pacifists, they refused to commit violence even against the animals of Ilbeor. Their rations were good, consisting of a sweeter hardtack, various dried vegetables, nuts, and fruits, but to humans used to consuming meat, they often felt lacking.

Tostig hummed while he expertly cleaned and spitted the rabbits. Alanda, absorbed in combing Alis, thought she recognized the tune: *An Old Man on a Mountaintop*. She smiled. The song was a happy one about an old man calling for his lost love from the top of the mountain, not realizing she could hear his calls as she made her way up to him. The song ended when she called back in a trill of pure joy.

They took turns turning the spit, talking of their villages. Alanda, who had never been to Lakeland, was intrigued by what it would be like to live near such a large body of water. True to its name, Lakeland was situated on the banks of the Irolam Lake, about a week's journey from Blackwell. She was not surprised to learn that Lakeland children learned to swim at a younger age than usual - sometimes as soon as their third birth celebration - to avoid accidental drownings.

Alanda told Tostig of Blackwell's namesake: an old well made entirely of shining black rock no one from the village had ever been able to identify. Clarifying that the well had dried up in times forgotten, she somewhat wistfully told him of the walks to the large stream bordering the village to fill her family's water buckets, and the longer treks to Wyntou Rill when they wanted to swim on a hot summer's day.

When the fat rabbits, well-seasoned and cooked to perfection, were ready, they both ate with a relish, sharing the meat with their dogs. Tostig and Alanda each added something from their packs to the meal: Alanda, some of the elves' dried berries, and Tostig, a loaf of the sweet hardtack made by the tselqs.

Though they had reached the tower in full daylight, the night was deepening by the time they finished: on the side of the Guilnora

Mountains, the sun set early and quickly. While Tostig buried the remains of their dinner and Alanda tossed more branches onto their fire, Alis and Ziva snuggled together, their sides touching, and watched their humans contentedly.

When Alanda and Tostig, their tasks finished, returned to sit by the fire, Tostig gestured at the dogs. "They seem to have the right idea," he whispered, and held out his hand to her, an invitation.

Alanda took his hand without hesitation, glorying in the warm shiver that ran down her spine. She didn't know what it was about Tostig, but she felt something for him she had never felt for any of the young men in her village, and she relished in the contact.

"I always wanted a family," Tostig said, his voice deeper than it had been when they were discussing other things. "I grew up with my mother and father and three sisters, and there's just something about having a home with everything running the way it should. You'd like my mother; she's a kind woman, but forceful when it comes to doing what's right. My father's a hunter, so he's gone a lot, but when he's home, he's hilarious."

"Mmmm," Alanda replied, somewhat distracted by the warm feeling of the fingers intertwined with hers.

"What about you? Do you want a family? I mean, you pursued a profession, which means you wouldn't need a husband, but - "

"No, I do want a family someday," Alanda interjected. "I haven't thought about it all that much, but I took a profession to help my family."

Tostig nodded but frowned. "What does your father do?" he asked.

"He's a leatherworker," Alanda answered. "And he's very good. It's just that..." She shook her head, not finishing what she had been about to say.

Tostig wasn't sure if he should press her or not. A good leather-worker usually made a decent living, decent enough for his family to be considered middies and to live in the town proper. But if Alanda had felt the need to take a profession to earn money for her family, they would have to be poor. It made little sense to him - he had expected her father either had no profession or was an unsuccessful farmer or shepherd.

"Just that what?" He asked the question softly, squeezing her hand in his. He wanted to know all about her, so he thought it was worth it to risk asking her the question.

Alanda sighed. "Well, my father is a wonderful man, but he's a drinker. He spends most of what he earns at the inn. We've asked Jenson not to serve him, but Jenson's never been one to turn down coin, so…" She trailed off, unsure of what else to say.

Tostig finally understood. He knew of several drinkers in Lakeland, and he had never envied their families. Not only did they spend much of their earnings on ale, mead, or wine, but they rarely worked as hard or as successfully as other tradesmen or artisans. It explained why, though her father had a skilled trade, his family needed the earnings of their children.

"What about your mother?" he asked.

Alanda brightened, which made him smile. "She's wonderful. She's very soft-spoken, but at the same time, has taught me and my brother well. She is good with a needle and thread and knows how to make soaps and oils from herbs and flowers, so we're able to survive even without my father bringing in too much."

Without even thinking about what he was going to do, Tostig withdrew his hand from hers and, before she could protest, put his arm around her and drew her to his side. He couldn't explain exactly why, but he wanted her close. Alanda seemed to have no objection as she snuggled into him, watching the fire all the while.

As she placed her left hand on her leg, Tostig caught a glance of the glittering ring on her fourth finger. "Whoa," he said, surprised. "Where'd you get that?" He pointed to the ring.

Alanda blushed. She had forgotten she was wearing it, and of course, Tostig wouldn't have seen it before because she had worn her gloves until the sun was safely behind the mountains. "The elves of Kilynelle gave it to me when they made me an elf-friend," she answered self-consciously. "It's called Moonshield."

Tostig took her hand in his free one and examined the gemstones glittering in the fire's light. "You're an elf-friend?" he asked, a hint of incredulity coloring his voice. "I thought elf-friends were only part of the old stories. I've never met one before, especially among messengers. What did you do for them to give you that?"

Alanda considered the question, for it was one she had asked herself many times after she had left Kilynelle. "I don't really know," she finally admitted. "I was sick and had to stay there a while. I got to know a few of the elves while I was healing, and I learned some of their language. A traveler named Grayson apparently thought well of me, but I don't know how that would have made any difference. Then, in the circle on my last night there, they gave me the ring and told me they had named me elf-friend. I'm not even sure what it means."

"Wait," Tostig said, flustered. He drew away from her just enough to look into her eyes. "You've met *Grayson*?" His voice, which had been politely incredulous at the idea of her being an elf-friend, rose in utter disbelief.

Alanda was confused. "Yes," she answered slowly. "He came to visit me while I was still bedridden. I thought it was unique that he could speak Yrui with Garrett and Myrine, and that's what gave me the idea of trying to learn it myself. He gave me a piece of wood when he saw a figurine I had carved for Myrine, who healed me."

Tostig shook his head. "There is more to you than anyone might have thought upon meeting you," he told her. "You sit there, casual as can be, and tell me you're an elf-friend and you've met Grayson the Traveler. Alanda, Grayson is a *legend* among the traveling professions. Had you never heard of him?"

"No, Alicia never mentioned him."

"He always seems to be everywhere anything interesting is happening, he carries gifts exactly suited to their recipients, and he knows all the languages of the land. No one knows who he really is, but he's in the old stories as well as the new. Everyone in the traveling professions hopes to meet him on their journeys."

"I thought he was human," Alanda said, even more confused now. "He looked and sounded human."

Tostig shook his head. "No one is exactly sure what he is, but it's clear that he's been around for generations. Maybe he's some kind of wizard; I don't know."

Alanda sat silently, contemplating. If it was true, then perhaps Grayson's commendation had meant more than she thought. But why would someone like that take an interest in her? It made no sense. She shook her head, trying to dispel the disconcerting thoughts.

Tostig placed his hand on her cheek to stop the motion, and a frisson of energy seemed to pass from his palm into her very skin. She shivered again and did not resist when he tilted her face towards his and kissed her.

WAKING up in Tostig's arms the next morning was an experience Alanda never wanted to forget. She opened her eyes, warmth suffusing her body as she nuzzled her head on his chest. She knew he was awake, too, when the arm that had stayed around her all night began lightly rubbing her back.

As she lay there, content in his arms, the soft light of *uht* only barely lightening the openings in the wall above them, she thought about the night before, what they had done, what she wished they could have done. She was still fully clothed, having agreed with Tostig that they should remain modest. That had not stopped them from kissing, though, and *oh* - the kisses! Alanda's cheeks burned as she thought of his mouth on hers, his tongue probing the inside of her mouth, the light tugs on her lips.

Tostig planted a chaste kiss on the top of her head. "I'm surprised Alis and Ziva haven't come in here to wake us," he murmured, his lips still against her hair.

Alanda reluctantly sat up, automatically smoothing her hair, which was a bit disheveled. Turning, she observed Tostig, who still lay at his ease atop the traveling blankets they had spread on the leafy floor. He grinned at her. "Surely we don't have to leave just yet," he said, patting the blanket beside him.

Alanda shook her head. "I still have several days of journey to get home," she told him. "Alis and I need to leave." Her voice was regretful but firm; she could not afford to tarry here, as much as she wanted to.

Tostig nodded, and sat up beside her. "Then we'd best break camp and get back onto the trail."

They both got to their feet and began rolling the blankets they had used the night before. When Alanda had stowed hers neatly in her pack, she leaned down and petted Alis. "You're ready to go, aren't you, girl?" she asked fondly.

Alis gave a soft bark, which Alanda took to indicate agreement.

"Shall we breakfast from our packs?" Tostig asked when the camp had been cleared and their packs and weapons stood ready against the wall of the tower. Before she could answer, he leaned in for a kiss, cupping his hand around the back of her head to pull her in.

When he pulled away, Alanda shook her head, regretful that the kiss hadn't lasted longer. She tried to return to the business at hand. "Yes, let's eat from our packs before we set off."

Tostig laughed, a light, cheerful sound that made Alanda smile ruefully. "Nothing can distract you, can it?" he asked, teasing mischief in his voice.

"It's not that I don't want to stay," Alanda protested. "It's just that I have these messages, and - "

"I know you want to get home," Tostig cut her off. "I don't blame you." He took the provisions he had separated out when he repacked his belongings and sat down in front of their banked fire. Alanda followed suit, and their dogs joined them as they ate in companionable silence.

By the time they had finished, the sun was rising in the east, casting an orange and pink glow over the small clearing. Alanda busied herself applying sun salve to her face and neck, and Tostig watched with some interest.

"Why do you have to do that?" he asked. "We're going to be mostly in the forest today."

As succinctly as she could, Alanda explained her extreme reaction to the sun and confessed it was the issue that had caused her to become so ill she had to remain in Kilynelle. He seemed anxious as she donned her cloak and then fastened her pack on over it, drawing the hood over her head and forehead so she looked much like she had when he had first met her.

"Are you going to be all right?" he asked anxiously. "We can wait - "

"I'll be fine," Alanda assured him. "You worry like an old gramma! This is always how I travel, and I don't have any trouble as long as I'm covered and use the sun salve." She pulled on her traveling gloves as she spoke. "There. I'm ready."

"Come on, then," Tostig invited, leading the way down the mountain and back into the forest.

The way back down to the messenger paths was difficult to navigate. Alanda and Tostig had to pick their way down a steep slope, grasping trees and branches to keep their balance. When they reached the trail nearly two hours later, Alanda was red-faced and sweaty even in the cool morning air, and Tostig's face looked ruddier than usual, too.

As they continued down the messenger path to the trailhead, they kept a running conversation about the settlements and villages they delivered messages to, the people they had met, and their own homes. Though she didn't comment on it, Alanda was delighted with the way he described his home, his parents, and his sisters. It was evident Tostig loved his family, and she thought he would make a good father and provider one day. She blushed a bit as she realized she was thinking of him as a potential match, but she knew their time together couldn't be easily dismissed. She felt something for him she had never felt before, and she thought her parents would approve if he came to ask to court her.

Tostig, for his part, didn't tell her in words that he was already planning on visiting her home in Blackwell to talk to her parents. Instead, he just took her hand as they journeyed down the trail together, enjoying the feel of it in his, even through her travelers' gloves. He had never thought so fervently about his own future as he did when they were heading down the trails; he couldn't explain the instant attraction and affection he felt, but neither could he dismiss it.

By the time they got to the trailhead in the late afternoon, neither was ready to part from the other. Alanda looked east toward the elven village of Isasari, which was almost in a direct line from the trailhead, about four days into the valley. Her home was south of that, another three days' journey, and she knew she had to make haste.

"I go east here," she told Tostig somewhat regretfully, knowing he would have to go northeast. Part of her hoped Tostig would choose to continue traveling with her, but she knew it was unlikely. Tostig needed to get another assignment and to visit his family.

Tostig looked at her. "May I call on you in Blackwell?" he asked, somewhat formally. He squeezed her hand, and Alanda was acutely aware of his fingers intertwined with hers.

"Yes. I should be home in a week. My mother will want me to stay awhile after being away so long, but I will have to take another assignment soon."

"I'll come as soon as I can," Tostig said. "Wait for me." It was not said in a tone of command, but yet Alanda felt herself wanting to obey him. She wanted to be there when he arrived to speak to her parents.

Just past the line of trees bordering the valley, he took her in his arms and kissed her long and deep. "I will come," he promised. "I won't take another assignment before I come to you."

"And I won't take another until you come," she promised in return. It was as much as either of them had to offer, but at that moment, it was enough. In the course of two short days, they both knew their lives had irrevocably changed.

Alanda made her deliveries to Isasari without incident. She was proud of the additional fifteen coppers she made in the elven village, but she did not stay even one night. She was eager to get home, to see her family, to smell the new concoctions her mother had made, to see how Kitz was progressing toward starting his apprenticeship with their father. Most of all, though, she wanted to see Tostig again, and she knew he was coming.

The three days through the valley from Isasari to Blackwell

seemed to last an eternity. Even focusing on the sound of her footsteps and the soft pats of Alis's paws on the dirt road, she found the journey tiresome. For the first time since early in her apprenticeship, she was impatient as she traveled. Impatience, Alicia had counseled, never made for a pleasant journey. Part of the beauty of being a messenger was enjoying the sights and sounds of nature, enjoying the journey as much as the destination. Alanda was finding it hard to follow that adage, though, as she increased her speed on the last day of the journey.

If I can continue at this pace, I'll make it home for the evening meal.

Try as she might, the time for the evening meal and her usual stopping point passed, though she continued pressing into the evening hours in her haste to reach home. Alis plodded patiently beside her; after alerting her it was time to stop and being ignored, she seemed resigned to walking into the night. Alanda knew they would reach home before dark, though.

When the thatched roof of the small house showed over the horizon, bordered on the south by her mother's flower field, she was surprised no smoke rose from the chimney. She frowned, wondering why a fire wasn't lit; the evening was cool enough, and the evening meal wouldn't have been long past. She hoped they hadn't run out of firewood. It was one of Kitz's responsibilities to cut and gather as much as he could, and she had thought he had started stockpiling for winter.

Maybe it's just too warm, she rationalized as she pressed forward. She smiled as she reached the front door and lifted the latch.

Inside the house, the fireplace was dark, and a lone figure sat at the table, her head down on her arms. Before Alanda even saw Dandelion sitting there, however, she registered how unruly and messy the house was. Chairs were overturned; their scant extra clothing was strewn along a dirty floor that obviously hadn't been swept in days.

Just as Alanda saw her mother sitting there, Dandelion raised her head. Her hair was disheveled, and foam dripped from her mouth as she snarled at her daughter. "Get out," she screeched, her voice not sounding at all like the sweet, moderated tone she usually took. "Get out!"

Alanda choked back a sob as she understood. As she was backing through the door, she saw her father and Kitz come into the main room from the sleeping room in quick succession, probably wanting to know what the commotion was. Her glance at them as she closed the door confirmed what she already knew: her family had The Hunger.

They were all going to die.

THE HUNGER

The broken wagon wheel that had leaned against the house for as long as Alanda remembered was heavier than she expected.

She heaved at it, her breath catching as she tried to keep her composure and do what she knew had to be done. After pushing it around the house and to the front door, Alanda lodged the wagon wheel under the latch, adding its weight to the frame as well as not allowing the latch to be disengaged from the inside. She stepped back and surveyed her handiwork, satisfied it would do the job.

The tears she had held back as she worked came in a torrent down her sweaty face. Her strength sapped, she collapsed to her knees in front of the house and sobbed for what seemed like hours, until her tears ran out and her breath came in small hiccups. She had seen all three members of her family, and she knew there was no way for them to leave the house now. They would cause more and more destruction until the disease overtook them and they died.

During her sobbing fit, Alanda had been aware of the door rattling behind the wagon wheel more than once; someone in her family had been trying to escape. Despite her desperate longing to see them one last time, Alanda knew she could not let them out for any reason.

The Hunger had taken a neighboring family less than a year before. People got it by eating the meat of an infected animal or being bitten by one. Often, a rabbit or flying squirrel was the culprit, but it could also be passed between people. This was why her family had to be kept in at all costs. It could spread to the entire village if they were allowed to roam, and The Hunger was incurable and fatal.

There was nothing anyone could do for them now.

Alanda thought of the small wild game Kitz sometimes brought home with his undersized bow and arrows. He might not have known or seen the signs of The Hunger and by the time it was dead and skinned, the meat wouldn't look or taste different. Alanda thought he had probably brought home a flying squirrel or two, as he was wont to do. Since the family could rarely afford the butcher, they depended upon Kitz or Alanda for meat.

As Alanda started to think more clearly, she knew what she had to do. Her heart broke all over again as she stood and ran toward Deena's hut near the center of the village. Alis streaked along beside her without any command, sensing Alanda's distress. Her cloak flew behind her, the hood down and forgotten, but it didn't matter. The sun had long since set.

When she reached Deena's hut, she knocked desperately at the door, hoping upon hope the herbalist was home. Within moments the door opened, and the pudgy, kind-looking woman looked at Alanda with something akin to wonder, birdsong in the background from the small aviary she had built onto her house.

"Alanda?" she asked in concern. "What's wrong?"

She noted Alanda's breathless state and surmised the girl had run from her house. Alanda looked absolutely shattered, as though her entire world had come down upon her head.

"The Hunger," Alanda gasped, her voice cracking and her eyes welling with tears again. "My family!"

"Were you exposed?" Deena asked quickly, stepping back in genuine alarm.

"No. I only saw them from across the house. They didn't get close to me. Mama screamed for me to get out. I blocked the door with the wagon wheel, and - "

Deena stepped forward, no longer worried about exposure, and put her hand on Alanda's cheek, warm from exertion and tight with grief. "My poor dear, you did the right thing. Let me gather my supplies and we will alert the leaders and go back to your house."

Alanda nodded, though the phrase "alert the leaders" almost made her cry again. She knew what their function would be, and she didn't want to think about it.

"While I do this, is there anyone that could be there for you?" Deena asked. "Is there anyone we could bring with us to provide support? You need support, dear."

She could tell by Alanda's voice and bearing that weathering this in the company only of herself and the village leaders was not an option.

"Maryah," Alanda answered mechanically. "Maryah's my best friend, my only friend, really. But she's married with a small child. I don't know if she could come."

"I will send a childless wife to stay with her son," Deena said reassuringly. "Go to Maryah. By the time you've finished explaining, I will have someone on the way."

Though nearly five years Alanda's senior, Maryah had been a staple throughout her life. She was the granddaughter of the blacksmith who had taken Alanda's mother in when she had arrived in Blackwell, alone and friendless. Maryah's mother and Dandelion had become fast friends, and despite their age difference, Maryah and Alanda had practically grown up together. Maryah had married Serill when she was sixteen, and Serill had taken over the smithy after Maryah's grandfather had retired. She had a small boy. Despite the changes in circumstances and responsibilities, she and Alanda had remained very close.

Alanda nodded numbly, and Deena clasped her on the shoulder. "Go! I will prepare," she commanded.

Night had fully fallen by the time Alanda, Deena, Maryah, and three of the seven men who led the village gathered around Alanda's home. They were all greatly relieved to find the wagon wheel had remained in place; no one could have left since Alanda had gone to Deena's. Even as they stood there, watching solemnly, the door rattled, and a crash came from inside. Each sound seemed to tear off another bit of Alanda's heart, and she wanted nothing more than to go to them, to save them, or even to die with them.

Alanda did not want to cry in front of all the people who had gathered, even Maryah, so she held her pain inside as she listened to the sounds of the destruction caused by The Hunger. She knew her family was crazed by this point, foaming at the mouth like her mother, perhaps enraged they couldn't leave.

Deena lit a bunch of dried herbs she held tied together in her hands, and soon, a pungent, healthy smell permeated the air. She walked all around the small plot of land, waving the smoldering herbs and chanting softly. To Alanda's surprise, Deena went right up to the door and swirled the herbs in a complicated pattern. By the time she had finished, the herbs burned so low Alanda thought they must be burning Deena's hand, but Deena paid them no notice. She simply doused them in the rainwater barrel then placed what was left in front of the door.

Next, she took out a sack containing a mixture of salt and herbs and walked around the house, sprinkling as she went. When she came back, she went straight to Alanda. "Now we wait," she said. "I brought something to help you sleep." She opened the bag hanging from her shoulder and gave Alanda a small bottle. "I know you won't want to take this, but as your herbalist and healer, I insist you do. Hard days are coming. You need your rest."

Alanda turned to Maryah. "Thank you for coming," she said sincerely, her voice somewhat stronger. "I - "

"I'm here until the end," Maryah said matter-of-factly. "Isaac is going to stay with Jessa and her husband until I return, and when I return, you will come with me. I asked Serill to prepare an extra bed. When you aren't delivering messages, you'll live with us."

"Thank you," Alanda replied, her voice hollow. She would need a place to stay, and as an unwed young woman, living alone was out of the question.

"Do you have blankets?" Deena broke in. "You will not need shelter; there is to be no rain tonight."

"In my pack," Alanda said. "I have food, too, enough for the vigil."

The vigil. She hated the way the words tasted in her mouth and hated the ending they foretold.

"Good," Deena replied brusquely. "I brought food and blankets, as did the leaders and, I assume, Maryah."

"Yes," Maryah confirmed.

"We are sorry for what has happened to your family." Theldan, one of the town leaders, met her eyes and finally spoke. "The village will care for you until you are ready to make your match." His voice was kind; an older man and longtime leader, he had completed several vigils for The Hunger, but it was unusual for one family member to survive while the rest perished. He knew Alanda only slightly; he was the village tanner, and his work sometimes brought him into contact with Jondolan and his family, though he lived in the village. Even so, he was sensitive enough to try to understand her immense pain.

"Thank you, Theldan."

The six watchers set up their blankets a fair distance from the house. As Alanda unrolled her blanket and got out Alis's comb - she would not fail to care for the one family member she had left - she heard Theldan talking with the other two leaders, Eugene and Terrick, about setting up a watch to make sure none of her family got out, and to monitor the noise to get a fair guess of when they had passed.

Alanda combed Alis, murmuring and humming to her more for her own comfort than the dog's. When she finished, she took out Deena's sleep potion and considered it. She did not want to sleep knowing her family might be gone by the time she woke, but she was so weary she could barely move her limbs. The tryst with Tostig seemed a lifetime ago. How could things have gone so badly, so quickly?

She uncorked the bottle and swallowed the potion in one gulp. It was not magical. Deena was not a magician, a witch, or a sorceress. The herbal concoction did not immediately send her into a dreamless sleep, but as Alanda lay on her blankets with one hand on Alis, she breathed steadily and felt her eyes close.

IT TOOK two interminable days for the door to stop rattling and the crashing noises to stop, but the leaders waited another day to inspect the inside. Early the third morning, their faces covered to the eyes by heavy cloth soaked in an herbal potion, Theldan, Eugene, and Terrick went inside the house.

Theldan had firmly but kindly denied Alanda's request to go with them. It was the duty of the village leaders to check for survivors, and any family or friends of the stricken were not allowed back into the house lest they be tempted to collect belongings or touch the bodies. Alanda watched helplessly as Eugene and Terrick moved the wagon wheel aside and pushed open the latch to enter her home; she thought of her parents and brother and hoped they were at peace.

After they had gone through the house, Theldan came directly to Alanda and pulled the cloth away from his face. "They are gone," he said gently. "I have seen all three: your mother, your father, and the boy. They have succumbed and suffer no longer. Blessed be."

Alanda nodded, her face working as she attempted to conceal her grief. She knew what came next, and she didn't know if she could bear it. She knew no one would fault her if she left, but upon reflection, she realized she had to see it through, no matter how painful it would be.

Maryah took her hand and squeezed it. "Are you ready?"

Alanda nodded, and Maryah gave a signal to the waiting leaders with her free hand.

As one, the three leaders picked up the torches they had brought with them to the vigil. Theldan lit his with flint and steel and turned to light the others. Without a word, Theldan, Eugene, and Terrick advanced and touched their torches to the thatched roof, the base of the walls, the door…they kept adding fire until the entire house was ablaze.

Alanda watched the house where she had grown up burn to the ground, her whole family inside. Even as the smell of burnt flesh met that of the burning wood and straw, she did not cry again. She simply stood, watching, her tearless face stark in its grief. She did not even notice Maryah still held her hand. Alis whined with discomfort at the scene; even she could tell how terribly wrong everything had become.

IT TOOK A SURPRISINGLY short time for the house to burn. With the dryness of summer and the age of both the wood of the house and the straw, the structure collapsed before Alanda's eyes only a short time after being set ablaze. She watched as the large fire was replaced by smaller ones around some of the hardier wood, and she knew the house would continue to smolder until there was nothing left but ash.

Except somehow it didn't. Not all of it.

Kitz stood in the middle of the burnt wreckage, visible as soon as the front wall collapsed, holding a blue scarf their mother had kept in a place of honor on the simple wooden mantlepiece over the stone fireplace. The fireplace was still standing, but the mantle had burned and fallen.

Kitz was naked and covered in soot, but unburned; even his hair had been spared. The scarf he held was still a brilliant blue, despite the soot on it. Alanda could not conceive how either her brother or the scarf had survived the blaze that had taken everything else.

He didn't stand on the wood floor; the floor was gone. Instead, he stood on the ash, somehow between the smoldering piles of wood around him. His mouth was wide open in a silent scream.

Alanda stared for what seemed like minutes before she sprang into action. Concerned only for her brother, she ran forward despite Maryah trying to hold her back. Dodging the burning parts of the house and furniture, she was only vaguely aware of the village leaders shouting and Deena sobbing as she reached Kitz. She took him into her arms, marveling that his skin was not hot with fever or from the fire and that he had yet to make a sound.

He was alive! He wasn't burned! But *how?*

She looked back. Theldan, Eugene, and Terrick were running away from the house as fast as they could, Terrick's elderly form looking as though it might fall apart from the impact of his footsteps.

What are they going to do, Alanda wondered, *sound the alarm? For a twelve-year-old boy? Are they afraid?*

Deena was furiously going through her bag, perhaps trying to find the right combination of herbs for such a situation. *Was* there a right combination of herbs? Maryah simply stood, watching somberly in the singularly calm way she always had.

Alanda turned back to Kitz.

"Kitz?" she asked urgently. "Talk to me! What happened? How did you survive? Did you not have The Hunger? Did you go out a window in the back? Why are you standing here like this? Where are your clothes?" She shot the words out rapid-fire, desperate for answers that weren't forthcoming.

She shook him gently, trying to break his stance, to make him speak or even to look at her. Anything.

Kitz said nothing. He closed his mouth and fixed his eyes on his sister. His gaze was older, more serious, than she had ever seen it. She felt inexplicably like he was trying to speak to her through his gaze instead of his voice, but she couldn't understand what he was trying to convey.

"Alanda?" Maryah called firmly. "Bring him here. Take him out of the wreckage."

Alanda obeyed. Neither of them needed to stand in the middle of their burnt house, the ashes of their parents perhaps settling on them.

Deena was still there, tears running down her face as she worked. She used water from the rainwater barrel and herbs she crushed with mortar and pestle to make some sort of tincture. It was dark red and smelled foul.

"I need to clean him," Deena said, her words almost sounding like a choked sob. "It won't hurt him. It will get the soot off and protect him against any lingering disease." Like Alanda, she could tell Kitz did not have The Hunger, if he ever had. There was no fever, no madness, no foaming at the mouth.

Alanda nodded, and Kitz stood impassively while Deena took Dandelion's blue scarf from him and put it into her bag. She used her own cloth to wipe the red tincture over his small form. She wetted another cloth in the rainwater barrel and cleaned the remnants of the tincture from his body. When she had finished, Kitz was no longer covered in soot and didn't smell as bad as Alanda had thought he would, given the stink of Deena's concoction.

Kitz still didn't speak, despite repeated questions from Deena and Alanda. Only Maryah remained quiet, observing, and it was Maryah who picked up her own sleeping blanket and wrapped it around him.

"I'm going back home," she said determinedly.

Alanda thought she meant to abandon them as the town leaders had.

"My neighbors have a boy Kitz's age - Saul; they probably know each other - and will lend me some clothes for Kitz while you and I, Alanda, make him some new ones. Serill will set up a larger bed. Kitz will come with us."

"Maryah, I - "

"Where else are you going to go, Alanda?" Maryah asked, a bit aggressively. "We are able and willing to help you. Shelve your pride, and once Deena speaks with you, bring Kitz to my house. We'll sort everything there."

Without another word, she turned and left.

Alanda looked at Kitz. "Do you know Saul?" she asked, simply for something to say, something to get him to speak.

Kitz's expression did not change. He didn't nod or shake his head, and he didn't speak.

"It's the trauma," Deena broke in. "If he somehow survived The Hunger, that means he watched your parents die from it, and he watched your house burn."

Alanda remembered what Theldan had said with a suddenness that almost made her jump. "Theldan said he saw all three bodies. He said it specifically, that he had seen the bodies of my mother, my father, and my brother. How can that be?"

As if in answer, a loud bell rang from the village. Alanda, exhausted and grieving, thought the village leaders had sounded the alarm. She realized after a moment that it was the sanctum bell.

"It's the fifth day," she said dully. Every villager was required to gather at the sanctum every fifth day for worship, followed by a village meeting.

"I will give excuse," Deena said. As the village healer, she was one of the few people allowed to do so. "I must go. The village leaders will expect me to report about what has happened. I'll come straight to Maryah and Serill's house when it's over. Go now, and if Maryah is still there, tell her I will give excuse for her. If she isn't, light a fire and sit with Kitz as close to it as you can. A good sweat will be beneficial for both of you." She tenderly touched Alanda's cheek. "All will be well, child. Be thankful for what you have been given."

Alanda nodded, and Deena took her leave. She and Kitz, orphans now, were left alone with the embers of their home, their parents, and their former life.

"Will you take my hand?" Alanda asked hopefully.

Kitz just stood there, no longer looking at Alanda, but staring into the distance. Alis surprised Alanda by going up to him, sniffing him curiously, and whining softly.

"It's Kitz, Alis, you know him," Alanda chided softly, reaching out to pet her dog reassuringly. She was sure that between the fire, the tincture, and his lack of clothing, Kitz smelled very different to Alis.

Alis whined again but nosed the blanket away from Kitz's hand and licked it several times.

"Good girl," Alanda praised. "See? It's our Kitz."

Alis retreated to Alanda's side, but she kept her eyes on Kitz.

Alanda took Kitz's hand into her own. The boy's hand remained limp, but he didn't pull away. Alanda tightened her grip. "It's going to be okay, Kitz. I promise. I'll take care of you until you're old enough to live on your own. You're going to grow into a man and have a good job as a leatherworker. You're going to marry and have children and grow old in the village, where you belong. You'll see."

She let go of his hand and quickly gathered her things. At Deena's chiding, she had put on her sun salve and cloak before the village leaders had burned the house, so she knew she was safe as she haphazardly packed. She went back to Kitz and took his hand again.

"Alis, heel," she said quietly, and they set off at a slow walk toward the village. Kitz kept pace with her, walking as though in a trance. Alanda noticed he did not stumble or fall. He was at least that aware of his surroundings, and she took hope from it.

Alanda was glad the village was quiet. Everyone was at the sanctum and the houses were empty, the shops closed. She didn't have to think as she walked, having treaded the path to Maryah's house so often it was imprinted in her mind and, it seemed, her legs. Practicing a trick she had learned as an apprentice, she let her mind empty, focusing on putting one foot in front of the other and on Kitz's small, limp hand in hers.

When she reached the familiar house, one made of newer boards with a shingled roof and three rooms, she knocked at the door, expecting no one would answer. No one did. It seemed Maryah and her family had obeyed the insistent bell and gone to the sanctum. Alanda was glad; she knew Maryah and Serill would not mind if she let herself in and started a fire.

She entered the familiar house and saw a set of clothes laid out on one of the wooden chairs surrounding the table. The light blue tunic brought her tears back to the surface; it was almost the same color as the tunic her mother had worn the last day Alanda had seen her. Also sitting out were underthings, stockings, brown linen pants, and short brown boots. Maryah had thought of everything.

Alanda did not dress Kitz right away. She didn't want him to sweat in the new clothes in front of the fire. She led him close to the fire-place and asked him to sit down. He silently obeyed, sitting cross-legged exactly where he had been standing. Alanda smiled amidst her pain; Kitz had understood her and listened! Perhaps once the shock had worn off, he would become more responsive.

She quickly started a fire with the tinder and logs that were waiting to be lit.

Behind Kitz's back, Alanda took off her cloak and all her clothes down to her own underthings and wrapped herself in a blanket she found hanging over the back of a rocking chair. She told herself she would wash both blankets as soon as she and Kitz were done, and she sat next to him, taking his hand again. They both started sweating as the fire heated the already warm room. Watching the flames dance, Alanda was painfully reminded of the house burning only an hour before, and her mind flashed back to the smell of burning wood and burning bodies. Try as she might to suppress it, her body shook with repressed grief and fear.

"It's going to be okay, Kitz," Alanda whispered repeatedly, squeezing his hand. "It's going to be okay."

She wasn't sure who she was trying to convince.

SANCTUM

Maryah pinched her son Isaac lightly through his yellow tunic. It was not a punishing pinch, but a reminder to stand still, his legs pressed against the wooden bench in the sanctum's main hall and demonstrate that he was listening to the chants of the High Priest and his deacons at the front of the room. After their third birth celebration, the children of Blackwell began to be held to the approved standards of behavior in the sanctum, and Isaac did very well other than some fidgeting when the services proceeded into their second hour.

She kept her eyes dutifully to the front, not looking at her son even as she silently reprimanded him for his slight movements and tried to concentrate on the familiar fifth-day ritual of services. She, like every other villager and the nobles that ruled Blackwell, had been attending them since the very week of her birth, and the words and chants were as familiar to her as household duties and daily rituals. She could feel Serill standing to her other side, his muscled back ramrod straight.

This day, however, Maryah felt a measure of sympathy for her son. She, too, was having trouble keeping her eyes focused and her attention on the ritual. Though she stood dutifully as a middie wife and mother, a little disheveled from her three-day vigil aside Alanda, her mind kept wandering to what she had seen not two hours before: Alanda's brother Kitz, standing naked and unburned in the ruins of his house, alive against all reason.

For Annuah watches us, Annuah follows us, Annuah points his finger unto us and gives fruit unto the land.

Maryah repeated the words, hardly hearing herself or noticing what she was saying. Her faith had always been a source of comfort and strength, and she had always felt blessed by Annuah with a good, useful life. But even considering all she had been taught, all she felt about Annuah, the words of the chants never meant much to her. She simply listened to them, repeated them, and did her duty by them. Her faith itself ran deeper than ritual; it was a steadfast and fulfilling belief that Annuah did indeed watch over her and that living a righteous life was not only right, but necessary.

She had not had much time to talk to Serill when she had returned; the bells had already summoned them, and the bells could not be disobeyed. She had told him, as the family had walked to the familiar wooden building, simply that Alanda and Kitz had survived The Hunger and they would provide housing for them until Alanda married. He had agreed, being a good-hearted man and feeling responsible for his wife's friend, now alone in the world, but had not commented other than to let her know he would get what they needed to house the two orphans.

As he stands astride the Great Mountain, Annuah chooses those with virtue for duty in the land and strikes down those who do not obey.

As one with the rest of the congregants, Maryah turned her back on the front of the building during the second half of the statement, showing her rejection of those who would not follow the word of their god. It was a symbolic act, for there were none in the village that rejected the sanctum's teaching and there hadn't been one in her lifetime. The fifth-day services, the authority of the village's High Priest, and the steadfastness of the god Annuah were such an inculcated part of village life that it was rare for anyone to challenge them. She had heard those who did so were forced away from village life and not seen again.

As she turned to face forward again, she patted Isaac on the shoulder, silently praising him for performing the movements correctly. Her breath caught inaudibly as she felt his shoulder blade through his tunic; her son was still so small, so helpless. As she felt a surge of motherly affection pulse through her, she withdrew her hand and her mind wandered again to Kitz, to Alanda's fierce protection of him, and to the sheer unlikeliness of his survival. *Where in Annuah's plan is a boy who doesn't travel to the otherworld after The Hunger and the subsequent burning?*

Maryah was startled when she felt the soft touch of Serill's hand on her arm as the congregants sat on their hard, backless benches to listen to the Saying, the High Priest's words to them about the lives they must lead in order to be righteous and steadfast. She had been so caught up in her visions of Kitz among the wreckage that she had not immediately sat when the rest did, and she knew Serill would be both surprised and displeased by her inattention, for it reflected poorly on his household leadership. She hoped no one else had noticed.

Chastened, Maryah tried to put her focus on the Saying, where it should be. This was always her favorite part about fifth-day services. The High Priest of Blackwell was a good, faithful, and true speaker, and he had a way of understanding the lives of the villagers that translated into sage advice on both religious and practical matters. With a slight bit of her attention on the small boy next to her, making sure he remained still and paid attention to the Saying, she tried to force her focus away from the plight of Alanda and Kitz.

"My children," the High Priest began, looking over his congregants benevolently from behind the wooden altar staged above the benches, "as the summer wanes, today I wish to speak to you of the impermanence of life in this world."

Maryah blinked, wondering if he was going to bring up the deaths of Jondolan and Dandelion in the actual Saying. It would be unusual for him to do such a thing; usually matters of village news and business were saved until the less formal village meeting after the service.

"Fall toils are soon to beset our farmers," the High Priest went on, "as they prepare sustenance for our village and our nobles to last through the winter. Our hunters are hard at work, and our tradesmen and artisans must keep pace. Truly, our village works as a tiny world within a bigger, and each person must perform their functions with patience and hard work, so all may thrive. But as the summer and fall wane and the winter sets upon us, we are reminded that just as Annuah gives us life, so he removes it when the time is right."

Though she tried to stay focused, Maryah had a sudden flash of Alanda's face as Theldan and the other village leaders had set fire to her home, the bodies of her parents and her brother locked inside. *Everything was taken away from her. Everything but Kitz. But how did he survive?*

"As we do not grieve the loss of the leaves and green grasses over the cold winter, knowing they will return to us in the fullness of spring, so we should not grieve overmuch the loss of life as the seasons change. For all righteous lives are given to the otherworld, to the hands of Annuah, for the good work of the land."

The High Priest did not mention the plight of Alanda's family in the Saying, and Maryah knew there had not been enough time for it to become common knowledge. Jondolan and Dandelion's family had lived rather remotely from the rest of the village, and the village leaders would not have thought it right to spread the word before the meeting. She couldn't help but wonder, though, as the High Priest continued speaking, if he was preparing them for the news. Jondolan and Dandelion, though poor and not without certain problems, were well liked, and many would take their loss to heart.

Try as she might to remain focused, Maryah's thoughts drifted to Alanda's mother as the Saying went on. She had been one of the most beautiful women in the village, despite the plain tunics and pants she had worn in keeping with her status. Her perfumes and soaps, supplied from the beautiful, wild-growing flower field she had kept seeded and cultivated herself, were sought after by all the middie women and even the noble ladies from the castle, and her prices had never been too exorbitant. Maryah herself had patronized Dandelion once she reached adulthood and married, and Serill had never objected to the expense. Dandelion had been like a second mother to

Maryah, one sweeter and less temperamental than her own. Maryah's heart ached as she thought of the talks she had as a young married woman with Dandelion, first on her own, and then in the company of her baby.

It is not for me to grieve her, she thought sternly. *Alanda lost her mother; I merely lost a friend.* Still, she couldn't help the sadness and regret that coursed through her as she thought of the talks they would never have, the gentle advice she would never again be given.

When the Saying was over some half an hour later, Maryah stood in unison with the rest of the congregants, not needing any reminders from Serill this time. While she had not strictly paid attention to the Saying, she had remained aware of her surroundings and did her duty faithfully as the last song was announced and sung, led by one of the two deacons in a clear, low voice.

In the ebb and flow of this life of toil
We give of ourselves to land and soil
We strive to be righteous, faithful, and true
As Annuah's will commands us to do.

THE STRICTURES of the sanctum rituals relaxed perceptibly as soon as the final song was done, and the villagers moved and spoke to one another as they transitioned into the more relaxed village meeting that always followed the service.

Isaac grinned at his mother as he sat wiggling on the seat next to her. "Meeting time, Mama," he told her, his voice only slightly quieter than his usual speaking voice.

Maryah smiled back at him, permitting him the comment as the High Priest moved away from the altar, his place to be taken by the seven village leaders. "You were a good boy today, Isaac," she praised him softly. "When we get home after the meeting, you may play in the yard while I make our midday meal."

Maryah's attention was drawn away from Isaac when Serill once again touched her arm. "Where was your mind today?" he asked in a whisper.

Maryah colored. She knew no one could hear Serill, and his voice was not harsh. The implied reproof still stung. Still, she had been inattentive, and it did not surprise her he had noticed. She answered him calmly. "I couldn't get my mind off Alanda and Kitz," she admitted. "The vigil was difficult."

Serill grunted and nodded, and she knew she had heard the last of it. He was not an unfeeling man, and he had accepted her answer.

The chatter among the villagers ceased as the seven leaders stood before them, placed one step down from the actual altar, as was appropriate for anyone not ordained.

"Blessed be," Theldan said, his deep voice ringing over the crowd, strong and sure.

Maryah noted he had changed his clothing and washed his face and hands before the meeting, and she idly wondered when he had found the time. It was good he had, though. As a village leader, part of his job was to appear strong for the village so they would trust his leadership.

"Today, we begin the meeting with news of great sadness," Theldan continued. "Jondolan and Dandelion were taken by The Hunger only this morning."

Mutters broke out among the crowd. It was clear that the news was distressing, not only because of the deaths, but due to the cause of them. The Hunger was one of the most feared conditions among the humans of Ilbeor.

Theldan held up a hand for silence. "The vigil was attended to, and none of the afflicted made contact with anyone outside their home. The house has been burned and the proper rituals observed. They suffer no more, and their children yet survive. Alanda and Kitz will be taken into the keeping of Serill and Maryah until a match can be arranged, but we ask that the village respect their time of mourning until they are ready to be seen again."

More mutters broke out at this matter-of-fact statement. Maryah caught Alanda's name from a few rows back as the baker asked his wife how the girl and her brother had survived and whether they were safe in Blackwell. Maryah bit back a retort. Did anyone really think the leaders would permit anyone affected by The Hunger to live in the village? It was simply not done.

"Remain calm," entreated another one of the village leaders, Drystan, who worked as the village peacekeeper in addition to his duties at the grain mill. "You have the assurances of the leaders that all has been conducted safely, and no one in Blackwell is in any danger at the present time. Theldan, Eugene, and Terrick attended to the vigil, and Deena did what must be done. Three days they waited, and they inspected the home before the burning. None escaped. We must be nothing but thankful that their children escaped infection."

But Kitz didn't, Maryah thought. *Kitz was in the house when it burned. Theldan checked his body himself.* She tried to reconcile herself to what the village was being told; would Kitz's strange survival ever be addressed, or would they simply see it as a blessing that he wasn't in the house when his parents got infected? Would the village even accept that, given that Kitz was only twelve and had not yet started an apprenticeship?

How had the boy survived?

The matter of Jondolan and Dandelion having now been dealt with, the village leaders turned to other matters in a businesslike fashion contrived to put the villagers' minds at ease. Maryah allowed her mind to wander more freely; the business being discussed mostly concerned the men of the village. Each of the leaders gave reports on the industries in the village and the needs the villagers would have to meet before the next fifth day service and into the fall season. Though Maryah knew issues of provision, supplies, and craft were vital, she was well outside of most of it as a wife and mother; her place was in her home with her son.

I wonder what we shall find when we return home. Will Kitz be speaking again? Will he be able to explain what happened?

I must remind Serill we will need meat from the butcher to supplement what he brought from his last hunt. We do not have enough to feed two addi-

tional people past today. Will he hunt tomorrow, or will the day be spent in work and getting Alanda and Kitz settled into our home?

The meeting concluded after the villagers to addressed concerns with the leaders. Today, there had not been many comments, and Maryah was thankful. The village meetings sometimes ran long, and she was eager to return home and talk with Serill, Alanda, and Deena.

They rose from their bench and Maryah took Isaac's hand, nodding at her husband, indicating she had things to discuss. She had to tell him the truth about Kitz; it was unfair for him to provide housing for the boy without knowing. She hoped he would not change his mind, but she was duty bound to tell him.

As they exited the sanctum through the large, thick double doors, Maryah began walking quickly. She wanted to get Serill away from the crowd. She pulled at Isaac's hand, encouraging him to hurry, but before they had made it ten steps away from the building, Theldan tapped Serill on the shoulder.

"I must speak with you," he said gravely. "Alone."

Serill nodded. "I will come. Maryah, take Isaac home. After I speak to Theldan, I will go to the woodworker and see what can be made ready for Alanda and Kitz. The shop should be open by then, and Randall can run the forges for me this afternoon."

"As you say," Maryah replied placidly, keeping her voice calm to hide the growing panic she felt. What would Theldan tell Serill? What did he know about Kitz's circumstances? She clearly pictured Theldan and the other two leaders running as fast as they could back toward the village after Kitz had appeared in the wreckage, and she could only guess what they had been thinking, what they had been afraid of, and what they might tell Serill.

"Mama!" Isaac called insistently, pulling on her hand after Serill walked away with Theldan. After three hours in the sanctum, the young boy was ready to go home and play.

"Yes," she said, recovering herself. "Let's go home."

AFTER THEY HAD SEPARATED themselves from the crowd thronging the entrance to the sanctum, Maryah dropped Isaac's hand but asked him to stay with her instead of running ahead.

"Isaac," she told him as he skipped beside her, happy to be free to move again, "I need to talk to you about something."

Isaac looked up at her, stopping his skipping and slowing to a walk. He looked slightly worried at his mother's tone and seemed almost as though he was afraid of a scolding.

"I'm going to need your help at home today. You see, my friend Alanda and her brother Kitz are going to come and live with us for a while."

Isaac grinned. "Alanda's going to live at our house? With you and me and Papa?" He seemed excited at the prospect; Alanda had always been kind to him.

"She is. And her brother, Kitz. He's twelve. Do you remember Kitz?"

"Kitz is a big boy," Isaac commented. "Why are they coming?"

Maryah stopped and knelt down on a level with her son. "Something very sad happened," she told him. "Were you listening to Theldan at the meeting today?"

Isaac looked down. He had not listened, even though he was supposed to. "No, Mama," he answered quietly.

"It's okay, Isaac. Mama's not cross with you," she reassured him. "But Theldan told the village what happened. Alanda and Kitz's mama and papa died this morning. They got sick and had to go live with Annuah in the otherworld."

Isaac's eyes went round. "They can't take care of Alanda and Kitz anymore?"

Maryah shook her head sadly. "No, they can't. They have to help Annuah take care of Ilbeor now. Alanda and Kitz are very sad today, and I wanted to know if you would help me make them happy and comfortable at our house."

"I'll let them play with my wooden horse," Isaac said, as though considering what else he might do. "And I'll be so, so good."

Maryah stood and began walking toward their house again.

"That's very good," she complimented him. "And I think they would like it if you smiled at them and let them know you are happy they are going to live with us. Are you happy?"

"Where will they sleep?"

"Papa's going to get them a new bed to put in the second sleeping room. We'll get some new chairs for the living room, too. Everyone will have a place."

Isaac smiled, satisfied. "I get to keep my own chair?" he confirmed.

"Yes, you can keep your chair. There's something else I need to tell you about, though. Something that I think you can help Mama and Papa and Alanda with."

"I'll help you," Isaac assured her.

"Good. Isaac, Kitz is very, very sad, and I think he's scared, too. It's scary not to have a mama and a papa anymore when you're still a child. Can you understand that?"

Isaac nodded hugely, seeming for a moment to enjoy the exaggerated movement.

"Kitz doesn't like talking right now," she told him. "He doesn't want to say anything to anyone. But you know what? I think he would like it if you would talk to him, even if he doesn't talk back to you. Do you think you can do that?"

"I can tell him lots of things," Isaac responded confidently. "About our house and our garden and my toys."

They had reached the front porch of their dwelling, and she stopped. "That's exactly right. Now, are you ready to greet our guests? You can still play in the yard while Mama makes the midday meal, just as I said. Alanda will watch you."

Isaac skipped in front of her and put his hand on the silver doorknob, struggling to turn it in his small hand. With a push, he entered the house ahead of his mother, already looking for Alanda and Kitz.

PROPHET

By the time Alanda heard the front door of Maryah's house open after fifth-day services, she was in the back sitting over a washtub of soapy water, scrubbing the two blankets she and Kitz had used. The wet, heavy fabric was comforting to her as she worked, the physical labor of scrubbing it over the ridged board a balm to her spirit. She had left Kitz sitting in Maryah's rocking chair after he had gotten dressed, and she listened hopefully as small Isaac greeted him. Kitz, however, didn't reply, and her heart sank.

Maryah opened the back door and joined her. "You started a fire?" she asked.

"Deena wanted to sweat out Kitz and I," Alanda told her. "I put it out, didn't I?" She suddenly couldn't remember what she had done after she had decided they had sweated enough.

"Yes, but it's stifling in there. Why didn't you air out the house?"

"I'm sorry, Maryah," Alanda said sincerely. "I was so focused on getting Kitz dressed and your blankets washed, I suppose I just forgot." She knew she should have opened the windows to let the air circulate when she was done. She felt a pang of regret more for leaving Kitz inside such a hot room than for inconveniencing Maryah.

Maryah's eyes softened. "Don't worry," she told Alanda. "It's okay;

we'll have the house aired out in no time. It's time for Isaac to play outside. Would you watch him while I open the windows and prepare the midday meal?" Maryah thought perhaps her four-year-old's cheerful disposition would help Alanda forget her sadness, if only for a moment.

Alanda nodded, and Maryah went back inside. Soon Isaac came bouncing out the door without a care in the world. At four years old, he was just coming into his own language and reason. Though he had been told Alanda and Kitz were going to live with him and why, it did not affect his mood. He seemed happy to have new friends to share his house with.

"Alanda!" he chirped. "Mama says you watch me!"

"That's right," Alanda told him in a falsely cheerful tone. "You go play while I wash these blankets, but stay where I can see you, all right?"

"Okay!" Isaac scampered off, carefully avoiding Maryah's vegetable garden. Soon, he had picked up a small shovel, no doubt made for him in his father's blacksmith shop, and began digging a hole in a patch of bare dirt in Alanda's line of sight. He sang nonsensically while he dug, and it did much to brighten her spirits.

Maryah called them in for the midday meal just as Alanda was hanging the second blanket to dry. Isaac ran in front of her, chanting, "Wash your hands, wash your hands, wash your hands, Alanda!"

She smiled a small but genuine smile, a smile holding a sadness that would never fully leave her. "You wash *your* hands, dirty boy! I haven't been digging in the mud!"

Her smile faded when she came in and saw Kitz still sitting mutely in the rocking chair. "Kitz, it's time for the midday meal. Come to the table," she said in what she hoped was a normal tone, as much for Isaac's sake as Kitz's.

Much to her surprise, Kitz got up, went to the table, and sat down in the chair Maryah pulled out for him. "Serill's letting his apprentice work the shop this afternoon," she told Alanda, busily spooning hot stew into four hardened clay bowls. "He's going to trade with the woodworker for two more chairs and a bedstead and mattress for you and Kitz."

Alanda felt bad that Serill had to take off work and trade for items and Kitz would need. "Maryah, I - "

"Shush. Don't worry about that now," Maryah chided her as she settled Isaac into a chair and pointed out where Alanda could sit. "You'll contribute when it's time, but for now, let us help. Don't pretend you wouldn't do the same for me if our situations were reversed."

"Kitz is hungry!" Isaac proclaimed suddenly in a singsong voice. "He wants stew!"

Maryah and Alanda looked at Isaac in surprise. Maryah was the first to find her voice. In a carefully casual tone, she asked, "And how do you know that?"

"He told me with his thinks," Isaac said matter-of-factly.

"Okay," Maryah said, as though this was the most normal thing in the world. "Well, Kitz is lucky because stew is what we're having! Does he like rabbit stew?" she asked, looking at Alanda.

"He loves it," Alanda answered, trying to shake off Isaac's uncanny announcement.

"Does he drink watered ale or plain water?" Maryah continued, determined their meal would be as if things were normal.

"Watered ale when he can get it," Alanda answered. "But plain water is fine as well."

"We have ale. You still won't drink it, I presume?" Maryah knew Alanda's distaste for any kind of spirit after she had seen what the overindulgence had done to her father.

"No, thank you. I'll just have water. Can I help?"

"Not a bit. You stay where you are," Maryah ordered.

The cool water and hot rabbit stew were very welcome, who had not had the heart to eat breakfast. She ate, remembering to compliment Maryah on her excellent cooking, and felt somewhat better. Through it all, Kitz ate mechanically, his expression unchanging as he drained both his cup and his bowl.

"Kitz wants more ale!" Isaac announced.

Without a word, Alanda got up and mixed the drink, half ale and half water, and handed it to Kitz. Just as Isaac had said, he seemed to be thirsty and drank the watered ale quickly.

"Okay, Isaac, it's time to wash the dishes," Maryah said. She gestured to the two tubs of water sitting on the floor near the back door, one murky with soap and the other clear. "Be very careful and don't break anything."

Alanda was strongly reminded of Kitz's childhood as Isaac, with exaggerated care, carried each of their bowls and cups to the first tub and placed them inside. This was the age children began helping around the house, and Alanda could tell this was far from the first time he had washed dishes. She continued to watch him, still seeing Kitz as a young boy as he wiped each of the dishes with a soapy rag and rinsed them in the clear water of the other tub.

"All done, Mama! You dry!" Isaac said proudly.

"Very good, Isaac. Go on and play, now."

Alanda got up before Maryah could protest and dried each dish, putting them where they went on the large hutch opposite her seat at the table. Kitz continued to sit in silence, staring into nowhere from his chair, his hands neatly folded in his lap and his back ramrod straight.

"Kitz," Maryah said, addressing him directly for the first time. "I want you to rest. Go into the first sleeping room, that door on the left, and lay down on the big bed in there, not Isaac's small one. There are blankets, but I daresay you won't need them."

Kitz got up without looking at anyone and followed her instructions. When the door closed behind him, Maryah addressed Alanda. "We'll talk about the difficult things in a bit," she said. "First, we need to get you into some cooler clothes. You look great in that leather, but you must be boiling."

Alanda wasn't sure what to say. Maryah was right; she was very hot in the traveling leathers, but on the other hand, they were the last thing she had from her parents, and she was loath to part with them.

Maryah seemed to read her mind. "I'm sure you'll get another assignment soon," she continued. "You'll put the leathers back on then.

But in the meantime, you should be comfortable. I have a light linen dress that would fit you well enough, and another piece of linen you can use for a scarf. I also have some gloves. My shoes won't fit you, but it's warm enough to be barefoot right now. You won't burn indoors, right? We'll deal with the winter when it comes."

"All right," Alanda heard herself say even as she caressed the fine leather of her sleeve and thought of her father and how he had stayed sober long enough to earn the money and make it for her. A tear ran down her cheek.

Maryah came in from the second sleeping room, where she stored her spare clothing. Seeing Alanda's face, she immediately came to her side and took her hand.

"You don't have to hide your sadness from me," she said, her voice dripping with sympathy for her friend.

"Thank you. It's just…" Alanda trailed off, not knowing how to complete the sentence.

"I know," Maryah said. "Well, I don't *know*, not exactly, but I can guess how you're feeling. You need time to grieve, and Kitz needs you here for the time being."

"I know," Alanda said woodenly, not bothering to wipe the tears trickling gently down her face. "I have to be strong for him."

"You do." Maryah nodded. "But strong doesn't mean unfeeling. Even if you never show it to him, you can always let your feelings out in front of me. Now, here's the dress and things," she said brusquely, letting go of Alanda's hand and placing a bundle of linen in front of Alanda. "Go into the second sleeping room and change. I'll clean your leather for you."

"No, I want to," Alanda told her. "Please."

"Of course. I'll set the supplies on the table."

Alanda disappeared with the dress Maryah had given her. She had to admit it was a good choice. Though the light green linen was fitted for Maryah, who was slightly taller and had more curves than Alanda, it fit decently. It had three-quarter sleeves, which meant the pair of gloves would likely cover her exposed skin when she went out, though she could use sun salve if necessary. The full skirt reached the top of her feet, and Alanda reminded herself to use sun salve there, as well. When she was done dressing, Alanda examined herself critically. She wasn't used to wearing dresses, and though plain, this one was one of the prettiest things she had ever worn. Poor women usually wore tunics and pants like the men, which made clothing easier to pass around.

She came back into the main area, and Maryah clapped her hands together from her seat at the table, where she had assembled the cleaning supplies for Alanda's leathers. "That works!" she said. "I'll alter it so it fits your figure better, and you can have it. Perhaps we can add some embroidery to the neckline and sleeves in time. I love the color, but I made the dress up plain for economy and work. It looks nice on you."

Alanda walked purposefully across the room to her pack, noticing the swishing of the soft material against her legs. Digging, she found her small coin purse and extracted three copper coins. She took Maryah's hand and pressed them into it. "For the dress," she said firmly.

"Alanda, you could buy a dress in the shop for three coppers, or at least the linen to make one," Maryah protested. "This is just an old thing I had lying around."

"It's a nice dress, and you're planning on altering it for me. Take the coin, or I'll put my leathers back on."

Maryah looked ready to protest again, but she saw the expression on Alanda's face and relented. This was a matter of pride. "Thank you," she said, getting up to place the coins in a small jar on the hutch.

Neither of them noticed the door to the first sleeping room had opened. Kitz stood in the doorway, watching the exchange impassively. He startled them when he spoke, his voice toneless and without inflection, yet strong and clear.

Burned in autumn twilight, wandering into spring
Returning to a place beyond memory
Crowned in white, stolen from lost longing
Whispers and threats, standing atop a spire of lies

Throne and scepter in waiting
For legacy's reluctant claim.

ALANDA AND MARYAH looked at each other in bewilderment and fear. Kitz had not spoken since they had taken him from the embers, but Alanda thought she would have preferred he not speak at all than to speak in such a toneless and emotionless voice, and to speak such abstract, almost nonsensical statements. Kitz had never spoken a riddle in his entire life.

"What did you say, Kitz?" Alanda tried to keep her voice from shaking. "What did you mean?"

Kitz stayed as silent and impassive as though he had never spoken. His dark blonde-brown hair was tousled from his recent rest and looked just like Alanda remembered from countless mornings at home, but his expression was so blank he appeared not to be alive, his usual olive tones pale in the light from the back window. Not noticing his sister's entreaty, he turned, walked back into the sleeping room, and closed the door behind himself. Alis moved to follow him, which was unusual, but Alanda called her back with a voice that did not entirely escape the effects of the trembles she felt in her body.

"Alanda, what *was* that?" Maryah looked worriedly at her friend.

The front door opened and Serill came in. A strapping man with a bulging chest and corded arm muscles from his work as a blacksmith, Serill had black hair and a thick beard. His overall visage contrasted magnificently with his wife's smaller but curvy frame and light brunette curls. Despite his imposing appearance, Serill had a friendly face and bearing and was known as a man who would stop at little to help others.

Alanda and Maryah looked at each other, and Alanda shook her head very slightly to show that she did not want to discuss Kitz's strange pronouncement with Serill.

"Were your successful, dear?" Maryah asked to cover the awkward silence.

"Yes," Serill grunted. "I'll take the wagon this afternoon to collect the goods. The woodworker already had what we needed."

"Good, good," Maryah said absently.

"Where's the boy?" Serill asked, looking around. "I saw Theldan, and he told me what happened. There's much to discuss."

"Kitz sleeping," Isaac said proudly, leaping into his father's brawny arms. "He's so, so tired."

"Is that so, little one?" Serill asked, ruffling Isaac's brown curls.

Maryah quickly filled him in on Kitz's silence and what she had done to make them comfortable, concluding by offering Serill some of the rabbit stew. He ate two bowlfuls while Isaac played with his set of glyph chips. He reminded Alanda of a bumblebee in his yellow tunic and dark brown pants, flitting around from one place to the next, placing the chips in various places around the main room.

It was clear he was playing some sort of game, but he kept to himself. Alanda knew he couldn't read the glyph chips yet. Meant to teach children the twenty-nine universal glyphs used by all five civilized races, wooden chips displaying the glyphs and their meanings were used by village parents to teach their offspring when they reached five years of age. The set Isaac was playing with had belonged to Kitz as a child.

"Alanda?" Serill broke through her thoughts, having finished eating, and moved to his big chair in the main room. "The village leaders want to see you tomorrow, after you've had a chance to rest and settle in. They need to talk to you about Kitz. In the meantime, I've been told to keep him well and keep him inside. The villagers only know he survived, not the circumstances."

"What about Kitz?" Alanda asked absently, still watching Isaac play. In her grief and confusion, Serill's words about hiding Kitz didn't quite register.

"The fact that Theldan, Eugene, and Terrick saw his body and burned the house themselves has given the leaders a fright. They haven't spread the word; they only told me because they knew you and Kitz were going to stay here, but the leaders don't know what to do about his rebirth."

"Rebirth?" Serill had Alanda's full attention at last. "What do you mean, rebirth? And what can they do about him, anyway? They're not going to exile him!"

"No, no. Theldan assured me they don't hold the boy or you to blame, but the circumstances are mysterious. They want to know your plans, and they want to know about anything Kitz has said since they took him from the house." Serill paused and took a long pipe and a leather pick from the shelf above the table. He said nothing else as he filled the bowl, tamped it down, and lit it with a taper. He puffed a small cloud of fragrant smoke into the air. "Alanda, they all saw Kitz's body, and Theldan himself checked it for signs of life. The boy was gone. To find him alive after seeing his body and burning the house is unheard of, and they don't know what he is now."

"He's a boy!" Alanda retorted hotly. "A boy who may have been to the otherworld and back, but still just a boy. He'll grow into a man just like anyone else."

"No, he won't," a voice interjected from the open front door. Everyone turned in surprise to find Deena standing there holding Dandelion's blue scarf in her hands. "Kitz is no longer like anyone else. He's not dangerous, at least not to anyone in the village, but he will never be an ordinary man. Alanda, I would like to speak to you privately."

Alanda stood from her chair at the table and made a move toward the herbalist, but Serill put up a hand and said, "Wait." His tone was so definitive and commanding that Alanda stopped obediently, looking at him with both impatience and expectation.

"The boy is now living under my roof. I will provide for him until he reaches manhood, if necessary, but my wife and I will be told everything there is to know if we are to do so. If he is to be shrouded in secrecy and lies, he will not stay here."

Deena looked at Alanda, who was momentarily undecided. She unconsciously fiddled with her braid as she thought, *I trust Serill and Maryah, but I don't know what Deena is going to say. What if it's something dangerous to Kitz? We don't have anywhere else to go, and I can't take him with me on assignments.*

She nodded reluctantly.

"Very well." Deena crossed the room and sat down in Maryah's rocking chair without being invited.

"Isaac, go out back and play," Maryah said, sitting down at the table across from where Alanda had returned to her seat.

"No!" Isaac protested defiantly. "Kitz needs me to say his thinks!"

Serill stood and crossed the room quickly, knelt, and took Isaac's upper arms gently but firmly in his huge hands, shaking him slightly. "You must never say 'no' to Mama," he rebuked sternly, his voice slightly raised with emphasis. "Never!"

Isaac looked startled, but then he said quietly, "Yes, Papa."

"Good." Serill released Isaac's arms and rocked back on his heels. He lifted Isaac's chin gently with one finger and looked at him. "Kitz is sleeping, so you don't need to say his thoughts right now. So go out and play as Mama bid you, and we'll call you in when he wakes up."

Isaac brightened as suddenly as the sun coming out after a rainstorm. Happy again, he ran out the back door, forgetting to close it behind him. Maryah got up and closed the door gently, then sat at the table next to the open window to supervise his play.

"What did Isaac mean by telling you he needs to say Kitz's thoughts?" Serill asked immediately.

"Yes, I'd like to know as well," Deena agreed.

Alanda and Maryah shared a brief look and Alanda, resigned, finally nodded. Maryah filled Serill and Deena in on everything, Alanda interjecting occasionally, up to Kitz's weird speech right before Serill had arrived. Neither Alanda nor Maryah could remember it word for word, but they conveyed the majority of it with enough accuracy to emphasize how strange and indecipherable it had been. "We don't know what he meant by it," Maryah finished. "He wouldn't say anything else; he just went back into the sleeping room and closed the door."

Serill sat silently, puffing on his pipe. Maryah knew he was turning everything over in his head and did not disturb him, though she hoped what she'd said wouldn't dissuade him from taking Alanda and

Kitz into their home. "I don't think Kitz is dangerous," she said rather lamely.

"He's not." Deena spoke up. "Kitz is a prophet."

Alanda leapt to her feet, knocking her wooden chair onto its back legs. For a moment, it seemed the chair would topple before it righted itself.

"What?" she shouted. Everyone looked at her in surprise; Alanda had never been one to raise her voice. Alis leapt to her feet and whined uncomfortably.

Chagrined, Alanda continued in a normal tone. "No. Kitz is traumatized. He witnessed something awful and was left for dead and nearly burned to death. He'll snap out of it, and he'll grow up like anyone else." Even as she spoke the words, she heard the ring of the lie in them; it was apparent by Kitz's weird speech that he was no longer himself.

Maryah stood and went over to her friend, urging her back into her seat. Alanda looked oddly small as she gazed at the others, and Deena's revelation seemed to diminish her further. "It can't be true," she whispered. She did not want this for Kitz. She did not want the life he should have had to be taken from him.

"It is true," Deena told her gently. "He has been through what all prophets have been through since the beginning of time: a death, a rebirth, a purification by fire. What Maryah said about his odd speech only confirmed what I already thought. What you heard was his first prophecy."

"What does this mean?" Serill asked before Alanda could interject again.

"For now, for Kitz, nothing. Let small Isaac interact with him and, if he continues to do so, tell you what Kitz is thinking. It is not unusual for prophets to have someone close to them, a child even, become attuned to their needs - or at least, so I have read in the histories. Kitz is healthy and needs food, drink, and sunshine like any growing boy, though I understand he must be kept inside until the next fifth-day meeting, when the village will be told about him. If he says something, write it down, starting with all you can remember about what he said today. Are you all literate?" she asked directly.

"Yes," said Alanda, Serill, and Maryah as one.

"Good. I will leave paper and, if you don't have them already, a pen and inkpot for you. It is important to write what he says exactly as he says it." She paused for a moment. "This is his profession. He will take no other, and you must accept and understand that. I can't decipher his first prophecy any more than the rest of you, but everything he says from here on is of great import."

Alanda heard a scratching noise, and she blinked in surprise as she realized Maryah was busily writing on a piece of thick yellow paper, a small writing pen poised in her graceful fingers, the inkpot just to her left. Alanda had not even noticed her get up to get the supplies; she was still reeling from everything Deena had said.

"There's something else," Deena said. "Alanda, the existence and survival of this scarf proves there is more to your mother's history than any of us knew." She held up Dandelion's blue scarf, and the bright color of the fabric and of the embroidered symbols on it almost seemed to glow in the light.

Alanda said nothing. Her stomach turned over at the thought that there might be more revelations, and she couldn't see how her mother's scarf could possibly have anything to do with their situation.

"The material is rare, almost unique. To test it, I tried to burn it in my fireplace," Deena said matter-of-factly.

Alanda still said nothing, though Deena had expected her to protest.

"The blue material, and the thread it was embroidered with, are interlaced with a fireproof material. I don't know the name of it, but I do know the only people who can find and use it are the witches and warlocks of Ferncombe, far in the north. It is so impervious to flame that those who own something made of it are apt to throw it into a clean fire to remove stains from it. As you can see, it bears no marks either from the house fire or my fire." She passed the scarf to Alanda. "This is yours. You're going to need it."

Alanda took it from her, realizing how *much* the herbalist knew.

Deena loved to read; everyone in the village knew that. She had read not only every book the sanctum offered, but every book owned by every family in Blackwell. Alanda wondered if she had even gone into the nobles' library.

She shook herself slightly and finally broke her silence. "Need it? I want it very much, of course. My mother prized it above any other possession and said it was one of the few things she brought with her when she came to Blackwell. But why do I need it?"

"There are only two explanations for a common villager to have such an item. Either your mother was descended from witches and warlocks, or she was a member of the nobility in Emelle. The embroidery contains many words and some runes, but it's not something I can read. I suggest you take it to the elves."

"What? And leave Kitz? No," Alanda protested.

"Kitz will be well taken care of," Maryah promised. "We will provide for all his needs and, as far as we are able, raise him as our own until you return. Right, Serill?"

A tense silence followed for several moments while Serill drew on his pipe, thinking while releasing large amounts of smoke into the room. Finally, he looked at his wife. "Yes," he said, his deep voice carrying no hint of indecision. "We will care for the boy."

Maryah breathed a sigh of relief.

"Alanda must go to the elves," Deena said. "I am certain the village leaders will agree with me. Is there an elven clan that will help you? Perhaps some you know from your profession?" Deena did not know about Alanda's crisis, Myrine's help, and Alanda's subsequent acceptance as an elf-friend. Aside from Tostig, no one knew.

In answer, Alanda carefully peeled the glove from her right hand and showed Deena her ring.

Everyone in the room gasped, even Maryah, who Alanda would have assumed to have seen it prior to her putting the gloves on after the midday meal. "When and where did you get *that*?" Deena asked incredulously. "And how?"

"The elves of Kilynelle gave it to me. It's supposed to be invisible by day unless I choose to show it," she said, remembering what

Garratt had told her. "I am an elf-friend. I believe any of the clans would help me now, though I would prefer to go back to Kilynelle. I know a few of the elves there."

Maryah and Serill exchanged a heavy look. Maryah had known Alanda since she was a baby, and Serill had gotten to know her after he had married Maryah. Besides her pale complexion and white-blonde hair, there had never seemed to be anything unusual about her; she was a normal girl, and Kitz was a normal boy. Now, they were hearing Kitz was a prophet, Alanda was an elf-friend, and both were descended from either witches or nobility. It challenged their sense of reality.

Deena stood. "I have said what was needed, and you should know I will report Kitz's status and yours to the village leaders and the High Priest. I am honor-bound to do so. Alanda, you must go to Kilynelle as soon as may be. Kitz will be fine here."

Without inviting questions or asking leave, Deena walked out, closing the front door behind her.

THE AFTERNOON and evening were busy. While Serill went to collect the new bedstead and chairs, Maryah bustled about, filling a new mattress with straw and visiting the shop to purchase two new feather pillows and some blankets. Alanda cleaned her leathers and boots, watching over Kitz, who simply sat where he was told and stared into space, and Isaac, who played on the floor of the main room with a small wooden horse and some other toys.

Kitz made no more odd pronouncements; he didn't speak at all. Isaac continued to cheerfully tell Maryah, Alanda, and Serill what Kitz wanted, and he grew impatient if they didn't attend to him immediately. After bringing the wagon home, Serill set to work installing the new furniture, heaving the straw mattress onto the bed, and adding additional hooks on the wall for their clothing.

By the first night, Alanda and Kitz were moved into the second sleeping room and were as comfortable as they ever had been in the big, new bed. Even Alis seemed relatively comfortable, having spent the afternoon and evening freely roaming the house and yard, sniffing everything and making her mark against the trees and buildings.

The second morning was much the same, but after the midday meal it was time for Alanda to meet Theldan and the other village leaders. Maryah had spent the morning altering the dress so it fit correctly, and Alanda dressed and braided her hair carefully. Instead of her cloak, which would look odd to the village leaders, Alanda donned the simple linen scarf Maryah had provided and tied it under her chin. She rubbed sun salve on her face, the exposed parts of her neck and arms, and on the tops of her feet. At Maryah's insistence, she dabbed on some of Dandelion's homemade perfume before she left. The scent made her feel like crying.

It was hard leaving Kitz even for the afternoon, but she had to obey the summons. Once she had ordered Alis to stay and closed the door behind her, she took a deep breath, emptied her mind, and walked alone toward the hall where the leaders met. Something was missing from the usual sounds of the empty-minded walking she was used to practicing: the footfalls from Alis's steady trot at her side. Alanda felt she could have used the reassurance of her constant companion, but she had felt that the village leaders would not welcome Alis into their hall for what she was sure would be a formal meeting.

To her surprise, Theldan stood alone in front of the hall to greet her when she arrived. "Not here," he said gruffly, but not unkindly. "We're meeting in the sanctum."

"The sanctum?" Alanda asked, surprised. The only meetings she knew of that were held in the sanctum were the village meetings that took place after worship on the fifth day.

"Yes," Theldan answered. "Come with me."

He softened at the uncertain look on her face, remembering how stricken she had been only the day before. His heart went out to her; survivors of The Hunger were rare, and he knew she must be afraid of what the future would hold. "All will be well, child," he said.

Alanda nodded and followed him across the square to the sanctum. It was an extensive structure, large enough to hold the entire village and the lesser nobles who technically ruled them. Though made of wood like all the other buildings, the sanctum was stained a very dark brown with an expensive concoction sent from the Sanctum of Oaos, the High Sanctum of the land, and was reapplied every few years. It had large windows set with thick, bubbled glass and imposing doors set under a tower holding a bell large enough to be heard throughout Blackwell and the surrounding valley.

Alanda silently followed Theldan through the doors, barely noting the smell of wood polish, the wooden benches, and the ornate decor. She had come here every fifth day since she had been born, and the surroundings were as familiar as her own home had been. What caught her attention was the people at the front of the sanctum blocking the carved wooden altar, talking quietly. She recognized the High Priest and all seven village leaders, but there were also two people she had only ever seen at sanctum services. By their fine, colorful clothing, Alanda knew they were the noble couple who lived in the small castle on the hill above Blackwell.

"Alanda," the High Priest greeted her, smiling. "Come. Do not be afraid."

The High Priest was a friendly, portly, older man who had been at the sanctum Alanda's entire life, first as a lower priest, advancing until he took the sanctum's top position. His smile comforted Alanda; she knew he was not devious and would not lie to her.

Unlike some priests she had heard about on her travels, he was not corrupt. His only minor crime seemed to be overindulgence in the food provided for him by sanctum members, including the nobles. He had a penchant for sugar-sweetened treats the likes of which Alanda had never tasted. Sugar had to be imported from the tselqs, and it rarely passed the lips of the poor or even the middies.

They joined the group standing in the area between the front benches and the steps leading up to the altar, and the High Priest invited them all to sit. Then he did something Alanda had never seen; he sat on the third step leading up to the altar, putting himself on a level with everyone else.

"We are here," the High Priest began, "to discuss Alanda and Kitz, their future in the village, and the safeguards we must take. Deena has relayed the circumstances of yesterday's incident and the changes wrought in Kitz and in yourself, Alanda."

"I would start, if that is agreeable," Theldan said. He remained seated, unusual for someone speaking to a group. It seemed almost as though they had orchestrated everything to make it appear they were all equals, which puzzled Alanda. "I would like to assure Alanda that neither she nor Kitz is to be exiled or persecuted. This meeting has not been called for such purpose. We are here only to determine what we can of their future."

Alanda visibly relaxed. Despite Serill's assurances, she had been afraid they would be asked to leave. She had already been planning where to go - Kilynelle most likely - but knew that, as friendly as the inhabitants of another settlement might be, it would never be like home.

"We have a prophet in our midst," the High Priest continued. "I do not doubt the word of Deena. Prophets are rare and must be cared for particularly. I would suggest Kitz come to live and be cared for here, with the priests. He is hidden for now, even from the villagers, but will not remain so for long."

"No." Alanda surprised everyone, herself included, by interrupting. "Kitz needs to be where he is comfortable. He has suffered, as have I. The best place is with Serill and Maryah. Did Deena tell you about Isaac?"

"Yes, my dear," the High Priest told her, apparently unperturbed by the interruption. "The child seems to be - what's the word Deena used - attuned to Kitz."

"That's only one reason Kitz should stay there," Alanda said. "He knows Maryah and Serill. He trusts them. They have already made a home for him."

The High Priest nodded, but the nobleman broke in. "Kitz's comfort is not the highest concern." He spoke unctuously, stroking his thin gray beard as he addressed them. "The boy's safety and training take priority. He will be safer here."

"I don't believe you can train a prophet," Eugene, another of the village leaders, interjected. "Prophets speak when they wish and say what has been given them to say." It was clear the others were listening; he had trained as a priest's acolyte but had left his apprenticeship before his final vows. He was literate and better-read than most in the village.

"Kitz has already given one prophecy," Alanda agreed, hating the feel of the word 'prophecy' on her tongue. "At Maryah and Serill's home. Isaac tells us when he is hungry, thirsty, tired, or uncomfortable. He has a warm bed and people who care for him, not people who would use him or attempt to train him for their own purposes."

The noblewoman seemed about to speak, but the High Priest cut across her, raising his voice slightly. "Alanda is right," he said. "The boy's spiritual welfare must be considered, and though it seems spiritual welfare would be best served at a sanctum, this may not be so. The boy, Isaac, is proof enough of this."

"Isaac's parents will not give him up to the sanctum," Eugene said. "I asked Serill this morning."

The nobles grew sour, the High Priest ran his hand over his bald head, and Theldan shifted in his seat. There could be no question of removing Isaac without his parents' permission; it was never done except in cases of mistreatment, neglect, or the death of the parents. The law was sacrosanct, and even the sanctum could not overturn it.

The noblewoman spoke, her voice honeyed and slightly accented. "Perhaps if the boy were to live at the castle," she said thoughtfully. "He would live in luxury, and the small child and his parents could come with him, so they all remain together." She smiled, pleased with herself and certain she had solved the problem. "We would prepare a room for you as well, dear," she added, treating Alanda as an afterthought.

"No," Alanda said again, still without heat. "The castle is an unfamiliar place with unfamiliar people. Kitz needs comfort, not luxury. You'll find, I think, those are two very different things. He may be a prophet, but he's still just a boy."

The noble couple looked affronted at what they perceived as a slight on their luxurious lifestyle, but both remained quiet.

"I think," Theldan said after a pause, "we have to listen to Alanda. She is Kitz's guardian. Though young, she has a profession and is an adult. She is unmarried, so there is no question of her living alone with him; it would not be proper. I have become convinced she is right: Kitz must stay with Serill, Maryah, and Isaac, especially while Alanda is away."

"It is settled," the High Priest said with finality. "I agree with Theldan."

"Serill has agreed to visits by Deena, the priests, and the village leaders," Eugene offered, "and has agreed either he or Maryah will record anything Kitz says and report it immediately. They are both literate."

"He must not be left alone," the nobleman said thoughtfully.

"He won't be," Alanda replied, a little tired of the nobles interfering. Though technically Blackwell's rulers and protectors, they rarely got involved in the village's affairs. If the villagers paid their taxes, the nobles didn't bother them. It worked for everyone, and Alanda didn't see why it should change now. "Maryah or Serill, as well as Issac, will be with Kitz when I am not." Alanda struggled to keep her voice even.

"As I said," the High Priest interjected, looking directly at the nobles, "we have settled this matter." He was the only person in the village who would dare to keep a noble from doing what they pleased.

The matter of Kitz put to rest, the meeting shifted to Alanda. It was quickly decided she should do as Deena had suggested and travel to Kilynelle as soon as possible to find answers about her mother's heritage. The High Priest had examined the scarf and was unable to read the embroidered words and runes. "It is possible you will have to travel farther than Kilynelle to find answers," he said, "but find them you must, for they will determine your and Kitz's future."

Then the conversation took an unwelcome turn.

"Now we must discuss a match for you, Alanda," Theldan said gently. "I know the prospect might be unwelcome, but you are of age and orphaned. Finding a good husband for you is of utmost importance, and it falls to us to broker the match."

"I don't want to talk about marriage," Alanda said firmly. "I want all my focus on caring for Kitz and my duties as a messenger. Though I intend to marry in time, now is not the moment." Because she had a profession and could support herself, marriage was not required, and she intended to remind them all of that. Most poor young women who took professions eventually married, but some, like Deena, continued to live single throughout their lives.

"My dear," the noblewoman said, her voice strained, "this is not a matter in which you have a choice. We must find you a husband. There are many messengers, but you now hold a unique position. You cannot expect to care properly for your brother and remain a traveler, and you have not yet reached an age to make a home for yourself."

Everyone was silent, giving her the gift of time to answer. Alanda immediately thought of Tostig and the plans they had made, but she thought the fact that he was from a different village might give them pause, especially given Kitz's position. If her parents were alive, she could have introduced him as a prospective suitor. She silently flailed for something, anything, to give her time to find Tostig and explain. After a few long moments, she hit on exactly what she needed to say.

"Deena said my mother's scarf proves she was either the daughter of witches or nobility. Either option changes my prospects. If she is rightfully a witch, then Kitz and I must go to Ferncombe." Alanda did not actually know if this was true, but she doubted the others did, either. "If she is nobility, I must marry a nobleman. Also, Deena may not have told you, but I have been named an elf-friend." She took off her glove and displayed Moonshield to the astonished eyes of the group, especially the noblewoman. "If I am not mistaken, the elves must be consulted in the matter of my match. If they are not, it is possible our trading status with them could change."

The noblewoman opened and closed her mouth, shifting uncomfortably. It could not have been clearer that the idea of Alanda, a poor village messenger, marrying a nobleman or being in close contact with the mysterious elven clans discomfited her.

"You are right," the nobleman said suddenly and decisively. "Your marriage cannot be resolved until we know your heritage and status and have consulted with the Council of Kilynelle." He did not seem uncomfortable, unlike his wife, who turned to him in disbelief. He held up a hand, stopping her from speaking. "Go learn what you can, and when you return with proof of your mother's former station, we will discuss your prospects."

Alanda nodded. They didn't need to know she would go to Lakeland first and try to find Tostig. She needed to talk to him and spend more time with him. She had no intention of being married off to a nobleman or traveling to Ferncombe; she wanted to marry Tostig, and she would do anything in her power to have the opportunity. She knew that because of Kitz's need for Isaac, she could not move to his village, as was custom if they made a match. He would have to move to Blackwell, and that might change his mind about marrying her. She hoped it wouldn't. Regardless of tradition and rules, she was determined to have a say in her marriage and of whom would become a brother or even a father-figure to Kitz.

The High Priest and Theldan concluded the meeting, wished Alanda well, and reassured her that Kitz would be well taken care of.

ALANDA WOKE BEFORE *UHT*. She knew Maryah and Serill and even Isaac would care for Kitz but leaving him so soon gave her pause. She lay in bed listening to his even breathing next to her.

Maybe it's not so urgent. Mama's heritage won't change. I can stay a few more days, even a week.

She turned the matter over and over until Alis woke and whined. She quietly got out of bed without waking Kitz and dressed quickly in the semidarkness of the predawn.

After she dressed, she took Alis outside. She was unsurprised to find Maryah and Serill awake and talking quietly at the table while Serill ate his porridge; he had to be at the forge early to feed the fires. They both looked at her, and Maryah opened her mouth to speak, but Alanda shook her head and proceeded quietly out the back door.

Alanda waited patiently while Alis sniffed around and found a spot, and Alis took position outside the outhouse door while Alanda attended to her own needs. When she returned to the main room of the house, Serill had finished his breakfast but waited at the table.

"Why are you wearing your dress?" Maryah asked immediately. There was no accusation in her voice, but Alanda reacted defensively.

"I decided to stay another few days to make sure Kitz is all right," she said a little defiantly.

"No," Serill said, surprising both women. As he spoke, he walked across the room in long strides, sitting on his chair to pull on his heavy boots. "You must go, Alanda. You are welcome here, but the village leaders, the High Priest, and the nobles have all spoken to me. They came to the shop after the meeting yesterday. They impressed upon me the importance of this journey and that it must not be delayed."

"Kitz is more important - " Alanda began.

"Yes," Maryah interrupted. "I agree with you, Alanda, but Kitz is in a good situation. Not only have we agreed to bring him into our home, not only is Isaac in accord with him, but the town leaders, the sanctum, and the nobles have all pledged support. They see him as a person of importance, a blessing to the village, even, and his every need will be met. They offered Serill everything from extra food to a larger house."

Alanda closed her mouth, stymied. It was clear Kitz would be taken care of better than ever, though nothing could replace their parents or the normal life he had once had.

In that moment, she realized all they had taken for granted. Despite their father's drinking and the family's subsequent poverty, they had been well loved and provided as normal and happy a life as any in Blackwell. She suddenly wondered if Kitz comprehended or even cared about all they had lost.

Maryah saw the flitting expressions on Alanda's face and knew there would be no more objections. She nodded silently at Serill, who stood.

"I must get to work." He pulled the door open. "Fair journey, Alanda. Fear not; you will return to find your brother healthy and comfortable."

"Go wake Kitz and change," Maryah ordered when the door had shut behind her husband. "The sooner you go, the sooner you'll return. I will hire a horseback messenger to Kilynelle should you be needed sooner." Horseback messengers were faster than regular messengers and traveled alone with their horses instead of with dogs, stopping less frequently and riding more hours each day. They were expensive to hire and usually only used for urgent messages. Maryah's offer touched Alanda. She inclined her head, conveying both gratitude and acceptance, and went to change.

After she had pulled on her leathers and her boots, Alanda woke Kitz.

"Kitz," she said softly, touching his small shoulder, then rubbing her hand down his back. "It's time to wake." She felt him stir. He sat up, looking sleepy and tousled but immediately focusing his gaze on the opposite wall. Alanda felt the familiar pang of sorrow, but she ignored it.

"I'm leaving for Kilynelle soon," she said. "Dress and come into the main room, please." As she left the room, she saw him stand and knew he would be out soon.

Isaac was already in the main room, still in his unbleached linen nightgown, looking sleepy. "Mornin', Alanda," he said in his small voice.

"Good morning, little one," she replied in a falsely cheerful voice.

He padded over to her and leaned against her leather-clad leg, putting one arm around her thigh. "I love Kitz for you while you go," he said.

Alanda felt tears prick her eyes. How could such a small child know what had been at the very center of her worries - that, despite all the care she knew would be lavished on him, there was no one left who would love Kitz like she did? She knelt and hugged the child for the first time. "Thank you," she whispered. "I know you will."

Maryah watched the scene without commenting. "Do you have time for some porridge?" she asked. "I know messengers usually leave before the sun rises, but you aren't on assignment today."

Alanda nodded and went to the table, Isaac padding along quietly beside her. As she sat in her chair, he sat in his.

"Isaac, you have to dress," Maryah chided him gently. "Go now; Alanda won't leave until you're back."

Isaac slid off his chair and ran into their sleeping room, slamming the door behind him. "Quietly, Isaac!" Maryah called in exasperation. She turned to Alanda, her face apologetic. "He hasn't learned all his manners yet."

"He's small," Alanda said with a slight, sad smile.

As Maryah handed her a bowl of porridge and a wooden spoon, the door to the second sleeping room opened and Kitz came out, fully dressed but for shoes. Like most children in Blackwell, Kitz was used to going barefoot in all but the winter months.

"Good morning, Kitz," Maryah said, smiling pleasantly at him even though he wasn't looking at her. She smoothed her hands on the blue apron she wore tied over her pale pink linen dress. "Come to the table, please. It's time for breakfast. Alanda, I have a treat for you."

She handed Alanda a mug of something steaming hot.

"Coffee!" Alanda exclaimed, taking the mug gratefully. She had not had coffee for at least a year; it was an extravagance even in middie households. She had been offered some by the tselqs the previous year, and she had loved it. She remembered telling Maryah about it.

Kitz silently took his place at the table.

"Serill got it for you yesterday. He remembered you talking about it. I know he's gruff, but he wants you to feel welcome and maybe even happy someday."

Alanda sipped the steaming hot coffee, and a wave of pleasure hit her as the rich taste rolled over her tongue. She thought Maryah's coffee was even better than the tselqs' had been, and she told her friend so.

"Thank you," Maryah said, setting out bowls of porridge for Kitz, Isaac, and herself. She added another steaming cup of coffee to her own place and put out fresh cow's milk for Kitz and Isaac.

Isaac came back, his yellow tunic on backwards, and after Maryah had fixed it, he sat down at the table. He chattered constantly, brightening Alanda's mood, and by the time she was ready to go, she felt more hopeful and secure in Kitz's safety and comfort.

She kissed Kitz on the forehead, hugged Maryah, and ruffled Isaac's hair. "I'll be back soon," she told them, knowing she needed to leave before she changed her mind again. "Alis, heel."

For the first time since the beginning of her training, Alis did not obey. Instead, she trotted to Kitz, who was still sitting in his chair with his empty porridge bowl in front of him. Alis whined and put both her front paws on his lap. Kitz looked at her, really seeming to see her, while Alanda and Maryah watched with bated breath. For a moment, dog and boy simply studied each other as though meeting for the first time, but Alis reached her face up to his and quickly licked his cheek.

"Alis!" Alanda exclaimed. Such displays of affection were usually reserved for dogs' owners and were not encouraged with others. Even as she made the exclamation, however, Alanda knew she should not chide her dog. Any affection Kitz received would only help. Kitz looked at Alis for another moment and then returned his attention to the dresser of dishes and kitchen utensils across from his place.

"Alis, heel," Alanda repeated firmly while exchanging a look of wonder with Maryah.

As she and the dog walked out the door, she heard Isaac proclaim, "Kitz wants more milk!"

She smiled sadly and set off on her journey.

MISSIVE FROM BLACKWELL

Altoneir barely moved as Iantris smoothed a section of his long hair behind his ear. Her touch was ambrosia to his skin and senses; soft and sensuous, every move she made seemed to proclaim her love for him. He shivered slightly as her fingers brushed the sensitive skin at the side of his neck. In that moment, he wanted her like he had never wanted anything in his life.

She drew away, and he released a breath he had not realized he had been holding. Of course, they were in his study, which was absolutely not the appropriate place for lovemaking.

I could take her to my bedchamber.

He dismissed the thought with some regret. They were dealing with the vital business of advancing his cause in Ilbeor, and he could not allow himself to be distracted by his feelings for her.

"You sent the Urothu to a neighboring village?" Iantris murmured the words as though they were foreplay, her voice somehow both husky and soft. She soundlessly crossed the room to the map table and gazed at the map of Claresea Valley still displayed there.

"Yes," Altoneir told her, his voice low and dripping with his desire for her. He could not help but gaze at the way her white water-cloth robes swayed against her shapely form as she bent to examine the map, the way her golden locks fell shining to her waist.

"Strikes and counterstrikes," she said approvingly, the whisper of her utterance barely registering even to his heightened senses. She spoke in a more normal tone as she continued. "Sending the Urothu was a stroke of genius, my heart. We must sow the seeds of doubt far and wide, and we must strike fear into the hearts of the humans at every opportunity. Fear and doubt are powerful allies."

She turned to face him, a small smile playing on her perfectly formed lips. With the arch of a slanted brow, she invited him to bring his gaze to her face. When his dark eyes met her blue ones, she whispered one more word to him, the muted sound a caress he could almost feel physically. "Ruthless."

Before Altoneir could reply, a tentative knock sounded through the arched wooden door. Altoneir, locked in Iantris's seductive gaze, didn't respond to it.

"Aren't you going to answer?" Iantris asked, gentle amusement evident in her tone. "Or shall I?"

Altoneir mastered himself with difficulty and found himself inexplicably irritated at the intrusion. "Enter," he snapped.

The young human servant who opened the door looked terrified; everyone knew disturbances to this room were only to be undertaken in an emergency. He wore the stark black and white livery of the castle servants, yet to Altoneir's eyes he looked like no more than a child.

"A message for you, m'lord," the servant stammered. "The master of messages bade me bring it to you with all haste." He tried to explain the intrusion, hoping to avoid the wrath of the elven lord.

Altoneir stood abruptly, striding to the door to take the message from the servant's shaking hand. "Go," he ordered before he opened it, and the servant made a bow and closed the door behind himself.

Iantris watched intently as Altoneir unfurled the small scroll. His eyes glittered dangerously as he made connections in his mind.

"What is it, my heart?" she asked softly.

"Word of a new prophet," he replied, stroking his long beard. "A human boy in the valley."

She stiffened slightly, but her voice was still honeyed sweetness when she asked, "And what is the import to you? Prophets are hardly valuable in the larger workings of the world."

"They aren't," he agreed absently, still turning the news over in his mind. Truthfully, he had never found prophets very interesting. Though they sometimes foretold events to come, their very nature made them accessories rather than power players; they were incapable of making decisions, incapable of discerning the movements of the powerful. He only had one prophet in his numbers, an elven maiden who had been but a child when she was reborn. He had convinced her parents to join his cause and had kept her close at first, but when it had become clear that most of the time, she was simply a mute young woman who didn't notice the world around her, he had relegated her to rooms in the castle with instructions to inform him of anything she had said. In the decades since she had come to the castle, she had only made six prophecies, and none had contained actionable information.

"What is troubling you?" Iantris pressed.

"The prophet is the younger brother of the elf-friend. Their parents died of the crazing disease, and it was through that process that the child was reborn."

Iantris's eyes flashed with a rage Altoneir had rarely seen in her, and that he didn't understand in the face of this news. She seemed infuriated, as though someone had deliberately ruined one of her plans. "Strikes and counterstrikes," she muttered again, and he could not discern the meaning of the words.

"Surely this is nothing but great coincidence," he protested. "It is not as though the elf-friend made her brother a prophet; such things do not happen."

Iantris regained her composure and her face relaxed into the coy and loving expression she had worn before. "No, of course she did not. Still, your master of messages was correct that this news is of import. Coincidence or not, this connection should be addressed."

Altoneir nodded. "There is something else. Apparently, the heritage of the elf-friend and her brother are in question. An artifact of their mother's that survived the fire hints her past may be other than what it had seemed. The village herbalist seems to think she was descended from Ferncombe or Emelle's nobility, according to my emissary in that village."

Iantris didn't seem surprised at this news; in fact, the expression she wore seemed to be more one of frustration than consideration.

"I could send the travelers to take the boy," he continued, perplexed by the emotions this news caused Iantris. "He could bear watching."

"It is not the boy we must watch," Iantris countered. "The girl, the elf-friend, could be positioned for a place of influence, and tracking her movements seems wise."

"She is to travel away from her village to discern the meaning of her mother's artifact," Altoneir answered. "To track her without detection would be difficult and take the talents of my best travelers. I will hear if anything of import happens in Kilynelle and will track her movements via my emissaries throughout the land. She still does not seem of the utmost consequence. She is only a human girl."

"Prophecy moves apace," Iantris murmured, seemingly to herself. She glided to him, placing her slender hands on his shoulders and looking him intently in the eye. "Do what you must," she said, "but do not forget this human child. I feel in my heart she will be the lynchpin upon which the world's events will turn. Do not underestimate her."

"I will not," Altoneir promised, but he was already becoming distracted by her closeness, the fresh scent she exuded, and the touch of her hands. He reached up and caressed her cheek. "What would I do without you?" he breathed. "Know this: your every utterance is a command to my ears."

She smiled gently at him, inclining her head to lean into his touch. The urges of his body pulled at him until he forgot the human elf-friend and her brother almost completely. He would do as Iantris had suggested and track the girl, and he would intervene if it seemed necessary, but at the moment, nothing was as important as the elf maiden. Sighing his acceptance of his body's desires, he took her hand and led her from the room.

A NEW PATH

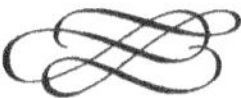

The two beings lay in a deep sleep, comfortable on soft blankets in a leaf-lined cave at the edge of the southeastern Guilnora Mountains. They were unaware of time's passage; it could have been a day, a week, even a year since they had fallen into slumber, and they would not have known the difference.

This was their work. They were the Watchers.

Simultaneously, the Watchers' dark eyelids fluttered as a vision came to them: a young man traveling alone, walking south in a land they had seen many times. There was nothing visually unusual about him; to all who saw him, he would have seemed an ordinary traveler. The Watchers knew differently.

Their eyes snapped open as though they were one creature separated into two bodies. Ancient, dark-skinned, and mysterious in deep purple robes, no one knew the origins of the Watchers, though many knew their purpose. Mirroring each other, they stood, packed their meager belongings, and left the cave for the valley below.

Tostig stood patiently in the front room of the house while his mother, Hawys, fussed over his pack, making sure he had enough provisions to last the week-long journey to Blackwell.

"You'll be hunting along the way?" she confirmed.

"Like I always do, Mother," Tostig replied tolerantly. Hawys was bustling about more than usual, perhaps because of the nature of his trip. He had told her and his father, Everard, about Alanda, and that he intended to ask her parents' permission to court and most likely marry her.

She tied the leather thongs of his pack deftly, with practiced movements showing her long years of experience. Everard was a hunter by profession, and she had been packing for him for years before Tostig became a messenger. Satisfied, she straightened and crossed the room to her son. She eyed him up and down, her eyes critical. Finally, her gaze softened. "You look good," she said with satisfaction. "I packed your red tunic for when you've reached Blackwell and gotten a room at the inn. Mind you take a bath before you go a'courting."

"I will," Tostig said.

"Is Tostig getting married?" asked Elia, the youngest of his sisters.

"That's yet to be seen," Hawys answered brusquely. "There's a lot goes into a marriage, especially with someone outside the village."

"Do you have the coin for the inn?" Everard asked solemnly.

"I do. Thank you, Father."

Tostig hefted the wood frame of his pack onto his back and clicked his fingers at Ziva, who had been nuzzling Miriel's hand. Miriel, who had just had her tenth birth celebration, often gave Ziva bits of cheese even when Tostig asked her not to. Ziva padded to Tostig's side obediently.

"I'll send word of my return," Tostig told his family. "I'm not sure how long I'll be. I might pick up some messages in Blackwell."

"Fare thee well," Hawys told him with a smile. "I hope you find what you're looking for."

Opening the front door, Tostig strode into the dim light of *uht*, Ziva at his side.

It was a week's journey down the southern valley road to Blackwell, and Tostig consulted his maps to see if he might reach the village more quickly cutting across the valley. Tracing a path from Lakeland to Blackwell, he concluded he could save a day's journey by doing so, and, anxious to reach Alanda, he set off through the valley grass, angling southwest.

The glorious colors of the sunrise felt like a good omen. Tinting the valley grass with brilliant pinks and oranges, the sky fairly burst with color. The grass, knee-high to Tostig and coming nearly up to Ziva's eyes, was not as easy to traverse as the road but Tostig found it much more beautiful and didn't mind the grass brushing against his legs. Ziva, who usually walked at his left, instead walked a pace behind in the path he left.

As he walked, Tostig saw several valley animals scurrying about, and even saw a small herd of deer grazing not far from him. The animals didn't seem to mind him and he left them alone - there would be time to hunt dinner later. As the sun rose in the sky, Tostig thought the small noises and movements of the animals a welcome addition to the beauty of the day.

I should take a deer to Alanda's family if I can, he thought. He hadn't forgotten the look on her face when she had tasted the rabbit stew during their tryst at the old tower.

They stopped for the night next to a burbling stream, somewhat later than usual. Though Ziva had barked softly at him at their usual time, she hadn't seemed to mind continuing the hike through the valley for another hour, until the sun set over the mountains. Enjoying the sounds the water made as it rushed over the small rocks, Tostig made camp. He felt content with his day's journey, and though he wouldn't be able to indulge in his evening hobby of woodworking, he could bathe in the spring, eat his cold dinner, and go to sleep early to make the time pass more quickly.

For the next five days, Ziva and Tostig traversed the high valley grass, sometimes stopping to hunt for their supper. The weather remained mostly fine, though he was caught in two rainstorms, and by the time he reached the outskirts of Blackwell on the afternoon of the sixth day, he knew he had to make himself presentable for Alanda's family.

Tostig's eyes wandered back and forth as he entered the village, taking the road to what he supposed would be the village square to find the inn. He was looking for Alanda, of course, though he knew she lived outside the village proper. He didn't see her, much to his disappointment, but upon reflection, he thought it would be better to see her after he had bathed, shaved, and changed clothes.

Blackwell's inn was a rather nondescript building of cut lumber with a wood-shingled roof. Two stories high, it wasn't as large as Lakeland's inn, but Tostig reflected that Blackwell probably didn't see many visitors, given its remote location. A battered sign reading "The Seaside Inn" with a rough carving of a seashell under the lettering announced its purpose, and Tostig hoped he would find a good meal in addition to a bed and a bath.

The Seaside Inn smelled like every inn he'd ever stopped at: ale, cooked meat, pipe smoke, and body odor. It looked familiar, too, though it was smaller than most. Six tables, each with four chairs, stood haphazardly around the common room, with just enough room between them for the serving maids and the innkeeper. Only two of the tables were occupied, one with a single man drinking deeply from a large tankard, and one with a young couple drinking wine and picking at a plate of cut cheese. Other than a cursory glance at him when he came into the room, none of them paid him any mind.

The walls were adorned with only two objects: a large set of antlers Tostig assumed had come from a buck, and the coat of arms of the noble family that ruled the village. A counter ran along the left side, and Tostig saw barrels of ale and bottles of wine and spirits lining the walls behind it. As he approached, he noticed that though the tables and bar were scratched and scuffed with use and age, they were clean. He took that as a good sign.

He waited patiently at the bar, and it was only moments before an overweight, sweaty man appeared from a door along the wall.

"I want food, ale, and a room for the night," Tostig said succinctly.

"Yeh can pay?"

"I have coin," Tostig assured him.

"Name's Jenson," the innkeeper told him. "Only got one room up for the night, but I s'pose it'll do for you. Yeh can pay now. Five coppers."

Tostig pulled out his coin purse. He'd done as well for himself as any middie without household expenses. He was saving to build his own house, but the pursuit of Alanda was worth parting with some coin. He handed Jenson six copper coins. "A bath, too," he requested.

"Aye, we have a tub." Jenson pocketed the coins. "But it won't be hot. Ain't got the stove space to heat no water for a traveler."

Tostig was a bit put off; he'd been looking forward to a hot bath. It appeared, however, that this inn didn't have a proper bathing room with its own stove, and he would have to make do. "No matter," he said with a sigh.

"Then come this way."

Tostig followed Jenson up a set of rickety wooden stairs that groaned with each of their steps. The room he was given was simple but clean, with a small wooden bedstead and straw-tick mattress, a table and chair, and a small, dim window.

"This'll do." Tostig set his pack down on the bed, signaling Ziva to take her place on the bare floor next to it.

Jenson eyed the dog distrustfully. "It bite?" he asked.

"She's a messenger's dog and is as well-trained as any," Tostig answered, annoyed at the question. Had this man never encountered a traveler's dog before? Not only messengers, but hunters traveled with them. "You'll see no problems from her."

"Leave it in yer room when yeh come downstairs," Jenson commanded. "I don't want no trouble."

"Fine," Tostig snapped, though he was not accustomed to leaving Ziva alone in unfamiliar places.

"I'll have the tub sent up with water to fill it," Jenson said, handing Tostig a small key. "Come down when yer ready. Got some roast beef for the dinner tonight an' the best ale you've ever drunk."

Tostig grunted, accepting the key and turning his back, hoping to be left alone. Jenson left without another word.

"Well, girl, we're here," Tostig said. "Now to find out what's what."

Ziva whimpered softly, and he caressed her head and sat on the bed to rummage in his pack for meat and cheese for her. He knew the cheese would cheer her up; she loved it, but he rarely shared it with her, saving it only for treats.

After his tepid bath, Tostig went downstairs to eat, leaving Ziva in the room. The food was good, hearty and well-seasoned, and though the ale was not the best he had ever had, it was adequate, and he enjoyed two tankards with his meal. After he finished, Tostig approached a serving maid at the bar. "I'm looking for a girl named Alanda," he said. "She's the leatherworker's daughter and lives on the outskirts." Knowing her father was a drinker, he wondered if the man was already at the inn. He glanced around; there were perhaps a dozen people in the inn that evening, but he did not know what Alanda's father looked like.

The serving maid didn't reply, but looked at him incredulously before disappearing behind the door to the kitchen. Within moments, Jenson came back out. "Lookin' for Jondolan's family?" he demanded.

"If Jondolan is the leatherworker in Blackwell, then yes," Tostig replied. "I need to speak with him."

"Yeh won't be speaking' to him anytime soon," Jenson informed him. "He's dead. Him and his wife."

Tostig's face twisted in horror. This had to have happened recently, for Alanda had spoken of her parents as though they were very much alive only weeks before. "What happened?" he asked, already wondering how he was going to find Alanda and making plans to talk to the village leaders about a match. He knew as an unwed adult woman, they would be eager to find her a husband.

"The Hunger," Jenson replied. "Whole place got burnt down, musta been a little over a week past."

Tostig reeled at the news, and it must have been clear on his face, for Jenson quickly brought out a tankard. "On me," he said gruffly. "Yeh look like yeh need it. Known the girl for long?"

"We're both messengers and met on the trails," Tostig answered as Jenson filled the tankard with dark ale from one of the barrels against the wall.

"Know what yeh must've been wantin' to speak to Jondolan about."

Tostig merely grunted, accepting the ale when it was offered. He drank quickly, noting that the ale was of a much finer quality than what he had been served with dinner. He knew he needed to move fast. "Where's the house?" he demanded. He had to see it if he was going to believe it; besides, Alanda might be there. *She could be anywhere*, he thought a bit frantically.

Jenson eyed him up and down without answering.

"Where's the house?" Tostig repeated when the innkeeper wasn't forthcoming.

Jenson relented. He had heard rumors about mysterious happenings around Jondolan's family and children, not the least of which was the news that had been spread at the most recent fifth day village meeting. He wasn't about to peddle the news to a stranger, however, so instead, he answered the boy's question without offering further information.

"Up the road a ways, past the sanctum, veer left when yeh hit the flowers in the field. That was the girl's mother's perfume field. Yeh'll see what's left o' the house right in front a yeh. Don't think yeh'll find her there, though. Word is, she's left the village on one of her journeys."

Tostig nodded and thanked Jenson for the ale. After hurrying to his room to collect his things and Ziva, deciding against spending the night in the inn after all, he left and ran in the direction Jenson had indicated, Ziva keeping pace with him. When he got there, it was as bad as he'd imagined. He saw the burnt wreckage, and he knew it was the only home Alanda had ever known. He also knew the bodies of her parents would have been there when it burned, and that if she had survived, she hadn't the chance to say goodbye.

"Alanda!" he called desperately, hoping she might have set up camp somewhere nearby. "Alanda, it's Tostig! It's me! Alanda!"

There was no answer, no smell but burnt wood and flesh and greenery.

After examining the ground near the house as well as he could in the deepening twilight, he ascertained that six people had stood vigil. There were still bits and pieces; a bone from a meal here, a burnt bundle of herbs at what would have been the front door, a faint salt trail around the house that he knew would have been made by Blackwell's herbalist. There were no recent signs of habitation.

Tostig's sadness, hurt, and desperation tore out of him all at once. He fell to his knees with a wordless shout into the skies and, as his knees hit the ground, a forked fragment of purple lightning struck the ground right where the center of the house would have been. It startled him; where had it come from? There wasn't a cloud in the sky.

He waited, but it didn't happen again, and he wrote it off as one of nature's freak moments. He began making plans to find Alanda, starting with more questions at the inn and a meeting with the village leaders, when he heard someone coming up behind him. Ziva growled.

The hackles on the back of his neck rose. If the newcomer had been Alanda or someone who seemed safe, Ziva wouldn't have growled, but barked softly to alert him. Instead, she was growling as fiercely as he had ever heard her do. Acting quickly, he drew his strung bow and nocked an arrow, spinning to face the intruder.

There was not one intruder, but two, and they stood impassively even as they were confronted by an arrow pointed only a few inches from their faces. Their skin was as black as an inky sky, so black it appeared the light was being directly absorbed around them; their heads were bald, and each wore a well-maintained mustache above thin lips. Upon examining them, Tostig could see they were absolutely identical down to the small moles on their right cheeks.

Something about them was different, something Tostig couldn't immediately place. It wasn't the color of their skin, for wide variations in color were common throughout the valley and most thought nothing of it. Their identical, deep purple robes put him off a bit; they were nothing like the tunics and pants worn by most humans.

They were human, though, as far as he could tell. "Who are you?" he demanded. "What are you doing here? Did you know this family?"

"We are the Watchers," the man on the left answered in a deep voice, exuding calm. "We have come to answer your questions."

"Where is Alanda?" he asked immediately. "And what do you mean, the Watchers? Are you from Blackwell?" He had never heard of such a title before.

"The girl is gone," the Watcher on the right told him. "She has taken her own path. Whether your paths will cross again, I cannot tell, but for now, you must speak with us. The gods of the Sashu have chosen you, young one."

This stopped Tostig short. He had heard of the Sashu; their existence and even approximate location was an open secret, though they were not known to exchange many messages or involve themselves much in trade. The Sashu adhered to an ancient religion that worshipped many gods and was considered blasphemous by most humans and even elves. Their practices involved magic.

Magic. Tostig's stomach tied itself into knots as a terrible possibility came to him. *Did I make that lighting?*

The Watchers looked at him expectantly. "You know who we are, and you know why we came. We found you in our dream state and knew where your first manifestation would come."

"My first...what?" Tostig felt like his head was spinning. First, there was worry and longing for Alanda, and now these Watchers were talking to him about manifestations. But he couldn't do magic, could he? *Had* he?

"Manifestation," the Watcher on the left said patiently. "The forked lightning came from you. It is not unusual for the first manifestation to be light or fire, and it often comes in a time of distress. Are you in distress, young man?"

"My name is Tostig."

"Tostig, well met. We have lost our names over time, but you may call us the Watchers all the same. You will have little contact with us after you reach the caves, however."

"The Sashu caves?" Tostig demanded, growing heated. "What

makes you think I will go there or anywhere else with you? I have an urgent situation here."

The ground rumbled and a small crack formed in the dirt between himself and the Watchers. He looked at it in dismay. Had he done *that*, too?

The Watchers looked down at the crack, not seeming surprised or the least bit perturbed. The Watcher on the right looked at Tostig and held up a placating hand. "Will you put the bow down, at least? I am certain you can see we mean you no harm."

Tostig glanced down at Ziva, who was leaning heavily on his left leg but no longer growling. He lowered the bow but kept it ready.

"We will no more force you to follow us to the caves than force you to do anything else," the Watcher continued. "Followers of the Sashu are never brought by coercion. You may go your own way, free from interference. However, there are some things you must know."

"Such as?" Tostig asked in a measured tone.

"The magic you have performed is but the beginning; the power will not fade with time. You are a magician, marked by the gods with the abilities you now possess, and without training, those abilities will be unpredictable and dangerous. Whenever you feel a potent emotion, be it positive or negative, magic will manifest whether or not you will it."

"And in these caves, I would receive training?"

"Yes, you would receive training in magic and the Sashu ways and beliefs. You would not be required to espouse those beliefs, though most do in the end." The Watcher on the left scratched his chin, the first truly human movement Tostig had seen either of them make.

"And what of my profession? My personal life? My family and friends?"

"There is no need to give up any of what you hold dear, though most magicians do not feel the need to keep a profession other than that of their calling. Your family and friends may remain as close as you wish; they may come to the caves, and you are free to leave at any time. You may marry inside or outside the circle; we have no prohibitions otherwise. All we ask, truly, is that you come and be trained."

"And what of Alanda?"

"The girl is on her own path, and you will not find her soon. Come with us, and we will help you find what you seek when the time is right."

"You can help me find her?"

"When the time is right, the Sashu will help you find what you seek. Her road is long and mostly unknown to us, but they will be able to find her if you wish."

The Watchers being so impassive, so unimpressed with his urgency, enraged him. Ziva whimpered softly. "What if I ask you to find her right now? What if that's what I asked as a symbol of trust?" His voice rose as his temper flared, and he didn't bother to contain it.

The Watchers did not react to his outburst, almost appearing as though they had expected it. "We cannot," the Watcher on the right said with a hint of regret. "We are the Watchers, and we find magicians as they manifest their powers; that is the power the gods have given us. When you are ready, and with the help of the most skilled magicians of the Sashu, you will find her yourself."

Tostig sighed, his anger deflating into a kind of hopelessness. If what he had done was magic, and it really was unpredictable, and it really would continue happening, he saw little choice. He had never heard of the Watchers, but he knew of the Sashu. He finally let his bow rest at his side.

"I need to send some messages first." His shoulders slumped. With the wreckage of Alanda's home behind him and the knowledge she was already gone, all he could feel was despair.

Tostig left a message for Alanda with Jenson at the Seaside Inn, who seemed surprised Tostig was leaving so quickly. He asked no questions, and promised Alanda would receive the message as soon as she returned to the village. He kept it short, not sure what to say other than he would find her as soon as he could and his promises from the forest still held, and would forever hold. He hoped she would wait for him; he hoped the village leaders would allow her to.

Next, he found the Messengers' Guild representative for Blackwell. As usual, the representative was old, nearing retirement age, and had given up running messages himself in favor of receiving messages and sending them on with the younger generation. Tostig composed a message to his father, explaining he had gone to the Sashu caves to learn magic and that he was not sure when he would return. Assuring his father of his safety, Tostig did not detail the circumstances, only that it was necessary. After paying the Guild and handing over the small scroll, he went to meet the Watchers on the outskirts of the village.

By the time Tostig and Ziva reached the Watchers, evening had become night, with little light to show the way. At first, the Watchers didn't seem inclined to wait for the sunrise, and Tostig wondered if they could somehow travel in the darkness, even though most humans couldn't see without some kind of light source. They only went a few minutes away from the village, however, before stopping next to a small pond just southwest of Blackwell.

"We will camp here," one of the Watchers said. "You may make a fire if you wish; we do not need one."

Tostig grumbled to himself as he took out the last pieces of firewood tied under his pack. He didn't like not knowing where they were going, and he didn't like that, though he was traveling with two other people, he seemed solely responsible for setting up camp.

"This is the last of my firewood," he informed the Watchers as he started the fire with flint and steel. "If we're not going into the forest, I'm going to need to find more before we camp tomorrow night."

"We are going into the forest of the southern Guilnora Mountains." The Watchers, with seemingly synchronous movements, settled down beside the fire. "You will find plenty of wood there."

Tostig grunted. At least he knew that much about where they were going, but he decided to ask some questions to see if he could glean some more information.

"Where are you taking me?" He asked the question without heat, but there was a certain edge to his voice.

"The caves are within the Guilnora Mountains. The messenger trails do not go there, and I doubt the caves are on your maps. However, you will find the trail no more strenuous than what you are accustomed to."

Tostig nodded. He had always been certain his map marked every settlement in the mountains; messenger maps were known for their accuracy. That he was going someplace not marked on his maps both worried and excited him. Perhaps he would be the one to add the Sashu caves to the messenger maps.

"What are the points of reference?" he asked. Points of reference were important for unknown destinations; they let the traveler know where he was in relation to known points on the map.

"We give no points of reference," one of the Watchers replied calmly.

Tostig bristled. With no points of reference, it would be hard for him to pinpoint his location, especially off the known trails. After a moment, he sighed. It was apparent he wasn't going to get more information. He would simply have to keep careful track as they traveled.

"Ziva," he called softly, and she padded to him. Rummaging in his pack, he pulled out her comb and began the nightly ritual of removing the day's debris from her fur. When he finished, her coat was soft and glossy, and she seemed content as he spread his blankets on the ground and tried to settle himself to sleep.

The Watchers spread no blankets, and he wondered if they were going to sleep on the bare ground or if they were going to sleep at all. It was disconcerting, but he eventually fell into a fitful and uncomfortable sleep, Ziva stretched out next to him.

Tostig followed the Watchers across the valley the next day, and they said little. They kept a steady but comfortable pace; Tostig had no trouble keeping up, but like them, he kept his thoughts to himself.

After two days of travel, the Watchers led him to a familiar trailhead into the southern Guilnora Mountains. Tostig had come this way many times on his travels, and at first, the trail was familiar to him. There was a tselq community known as Telchoa near where they entered the range, and he had delivered messages there. After about an hour, however, the Watchers turned further south onto a trail artfully concealed by vines hanging from trees and brush on the ground. Past this, the woods looked like they always did, but Tostig knew he was traveling beyond the boundaries of his maps.

He tried to keep track of the various twists and turns, first east, then north, then west, then switching back to the east, but after a while, even his keen sense of direction failed. It seemed the trail and its offshoots were deliberately confusing, so no one could actually get there without being told the way. Tostig was certain he would not be able to return to the caves without a map or more practice, and this disconcerted him. If his family and friends, if Alanda were to be allowed to join him at the caves, how were they supposed to get there?

"Will I receive maps to this place?" he asked irritably after they had taken yet another switchback turn.

"You will not need them," one of the Watchers said without turning around. "You will know the way."

"And if I want others to join me?"

"You will bring them," the same Watcher said simply. "You will see when we reach the caves that there are folk of all kinds there; though it is not easy to reach, neither is it hidden."

Not easy to reach, but not hidden. How could he ever send for his family or Alanda from a cave system so far off the mapped trails? He stopped. "I go no further until I am given a map or clear directions to send to Ala-, erm, to send to my family."

The Watchers finally stopped and looked at him, but instead of the anger or annoyance he expected, he saw only patience and, if it were possible, amusement. "How would you find your way back?" the first Watcher asked.

"And what will you do with your magic?" the second added.

"You are free to go, but we have no map and will give no direction. When you have learned, you will know," the first concluded.

"What does that even mean?" Tostig demanded. "When I have learned, I will know? What kind of dragon dung is this?"

"The kind which will lead you to your destiny, if you will allow it to," the second Watcher said, rubbing a hand over his bald head. "This is one moment in your life, young man, in which your decision will determine your ultimate fate. Will you come, or will you go?"

After days of following the Watchers over this twisted path, his mind had cleared somewhat, and he had thought of several places he could look for Alanda, places he cursed himself for not thinking of before. If she wasn't in Blackwell, then perhaps she had gone to Kilynelle, or even crossed his path and gone to Lakeland. She could have even gone back to the old tower. He was suddenly eager to be rid of the Watchers and get back to the trails he was certain she would tread. Whatever waited for him at the end of this path, it wasn't her.

Before he could speak, the first Watcher said, "I see you are conflicted. Most are, and we do not fault you for that, but you must decide. You may make your way back and find the young woman you dream of, or find her not, or you may make your way forward, learn how to control and use your magic, and build a better life for both of you."

"The Sashu and the people you will serve using your skill will provide a comfortable and highly respectable life for you, your family, and even your children, should you choose to have them. You will want for nothing; you will be elevated among your peers, able to perform tasks that would otherwise take much time and effort, or that could not take place at all. You will bring honor to all you touch," the second Watcher said with no hint of hurry or impatience. It seemed to Tostig that they must have given this exact speech before, perhaps many times. It had a rote quality to it that made it sound almost rehearsed.

It was apparent to Tostig that his outburst was not abnormal. He turned away, thinking hard about Alanda, about his family, and about what he wanted out of life.

He had met a non-elf magician once. She had been a tselq visiting one of the communities he delivered to during his apprenticeship. She had been called after a particularly devastating storm, sometimes known as a rock-eater, had razed the entire place to the ground. Homes, crops, community buildings, and living creatures had all been wiped away, and the remaining shamans had been overwhelmed. The tselq magician, whose name Tostig had never learned, had moved calmly among the chaos, offering healing, magical assistance in erecting buildings, and had even called back most of the dog breeders' dogs from their hiding places in the surrounding woods. Tostig remembered the feeling of awe he had experienced in her presence… she was so capable, so calm, so in control of the situation.

Could that be my fate if I get training? Could I do that much good?

Thoughts of Alanda came unbidden. He knew the true weight of what he was considering. He was mature enough to understand he had only just met Alanda, but there had been something there, something he would never find again. People made lifetime matches based on much less, and they had made promises to one another. Could he give her up?

They said I could find her after my training, that they would even help. She's off on her own journey now, a journey I know nothing about. I could try to find her, but would I even be successful?

Tostig thought again of the tselq magician and how much good she had done, and he thought of the elves, who were born with magical ability. "Do the elves come to the Sashu caves for training?" he asked to buy himself more time to think, keeping his back turned.

"No. Their ability is innate, and their training is a matter of family and clan education," the second Watcher told him calmly. Tostig detected a note in the Watcher's voice suggesting the matter was settled and they were simply discussing details. "Tselqs, humans, and dwarves manifest the ability as young adults. As Watchers, it is our job to find them and bring them into their rightful place."

My rightful place. Is this to be my rightful place? I am a messenger from a poor village, and yet…and yet, now I'm a magician. That's what they said. Whether or not I get trained, I'm a magician.

He blinked at the realization he had been struggling against. He was no longer the same. He was no longer a simple messenger, no longer just a man. He was a magician.

Without a word, he turned back toward the Watchers and motioned to them he was ready. They nodded in unison and continued to lead the way.

THE WATCHERS LED him along the twisting, rising trails for four full days. Nearing the afternoon of the fifth day, they finally reached their destination, a large clearing that appeared as suddenly as though by magic.

The Sashu caves were nothing like Tostig had imagined. He had imagined something like a community or village, a circle or square surrounded by caves used for habitation. In their own ways, the four races he had come into contact with had all followed the same basic method of building communities.

Instead, he was led across the clearing to a crack between two boulders, barely large enough for the Watchers to fit their bulk through. When he and Ziva had made their way through, he gaped in awe.

He was standing at the entrance to an enormous cavern, larger than the largest hall he had ever seen, with high ceilings and reddish-orange stone walls set with gigantic human-like figures carved from the wall itself. He wondered if they were the Sashu gods, but he didn't have time to ask.

"We have come!" the first Watcher proclaimed in a booming voice. He said no more, but Tostig thought this must have been a ritual. The large room, empty at first, suddenly came to life as humans, tselqs, and dwarves rushed out of passageways connecting to what he thought was a large cave system in the side of the mountain itself.

"Who is this?" A tall, honey-skinned woman with dark hair and eyes asked the Watchers calmly.

"He is Tostig, who first manifested his power seven days prior, in the southern valley," the second Watcher said.

Tostig felt awkward and left out. They were speaking of him as if he weren't there. He stepped forward, and the gathered people looked at him expectantly. Looking back at them, he suddenly lost track of what he had impulsively planned to say.

A few chuckles ran through the small crowd, and one dwarf let out of a loud guffaw of merriment. Tostig frowned.

"Do not worry," the honey-skinned woman said, smiling genuinely. "You and your companion are safe here, and we will teach you all that you would learn. I know you have left a life behind; we all did. You will find it again, if you wish. My name is Cecy, and I am the leader here."

"You're so young," Tostig blurted out, flushing red as another chuckle rang out. Elders and leaders, in his experience, were always older and nearly always male. To find a young woman at the head of a such a large, powerful group surprised him.

"Age is nothing," a tselq man grunted from behind her. He was more like what Tostig expected from a leader. Though he spoke the common tongue, there was a slight accent from his native language. His earthy green skin seemed to glow from the large fire at the opposite end of the cave, and the horns protruding from his forehead were curled many times, indicating great age.

"I am older than I look," Cecy told him, "But as Joque has said, age matters little among the Sashu."

Tostig nodded, accepting what she had said. "What do I do now?" he asked, ashamed of the question even as he asked it. He had never felt so out of place.

"You will settle in," Cecy said simply. "You will find your place, and your training will begin after you have bathed and been given your supplies and a meal. We have many newcomers; you will find the process quite smooth."

"We have completed our work today," one of the Watchers announced. "We will return to our place."

"Would you not sup with us?" asked another person, a small, pale young man near the middle of the crowd. "I would know more about how you found this one."

"There is no time for stories," the Watcher replied. "We must return to our dreams until we find others." They both turned and, nodding at Tostig, disappeared through the entrance.

Cecy came up to Tostig and took both his hands in hers. Her touch was warm, but not overly so, and her skin was soft against the roughness of his own. "Are you ready?" she asked, her voice kind.

Tostig swallowed. "Yes."

PART II

FROM THE PROPHECY OF
BEIANARIAN AND THE MAGUS

Small pleasures thrive in a duty-bound life
Traveling a small world on well-worn paths
Finding a lover sheathed in sunlight pure
Brings hope of the future long desired.
Stolen away, the silent cry of lost love
Ignites anguish never known or sought
Magic draws him from sky and under earth
Wresting from despair unwanted power.

A journey away from love and known worlds,
A strength long shared, yet in him set above,
Of the breath of the gods, he is reborn.
Succored by spirit of those come before
Magic within as a gale finally freed,
Taming his power and his realized might
He communes with the divine of the land
Rendering aid to those he once had been.

Remembering passion gone long ago
He journeys are in search of what he lost

As new duties summon him far afield
His heart cries out for a future faded.

from The Prophecy of Beianarian and the Magus
set forth by Algernon of House Agelon
Second Age, 246

SUMMER'S END

Alanda's training served her well as she and Alis trekked up the familiar trails toward Kilynelle. She cleared her mind, focusing only on her own soft footfalls and the quiet padding of Alis's paws. The dappled light filtering through the late-summer greenery of the forest didn't concern her any more than the bright sunlight of the valley had. She had her leathers, her cloak, and her sun salve, and the days were growing cooler.

It had been harder to fall into her meditative rhythm while traveling up the valley from Blackwell to Lakeland. She could not settle into her usual calm. Instead of focusing on the sights, sounds, and experiences of the road, she had repeatedly rehearsed what she would say to Tostig, and whether their connection and promises would turn into something more. In her most honest moments, she had to admit she hoped it would turn into something more...something much, much more.

All her planning and rehearsing had been for naught. When she had reached Lakeland, she had been directed to a nice-sized middie dwelling just outside the village square. A thin, pleasant woman had opened the door at Alanda's knock and had seemed both surprised and delighted to see her. Over tea, Alanda learned Tostig had left only days before to seek her out in Blackwell and to speak to her parents.

Alanda had made her excuses and left after tea, angling back south along the road to Blackwell, hoping to meet Tostig along the way. She had known she would be unlikely to see him on the road and hoped he would remain in Blackwell long enough for her to return. She knew the village leaders would not be happy to see her back so soon, but she had supposed meeting her potential match would reconcile them to it.

The village leaders, Maryah, and Serill had not seen Tostig. It had only been when she had asked Jenson that she had learned he had been there, but had left abruptly. He gave her Tostig's hastily written message, which only told her he had to leave but he hoped to meet her again soon. She could not determine from it why he had left, but she took some hope in knowing he had not wanted to abandon her.

After checking in on Kitz, the village leaders had encouraged her to continue her own journey, assuring her they would consider Tostig as a match. She spent only one night at Maryah and Serill's before heading into the mountains.

Alanda's attention was diverted from her reminiscences by a soft whine from Alis. "What is it, girl?" She reached down to scratch between Alis's ears.

She glanced up. The light had changed, and Alis's whine reminded her it was time to leave the trail for the night.

With a sigh, Alanda pulled her bow from its leather tube and strung it while prowling around, looking for small game. At one point, she caught movement in the brush that she thought might have been a wild rabbit or squirrel, she hadn't found it. After an hour, she decided not to continue trying.

"Dried meat tonight, Alis." Maryah had resupplied her well, and she had been lucky until that night's hunt. It would be no great loss to eat from her pack.

It didn't take long to find a suitable spot. Though not exactly a clearing, Alanda found a break in the trees. After she settled in, she called Alis for her nightly combing. Alis padded obediently to her but leaned into Alanda instead of sitting separately. Though this made it impossible to comb her, Alanda was touched.

"It's just us now, isn't it, Alis?" Alanda crooned, stroking Alis's silky fur. "Just us in this big world. What's going to happen to us, hmm?" Impulsively, she leaned over and planted a kiss on the dog's head. She laughed aloud when Alis immediately shook her head, her ears flopping back and forth. "Okay, girl, up you get. Time for the comb."

After the tangles, dust, and debris from the day had been combed out, Alanda prepared a cold dinner. She pulled the packet of dried meat strips out first, and then considered a medium-sized fabric bundle Maryah had placed in her pack the morning she had left the second time.

"Wait on this," Maryah had said, "until you're having a lonely day and need a taste of home." Obediently, Alanda had ignored the bundle during her trek, but she thought tonight might be a good time for whatever Maryah had given her.

The bundle wasn't heavy, but as she felt the shape of it, she knew immediately what it was. Unbidden, tears pricked her eyes as she untied the bundle and removed the fabric covering. To anyone else, it would not have seemed unusual. It looked like normal hardtack. Sturdy and long-lasting, hardtack had the consistency of a strong cracker and was as thick as a slice of bread; most travelers soaked it in water or ale to make it softer.

It wasn't the hardtack that caused a flood of memories, but how it was made. Maryah had baked the hardtack, but instead of leaving it as-is, she had taken a long, serrated knife and cut it lengthwise. Alanda knew before she opened it what she would find inside: a thick layer of fruit preserves to sweeten the bread and turn a necessity into a treat.

Dandelion had made this for her when she had started her apprenticeship, and Alanda had been so envied for it that Dandelion had started making loaves for her trainer and any traveling companions. She had never said where she had gotten the idea to do it, but it had never been heard of before by the travelers of the valley.

I don't know if I can eat this. She thought of Maryah and the extra work and supplies that had gone into the gesture, and she knew she couldn't refuse it. Rather than break into it right away, Alanda set it aside to give herself time and offered three strips of dried meat to Alis, who snapped them up eagerly.

After her own meat and cheese, Alanda once again took the special hardtack into her lap, her tin cup full of water next to her. Quelling the memories, Alanda broke a corner off and dipped it into the water. When she brought it to her mouth, she closed her eyes as the sweet taste of fruit preserves flooded her taste buds.

Dandelion, smiling as she placed supplies in Alanda's first pack when she was an apprentice at twelve, telling her there was a little treat for her when the road got long...the first taste of the preserves on the hardtack the first night of her first journey, her trainer asking for a taste...the tradition she had made for herself of waiting until everything else in her pack was gone before eating the treat...

Alanda chewed and swallowed over a lump in her throat. Since she had last seen her mother on that horrible evening Dandelion had screamed for her to get out, Alanda had been so busy with Kitz and the village leaders that she had not let herself think too much about her parents. Sitting with Alis in the leathers her father had made for her, eating the treat her mother had invented for her, she allowed herself to miss them.

Alis moved from a spot a few feet away and rested her head on Alanda's thigh. Alanda methodically broke pieces from the hardtack, soaked them, and ate them mechanically, barely noticing the silent tears running down her own cheeks. She wrapped the remainder in the linen cloth. Instead of putting it back into her pack, she got up and walked into the surrounding trees and buried the bundle under a mound of forest-floor detritus. She knew that, as kind as Maryah's gesture had been, she would never let the treat pass her lips again. It had been something special between her and her mother, and she preferred to leave it that way.

Sleep did not come easily. Alanda's mind remained on her mother and father, on Kitz, and on the complicated mess her once-simple life had become. She had held her ground when the issues of Kitz's living situation and her own match had been brought up, but Alanda had never really stopped to wonder what was going to happen to her.

Was she to be Kitz's minder for the rest of her life, living with Maryah and Serill and Isaac for her brother's sake? Was she to be married to a village man, living the life she had once expected as a wife and a mother? Would she ever find Tostig? Was her mother's mysterious heritage going to change anything?

What was she supposed to do?

ALANDA AND ALIS did not stray from the trails other than to camp; Alanda had no desire to explore. Other than a brief rainstorm halfway through her trip, even the weather cooperated with her wish for a short, uneventful journey.

As usual, Alanda heard Kilynelle before it came into view. The whistling of Yrui still reminded her of Deena's aviary, though as she got closer, her familiarity with the language allowed her to realize something was different this time. As she neared the bend concealing the entrance to Kilynelle, she realized many of the elves were whistling the same things in unison and perhaps even repetitively.

Alanda set her pack down and go out her whittled flute, ready to greet her friends in their own language. She rounded the bend and came into full view of the Kilynelle community circle, the flute already at her lips.

She stopped. The elves were in the midst of some kind of celebration or ritual that she had never seen before. The entire clan had gathered in the circle but were not sitting around the edges as she had expected. Instead, they were standing in concentric shapes, fanning in and out to Yrui music led by Julen. Each elf was garbed in shocking white, brighter than any white Alanda had ever seen, and the only differences between them were the colors of their belts and the arrangements of their hair. Alanda was glad no one seemed to have noticed her. She felt very out of place in her black leathers and cloak, with her hair in a simple braid.

Just as Alanda had decided to leave and camp for the night, Alis barked. It was only one sound, but it seemed amplified so no elf within the circle could miss it.

The Yrui music didn't stop, nor did the strange, concentric dance, but one elf detached himself from the crowd and came to greet the newcomers. Though she did not think she had met him before, she automatically brought her flute back to her lips and played the Yrui greeting. His smile, already welcoming, widened into a grin. He whistled a return and switched to the common tongue as he approached. "Elf-friend Alanda!" he said jovially. "My name is Dmeter. My partner, Julen, has told me much about you." He inclined his head and touched two fingers to his forehead, and Alanda imitated the gesture of respect.

Dmeter, wearing the same shocking white robes as the rest of the clan, had accented them with a deep blue belt and had braided his long black hair in a complicated configuration Alanda couldn't follow with her eyes. His skin was darker than most elves, a rich cinnamon brown with twinkling brown eyes. Alanda liked him immediately, and, forgetting her troubles for the moment, smiled widely at him. "Well met, Dmeter," she said. "This is Alis," she added, gesturing.

Dmeter's smile widened. "May I?" he asked, reaching down.

"Of course."

While Dmeter scratched Alis behind her ears in the way she loved most, she scanned the crowd in the circle for more familiar faces. Though she thought she knew a few of the elves rather well, she found it hard to pick them out in the crowd. Finally, just as Dmeter was straightening to look at her again, she spotted Myrine near the middle of the dancers.

"My dog Gabi enjoys being scratched in just that way," Dmeter commented. "Alis is beautiful. I can see that you take wonderful care of one another."

"You have a dog?" Alanda blurted, surprised. She couldn't remember having seen any other dogs, though there were plenty of cats among the elven families.

"We have much in common," Dmeter told her. "I am a messenger, and have a dog very similar to Alis, though Gabi's fur matches my skin more closely than she does yours." He laughed. "Come!"

He surprised her by taking her hand and pulling her forward. She stumbled a bit and barely had time to tell Alis to come with her as he pulled her around the circle of dancing elves to a roundhouse on the edge of the festivities. Despite everything, including not liking to be touched without permission, she found herself laughing at Dmeter's enthusiasm.

Alanda gasped softly as she neared the roundhouse she assumed Dmeter and Julen shared. It differed greatly from Garratt's roundhouse, which had been decorated nicely but sparsely. This roundhouse was surrounded by a flower garden boasting blooms Alanda had never seen before, growing in a wild effusiveness that reminded her of her mother's flower field. Inside, the small, magical lights blinked not only from the junction of the wall and ceiling, but trailed up the curved underside of the roof, giving the impression of fireflies.

"Now, we must prepare you for the festivities," Dmeter announced. "Though we were not expecting you, it so happens that Julen and I have an extra robe and sash for a friend from another clan who was originally supposed to come."

"No," Alanda protested. "I'm not familiar with your celebrations. Please, with your permission, Alis and I will rest in your roundhouse until the festivities are over."

"We wouldn't hear of it," Dmeter countered, grinning. "You are an elf-friend, and it is time you learned some of our customs. It just so happens you came upon one of our most important festivals, that of Summer's End."

"Summer's not over yet."

"Perhaps so for valley-dwellers," Dmeter said, pulling white robes from behind a curtain. "Here on the mountain, we celebrate Summer's End when frost forms on the ground in the bright morns."

Alanda had never considered that even the seasons were different on the mountains. Seasons had always seemed immutable, changing on designated dates regardless of weather or natural phenomena.

"So, how do you know when to hold the celebration?" She accepted the robes from Dmeter.

"Why, hello, Gabi!" Dmeter said suddenly, looking past Alanda at the doorway to the roundhouse. "Did you enjoy the dance?"

Alanda looked around to see a brown messenger dog, somewhat bigger than Alis, entering the roundhouse at a slow amble. Alanda had never seen a messenger dog move with the easy grace this one did; it seemed somehow Gabi had inherited some of the style of her elven master. She approached Alis, who stiffened slightly while the other dog examined her. Apparently content with her canine visitor, Gabi barked softly and moved to Alanda.

Alanda knelt, careful not to allow the white robes in her arms to touch the floor, and extended one hand to Gabi. Gabi dutifully sniffed the gloved hand and licked it. Alanda giggled and stood up, knowing she had been accepted.

Dmeter watched the scene with his characteristic smile, then clapped his hands together in a businesslike way. "Come Gabi, Alis," he announced. "We shall take a turn around the settlement while Alanda changes her clothing and prepares herself." Before Alanda could argue, both dogs followed him out.

Alanda sighed. She would look like a ghost garbed in white; her skin and hair would not offer much contrast. Feeling beleaguered, she changed her clothes, placing her travel-worn leathers on a wooden chair.

By the time Dmeter returned, Alanda was garbed in the white robes. He pursed his lips as he looked at her.

"I know I look like a ghost," Alanda said, a bit defensively. She felt silly. She had never been one to wear white.

"No, child, it is not that," Dmeter said. "There are simply a couple of adjustments we must make before you are ready to join us." He bustled over to the curtained area and returned with a bright purple sash. Without asking permission, he wound the sash around Alanda's slight waist and tied it at her side.

"Now, my dear, there is but one more thing we must do. Will you sit and allow me to arrange your hair?"

"What are you going to do with it?" Alanda asked, placing her hand on her head.

"Just refresh the braid it and wind it around the back of your head," Dmeter said reassuringly. "It will not hurt."

Alanda didn't smile as she seated herself and slowly undid her simple braid, carefully holding her black hair tie so it would not get lost. She tried to concentrate on the sound of the celebration outside, on the gentle weight of Alis's head resting on her foot, on anything besides the gentle feeling of Dmeter's long fingers in her hair.

She could not suppress the memories as he arranged her hair. Dandelion had loved arranging her daughter's hair for fifth-day services, often braiding it into configurations the village had never seen. Dandelion, like Dmeter, had been very gentle and only rarely pulled the hair as she worked.

Alanda closed her eyes as Dmeter wound her braided hair around the back of her head, using smooth wooden combs to keep it in place. It felt strange to have her hair off her neck, exposed, and even unsafe as the sun had yet to go down.

"There," Dmeter said, satisfied as he stepped back to admire his handiwork. "You are truly ready to join us now."

"She is," a deep voice agreed from the doorway.

Dmeter and Alanda both turned to see Julen in the doorway, his tall frame blocking most of the sunlight. Dmeter's eyes lit up as he quickly crossed the room, taking Julen's hands and kissing him chastely. "Have the festivities reached a break?" he asked, stepping back to allow Julen to green Alanda.

"Yes, but for a few moments only," Julen answered. "Alanda, it is wonderful to see you again. Welcome to Summer's End. Myrine asked me to remind you to cover yourself well with sun salve."

Alanda nodded and stood, causing Alis to also spring to her feet. "Hello, Julen," she said, feeling silly in her white garb even though she matched the two elves. She opened her pack and took out a small pot of the sun salve, applying it to every bit of exposed skin, not forgetting the back of her neck or the part at the top of her head.

While she did this, Julen and Dmeter held a brief conversation in

Yrui, and though Alanda didn't understand everything, she under-stood enough to realize they were discussing her part in the rest of the day's activities.

"Really," she protested in the common tongue, not knowing enough Yrui to express herself, "I would rather observe. Alis and I don't know how to do your dances or even what the meaning behind the festival is."

"The magic will lead you," Julen told her. "You have never been part of an elven ceremony, have you, child?"

"No," Alanda admitted.

Julen came to her and placed his hands on her shoulders, looking her in the eye. His brown eyes, as always, were pools of compassion and kindness. "Close your eyes," he instructed.

Putting one hand on Alis's head to reassure herself, Alanda did so.

"Now, breathe deeply," Julen instructed before beginning to whis-tle, the lower, more melodic tone alerting Alanda he was calling upon a spell.

Alanda jumped slightly as she felt something pass into her from his hands. She wasn't sure what it was; it didn't hurt, but it felt as though small bolts of energy had transferred between his hands and her body. Suddenly, she felt more alive than she had since she had been with Tostig. Her body hummed with energy and without meaning to, she swayed to the melody of Julen's spell.

"Yes," Dmeter whispered, watching as the spell took effect. "An elf-friend, indeed. Come, Julen."

Alanda no longer objected to joining the elves. Pulled along by the magic of Julen's spell and the magic suffusing the air, she willingly followed him and Dmeter out of the roundhouse.

Blinking against the bright daylight, she noticed at once that the dance was over and the elves were seated around the circle. She found herself disappointed. She sat herself down next to Garratt, Myrine, and, to her surprise, Kataryna.

Garratt and Myrine greeted her in Yrui, and Alanda realized she had left her flute in Dmeter and Julen's house. Undaunted, she pursed her lips and attempted to repeat the greeting, though she had never been good at whistling. Judging by their smiles, she met with some success. Kataryna, though she did not get up and move as Alanda had expected her to, did not return the greeting or meet Alanda's eyes.

"Friends," Julen called from the center of the circle, surprising Alanda with his use of the common tongue. "Forgive me the use of the human language for the time being, for we have a visitor who is not yet fluent in our tongue."

The elves around Alanda murmured at this, but she thought that most of them agreed with Julen.

Julen continued with a smile. "We gather today for the celebration of Summer's End, in which our forest sheds her previous garb and puts on the colors of autumn and winter. Allow yourself to feel the change in the air, to feel the change in the forest, and to feel the change in yourselves. Harvest is upon us, and we are grateful for the bounties of our place in this world." He clapped his hands twice, and Alanda gazed in wonder as the circle was suddenly the site of a rainfall of colorful autumn leaves, which danced their way to the forest floor.

"It's beautiful," she murmured to Myrine, who smiled as a bright orange leaf caught in her curled blonde hair.

While Julen continued speaking about the changes wrought by autumn, Alanda came to a realization. She had been taught elves worshipped no deity and recognized no afterlife. Now, watching and taking part in this celebration of autumn, she thought a more accurate representation of the elves would be to say they worshipped nature and the world around them.

She was so absorbed in her thoughts that it surprised her when Myrine nudged her. Julen had finished speaking, and the elves were getting to their feet amidst the autumn leaves. Alanda stood, unsure, but her uncertainty disappeared as the elves began again what she had seen as she had entered Kilynelle, the melodic recitation of what Alanda suspected were ancient songs and possibly incantations, some in unison, some in harmony. Next to her, Alis barked. Automatically, Alanda turned to shush her; barking without reason was discouraged.

"Let her be," Garratt advised her softly, taking her upper arm gently. "She, too, feels the magic."

Alanda nodded as Alis continued to bark; now that Garratt had said something, she noticed other animals in and around the settlement had also joined in. She heard Gabi barking from across the circle, many cats meowing and yowling, and various forest sounds she assumed came from animals surrounding them.

Magic really affects everything here. She wondered how she had failed to notice it during her previous visits.

"Come." Myrine took her hand and led her into the circle. "You do not know our songs, child, but allow the magic and the beauty of the world into your heart and dance with us to welcome the new season."

Alanda tried to clear her mind of all but the melodic music around her and the leaves falling around them and allowed herself to be led. Myrine didn't let go of her hand when they reached the center; instead, she encouraged Alanda to take the hand of an unknown elf on her other side. As soon as she did, she felt herself be pulled inward toward the center and then outward, sometimes mingling with the elves in the outer circles, always in sync with Myrine and the unknown elf on her other side.

With wonder, Alanda realized she was actually part of the swirling shapes of the elven dance, and she felt free and happy, smiling and laughing. Afternoon passed into evening in what felt like an instant, and by the end of the dance, she had found herself joining in the Yrui music. No one, herself included, minded when she made mistakes. They welcomed her as one of their own, and she almost forgot her own humanity and her own pain.

A grand feast followed, and as Alanda sat at one of the long tables in a clearing she had never seen before, she thought she had never tasted anything as delicious as the wheaten bread, berries drizzled in sweet sauces, venison coated with savory spices, and what seemed a thousand other dishes. She laughed and chatted, sometimes in the common tongue and sometimes in her clumsy Yrui, ate more than she had in her life, and was disappointed when Garratt called an end to the festivities.

"Come, elf-friend," Dmeter whispered, appearing at her side. "I will show you to your quarters." Seeing that Alanda was too caught up in the moment and the magic to attend to such ordinary matters, he took her hand and guided her to a small roundhouse.

Alanda was surprised to see her things already arranged in a small room decorated with tiny, flickering elf lights, flowering plants, and a painting on a curved canvas. The bed was made with fresh linens and the mattress looked like it might be the softest thing she had ever slept on. Next to it was a small, similar mattress on the floor, lined with soft blankets, clearly meant for Alis.

Alanda turned to thank Dmeter, only to realize he was already gone. Sighing, she changed clothes and settled into the comfortable bed. Though she had felt full of energy only moments before, she almost immediately fell into a deep sleep.

SHE AWOKE IN TOTAL DARKNESS.

The elf-lights had gone out while she slept, and she could hear Alis snoring lightly on the pallet next to her bed. Alanda gazed straight up, but the darkness was so complete she couldn't make out the curved beams of the ceiling.

After the bliss of the festivities, Alanda wasn't prepared for the emptiness and sadness she felt upon waking. It was as though the brief respite from grief, uncertainty, and fear had done nothing more than allow those feelings to be released all at once when the magic left her. She lay there, not wanting to wake Alis, again thinking about all she had lost. Her mother, her father, and her brother as he had once been all floated through her mind, and the life she had planned for herself felt like ashes in the wind.

Her dark thoughts were interrupted when the elf-lights suddenly blinked on, though it wasn't even *uht* yet. Alis jumped to attention, poking her nose at Alanda's face and whining loudly. Alanda comforted her, patting her head and murmuring softly until Alis calmed, sitting next to the bed.

Alanda wondered what had caused the lights to blink on and made a mental note to ask. Knowing she would not be returning to sleep, she decided to take a walk with Alis. Rising from the warm feather mattress, she realized quickly that Dmeter hadn't been kidding when he had talked about Summer's End occurring when it had become chilly enough for frost to cover the ground. She shivered and quickly dressed in her leathers, putting on her cloak even though the sun was not even peeking over the horizon.

Calling Alis, Alanda opened the door to be greeted by complete darkness. She wondered how she was supposed to get around with no light. As she scanned the roundhouse, she spied a small lantern sitting on the table. Crossing to it, she examined it under the twinkling elf-lights, wondering if she was supposed to light it with her flint and steel or if this was another magical creation.

There was no wick, nor lamp oil. It was simply a hollow glass ball, empty, encircled by a well-wrought metal design of flowers and leaves curving into a handle on top.

I really didn't learn as much about the elves as I thought I did.

Alanda continued examining the strange lantern. She had spent much of her previous visit unable to see her surroundings and had almost always been accompanied by an elf both in Myrine's round-house and when she had ventured outside.

"How does this work, Alis?" she asked aloud, holding the lantern in front of the dog's face as though she might find an answer.

"You ask it to alight," said a voice from the doorway.

Alanda jumped and turned toward the sound. Myrine, fully dressed in turquoise robes with her hair again straight and hanging down her back, stood just outside the room, gazing in with amusement.

"Do you ever rest?" Alanda asked, finally voicing the question she had wanted to ask since her last visit. She had never caught Myrine sleeping or even in bed.

"I do, but I do not require as much sleep as most elves, and certainly not as much as humans," Myrine replied calmly. "Now, retrieve your flute, and I will teach you how to activate the lantern."

Alanda did as she was bidden and listened attentively as Myrine taught her the simple Yrui intonation for "light". She had no trouble repeating it and smiled in spite of herself when a round, yellow light appeared inside the glass globe.

"There," Myrine said approvingly. "Now you will not have to wander in the darkness. Would you like company, or would you prefer to be alone with Alis?"

Alanda decided she would rather walk with Myrine than alone. She did not want to dwell on her sadness when there were so many other things she needed to attend to. "Join me," she invited before calling Alis to her side.

As she and Myrine walked, their path lit only by the slightly pulsing light of the lantern, Alanda spoke of what had occurred since she had left Kilynelle. Myrine appeared stricken when she heard the fate of Jondolan and Dandelion, and though she sympathized with Alanda's feelings over the changes wrought in Kitz, she was very interested in the prophecy he had given.

"And you know nothing of your mother's past before she appeared in Blackwell, alone and friendless?" she asked.

"Nothing," Alanda confirmed. "She had some skills unusual for the women of the village. She knew how to make perfumes and sweet-smelling soaps, and when she could get the materials, her needlework was wonderful. Those skills kept the family fed when my father spent his earnings at the inn. I asked her once where she had learned, but she only said she learned as a child. She wouldn't answer any of my other questions."

"Interesting indeed," Myrine said wonderingly. "And what of this scarf left behind after the fire, the one you say cannot be burned?"

"It has runes on it," Alanda said, "and a lot of embroidered pictures. Neither Deena, the village herbalist, nor the High Priest could read them. That's the main reason I traveled here. I was hoping perhaps the elves could help me understand."

"Perhaps," Myrine answered, "though none of the elves in Kilynelle specialize in human lore, I am afraid. But why is it so important for you to understand your mother's heritage now, after her death?"

Alanda thought for a moment before she answered, "A lot is shrouded in mystery since my parents passed," she said slowly. "Kitz's condition, my mother's origins, and even my own future are all in question. The village leaders felt finding the meaning behind my mother's scarf and perhaps where she came from might help answer some of those questions. Deena said the material the scarf is made from can only be found in Ferncombe and among the nobility in Emelle."

Myrine stopped and bent down, picking a small white flower from the base of a tree. Twirling it in her fingers, she asked, "And you, Alanda? What do you want for your future?"

Alanda didn't answer because the truth was that she didn't know. All she was sure of was her need to protect and care for her brother, the only family she had left. After a beat, she told Myrine so.

Myrine was silent for several moments, simply gazing at the white flower in her hand. Finally, she looked directly into Alanda's eyes. "We will assist you in any way we can," she said. "If you entrust your mother's scarf to me, I will take it to the council and see what can be divined from it, and if we cannot interpret it, we may be able to point you in the correct direction. I worry, though, child, what you seek will not bring you happiness, but only greater sorrow. Will you not return to Blackwell and live the life you would have lived if The Hunger had not taken your family, perhaps with the young man you mentioned? I am certain a member of the council would consent to accompany you and help plead your case. You are an elf-friend, and we also have a vested interest in your future."

"There is no life for me there now," Alanda said, looking down. It was the first time she had voiced the thought aloud, but she knew it to be true as the words fell from her mouth "It would only be a life of loneliness and convenience for others, and though a life of service is a noble thing, I feel…I feel there is something else out there, something else I am meant for." The words sounded absurd to her own ears even as she said them, but it was the best way to describe the feeling that had beset her in the days since her family's tragedy.

Myrine gently took Alanda's chin in her free hand, tucking the flower behind her ear and then stepping back to study her carefully. "Elf-friend Alanda," she said, addressing her as such for the first time, "I believe you are right. Let us see what can be done. Come, child, the sun begins to rise, and we must prepare for the day."

As PROMISED, Myrine took Dandelion's scarf to the settlement's council, the oldest and wisest of the elves in Kilynelle. None of them could interpret the runes, saying only that Deena had been correct that the inflammable material had originated in Ferncombe and that Dandelion had gotten it there or from the nobility in the royal city.

"The language is ancient," said Garratt, holding the scarf out to Alanda, "and though I believe it to be human in origin, it is nothing I have ever seen before. I would be surprised if even your mother could have translated it."

Alanda let her frustration show. *What am I supposed to do now?* She was sorely tempted to simply return to Blackwell and inform the village leaders the origins of the scarf were unknown, and her mother's heritage was no longer of any interest to her, but she wasn't certain they would accept that. They had been too spooked by her brother's transformation and too intrigued about her family's past to let it go. *Besides*, she reflected, *it isn't exactly true that I'm no longer interested in the answers.* She couldn't put her finger on exactly why, but it still felt important to her.

Analiese, a raven-haired and serious elf, addressed her for the first time. Though Alanda had not met her before, she had to admit the elf's attentiveness to the problem at hand impressed her. From what Myrine told her, Analiese took her responsibilities as one of the elders to heart and rarely let a problem go unsolved. "Ferncombe, of course, would probably be the most direct way of tracing the origins of the artifact," she said, "but Ferncombe is in the extreme northeast and it would be an incredible journey for one as young as yourself to undertake alone."

Alanda shuffled her feet, offended by the implication she was unsuited for the solo journey; after all, journeys alone were what she did for a living. Before she could reply, however, Kataryna spoke directly to her for the first time.

"There is another option," she said, her voice hard and brittle. She would not meet Alanda's eyes.

"Kataryna," Garratt protested, "we agreed - "

"The girl should know the different paths available to her," Kataryna interrupted him.

"I would like to know," Alanda said softly. Though she was not afraid to journey to Ferncombe with only Alis for company, the journey would take her away from Kitz for months, if not longer. If there was a way to solve this mystery without being away for so long, she would be inclined to take it.

"The tselqs have a compound on the other side of one of the mountain peaks, over Anneau's Field, that holds a library. The custodians of this library are an order of tselqs dedicated to the preservation of knowledge of all the races of Ilbeor, and it has existed since long before *humans*," she spat the word as though it were a curse, "came to this land. If there is a translation, there is a good chance they would have it."

"How far is this compound?" Alanda asked evenly.

"It is in the Guilnora Mountains," Garratt answered slowly, almost unwillingly, "over the peak known as Tonchun's Rest. You will not find it on your maps, which end at the edge of the glacial top of the mountains."

Alanda did some quick thinking. Tonchun's Rest was known to her; it was marked on her map of the Guilnora, though she knew Garratt was right; her maps ended at the glacial sheet known as Anneau's Field. In her training, they had warned her never to venture above the tree line and onto the ice, for the air was thin and temperatures frigid. Humans who attempted to cross it rarely returned home.

The journey would be much shorter if she could remain in this range rather than traversing the entirety of Ilbeor to reach Ferncombe. She thought, foolishly perhaps, if she prepared herself well enough, she might be able to cross the glacier safely and return to her brother in weeks rather than months.

"How do I get there?" she asked. "What are the points of reference?"

"Wait a moment," Garratt said, holding up two hands to stop her. "This is an incredibly risky endeavor you are proposing. You will not be of aid to your brother or anyone else if you die in the attempt."

Alanda stared at him steadily, a steely glint in her eyes that none of the elves had ever seen before. "What are the points of reference?" she asked again.

It was Kataryna who answered, again without meeting her eyes. "You would want to travel first to the tselq community of Chinnua. I believe it is marked on your map. There, they will share the points of reference and, I believe, assign a guide to escort you to their library."

Alanda nodded; she was familiar with Chinnua, having delivered messages there during her apprenticeship. The settlement was friendly and welcoming, and she thought it likely she would find help there. It would take her a bit more than a week to reach it from Kilynelle, but she thought it a better alternative to the journey to Ferncombe.

"Elf-friend Alanda," a blonde elf she didn't know said suddenly, "do not do this. Kataryna cares nothing for human life, even that of an elf-friend. She will care nothing for your death, and your death would almost certainly be the result of an attempt to cross the glacier. Humans are not built for that endeavor. Even elves find it difficult."

Kataryna made a noise between disgust and dismay, and abruptly got up and left the council house without so much as a glance at her mate or any of the other council members. They watched her leave without comment.

Alanda sat silently for a moment, feeling the elven council's eyes return to her after Kataryna's departure. "I will travel to Chinnua at least," she said finally, "and find out if there is a way the thing can be done."

"You are determined?" Garratt asked her, gazing at her sadly.

"I am," Alanda said.

"Then so be it."

~

BETWEEN THE SAD looks Garratt kept giving her and the admonishments from both Julen and Myrine about her upcoming journey, Alanda was glad to leave Kilynelle the next day. Myrine provisioned her pack generously with more sun salve and all the food she could carry, and as Alanda thanked her for the consideration, Myrine could not help one last plea for Alanda to change her course.

"You are more than just elf-friend to me, Alanda," Myrine told her as she prepared to leave from the small roundhouse. "You are a personal friend as well, and I care what happens to you. I know you could make the journey to Ferncombe, so won't you reconsider?"

Alanda only shook her head, hefting her pack onto her back. "Thank you for everything," she said sincerely, "but my duty is to return to my brother as soon as may be. I will take every precaution possible, I promise you."

Myrine, understanding she would not change Alanda's mind, gave her a hug and wished her well, an anxious look in her eye that Alanda did not soon forget.

She and Alis journeyed as quickly as they could, traveling the cross-range trails without deviation, Alanda's gait rather faster than usual. Alis did not complain, but dutifully stayed with her mistress even when they both panted from traveling uphill.

On the eighth day after leaving Kilynelle, Alanda and Alis reached the outskirts of Chinnua. Tselq communities were the quietest of any race, and the only sign of its proximity was a slight thinning of the trees, a result of the forestry necessary to build their homes. A hardy, earthy green people with defined musculature, white horns protruding from their foreheads, and long, thin hair, the tselqs were considered monsters by many of the other races, but Alanda knew them to be talented builders and peaceful companions.

"I think - " Alanda started to say to Alis, but stopped when she was knocked off her feet by a violent shaking of the earth. Her breath was knocked out of her as her back hit a tree, and she sat stunned on the ground, barely able to stay upright, as the ground continued to roll and tumble beneath her for nearly an entire minute. The thick trunk of the tree at her back swayed and moved, and she saw lesser trees uprooted. She watched boulders become displaced, moving and even rolling with the swells of the earth, and she was knocked on her side by the tremors, scraping the side of her face painfully on a tree root.

As the earth settled, Alanda stood with difficulty. Her right knee seemed to have been wrenched as she was thrown off balance, but she was relieved to discover no broken bones or major injuries. She looked around and in a heart-stopping moment realized she couldn't see Alis anywhere.

"Alis!" she screamed, terrified something had happened to her beloved companion. She looked around wildly but did not see even a hint of Alis's white fur anywhere. Her heart pounded painfully, and her fear spiked. She didn't think she could bear to lose Alis on top of everything else.

After what seemed like an eternity, she heard the unmistakable sound of Alis's bark coming from some distance away. "Alis, heel!" she shouted firmly in the direction from which the barks seemed to come.

To her surprise, Alis did not obey, but continued barking. From the sound of it, Alanda surmised she had stayed exactly where she was. *I hope she's not hurt*, Alanda thought as she hurried toward the sound, limping slightly as she picked her way around the fallen trees and displaced rocks that had completely obscured the trail.

She found Alis a short distance away, standing alertly and barking at a large pile of rocks that must have fallen during the earthquake. After a quick scan, Alanda determined that Alis's only injury was a minor scrape on her right front leg, but no matter what command she gave, the dog would not stop barking.

Alanda looked at the pile of rocks, wondering what had Alis so worked up. Then she saw it: a large hand, earthy green, protruding from underneath one of the rocks. As she knelt to examine it, Alis finally quieted.

In the sudden stillness, Alanda finally heard what Alis had heard all along: a male voice, weak but clear, calling out in the tselq tongue. Alanda urgently shifted the rocks as best she could, feeling fortunate they were not too large. There were many of them, however, and it took at least an hour before she unearthed the top half of the injured tselq. He blinked up at her, finally opening his eyes and able to breathe freely even though he could not yet unearth himself.

"Are you a spirit?" he asked in a raspy voice, his eyes wide. He had never seen a person of any race as pale as the figure kneeling over him.

Alanda almost laughed. She couldn't imagine what kind of spirit she could be with blood dripping down her face. "No," she answered, "I'm just a girl. Now that your head and chest are out, I'm going to run to Chinnua for help. What's your name?"

"Rinayai," the tselq said wearily. "Thank you...for saving my life." He took a deep breath with some difficulty and closed his eyes.

Alanda, alarmed and fearing he was more injured than she had imagined, ordered Alis to stay with him and ran as fast as her injured knee would carry her, straight into the heart of the community of Chinnua.

CHINNUA

$\mathcal{A}$landa ran into the tselq community as fast as she could, her black cloak streaming behind her. As she entered the community, she was struck by something that seemed impossible: although trees had been uprooted and the terracing of their gardens displaced, none of the huts or buildings had fallen.

She had barely registered this when the tselqs noticed her, and their work stopped at once. It did not shock her they had stopped work to gape at her; running was unseemly in the tselq culture, and she was not expected. She supposed the sight of her pale figure streaking in, her cloak flying behind her, was just as unexpected. She had been there before, but not since her apprenticeship.

One of the tselqs, an earthy-green male wearing an unbleached linen shirt and trousers, walked to her at what felt like a maddeningly slow pace.

"Rinayai is in trouble," she said in the common tongue before anyone could ask. "The cave he was in collapsed, and I can't get him out!"

Her words were met with immediate, silent action. The tselq who had approached her signaled to a large group of his kin who were rebuilding part of the terrace wall, and all of them dropped what they were holding and strode to Alanda. Gasping from her run, she told them where to go, and tried to keep up with their long strides as they hurried in the direction she had pointed.

When they got there a few short minutes later, the tselqs, male and female alike, immediately set to work. Alanda, knowing she was no match for them in strength, called Alis to her side and stood out of the way, watching and hoping Rinayai would survive.

She marveled that the female tselqs took on just as much work as the males; there was really no difference between the genders other than their clothing. She remembered being told the tselqs didn't tolerate weakness in any of their community and were brought up to be strong and self-sufficient, but she still found herself surprised by the equality of the genders.

It took very little time for the tselqs to unearth Rinayai, especially compared to how long it had taken Alanda to just get him free enough he could breathe. She sighed with relief as they dug him out, noting he was standing even if he was being supported on both sides. His eyes were open, and he seemed to be breathing normally.

Tselqs really are a hardy folk. If the same thing had happened to a human, they would likely have died before they could be rescued.

The duo of tselqs supporting Rinayai brought him directly to Alanda. "I...am in your debt," Rinayai said, his low voice croaky from the dust.

"It's nothing," Alanda replied automatically. "I'm glad I could help, but it was Alis who found you." She gestured toward the dog.

"Then I am in Alis's debt as well," Rinayai said, nodding. "Come back with us to Chinnua. We would hear your tale and learn why you have come." His eyes, clear and penetrating, seemed to study everything about her.

Agreeing, Alanda found her belongings. Luckily, her pack had remained intact, and nothing had spilled; her knot work was too good for that. Picking it up, she followed the tselqs back to Chinnua, but was surprised when they stopped in front of a round hut, the only one in a sea of rectangular houses. She knew this was the shaman's hut, but she had never been this close to it, much less inside. Nevertheless, the tselqs indicated she should follow them in as they helped Rinayai through the fabric-covered doorway and into the semi-darkness.

Looking around, Alanda felt slightly claustrophobic. The round hut had no windows; the only light came through the doorway, stained red from the fabric, and a beam of light shining through a small hole in the roof. *I wonder what that's for.*

"The dog must stay outside," one of the tselqs informed her in a low, guttural voice, as he and a companion helped Rinayai through the doorway and into the hut.

Alanda was not pleased by that, but knowing how important it was to obey customs to the best of her ability, she took Alis out and told her to stay by the door. Alis whined but obeyed.

Rinayai was situated across from the door, his back to the far curve of the wall, his legs crossed. He said something in tselq, and the others quickly left, returning in a few moments with a large stump. Situating it behind Rinayai's back, they helped him rest against it. Rinayai closed his eyes for a moment and sighed. Alanda wondered if he was in more pain than he let on.

The other two tselqs cleared out of the hut once Rinayai seemed to be resting as comfortably as possible. Not knowing what to say and feeling distinctly uncomfortable, Alanda picked at a small piece of threading coming loose from her leather pants. She would have to fix it soon.

Rinayai didn't break the silence for several minutes, seeming content to rest against the stump and study Alanda with an unblinking gaze. Finally, he said, "I do not know if you know the service you provided not just for me, but for my people, when you saved my life."

Alanda wasn't sure what he meant, though the location of their conversation gave her some clue.

"I am Chinnua's shaman," he told her seriously. "We do have another, but he is old and has retired from his duties. I became fully qualified only several months ago. I was meditating in the cave when the earthquake hit. I have not yet begun training my successor; that will not happen for many years. If I had not survived, my community would be in peril."

"I am grateful you survived, Rinayai," Alanda said respectfully, inclining her head. She wasn't certain that was the right thing to do, but figured it was a fairly universal sign of respect for the elderly or high-ranking of any race.

"It is the custom of my people that when one save's another's life, that one is in the debt of his rescuer until the favor has been repaid."

"Thank you, Rinayai, but that isn't necessary," Alanda protested. "You would have done the same in my place."

"Yes, but that is not the issue. I did not save you; you saved me. The debt has been incurred, whether or not you would have it." His use of the common tongue was thickly accented with the more guttural intonations of the tselq language, but he spoke clearly and gravely.

"I can't stay here," Alanda said. "I came for help of a different sort, and I would beg you to assist me in that way so I can go home to my brother soon."

She turned her head slightly as she heard Alis bark from outside, but as the bark was not one of distress or pain, she did not get up from where she sat.

Rinayai's stare bored into her, but occasionally his eyes closed for brief periods. Alanda bore the scrutiny without complaint; though she was not as acquainted with tselqs as she was with elves, she knew both races had a greater penchant for silent reflection than humans.

Rinayai suddenly opened his eyes wide, seeming somewhat surprised. His mouth moved silently as he resumed staring at Alanda, but something in his gaze told her he was not really seeing her but something entirely different.

He finally nodded to himself. "You have a great journey ahead of you, young one." His voice had a tone she had not heard from any other tselq before, like he was making a portentous pronouncement. "You do not yet know how great."

Alanda shifted uncomfortably. "I'm hoping my journey will end sooner rather than later. I have responsibilities to my brother and my friends who are taking care of him."

"You will not return to your village."

"For how long?" Alanda asked, her heart quickening in her chest. She did not like the certainty with which he spoke.

"You will never return to your village." Rinayai's voice still rung with absolute sureness.

Alanda looked at him seriously, actually taking the time to study him, noting in the red-tinted light of the shaman's hut, he looked much older than he had when she unearthed him from the rubble. In his eyes, she thought she saw a hint of the ancient wisdom sometimes said to be hereditary to the tselqs.

Finally, she said, "I must return to Blackwell."

"You will see," was Rinayai's only reply. He lapsed into silence, his eyes closed, breathing deeply. Alanda wondered if he was attempting to contact the spirit world of his ancestors, for she knew ancestor-worship was much of the tselq religion.

"Rinayai?" she asked when he had been silent for several long moments. "I really need to talk to you and to your council of elders. I have something important to show you, something I need answers about."

Rinayai opened his eyes, and she was discomfited to notice the ancient-looking aspect of them had vanished, replaced by the eyes of a young tselq. "Of course," he said smoothly. "You go ahead. Tell the others I will require help to join you in the council hall."

Alanda nodded and stood, feeling she couldn't get out of the shaman's hut quickly enough. Pushing the red curtain aside, she took a deep breath of the chilly air and felt herself return to some semblance of reality. She knew Rinayai wasn't right about never returning to Blackwell. It was her home. Kitz was there, and he needed her.

"Alis," she said, reaching down to scratch between the dog's ears, "sometimes things are just too strange to be believed."

She found two of the tselqs who had helped unearth Rinayai. She told them Rinayai needed help to get to the council hall, and then she asked for directions herself. Startled and clearly wondering who she was to have the right to call the council, they told her where to go and hurried inside the shaman's hut.

❧

IT TOOK two full hours to assemble the council of elders, and though Alanda was anxious, she didn't dare try to hurry the process. Some of the elders were old enough to be retired from manual work; they arrived first. She nodded as they came in, trying to remember their names as they said them: Toncha, Haran-wari, and Qonsi were the only three she could identify after they had seated themselves. Each tselq had many curls to their horns, indicating great age, and their skin did not seem as vibrantly green as that of their younger counter-parts. They were friendly enough as they waited, but mostly conversed in their own tongue.

Later, five additional tselqs, clearly aged but not yet retired, entered the hall. These three men and two women were not as friendly. They had been pulled from the work of rebuilding the community, and being pulled from important work was not something any tselq tolerated well. When Rinayai finally arrived, Alanda was surprised to find him accompanying an ancient tselq with eight full curls of his horns and skin even paler than the rest.

"This is Pallin," Rinayai said as the tselqs helped them both take their seats at the long wooden table. "He was shaman before me and will have a say in some of the matters we are here to discuss."

Alanda nodded, noticing some of the tselqs at the table appeared less than happy about Pallin's presence. She wondered why, but her unspoken question was answered when one of the five younger tselqs, a male, said brusquely in the common tongue, "Pallin should be at his rest. He is no longer required to take part in the work of leading this community."

Several of the council members nodded their agreement, but Rinayai held up one hand in a placating gesture. "This is to be an unusual meeting," he said calmly. "This young human has questions of great import, the answers of which may shape the very world we live in."

This statement startled Alanda. *Shape the world we live in?* It was simply a question of a poor village woman's heritage and her brother's transformation from normal boy to prophet. Admittedly, she knew there were few prophets, but she could not see how her mother's heritage or Kitz's transformation would change the entire world. And how did Rinayai even know what she was going to ask? Remembering the strange tone of his voice when he had said she would never return to Blackwell, she had to wonder what else he thought he knew about her, and why.

She shook herself out of her thoughts when she realized all the tselqs were looking at her expectantly. Sighing, she took a reassuring look at Alis, who was sitting alertly beside her, and reached into her pack for her mother's scarf. Not mentioning Kitz at all, she simply told the tselqs she was seeking a translation of the runes on her mother's scarf to better understand where her mother had come from and how it might impact her family and her village.

The tselq closest to her, Haran-wari, looked at her with raised eyebrows and held out her large hand for the scarf. Her thin, gray hair, tied back with a linen thong, swayed slightly as she moved, and Alanda wondered if the gray was from age or was the color she had always had.

Alanda willingly handed the scarf over, trusting that the gentle giants would not damage it. One by one, they passed it around the table, each examining it in the light of the large windows on each side of the hall. Pallin kept it the longest, turning it over and over in his withered hands, examining what seemed to be every square inch. Alanda watched him closely. If anyone in the room could explain the runes, it would be him.

Pallin spoke in a frail, gravelly voice. "She must go to Dachilon," he dictated, looking at each council member in turn. "She must seek answers with the guardians there."

"Dachilon?" Alanda asked, confused. She had never heard of it, nor seen it on any map. Making the connection in the next moment, however, she realized it must be the library across Anneau's Field the elves told her of.

Rinayai confirmed her assumption. "Dachilon is an ancient and sacred place to us," he said. "It contains the heart of our knowledge and the spirits of our ancestors. The guardians there have great knowledge. They commit themselves to the pursuit of it, some traveling over the wide expanses of Ilbeor's mountains and valleys to learn, and some remaining in Dachilon their entire adult lives, cataloguing what has been learned so it may be preserved for future generations. They do not mate nor procreate, and they are all there by choice. It has been as it is for millennia."

Alanda nodded, marveling at the idea that any one place or tradition in Ilbeor was that old. Humans, as far as her mother had taught her, had arrived in Ilbeor later than all but the Twanai. It had once seemed a long time to her regardless - generations upon generations - but compared to Rinayai's claim that Dachilon had existed for millennia, she realized just how ancient the tselqs' history was. "Will these guardians be able to understand the runes?" she asked directly. If she was going to make the trip, she wanted to be reasonably sure it would be worth it.

"Certainly," Toncha said in a booming voice. "If there is a translation for these runes, be it human, elf, dwarf, or otherwise, the guardians will have it. You will not find a more complete store of knowledge anywhere in Ilbeor, even at the humans' Sanctum of Oaos, which is, I believe, the heart of your knowledge and religion."

"It is," Alanda agreed, her voice flat. She was already planning her journey across the glacier and wondering how much the tselqs would be willing to help her. "What are the points of reference?"

At this question, several of the tselqs began talking at once, protesting. She could not possibly be allowed to journey to Dachilon. It was not done; only tselqs, and usually only shamans or those who had pledged themselves to become guardians, were allowed to enter.

Rinayai held up a hand again, immediately silencing everyone. "This is not a typical situation," he said gravely. "As I have said, and as I have seen, this young human's quest for this knowledge will cause waves which will shake the very foundations of our land. She is to be allowed to go, but she will not go alone. I will accompany her. It is my fate to be her companion for as long as she has need of me."

Another storm of protest greeted this, and this time Alanda understood why. Rinayai had told her just hours before he was the only shaman in Chinnua and that he had not yet begun preparing the next tselq to take the post. The idea of him leaving the people who had chosen him to lead was preposterous.

Rinayai held up his hand again, and again silence reigned. "Pallin and I have spoken. He is to take a new apprentice immediately; we have already identified who will be the next shaman. She will begin her training before the day is done. Even her name speaks of the heritage of the shamans: Sincha will take up the mantle in my place."

Alanda lost track of the conversation at that point because the tselq council and even Rinayai stopped speaking the common tongue. After a while, she quietly stood, nudged Alis, and left the hall.

Alanda always enjoyed looking at tselq communities because they were so different from human or elven settlements. The tselqs had developed a technique for adding pigments to a substance they wouldn't share with the other races, and as a result, their houses, shops, and various other buildings were brightly colored and chaotically arranged. The substance didn't fade even in the harsh mountain weather. Alanda, used to the squared organization of the human villages in the valley and the circular orientation of elven settlements, enjoyed how the tselq buildings seemed to be placed in no particular order or shape.

She stood with Alis, watching the tselqs work to restore their community, and she relaxed somewhat. She was tired and she hoped the tselqs would offer her one of their small guest huts; it would be nice to sleep out of the elements.

Her attention drifted to the terraced gardens being worked by tselq children with barely a curl to their small horns, all clearing rubble . Tselqs believed children ought to be contributing members of the community as early as possible, so they became the primary farmers and gardeners at a young age. While they worked, adult tselqs taught them songs of history and heritage, of the mores and traditions that made them who they were, and of the earth and the farming techniques they would need all their lives. It made a pleasant, melodic addition to the sounds of the mountain and wilderness around them, and though she couldn't understand the words, Alanda enjoyed listening.

She and Alis stood, their backs to the council hall, watching the work and listening to the songs. Alanda was startled when Rinayai tapped her shoulder from behind.

"It is decided," he said in the common tongue. "We travel together."

THE SONGS OF THE CHILDREN

Alanda was given the nicest guest accommodation Chinnua offered. With two rooms and a view of the terraced gardens, the vibrantly purple hut was usually used for visiting shamans and other high-ranking members of tselq society.

She woke at *uht* to find that while fire in the hearth had burnt to embers, the chill of the early fall morning had not completely over-taken the space. Petting Alis, she sat up on the soft pallet on the floor of the main room and blinked in surprise as she recognized the songs of the children outside. How could they be at work already?

Puzzled, Alanda got off the pallet and stood, stretching. Even in the simple shift she slept in, the room was warm enough, and she quickly dressed in a soft blue wool tunic and brown wool pants, glad she had packed them for her journey. Her leathers needed repair, and she would look far less odd to the tselqs in this outfit. Smoothing sun salve over her exposed skin and head, she wondered about breakfast. She wasn't sure where she was supposed to go to eat, but even as she considered eating from the scant provisions left in her pack, a knock sounded on the door to the hut.

"Come in," Alanda called, glad she was already dressed for the day.

Two tselqs Alanda didn't recognize came in at her summons, one male and one female, each bearing a wooden tray. The male wore an unbleached linen shirt and brown linen pants, but the female's dress surprised her. It was a simple enough dress without tucks or frills about it, very similar to what she had seen on other tselq women, but at the neck and the ends of the sleeves was some fine embroidery work in geometric shapes in reds and browns.

The tselqs sat the trays down on the small table in the main room and made to leave without speaking to Alanda, but this didn't sit well with her. "Wait," she said as they reached the door to the hut. "What are your names?"

"Karuk," the male grunted, turning back toward her. She counted three curls to his horns, and the muscles in his arms bulged under the sleeves of his shirt. She wondered if he was more accustomed to manual labor, or if his muscles were that way, regardless.

"Karuk-wari," said the female. She, too, had three curls to her horns. Alanda knew from her name that she was married to Karuk; tselq women took the names of their husbands followed by the moniker "wari" when they were bound.

"Karuk-wari," she said respectfully. "I like your dress. The embroidery is beautiful. Did you do that yourself?"

Karuk-wari brightened, bestowing a smile upon Alanda. "Yes," she said, her voice only slightly higher in pitch and gentler than Karuk's guttural utterances. "My mother is thread-mistress and taught me when I was a child, though it is not my work now."

Alanda was surprised. Given the unadorned nature of most tselq clothing, she had not realized embroidery was a skill prized among them. She wondered if the thread-mistress was the one who made the shamans' ceremonial garb, which she had only seen once during her apprenticeship. "What is your work?" she asked, genuinely curious.

"Karuk is the master of sustenance," Karuk-wari told her. "He sees that the community remains fed through both hard and bounteous times. My place is with our children, but as they are all old enough to work the gardens, I have taken on duties as my mate's helper."

Alanda realized that Karuk's position was one of importance and honor among the community, and she wondered why he had delivered her breakfast himself. She knew it would be rude to ask, so instead she extended her hand, palm-up, in the tselq's gesture of goodwill and respect. "Thank you for bringing my breakfast," she said sincerely.

Karuk and Karuk-wari both placed their hands atop hers, palms down, in acceptance of her gesture. "It was our pleasure," Karuk said. "Your presence brings honor to our community." They turned and left the hut, closing the door softly behind them.

Alanda was touched. She did not consider her presence any more special than anyone else's, but knowing she was welcomed by the community and not just Rinayai made her feel warm inside.

Before she sat at the table to eat, Alanda opened the door so she could more clearly hear the songs coming from the terraced gardens. Though they were not in the common tongue and the tselq language was as foreign to her as the elves' Yrui had once been, she liked the effortless harmony of the music.

Breakfast consisted of a large quantity of fruit drizzled with a sweet sauce Alanda had never tasted before, brown bread and butter, and a steaming mug of coffee. On the second tray was a bowl full of food for Alis, which looked different from anything Alanda had seen before: mostly the color of mush, the soft meal was interspersed with brighter colors that Alanda surmised came from fruits and vegetables. She wondered what was in the food; tselqs didn't consume any sort of meat, and Alis had eaten meat for as long as Alanda had owned her.

Alis had no reservations about her allotted meal. Scarfing down the contents of the bowl while Alanda ate her ration more slowly, Alis soon finished and whined at Alanda for permission to venture outside the hut. Patting her head between delicious bites of the sweet fruit, Alanda said, "Go explore, girl, and enjoy yourself." With one bark of contentment, Alis left the hut.

Alanda enjoyed her breakfast immensely, even given the lack of meat or cheese. The sweet sauce reminded her of something she had tasted at the elves' Summer's End feast, and she wondered if sugar had been one of the ingredients. The brown bread was nutty and fresh with the welcome addition of the honey-sweetened butter, and the coffee, while not as good as Maryah's had been, was rich and hot.

After she had finished and stacked the wooden plates and bowls neatly on one of the trays, Alanda ventured outside. Stepping outside the door, she wrapped her arms around herself to fend off the chill and watched the children at work.

Tselq children, at least the ones old enough to work the gardens, were much bigger and bulkier than human children of similar age, some of the older ones even reaching the height of an average human adult. They labored easily, some still clearing rubble from the previous day's earthquake, while others tended the plants, most of which looked ready for fall harvest. At the head of each row of children was an adult with several curls to their horns, leading the singing as they worked alongside them. Given the apparent advanced age of the children's leaders, Alanda wondered if adult tselqs took those positions after they had retired from other work; one adult, some distance from the house, appeared to have as many as five curls to his horns.

Alanda could not help but wonder at the early hour the children had begun. In the valley, children usually woke before sunrise with their parents, but unless something emergent required them to start earlier, they ate breakfast and attended to household chores before starting the harder work in the gardens and fields. To already be working at *uht*, the tselq children would have had to wake and breakfast in full darkness. It seemed harsh to Alanda, and she wondered whether the tselq children were given the chance to enjoy their childhood as human children were.

Another unknown tselq woman came up to Alanda as she watched the children work in the gardens. Dressed in a long, tunic-style dress of blue wool with heavy embroidery at the neck, sleeves, and chest, the woman looked different from any tselq woman Alanda had ever seen, and she wondered at the distinction but didn't know how to ask about it.

"I am Sincha," the tselq woman announced, her pronunciation in the common tongue somewhat less accented than the other tselqs

Alanda had met. "Well met, Alanda of Blackwell." She extended her large, green hand, palm-up, to Alanda.

Alanda placed her hand atop the woman's. "Well met," she said, trying not to stare.

Sincha's features, even aside from her dress, seemed distinctive from the other tselqs. Her face was broad like that of everyone of her race, but her cheekbones were well-defined and her nose smaller than usual. Her horns curled only twice; she was obviously still young, but she carried herself with an authority that did not seem completely comfortable to her yet. It was almost forced.

Alanda realized who she was a moment later. "You're the new shaman," she blurted out.

Sincha smiled. "I am," she said. "I was called only yesterday, as I am sure you know from your meeting with the elders."

Alanda nodded. "I really enjoy listening to the children sing as they work."

"I always enjoyed it as a child. I am only a few years gone from the work myself. Would you like to know what they are singing this morning? I do not imagine you are familiar with our language and customs."

"I'm not," Alanda admitted. "I would love to hear a translation of their song if you have the time."

"This morning they are singing of our distant past, of our arrival on Ilbeor," Sincha told her. "They sing of the ships that brought us to this beautiful land from the harsh reality of the former one, large ships holding the entirety of our race safe on a long journey over endless seas."

"Your race still remembers their arrival here?" Alanda asked in surprise. "I would think, given how long you have been in the land, that your arrival would have been forgotten by now."

"We remember through our songs and stories," Sincha said, looking contemplative. "Our ancestors should not be forgotten."

Alanda thought of the songs she had learned as a child, usually silly things about people falling in love or venturing to unknown places. None of them spoke overmuch of human history and, listening to

Sincha talk about the history of her people as though it were an affront not to remember it, she thought it was a shame.

"Which sea did your ancestors cross?" she asked curiously.

"We came across the Unresting Sea from a land called Moacha, a harsh land with many enemies. We found Ilbeor through the dreams of the old shamans, who saw a land bounteous and beautiful in our futures. And so it was, and we have lived here in peace ever since."

Alanda thought it both astounding and wonderful that the tselqs had found Ilbeor through dreams. What a journey to undertake, having no actual way of knowing where it would end! They were lucky to find Ilbeor. Sincha was right; the land was beautiful.

Sincha seemed to come to herself, almost as though coming out of a trance. "I am here to see what you need for your stay," she said, her voice becoming more businesslike. "We require time to make you appropriate protective clothing for your crossing, and we would have you be comfortable here."

"I need materials to repair my leathers," Alanda said, hoping she would not offend Sincha with the mention of the material. "Just strong needles and black thread."

"You may find those materials at the shop of the thread-mistress," Sincha told her, seemingly unperturbed by the mention of leather. She pointed through the jumble of huts and other buildings. "Hers is a small, square hut painted green. You'll see a sign above it, but it is not in the common tongue."

"I'm sure I can find it," Alanda said gratefully. "Thank you, Sincha."

"Should you have need of anything, call upon any of the tselqs. They are all thankful to you for your rescue of Rinayai and will willingly aid you. Would you sup with me tonight?"

Alanda agreed, glad not to spend her days in solitude. Sincha smiled at her and ambled away, her pace slow, still with the sense of forced authority in her bearing.

As Alanda watched Sincha wind through the chaotically arranged buildings, Alis came to her side, panting happily. It was clear that she'd enjoyed exploring. Alanda petted her in long, rhythmic strokes, and the children continued to sing. She was going to enjoy staying in Chinnua.

As Alanda walked through the community of brightly colored buildings, she saw that, despite the early hour, all the tselqs seemed to be up and about. She saw women with babies on their hips or breasts, using their free hands to tend small gardens or clean dishes from the morning meal. She saw tselq men at work in what looked almost exactly like a human smithy, pumping bellows and wielding huge hammers on metal so hot it was brightly colored in orange and yellow.

Although all tselqs were muscular, the tselq men working the smithy had muscles that seemed almost unbelievable to her human eyes. She had thought Serill to be strong, but she privately wondered if his strength could even come close to competing with the strength of the tselq blacksmiths.

When she reached the square green hut with the sign over the door, Alanda thought she had found the thread-mistress's shop. The door was closed and, not knowing if the customs were the same, Alanda knocked politely.

A guttural response in tselq came through the door. After a moment, the phrase was repeated, so she took her chances and pushed the door open. It felt strange to her not to make the usual gesture of offering her open hands at the door, but she knew it wasn't the tselq custom, so she simply stood a step in from the doorway and waited.

The shop looked similar to what she had been expecting: a long counter ran the length of the back of the square room, and the walls were lined with various threads and hues of woolen and linen fabric. Behind the counter, the tools of the trade were displayed: sharp knives and awls hung on the wall, two different looms both set with fabric being made rested unused, and a spinning wheel spun with a rhythmic clicking as a tselq woman with five curls to her horns worked it.

The spinning stopped as the tselq turned to greet her visitor. As soon as she saw Alanda, the thread-mistress's broad face split into a friendly, welcoming grin. "Hello," she said in the common tongue, though her stilted pronunciation of the word suggested she had not had much practice speaking to outsiders.

Alanda smiled in return, glad for the warm reception. "Hello," she replied. "I'm Alanda, and I'm visiting Chinnua from my village in the valley. Are you the thread-mistress?"

"Yes," the woman replied. "I am Akunda-ikma." She named herself as the widow of a man named Akunda, though Alanda detected no hints of grief. She went on to say, "I have been charged with making you warm clothing for your journey over Anneau's Field, as I believe the humans call it."

"Thank you," Alanda said. "I'm very grateful for your help." She wondered how to make her requests without seeming rude.

Akunda-ikma solved her quandary by asking, "Why have you come to my shop today, young human?"

Alanda was relieved by the opening. "I need materials to repair my traveling lea-, I mean, clothing. Black thread, if you have it, and strong needles."

Akunda-ikma grimaced, and Alanda wondered if it was because she knew what kind of clothing Alanda had worn into the settlement. Just as they didn't eat meat, neither did tselqs wear leather or fur. "I know why you need strong needles," the woman said, confirming Alanda's suspicions. She was surprised, however, when Akunda-ikma continued, "I do not fault you for it. You are human, and it is your way. I think I have what you will need to repair your clothing." She stood up from the stool in front of her spinning wheel and went to a medium-sized wooden box on the counter.

Alanda watched as Akunda-ikma selected several metal needles from the box, all of which looked well-suited to her task. Next, she came out from behind the counter to examine the skeins of thread on one wall of the shop. Selecting one, she invited Alanda to come examine it.

The thread was thicker than what Alanda was used to but seemed strong and serviceable. She ran her hand along the length of it and nodded. It would be perfect for repairing both her linen shirt and the small area of her pants that needed restitching.

Alanda reached into her belt pouch, but Akunda-ikma stopped her as she drew out a silver coin. "We do not trade in money here," she said kindly. "I cannot accept that."

Alanda was confused. "How do you want me to pay for the supplies?" she asked, unsure of what she had to trade with otherwise.

"There is no need for payment of that sort. In the tselq communities, each contributes to the fullest of their ability and, in turn, has their needs met. You have contributed to our community already, and thus, you are entitled to these supplies from my shop." Akunda-ikma deftly wrapped the length of thread and three of the needles in a small, brown paper parcel similar to what Alanda would have received in a human shop. With a kind smile, she handed it to Alanda.

Alanda accepted the package uncertainly. Never, in all the various lessons during her apprenticeship, had she learned that tselqs did not use money for trades between themselves. When she delivered messages to a tselq community, she had always received coin, just as she did everywhere else. It seemed wrong to take supplies from the shop without paying, but she didn't know how to protest without breaking tselq customs.

"If there is nothing else you need, I must return to spinning," Akunda-ikma said firmly, ready to continue with her business for the day.

"Thank you," Alanda said, still feeling uncertain, and made to leave.

"Have a pleasant stay, Alanda." The way the tselq woman pronounced her name made it sound exotic, like some creature from another land altogether.

Alanda ventured back to the guest hut with her needles and thread, deciding she would repair her leathers right away instead of waiting for another day. The air was warming as the sun rose, and she was glad for the beautiful day following the stress of the earthquake. If she had not been afraid she would offend the tselqs with her leathers, she would have done her repairs outside her hut, but as it was, she chose to remain indoors. Alis padded along comfortably beside her, stopping occasionally to sniff, and took her place beside Alanda as Alanda sat at the table to work.

THOUGH HER BREAKFAST and midday meal were usually undertaken with only Alis for company, Alanda rarely spent the entire day alone. Starting with her evening meal with Sincha and her parents, Alanda supped with a different member of the community almost every night. Sometimes, the meals were sumptuous affairs with members of the council or Rinayai and Pallin, but more often she supped simply with the everyday members of the community. It seemed she was not only an honored guest for what she had done for Rinayai, but also a curiosity. Human visitors this far up in the mountains were rare, and her pale coloring and hair made her unique even among the humans they had seen.

One night, the twelfth since she had come to Chinnua, she ate with Karuk, Karuk-wari, and their children. Their meal was later than those of the other community members, because Karuk saw to the provisions of the rest of the community before his own. Alanda was surprised upon her arrival to find Karuk tending the pot of vegetable stew hanging on a trivet over the fire, rather than Karuk-wari, who was sitting in a cushioned chair in the main room, knitting.

Karuk-wari noticed her look of surprise and laughed, much to Alanda's discomfiture. Tselqs rarely laughed and had a strange sense of humor. "Our ways are not yours, I see," she said, putting down her needles and standing to greet her guest. "In tselq households, the partner who enjoys cookery more is the one to prepare the meals. Here, that is Karuk. He enjoys preparing our small repasts after his work with larger amounts of food is done for the day. You will find his food satisfactory, I think."

"I'm sure it will be wonderful," Alanda said politely, and truthfully, the smells coming from the pot over the fire were very enticing. Alanda had paid attention to the various meals she had been served;

the tselqs used different seasonings than those found in the valley. The results, Alanda thought, were more appetizing than even the best human food she had tasted.

Each of Karuk-wari's three children attended to tasks around the house as they waited for the meal to be ready. One, the smallest, ran a small cloth over each of the surfaces of the room, removing dust. The middle child, a female named Kateri, busily sewed something that looked like the beginnings of a child's tunic. The oldest, a strapping male soon to be released from his work in the gardens to pursue a profession, sharpened a collection of kitchen knives much more extensive than Alanda was used to seeing in human kitchens, most of which only had one or two knives.

The musky smell common to the tselqs was strong inside the house, even over the enticing scent of the stew. Alanda had learned on her first day that in the afternoons, the garden work stopped and the children were allowed several hours for free play. Tselq children played raucously, stopping only when the sun dipped below the horizon. Then, they attended to daily chores at home. Alanda concluded the childhoods of the tselqs were just as happy as those of humans, even if they were quite different.

The stew was every bit as delicious as the scent had promised, especially when one sopped the broth up with more of the nutty brown bread she was served at each meal. Alanda complimented Karuk on it, saying honestly that the meal had been one of the best she'd had since she had come to Chinnua.

"Thank you," he grunted, then addressed his children in the tselq language. The words were apparently an order to clean the remains of the meal, for all three children jumped up and began taking the wooden dishes and metal cutlery to be scoured.

Alanda only remained a short time after the meal had concluded to talk to her hosts. She had learned that tselqs went to sleep soon after nightfall, both to conserve resources and because they awoke so early. She bid her goodbyes and made her way back to her hut by the light of a large lantern, made for tselq hands rather than human. Alis's paws drummed their familiar beat as they walked.

Alis had been welcomed freely into every hut and building they had entered during their stay, except the shaman's hut. The tselqs only kept pets deemed unsuitable to be companions to the travelers of the land, and they loved all animals. Alanda found their pets charming; though all had some defect in size, shape, or form that made them unable to complete the rigorous training and lifestyle of the traveling professions, they had all been trained and cared for, and they all responded to both her and Alis with dispositions almost too sweet to be believed. The love tselqs had for animals of all kinds was reflected in the animals' lack of fear and aggression to any who crossed their path.

As she approached the hut, Alanda reflected that no race was as peaceful as the tselqs, including the even-tempered elves. Even during the heavy work of the day in the mountainside community, voices remained tranquil, everyone seemed happy, and she had yet to see any kind of serious disagreement, even among the children.

This would be a wonderful place to raise a family, Alanda thought, then laughed at herself. Humans wouldn't last long in a community like this; though the land itself was at peace and most of the humans in each village worked well with one another, humans were much more temperamental than the peace-loving tselqs.

The air had become increasingly crisp that evening, and Alanda added logs to her fire from the ever-present supply. The snows had not come yet, but she knew it would not be long. Alanda extinguished the lantern, and, by the light of her fire, changed into her shift and snuggled into the blankets of the soft pallet while Alis circled her own small pallet and found a comfortable position.

Alanda soon drifted into sleep herself, feeling content and safer than she had since her parents had died.

ALANDA WAS FINISHING her breakfast on her thirteenth day when a soft knock sounded at her door. When she opened it, a small tselq child, perhaps four or five years of age and without a single curl to his horns, brought Alanda the protective clothing Akunda-ikma had made for her journey over Anneau's Field. After a moment, she recognized the small child as Karuk and Karuk-wari's youngest child.

"Ulo!" She greeted him enthusiastically, taking the large bundle from his arms and placing it on her table. "Thank you!"

The child beamed at her and said something in tselq she did not understand.

Alanda, realizing he had not yet learned the common tongue, offered the tselq sign of goodwill to the child. She extended her hand, palm-up, to him.

Ulo smiled widely at her and placed his small hand atop hers. He left, pleased, and Alanda examined what she had been given.

As she opened the bundle, she could not help but wrinkle her nose. To her eyes, used to solid-color clothing, the patchwork appearance of the clothing was quite ugly. She much preferred her black and green water-cloth cloak to the puffy, multicolored coat she pulled from the bundle. It was stuffed with scraps of fabric, much like tselq pillows and mattresses. It was thick and unwieldy, made of various colors and types of fabric sewn together with thick thread. Alanda sighed, thinking of the fine, small stitches her mother had used even when sewing the simplest of her clothing and considering the considerable trouble she had gone to in order to repair her leathers while waiting for her departure.

Well, it does look like it will keep me warm.

She thought of the work Akunda-ikma must have gone through to make the coat, and she felt a pang of guilt for her distaste. After all, the Chinnua tselqs must know much better than she what it would take to survive the crossing.

Sifting through the rest of the bundle, she found three pairs of thick, woolen socks, four small, puffy boots that had to be for Alis, and two sets of woolen undergarments she supposed were meant to be worn under her leathers; there weren't any other clothes for her. Alanda was a bit relieved by that. Besides her ridiculous coat, she could at least look like herself when she was presented to the guardians.

She smiled at the thought of putting the puffy boots on Alis's feet - clothing for a dog had seemed so ridiculous when Rinayai had first mentioned it several days before - but upon reflection, she thought it was probably a good thing. Alis's coat protected her well from the elements, but she didn't have fur on the bottom of her paws, and the ice would be frigid.

As she was putting things away and preparing her pack for the journey, she was slightly startled by another knock at the door, this one stronger and surer. She answered it to find Rinayai, Pallin, and Sincha.

Sincha was not dressed in the shamans' traditional garb, but in a simple linen dress. As she came in, she did as she always did and examined Alis from head to tail. "I never asked you where she was bred," she said by way of greeting. "Not here, I think. We rarely have white pups among our litters."

"Not here," Alanda agreed. "Alis was bred in Barichon in the southern range. My trainer picked her especially for me, since I am so pale."

"It was a good choice," Sincha said, nodding seriously. "Alis is your match in more than coloring. Your spirits roam together."

Alanda wasn't sure what to say to that and was relieved when Rinayai stepped forward, ending the conversation. "We have much to discuss. May we enter?"

Alanda mentally shook herself. "Of course. Please, come in." She stood aside to let the three tselqs in. Alis barked once as Pallin passed her, and Alanda shushed her, mortified by her lack of manners.

"It is well," Pallin assured her in his gravelly voice. "I am old, and my scent differs."

Alanda followed them into the small sitting room, where they each took seats on the low upholstered chairs facing one another. Alis positioned herself next to Alanda and, at Alanda's signal, relaxed into a sitting position.

"We will begin our journey at first light tomorrow," Rinayai announced. "That is, if you have had sufficient rest?"

"Yes, thank you," Alanda said. "Alis and I are well rested and very grateful for the accommodations. I like waking to the songs of the children each morning." She smiled.

"The songs of the children hold the beauty of our race," Pallin agreed, nodding sagely. Alanda idly wondered whether the many curls of his long horns made his head too heavy on his neck, which appeared thin and frail.

"It will take us approximately five days to reach the edge of the ice sheet," Rinayai continued. "Until then, I would suggest you wear your normal traveling clothes, for though the chill has set in, winter is not yet upon us. I would not want you to overheat."

"Of course, Rinayai," Alanda said respectfully, appreciating the advice.

"Humans do not cross the ice," Pallin commented. "It is not done. We have prepared as well as we can for you, but your bodies are frail, and the glacier is an extreme and unpredictable environment. I am concerned for your safety."

Alanda said nothing for a long moment, studying the tselqs as she had never done before. They were taller than humans, ranging from six to over seven feet tall, but what really struck her was how much hardier they were. Tselqs were well-muscled by default; their bodies developed that way regardless of the work they put in, and the demanding nature of their lifestyle in the mountains only added to it. The average tselq was more muscular than the strongest human male, one who had performed hard labor all his life. Even Sincha, who did not perform hard labor in her profession, had corded muscles running up her arms and legs under her dress.

Suddenly, Alanda felt frail and small. She was fit and healthy from her long journeys and a diet bereft of most sugars, but her frame was slight and not overly muscular. Compared to the tselqs with their earthy green skin and robust, muscled frames, she felt as though she were but a ghost.

"You will be well protected," Sincha assured her, seeing Alanda's expression and correctly guessing her feelings. "Not only will you be wearing protective clothing, but Rinayai will carry equipment to keep you warm at night."

Alanda nodded her thanks, and the discussion turned to logistics. Alanda learned they would be on the glacier for at least seven days, and when she heard that, she was truly frightened for the first time since conceiving of the journey back in Kilynelle. Seven days was an eternity in frigid conditions, with no food or cover to be found. She hid her fears behind an impassive expression, and no one thought to reassure her.

By the time the three tselqs left and she had eaten, she was overwhelmed, tired, and nervous. She spent the rest of the day preparing for the journey, supped with Rinayai, and returned to the house not much less worried than she had been before. Her last thoughts before she went to sleep were about Kitz, and whether she had doomed him to a life without a family.

She wondered if he would even notice.

WHEN ALIS WOKE Alanda at *uht*, Alanda stretched on her pallet and smiled as she heard the voices of the tselq children in the gardens. Her smile faded as she sat up and remembered what the day would bring: the first day of her journey toward the glacier. Though she loved traveling, she did not know Rinayai well and had never traveled with a tselq. Additionally, she was nervous about crossing Anneau's Field, though not as frightened as she had been.

"Alis," she said, stroking her dog from her head down her back, "this is going to be interesting, at the very least. I'm so glad I've got you." Alis licked her hand.

By the time Rinayai came to her door at dawn, Alanda was packed and ready, having eaten a light breakfast and fed Alis the specially made mix the tselq breeders fed all their dogs. She still didn't know what was in it, but the tselqs bred all the messenger dogs, and they were known for their health and vitality. Alanda knew it was quite possible her dog had supped more sumptuously than she had.

After receiving a blessing from Pallin and Sincha conducted in fluent, rolling tselq, Rinayai, Alanda, and Alis shouldered their heavy packs and began their journey up the mountain.

For most of the first day, they talked little other than to note changes in direction as they ascended. When Alanda reapplied her sun salve at midday, Rinayai asked her about it, and she explained her sensitivity to the sun. He seemed more worried than she had expected, given she had spent two weeks in their community without incident, and when she questioned him, he explained.

On the glacier, the sun reflected off the ground as well as from the sky. Alanda shrugged off his worries, telling him the sun salve would protect her regardless of which direction the light came from, but she would keep it in mind and apply the salve more often.

The first night, when they made camp, Rinayai surprised Alanda by saying a few unknown words over the logs and snapping his fingers, causing a bright blaze to immediately appear.

Alanda paused as she unpacked her evening supplies. "You're a magician," she said in amazement.

"Yes, but not trained as well as most," Rinayai replied modestly. "By the time the Sashu came for me, I had already been in training to be the next shaman for more than a year, and I declined to go with them to the place where I would learn to use my gift. An older tselq magician who had returned to our community trained me in some words and methods, but he died before I could learn much."

"The Sashu," Alanda said wonderingly. "What were they like?"

"The ones who came for me were called the Watchers," Rinayai said, busying himself with his own pack. "They were very…strange. They seemed ancient but looked like large adult humans with dark skin, almost black. They spoke my language with ease, and when I explained I could not go with them, they accepted what I said and departed. I never heard from them again."

"What all can you do?" Alanda asked curiously, beginning Alis's nightly combing.

"Not much," Rinayai replied. "Start fires, and sometimes if I concentrate hard enough, I can move things with my mind. It has proven helpful when there are heavy things to be moved, but I found myself unable to use my power when I was buried in the rubble before you found me. True magicians can perform wonders the likes of which you may not have seen."

"I've seen magic among the elves," Alanda told him. "The elf healer, Myrine, who treated me when I was very ill, used magic as well as herbal remedies. I have also taken part in one of their festivals, and the magic was intoxicating. It got into my body and, I think, my soul. I've never met a human magician, though. We didn't have one in Blackwell."

"Most human magicians stay with the Sashu, or so I was told, which is why you have never met them. The Sashu do not use messengers other than their own, and they don't engage in much trade. They are sent out to places when there has been tragedy on a large scale, like plague, fire, or natural disaster."

Alanda nodded. It made sense. She had never even heard of the Sashu before her apprenticeship, and even then, the information had been vague. She had heard tales of magic in her childhood, of course, but they were often stories of dark witches and sorcerers meant to frighten children into good behavior instead of reflections on what she now knew was the truth about magic.

"Our evening meal does not require cooking," Rinayai said, pulling an assortment of preserved fruits and bread from his pack. "You have food for Alis, yes?"

"Yes," Alanda answered. "Sincha brought me a large supply yesterday evening. Though it adds weight to my pack, I was grateful for it. Our road is long."

"Sincha was originally trained as a dog breeder," Rinayai explained. "She has a great love of animals."

"She told me," Alanda replied. "Do you think she minded being pulled from her chosen profession to become a shaman?" It was a question she had not dared to ask Sincha herself, but knowing how much the tselq woman loved animals, she wondered about it.

"To serve as shaman is a great honor among my people. Though Sincha may have had some pangs about leaving the dogs she loves, she was properly willing to take on the mantle when asked. No tselq would refuse that call."

After this, they ate in silence, though as she chewed on her preserved apples, Alanda wondered if she was truly expected not to consume meat at all while she traveled with Rinayai. The thought dismayed her. Though she understood the tselqs' distaste for violence and their love for living things, she had been raised eating meat. Understanding Rinayai meant to accompany her on her travels even past Dachilon, she knew she would have to discuss it with him at some point. She decided their first night traveling together was not the time.

When everything was settled for the night, Alanda once again got out the block of strange wood Grayson had given her. During her stay in Chinnua, she had begun carving a new dragon for Kitz, though she had already missed his thirteenth birth celebration. She knew he might not be interested in it anymore, but had some thoughts about giving it to Isaac if Kitz didn't want it. Enjoying the familiar feel of her whittling knife in her hand, she worked, humming unconsciously while she carved.

Rinayai smiled as he watched her. He knew messengers often had evening hobbies ranging from writing poems to hunting, and he liked the look of ease and contentment on Alanda's face as she worked. Not having seen any of her completed work, he did not know the extent of her skill, but to him, that she seemed to be truly enjoying herself was the most important thing.

When the darkness became complete, they took to their blankets on opposite sides of the fire. Alanda, used to sleeping outdoors, fell asleep quickly and easily among her familiar blankets with Alis nestled close, but Rinayai had a hard time acclimatizing to the sounds of the forest and sleeping on the ground. As Alanda began to lightly snore, Rinayai readjusted himself for the tenth time as an owl hooted somewhere above him. The moon had almost reached its zenith before he finally fell asleep out of sheer exhaustion.

The journey grew more difficult as they angled up the mountain, heading north as they climbed. By the third day, Alanda was having trouble keeping her breathing steady. She had never traveled so high before, and the thinner air was difficult for her. Rinayai had an easier time but was considerate of her need to pause and catch her breath. Though he did not mention it to Alanda, he grew increasingly concerned throughout the journey that traveling across the ice would prove too difficult, if not impossible, for her. He was impressed with her determination, however.

As Rinayai had predicted, by the afternoon of the fifth day they had reached the tree line and the edge of the glacier, Anneau's Field. "We stop here," Rinayai said in a tone allowing no argument. "We must prepare for the crossing and get as much rest as we can."

Alanda agreed, wrapping her arms around herself to suppress a shiver. The days and nights had grown colder the higher they traveled, and snow had begun to fall and coat the ground earlier that day. Staring at the vast expanse of blue-white ice spread out in front of them as far as the eye could see, she felt some of her previous fear return as she imagined just how very cold it must be to have ice under her feet in addition to the weather.

Rinayai led them back amongst the trees, and they found a clearing without a view of the ice sheet, which Alanda was thankful for. They went to work sweeping the snow aside to give themselves enough dry space for their fire and their sleeping blankets, and Rinayai once again gathered wood and started the fire by magic. Alanda was grateful for the warmth of the blaze and encouraged Alis to join her near the fire for her nightly combing.

After they had eaten, Alanda asked Rinayai to turn his back so she could put on the warm underclothes the tselqs had provided for her, knowing she would appreciate them during what would be a freezing night. She was pleased when he not only did, but actually left the clearing altogether to give her privacy.

Shivering violently, Alanda pulled off her leathers and put on both sets of the warm underclothes as quickly as she could, wrinkling her nose as she realized she hadn't bathed since leaving Chinnua; the water in the abundant streams and ponds had simply been too cold. Longing for the nights when her father had brought water into the house and her mother had heated it for warm baths, she struggled to lace the tight leathers over the thick undergarments. Once she had managed that, she pulled her boots on over a pair of the thick woolen socks.

Rinayai's return was so perfectly timed she secretly wondered if he had been watching her from the surrounding forest, but she dismissed the thought. He had too much honor for that.

They sat companionably next to the fire, not speaking until Rinayai asked her why she wasn't working on her evening hobby.

"I can't carve with my gloves on," Alanda explained. "I work as much by touch as by sight, and it's too cold to go without my gloves."

Rinayai could feel the chill on his skin, of course, but tselqs were more acclimated to cold, and their bodies were well suited to extreme weather. His only concession to the colder weather and the snow had been to change his short-sleeved tunic for a long-sleeved one and to put shoes on his usually bare feet.

"What do you do when you must deliver messages in the winter?" Rinayai asked curiously.

"Last winter, I was still in my apprenticeship," she said, "and so Alicia and I would spend the evenings telling stories or talking over the fire until it was time to sleep. This winter, I don't know what I will do."

"This winter, I will be with you," Rinayai replied confidently, as though this were a foregone conclusion. "You and I will talk and tell stories as well."

They chatted for a while about the differences between their lives and cultures, and their upcoming journey, but Alanda was clearly tired from exertion at the high altitude. It was not completely dark when Rinayai insisted they go to bed, and Alanda did not argue.

Even though she knew her tightly woven traveling blankets would provide warmth, Alanda didn't remove her boots or gloves before curling up with Alis and pulling the blankets up to her chin. Anticipation ran through her as she settled down, rhythmically petting Alis to soothe herself until her eyes finally closed.

Tomorrow, they would begin crossing Anneau's Field.

UROTHU

Herve closed the door to his bakery with a finality that showed just how anxious he was to be done with the business of the day. His customers, all villagers from Basendale today, had seemed particularly difficult to please, and he had made several special orders, including a cake for the birth celebration of one of the noble children.

Herve did not like making celebration cakes. They seemed to him exceptionally superfluous, and the resources he had to use for the sugary cakes and the decoration meant that, even at the premium prices he charged, his profit was not appreciably more than it was when he made a simple loaf of brown bread. No, celebration cakes were not his favorite part of the job, and he was glad this one was done and sold.

He washed his hands in the basin behind the counter for a final time before making the walk back to his home just off Basendale's village square. Barnaby, his oldest son and the one who stood to inherit the bakery, had already left for the evening. The shop was quiet, and the flour from the day's baking had settled into a fine layer of light brown powder on the shop's surfaces.

Herve scowled as he always did at the mess of the day's end, and he continued scrubbing his hands with the harsh green soap he always kept beside the basin. He would have to clean the shop in the morning as the first bread of the day baked, and it was not a task he ever relished. No matter how hard he tried, that fine flour dust could never be fully eradicated.

Rinsing his hands, he dried them on the small white cloth next to the basin and reached behind his plump form to untie the white apron he always wore. *Soon enough, I'll be rid of the place*, he thought sourly as he hung the apron on its peg.

He had not chosen baking as his profession; not exactly, anyhow. He had been one of the rare village children who had no siblings, and when it had come time for his apprenticeship some forty years before, it was assumed he would follow in his father's footsteps. His father had taught him well, and Herve had inherited and improved a robust business that more than provided for his family and kept his status as a well-to-do middie secure. Sometimes, though, he found it hard to appreciate the rewards of his hard work over the years, because the truth was that he hated the bakery and everything about it.

Given the chance, he would have taken an apprenticeship as a hunter. Herve enjoyed the hunt; he enjoyed the solitude of the outdoors, enjoyed the tools of the trade, enjoyed the precision required to put meat on the tables of not just his own, but all the families in Basendale. Hunting was an honorable profession, a vital profession, and hunters were afforded a certain importance he was not, for all that he did provide the bread for everyone who could afford to buy it.

Herve grunted as he exited the front door of the bakery, carefully latching and locking it behind him. Though he had grown portly in his older years and was no longer as agile as he would like, he still hunted on the traditional sixth day and also on the fourth. Barnaby, who had worked in his father's kitchen and shop for over twenty years, was perfectly capable of keeping the customers happy while his father indulged in the profession he wished he had taken. Today, however, was the first day, and he had two more days of work in the bakery to endure before he could hunt again.

His mood improved slightly as he walked through the village square towards the two-story, shingled house he and his wife Brigit had called home their entire married lives. Brigit was a superb cook, and he was hungry. He hoped she would have the evening meal on the table when he arrived; sometimes she lost track of the hours as she attended the other household chores or indulged in her former profession as a seamstress. If he was being honest with himself, he faulted her for the lack of punctuality in providing his evening meals. It seemed to him that if all the other wives in Basendale could adhere to a set schedule, she should be able to as well.

He grumbled to himself as he approached the house and didn't smell the tantalizing scent of stew or fried meat. He had brought home a deer from his latest hunt, and the butcher had provided him with some choice cuts in exchange for the rest of the animal.

Damn the woman. Probably hunched over some child's dress instead of attending to her own house.

Herve was planning just what he would say to her when he got inside when the first scream ripped through the air and erased all thoughts of the evening meal and his negligent wife.

The scream had come from the outskirts of the village to the north, from the small community of houses reserved for elderly villagers who had retired. Having it come from that direction was particularly jarring for Herve and the rest of the village because that community was normally the quietest place in Basendale, intentionally separated from the bustle of daily life and absent the cries and babble of playing children and scolding parents. It was a place of peace and repose. No screams should come from the village's elderly.

Just as Herve had decided to go investigate, a second scream sounded but was cut off abruptly, as though the person responsible had clamped their mouth shut. A third scream, and then it seemed as though all the voices of Basendale's elderly rose together in a chorus of shrieks.

Herve ran, urgency and adrenaline pumping his limbs seemingly of their own accord as front doors to houses all along the road opened and the men of the village joined him in his sprint.

The clamor of weapons joined the running footfalls, and Herve noticed that while two had brought aging swords that had probably hung over their mantlepieces for years, most carried weapons consisting of tools such as shovels or pitchforks.

Herve hardly needed the warning shout as the first of the men reached the homes of the elderly. Only one thing could have caused the genuine distress and abject fear of those shrieks: Urothu. Herve didn't know how and he didn't know why, but he knew at least one band of Urothu had infiltrated the village's borders this evening, and Urothu only ever had one aim: the total destruction of anything and everything in their path.

As Herve reached the edge of the village, he knew at a glance that nothing he or anyone else could do would help. He stopped, struck momentarily motionless and dumb by the scene before him.

His eye first caught Martha, who had been Basendale's herbalist before her retirement, cowering behind the rain barrel in front of her home hoping to escape the notice of the gray-skinned creatures throwing fire and blue light at everything they came across.

Herve had never seen Urothu before, though he'd heard tales of them. Those tales had always seemed like they had been more to scare children than actual fact, for no one from Basendale had ever seen one. In fact, it was said stories of Urothu were ancient, told originally by powerful elves, because no human had ever survived an encounter with one. Gray-skinned, as short as children, long-limbed, and bald, Urothu were said to be the most powerfully magical creatures in Ilbeor, their power surpassing even the elves.

In the split second he took to take in the scene before him, a creature detached from the main group and saw Martha. As it approached, Martha screamed, but her scream was cut off as a blade of blue light slashed from between the Urothu's outstretched hands. Herve watched, frozen in horror, as her entire body was slashed in half, the upper part of her torso detaching with a sickening finality from the lower.

As both halves of the woman who had once been Martha dropped to the ground, Herve felt frozen as he realized she had not bled - the magical blade, whatever it had been made of, had cauterized the halves of her body as it had passed through.

What is this evil?

Herve had seen enough. Without a weapon, he could not help, he turned and ran back into the village as fast as his thick legs would carry him, bellowing an unnecessary warning as he hurried back to his own home.

Somewhere inside himself, Herve knew that night would be his last. He knew that, but he did not acknowledge it as he thought wildly of his longbow and hunting knife, both stored carefully just inside the back door of his house. Even knowing, after what he had seen, that to fight was useless, he held onto the thin threads of hope as though they were the last crumbles of rock left to grasp as he fell over a cliff.

He had never been one to pray. He had been a dutiful participant in fifth-day sanctum services all his life, but he had never been one to ask for Annuah's gifts alone. He did not pray tonight, and neither were his thoughts on his wife, his children, or his grandchildren. His entire focus, his entire reason for being as he ran, was retrieving his weapons before the Urothu made it into the village proper.

The screams followed him through the village, coming nearer and nearer. He knew he had moments, if that, before the deadly magicians reached his home. He had to retrieve his weapons before they did; it was his only chance.

Herve nearly crashed through the front door of his home. As he grabbed the longbow and quiver from the back wall and hurriedly strung the bow, only one part of his mind registered that Brigit did not seem to be in the house. He did not spare enough thought to wonder where she might be, fastening the knife to his belt as he rushed back to the front door.

"Herve!"

The shout, almost a scream of fright, came from up the steep wooden staircase. Of course, Brigit was hiding up there, thinking she would be safe.

He did not answer her, only feeling a split second of regret that her hiding place would not likely save her. It was said these inhuman creatures burned every dwelling, every building. Brigit would either be burned with the house or would be killed as she ran out to escape the flames.

He shook his head as he reached the front door and opened it, ignoring another scream of his name from his terrified wife. Glancing north, his earlier thought was confirmed: thick plumes of black smoke rose from the community of the elderly.

Everyone's dead, then.

On the front porch of his home, Herve expertly nocked an arrow and drew the string back, the back of his hand caressing the side of his rough face in a gesture so familiar it should have been comforting. The rote act of self-intimacy went unnoticed, however, as he carefully listened to the sounds coming down from the north: the Urothu were getting closer, killing everyone in their path with their destructive magic. Screams rose and were abruptly cut off; the clamor of metal weapons similarly rose and fell as, Herve assumed, their wielders were killed.

Herve didn't move, only widened his stance to give himself more stability as he waited. He was not stupid; he knew he was not fast enough to outrun them, not skilled enough at close range to do anything other than get himself killed. No, his only hope lay in the true arc of his arrows, fast and deadly, that still netted him comparable kills to the village hunters, even considering his advanced age and decreased agility. He could take them down from where he stood, so he waited.

A fireball larger than anything he had ever seen rose from the north side of the village, and Herve knew that Holger's blacksmith shop must have been hit. Strangely, Herve felt no sense of loss for what he knew must have been the end of Holger and his family, only a detached realization that the blacksmith would never have let the Urothu near his home or his smithy without a fight. There was only one outcome of such a stand, and the fire raging through the shop showed that the outcome had been attained.

They're getting closer.

Herve remained absolutely still, not even noticing the cramp in the small muscles of his hand from holding the bowstring drawn for so long. These feelings were familiar, even down to the lingering discomfort in the small of his back.

They came in a wave from the gaps between the buildings of the village. Perhaps fifty of the small, frail-looking creatures, most of them seeming to carry balls of fire or light between their hands. Their faces were strangely illuminated by their magic, and Herve used that to his advantage as he made his first shot. His aim was true, and one creature went down, the crackling firelight between its hands blinking out as it died.

Herve didn't stop to congratulate himself or celebrate his small victory. He barely even acknowledged it as he removed another arrow from his quiver, nocked it, and shot. Another creature went down with an arrow shaft sticking from its wide forehead. Another spot of magic extinguished.

As he shot, Herve was surprised to note that the creatures did not immediately make a beeline to him as he had expected. Seemingly undisturbed by their losses, the creatures continued to kill everyone they met, sometimes with a ball of fire, sometimes a ball of blue light, sometimes with a blade of magic. The results were always the same: immediate death with no blood in evidence. The Urothu seemed to take no particular pleasure in their conquest, never uttering a single sound from their strange, thin-lipped mouths. As they killed and burned with their magic, the band moved inexorably forward, not in sync, but still somehow seeming to be one unit in the deepening dusk.

The villagers had long since stopped screaming, and the silencing of the voices was more ominous than the clamor of weapons. The silence was the futility of people who knew there was no hope, who fought only because fighting might buy them one more precious moment of life.

As the Urothu got closer, Herve could discern, even over the repeated twang of his bowstring, the low whooshes of the magical weapons as they raced toward their marks.

He even heard the one that came for him.

~

GEFROI WHISTLED an old dancing song as he plodded beside the graying carthorse pulling Jenson's barrels of ale along the well-worn road to Basendale. A little over a year into his apprenticeship to Blackwell's innkeeper, he had finally been trusted to make the exchange on his own. It was always the same: three barrels of Jenson's finest ale for six bottles of a wine the Basendale innkeeper bought from the city of Bergefort. Gefroi privately thought the exchange was weighted on the side of Basendale's innkeeper: three barrels of ale would serve many more people than six bottles of wine, no matter how fine.

The morning, if one could call it that, was still dark - it was not even *uht* yet, but Gefroi had been taught that on the third and final day of the journey he should rise early and arrive at the inn before they served breakfast. At this time, Tomkin, the innkeeper, was usually affable and ready to make the trade with as little fuss as possible. Gefroi wasn't afraid of the dark; he could see well enough by the light of the moon, and in the vast expanses of Claresea Valley, he was not likely to be taken by surprise by anything larger than a rabbit.

He knew he would reach Basendale before *uht* broke into dawn, and he was unhurried as swung his unencumbered arms back and forth in time to his whistling. He thought he had done very well on his first solo journey: the barrels of ale, padded with straw in the horse-drawn cart, were undisturbed, he had cheerfully interacted with several people he met on the road, and he had carefully measured his meals to not exhaust his rations. For perhaps the first time in his life, Gefroi felt like an adult.

Pretty Millie Mae, rosy and sweet,
Light in her dress and light on her feet,
She'll pour you a pint with a wink and a grin,
And you'll forget all your troubles as you drink it in.

. . .

Raise your glass high, a song in the air,
Drink to Millie Mae, her smile so fair,
Sing of her beauties, sing of her face,
Sing of her bosoms and tiny waist.

Dance, Millie Mae! Twirl all around
In the arms of a man so strong and so sound
Dance, Millie Mae, till the night's end
And till our cups need filling again!

GEFROI DIDN'T EVEN REALIZE he was singing at first, but the realization didn't disturb him; there was no one on the road to hear him, and even if there was, singing while traveling was common. Feeling more cheerful by the moment at the thought of a hot meal at *The Gray Fairy* after making the exchange, he bellowed the second verse much louder than he would have sung it in company, making his voice boom with glee.

From the first light of dawn to the end of the night,
Millie Mae fills cups and offers the sight
Of a fair maiden with capable hands
To strike dreams in the heart of every man

Raise your glass high, a song in the air,
Drink to Millie Mae, her smile so fair,
Sing of her beauties, sing of her face,

Sing of her bosoms and tiny waist.

Dance, Millie Mae! Twirl all around
In the arms of a man so strong and so sound
Dance, Millie Mae, till the night's end
And till our cups need filling again!

THE SOUND of his cheerful song spread through the empty valley as he walked, occasionally giving the carthorse a commiserating pat. The cart made rumbling noises as it rolled over the dirt road, occasionally hitting an uneven spot with a jolt and the clatter of the metal joints of the hitch. Gefroi made a cheerful picture for anyone who might have seen him, a sandy-haired, gangly teen singing on his first solo journey.

His thoughts wandered as he ended the drinking song and walked in contemplative silence. He thought about Millie Mae, the pretty girl in the song who set all the men's hearts ablaze. Was there such a girl? He had met no one in Blackwell that held that kind of attraction, at least to him, and he was of an age where he should have been looking. After all, his own parents had married when his father was seventeen and his mother was sixteen. So far, though, none of the village girls had caught his attention as someone he would want to spend time with, never mind the rest of his life.

Gefroi didn't want to spend the rest of his life in Blackwell, anyway. He knew that at the end of his apprenticeship, his choices would be simple: continue working for Jenson at a wage that would enable him to marry and even possibly build a small house in the village, or find an inn in some village whose keeper was ready to sell. Neither option appealed; what was the point of leaving home, only to live the same life in another village? No, Gefroi wanted to move into one of the big cities: Bergefort was closest, but he thought he might like to go even farther, to Stormacre on the coast of the

Unresting Sea, or even all the way to Emelle, where the king and queen lived.

The carthorse stopped suddenly and gave a nervous whinny. Gefroi stopped too, confused because the carthorse never stopped unless he stopped her. "What is it, Cassie?" he asked, looking around to see if he could see the source of her nervousness.

Cassie pawed the ground and whinnied again, tossing her head.

Gefroi looked around, even more confused. The valley looked like it always did in the dark; waving dark grass in the moonlight, and the reddish-brown packed dirt of the road seeming to have a bit of a glow. He could see no one on the road ahead, and the road was empty behind him. He squinted into the surrounding grasses; was there a predator, some sort of animal that had Cassie's hackles up?

After another minute, Gefroi sighed. Animals could be strange. He had never fully figured out the behavior of the oxen or sheep on his father's farm, and he put this down as just another eccentricity. "Come on, Cassie. Geeyup."

The carthorse started forward obediently, but Gefroi could tell something was still bothering her. For the next couple miles, he didn't sing or whistle or even think, but kept his eyes open. As he got within a mile of the outskirts of Basendale, just as the pale almost-light of *uht* was lightening the sky, he caught the first scent of burning.

Gefroi frowned. Though the smell of cook fires wouldn't have been unusual even at this early hour - after all, the inn and the bakery had to prepare for their morning custom, and families had to prepare for their breadwinners to go work - the scent was somehow different from what he was used to. He couldn't figure out exactly how, but it definitely felt more threatening, somehow.

Gefroi quickened his pace, and Cassie kept up with him. He wondered if one of the buildings had burned down; with all the buildings in most villages built of wood, fire was always a danger.

The smell got stronger as he went, but nothing prepared him for what he saw when he reached the southern outskirts of the village: every single dwelling and building was burned to the ground.

He stopped Cassie; clearly, there was going to be no exchange of ale and wine this morning. He wondered if he was the first outsider to come since the burning; it was possible, as several of the ruins still had small flames and smoke. He had to see if anyone needed help.

Before he went into the village, Gefroi knew what he needed to do. Searching for small pebbles, he quickly gathered a handful and went back to stand beside Cassie. Bending over, he quickly formed the pebbles into the fourth universal glyph, the glyph signaling someone needed help. If anyone came behind him on the road, they would know he had gone into the village and would hurry to his aid.

Breaking into a trot, Gefroi jogged the rest of the way. He called out when he got there, hoping to find a villager who could tell him what had happened. No one answered. He kept calling out as he reached the first of the burnt houses, but his calls abruptly stopped when he saw the first body.

A child who could not have even had their fifth birth celebration yet lay in front of one of the ruins. It was clear the child was dead; there was a large, burned circle on his chest, and his eyes were open in surprise, but glazed completely over.

Gefroi's breath caught. What had happened here?

Trying to ignore what he had seen, Gefroi, now walking cautiously, called out again. "Hello? Is there anyone here?" He shouted as loud as he could, hoping fervently for an answer.

He got none.

He saw the second and third bodies at the same time, and his stomach turned. Something had obviously attacked this village. None of the bodies bore signs of burning other than the strange circles on their chests.

Urothu.

Just thinking the word made Gefroi tremble. He had been raised to fear the Urothu, savage magic-wielders who killed everything in sight. Some stories said they targeted naughty children, but from what Gefroi saw as he continued forward, now running from house to house, they had spared no one.

He stopped abruptly inside what had once been the village square. He could not count the number of bodies, and he was certain no one had survived, but it was the condition of Tomkin, in front of the ruins of The Gray Fairy, that caused his stomach to heave.

The man, the kind man who had always given him a meal when he had come for an exchange, had been cleanly sliced in two, the halves of his body lying roughshod in the road. Not far from him were five more bodies: two serving maids and Tomkin's wife and children. None of them had been severed in twain like the innkeeper, but all bore the strange burnt circles somewhere on their bodies; on one of the serving girls, the circle had all but eradicated her face.

This was too much for Gefroi. Bending over, he vomited everything in his stomach onto the street, not even noticing the tears running down his face as he wiped his mouth. He squeezed his eyes shut, determinedly not looking at the remains of Tomkin or his family, trying not to notice the buzzing of the flies or the smell of burnt buildings. He had to get out of the village - were any of the Urothu still here? - and return to Blackwell to raise the alarm.

Turning, the boy sprinted, avoiding the bodies lying everywhere, out of the decimated village and back to the road. He barely saw Cassie and the cart in the road as he raced past them, completely forgetting his own belongings and the barrels of ale Jenson would surely ask about when he returned. Nothing mattered but to get home as quickly as he could.

He wondered if he would even have a home left.

THE CHOSEN

ecy led him down one of the many passages branching from the main cavern and into a small, rounded room clearly carved from the cave wall. In it, he found a straw-tick mattress covered in colorful blankets, a pillow at the top, a small wooden table and chair, a few pegs bored into the walls, and several round globes with metal fastenings. Tostig frowned as Cecy drew the dark wool curtain back over the entrance; without the light from the globes in the passageway, the room was dark as pitch.

Cecy said something under her breath and the globes came to life with a soft yellow light. "We'll bring a small mattress for your dog," she told him, "as well as blankets, should she want them. We have few animals in the caves, but you will find those dwelling here are treated well."

Tostig nodded his thanks. He was glad to hear her words; he had not seen a single animal as they walked through the caverns and had been worried Ziva would not be welcome.

"Now, which would you like first, a bath or a meal?" she asked. "I know the Watchers bring scant provisions, and many newcomers arrive hungry."

"A bath," Tostig replied. "I was taught to hunt by my father at a young age, and I provided myself and Ziva ample food. You eat meat here, do you not?" He hadn't thought to ask the Watchers, but remembering tselqs didn't eat meat, he wondered if the Sashu were similar.

"To eat meat is part of the natural order of things," Cecy assured him. "We partake in all the foods you are accustomed to, and many you are not. Now, relieve yourself of your pack and follow me to the bathing room. Would you like to bathe your dog as well?"

"Her name is Ziva," Tostig replied, "and yes, she could use a bath if you have enough water for it."

"We have a natural water source running right into the caves," Cecy told him. "You will be expected to bathe daily, and you can bathe Ziva as often as you like." She opened the curtain once again, and Tostig wondered if she had only closed it to show him that even the lamps were lit with magic.

Tostig did as he was told, placing his pack beside the mattress and commanding Ziva to follow him. She hardly needed the command; in these unfamiliar surroundings, she was staying as close as possible. Cecy led them through the passage and into another one that forked to the left. As they walked, Tostig tried to determine which parts of the cave system were natural and which parts had been carved out by the Sashu over the centuries. In most places, it was fairly easy to tell. The natural walls were rougher, and in some places stalactites and stalagmites had formed from the floors and ceilings.

As they walked, Cecy pointed out various places of interest in the caves: teaching rooms, her own quarters, and a passage leading to the dining hall. They walked for nearly ten minutes before finally stopping. "Inside, you will find the bathing area for males. If you are modest with your body, come in the very early morning or late at night; otherwise, there will likely be others. The pool is fed by a spring and drains naturally, so the water stays fresh. We ask, of course, that you do not produce any waste in the bathing pool. We have a separate area for those needs." She pointed at the next opening along the passage.

Tostig wasn't bothered by the idea of there being other males in the bathing pool while he was there; it was not unusual for those of the same gender. He was glad, however, that there was a separate area for females. Human custom dictated adults should only see the bodies of the other gender if they were married, and that rule had been drilled into him as he had grown up with his three sisters.

"Do I bathe Ziva here as well?" he asked.

"Yes," Cecy answered. "You will find soap and cloths inside the cave, and I will see to it clothing is left for you on the side of the pool. Your current clothing will be cleaned and put away; you will not need it for your stay here."

Tostig frowned. He had noticed the different colored robes worn by the people when he had arrived, but he had not realized they were mandatory. He had worn trousers, tunics, and boots all his life and was not looking forward to the change.

"You will adjust," said Cecy, correctly reading his expression. "Everyone does. Now, go perform your ablutions. I will wait with a hot meal in your room when you have finished."

"How will I find my way back?" Tostig asked. Though he had tried to keep track of the many twists and turns they had traveled through, he knew he hadn't memorized them yet.

"Simply ask anyone you come across," Cecy told him. "Everyone here will help newcomers find their way."

Tostig nodded, knowing this was the best answer he was going to get. He and Ziva walked through the entrance to the cavern. The pool was quite wide and seemed deep in the middle. Steam wafting from the water warned it would be warm, maybe even hot. Two men, a tselq, and a dwarf, were already bathing. They took no notice of him as he disrobed and entered the water, coaxing Ziva to come in with him.

The water was warm, but not overly hot, and Tostig could feel his muscles relax as he waded in waist deep. Taking a piece of soap and a cloth, he set to work cleaning the traveling grime from himself and Ziva.

When they finished, Tostig found his traveling clothes missing and a set of new clothing set out for him. The underclothes were not much different, but he glared at the muted blue robes that would cover him from neck to feet.

Sighing, he put them on, noting they were nearly perfectly sized. As he and Ziva left the cavern, he did not enjoy the way the robes swept around him, brushing against his arms and legs. He had to stop several times as Ziva shook, and each time he did so, Tostig examined different parts of his new garments.

He did not have to travel far before he met a tselq. Garbed in robes identical to Tostig's but for their color, the tselq's earthy green skin appeared darker than he was used to in the muted light. Her horns were curled twice, with a third beginning, and her face was kind as she led him back to his sleeping quarters.

Cecy sat cross-legged on his mattress, waiting for him in the room that was still illuminated by the mysterious globes attached to the wall. On the small table, there was a bowl of stew alongside a loaf of bread and a goblet of red liquid, perhaps wine, and he noticed a small mattress with a red blanket folded atop it.

"Come, Tostig," Cecy said, smiling warmly at him. "We have much to discuss."

Tostig smiled uncertainly. He wasn't sure if he was supposed to sit with her on the mattress, but he was hungry, and the food smelled appetizing.

"Please eat," Cecy encouraged him when she saw his hesitation.

Tostig sat down at the small table, not sure how to arrange his new robes, and tasted the stew. It was venison, and the gravy was thicker and more flavorful than he was used to. He ate quickly, savoring the meal, while Cecy told him about life in the caves and what he could expect.

"You will have several lessons each day," she said, "in magic, as well as other subjects. Are you literate?"

"Yes," Tostig answered, swallowing a bite of brown bread too quickly and choking slightly on it.

Cecy waited until he had regained his composure. "You will learn how to use your magic both for your own ends and to help those across Ilbeor. That is, I'm sure the Watchers told you, our primary aim."

Tostig told her about the tselq magician he had met on his travels, and she nodded. "You met Nita," she said. "She prefers assignments to tselq communities, though she is willing to go where she is sent. She is not in the caves just now, but I will arrange for you to meet her properly when she returns. I am sure she will appreciate that you remembered and were inspired by her actions."

Tostig drained the last of the dry red wine. He wished he had some water, and it was then that he noticed his pack was no longer in his room. Frowning, he asked Cecy about it.

"Novitiates don't require any supplies besides that which they are given," she said seriously. "We do not want any distractions to your studies." She saw him about to protest and held up a calming hand. "When you become an apprentice, you will see your things returned to you in just the same condition you left them."

Tostig held his tongue, though he did not like that they had taken his possessions from him.

"You have had a long day of travel, and it is late," Cecy said. "You cannot tell in the caves, but it is full dark outside. You should sleep. I am sure you can see you have clothes for sleep as well as more daywear on the pegs."

"The lights - " Tostig began.

Cecy waved an arm almost lazily and then said, "They will extinguish themselves in ten minutes. When you wake and wish for the light again, the spell is *iluma*."

"But I don't know how to work spells yet," Tostig protested.

"The best way to learn is to try for yourself. Find the spark of magic within you - you will feel it near your heart if you concentrate hard enough. In time, you will not need to search but will have access to it at will."

"Yes, but what do I do after that?"

"Concentrate on what you wish to do and say the word," Cecy told him. "It may take you many tries, but I have confidence you will be able to light your way come morning. Good night, Tostig." Without another word, she left the room, closing the curtain behind her.

Tostig changed quickly. His new night clothes consisted of a soft wool tunic with matching pants, and he thought they would be more comfortable than the nightshirt he wore at home. He hung the blue robes on a peg next to two more identical sets and quickly crawled onto his mattress, wanting to be there before the lights went out.

Patting the small mattress next to his own, Tostig encouraged Ziva to try her new bed. She used her mouth to arrange the blanket to her liking and lay down, seeming content.

A few moments later, the lights blinked out.

TOSTIG AWOKE in the darkness to Ziva's whine. He guessed it must be *uht*; Ziva's internal clock was nearly infallible. He could not tell for certain. There were no windows, and it could have been midday for all he knew.

As he had eaten dinner the previous night, Cecy had explained that the first full day was a day of exploration. He could go anywhere, ask questions of anyone he met, and get an introduction to the Sashu way of life. The only requirements were that he bathe, eat meals with the community, and wear his newly assigned robes. He had also learned that the muted blue robes were for novitiates and after he had finished his novitiate stage, he would be free to choose colors. Tostig already knew he would dispose of the blue robes at his first opportunity.

Tostig's eyes could not adjust to the darkness because there was no light to adjust to. He took a deep breath, thinking of the word Cecy had taught him. Tostig did as he had been instructed, thinking hard about his purpose and intention, trying to find the spark inside of him Cecy had assured him was there.

He closed his eyes, concentrating. He had never summoned magic purposely, but he knew he had to do it now unless he wanted to prepare for the day in complete darkness. To his surprise, after a few minutes of an almost meditative state, he felt something stir in his chest right where Cecy had said it would be. It was slight, only a tickle, but somehow Tostig knew it was the spark of magic.

He instinctively extended his right hand toward the wall of his quarters. *"Iluma,"* he said, his voice deeper than usual as he tried to make it sound authoritative.

The globes surrounding him flickered in unison, but quickly became dark again. Tostig grunted.

Again, he closed his eyes and tried to find the tickle of magic in his chest. When he felt it, he concentrated again. *"Iluma!"* He spoke with more confidence, his voice booming.

The lights blinked on, steady and comforting. They remained on as he put his hand back down. He couldn't stifle a grin. He had done it, and on his second try, too! Cecy had warned him it might take him quite some time, and he felt accomplished.

Next to him, Ziva whined uncomfortably. "It's okay, girl," he assured her, but when he reached out to scratch between her ears, she shied away from him.

He frowned. Was she *afraid* of him? They had been together since she was a newly weaned puppy. He was going to have to mend this rift, and quickly. He did not want to lose his companion, *would* not lose his companion.

"Ziva," he said, his voice soft and exceptionally calm. "Come here."

The dog did not move from her place on her mattress a couple feet away, but she looked at him, appraising.

"Come here," he repeated, allowing no impatience in his voice. He gestured with his fingers, their silent signal for her to come.

She hesitated, but slowly came to rest next to his crossed legs. This time, she allowed him to slowly extend his hand to scratch between her ears in the particular way she loved. After a moment, she leaned into the contact.

Tostig sighed with relief. Ziva was wary of magic, and he would have to be very sensitive to her needs as he explored and learned in the coming weeks. He hoped it would not take her long adjust. That she had come to him and let him touch her, though, told him it could be done, and he wouldn't lose her as he became a magician.

Tostig changed into the hated blue robes. He had been told they served the first meal at dawn and a bell would chime when it was time to go to the dining hall. Since the caves boasted no natural light, a series of different sounds were used to alert occupants of various happenings.

"Ziva, heel," he said, and he was glad when she obeyed. Together, they set off to explore the cave system until it was time to meet the rest of the community.

TOSTIG HAD no particular destination in mind as he and Ziva set off. If he had wanted to go to a certain place, he would have had to find someone to give him directions. The cave system was naturally vast and had been added to over centuries by the Sashu until it was a complex maze of passages, rooms, and caverns. Cecy had warned him it was easy to become lost and if he found an entranceway too narrow to fit through, he should not try.

"All the entrances to the purposed areas of our system are large enough even for the Watchers," she had said. "The smaller crevices lead to unexplored areas, and many who have sought their mysteries have never returned."

Tostig eventually found himself in the gigantic cavern serving as the main room and entrance to the cave system. He was glad to be there; he had not had a chance to look at the various statues and cave drawings scattered throughout, and he was curious. He knew the Sashu followed a polytheistic religion seen as blasphemous to the human sanctum, but otherwise, their beliefs were shrouded in mystery.

He crossed to the largest statue, Ziva staying close. The cavern was dimly lit; a few of the magical globes dotted the walls, but small fires in stone braziers in front of each statue provided most of the scant light. The large fire he had noticed the night before at the head of the cavern had not yet been lit.

The statue, which seemed to have been carved from the cave wall itself, stood at least twenty feet tall and five feet wide. It depicted a bald man with a kind expression, though not an outright smile, flowing robes, and a protruding belly. On his feet were sandals the like of which Tostig had never seen; the stone straps crisscrossed in an intricate pattern. After he had finished trying to understand the sandals, his eyes were drawn back up to the statue's face. It seemed familiar somehow, though he didn't think he'd ever seen it before.

"That is Sado," said a male voice next to him, startling him. "He is the mightiest of the Nine, creator of the world and of magic, creator of the seas and skies, and father of all."

"Sado," Tostig repeated, committing the name to memory. "And who are you?"

The man, a human who Tostig estimated to be in his forties by the fine wrinkles on his face and the graying of his hair, smiled warmly at him. "I am Maxwell," he said simply. He did not offer his hand to shake Tostig's.

"I'm Tostig, and this is Ziva."

"Well met," Maxwell said. Tostig noticed Maxwell was not garbed in the robes he had thought were mandatory. Instead, he wore a long tunic and leather breeches.

"I hope I'm not being rude," Tostig said, "but why aren't you dressed like me?"

"I'm not a magician," Maxwell explained. "I came to the Sashu as a young man disillusioned by the corruption I found in the sanctum. You see, I was once an acolyte and was sent to Sanctum of Oaos to spend my days working for the good of the sanctum and in service to the Most High Priest."

"I'm sorry," Tostig apologized. "I didn't know people who weren't magicians came here."

"All are welcome here, though many wander for a long time before they find this place. Without the aid of the Watchers, it often takes years before the gods see fit to lead new adherents to the caves. I was one of the lucky ones, if you could call it luck. Sado sent me here in a dream, and I was able to find my way a mere year after I left Sanctum of Oaos. I now serve the Nine and do what I can for the magicians who come here. We know you as the Chosen."

Tostig was silent for a few moments as he pondered what he had been told. "How many of you are there?" he asked finally, referring to non-magicians.

"Perhaps thirty," Maxwell answered. "We come and we go as we please, as do the Chosen once they are trained, and our numbers vary. There are many more Chosen than non-magicians. Would you like to hear about the rest of the Nine? We should have just enough time before they ring the bell for the morning meal."

Tostig nodded. He supposed he ought to learn as much as he could about the Sashu faith, although he vowed to adhere to the Covenant of Annuah. The idea there was more than one god was preposterous.

Over the next half hour, Maxwell tutored him on the Nine and their domains. He learned about Aaldir, god of the rains, responsible for both life-giving precipitation and the rock-eater storms that devastated entire villages. Iarae, goddess of the harvest and flowers, presided over all the growing things, from foodstuffs to ornamental flowers, including the most poisonous of plants. Ybus, god of the rock, was the most somnolent of the gods, for his work had been done when he created the mountains from the clay of the earth, hardening them into their various forms. The Sashu thanked him for their cave system, though many believed he no longer listened.

Qhalina was the goddess who interested Tostig most besides Sado himself, for she reigned over all animals wild and domestic. Her statue portrayed a young woman with curly hair, surrounded by a number of various animals. As a hunter and as Ziva's master, Tostig respected all living things and what they provided. He learned Qhalina was not opposed to hunting for meat, but she exacted revenge on those who abused or caused unnecessary pain to the creatures she protected.

Etuna, the goddess of children, presided over all aspects of child-hood, imagination, and creativity. Maxwell somberly informed Tostig the Sashu believed flights of imagination and creativity were to be cherished, as they were manifestations of Etuna's child still present in every sentient being.

"Here, you will not only learn the magical arts, but poetry and prose, drawing and painting. After you learn the basics, you will be allowed to choose the skill in which you would like to achieve mastery."

The statue of Annukai, god of knowledge, attracted Tostig's attention even before Maxwell explained his role. Tostig would have expected the god of knowledge to be a serious, scholarly type, but the statue wore a broad grin. Somehow, even set in stone, he seemed to laugh at some sort of private joke.

"He is the only god who currently walks in Ilbeor with those of us who exist in the flesh," Maxwell said. "His interest lies not only in scholarly pursuits, but in the pursuit of the lore and practices of all the races and the individuals within them."

"He walks…in flesh, like us?" Tostig asked, confused. He had never heard of any sort of deity who would deign to share the land with the mortals, or even the immortal elves, who inhabited it. Annuah certainly would never do such a thing; he belonged on the Great Mountain that sat far above in the skies of Ilbeor.

"Yes," Maxwell said simply, offering no other explanation. "You are unlikely to meet him here, as the process of training new magicians is of little interest to him, but as you go out into the world as one of the Chosen, you may see him as you render aid or otherwise do your duty as a magician. He is often present where momentous events occur."

Before Tostig could ask any other questions, Maxwell moved to the next statue, a serene-looking male with long, flowing hair and billowing robes that seemed, even in stone, to blow in the wind. It was, Maxwell explained, Cherasil, the god of love. Responsible for all romances, partnerships, marriages, and sexual relations, he was said to be a tricky, unpredictable god who changed his mind as often as he kept his promises. Inevitably, Tostig thought of Alanda as he gazed at the statue, wondering if the supposed god would keep the unspoken promises made during their tryst. Already that seemed to be so long ago, part of a different life, but he still longed for her and wondered if he would ever find her again.

Finally, they moved to the last statue, that of Xatra, the goddess of death. She looked exactly like Tostig would have pictured her if he had ever pictured her at all. Thin, stern, and forbidding, she gazed off into the distance with eyes that seemed cold even in statue form. Though the statue's coloring was the same red-brown of the cave walls, Tostig knew she was wearing black robes. "She is inexorable," Maxwell said, gazing at the statue. "She is the one who comes for all, even the elves, in the end. It is she who determines our eternal fate."

Tostig shivered even in the warmth from the fire in Xatra's brazier. He had been raised to believe any man who lived a righteous life and participated in the rites of the sanctum would become one with Annuah after death and help him with the affairs of the land. This determination of eternal fate by Xatra was a frightening concept he could not quite wrap his mind around.

Just then, a single toll of a bell, loud yet pleasing, sounded. It echoed off the walls in shadows of itself long after the initial sound had ended.

"Come," Maxwell said, smiling. "Let us break our fast together."

Tostig and Ziva followed Maxwell through the cavern and into one of the passages they had not explored. This passage was not like the one leading into the sleeping quarters. After a short distance, they made a sharp right turn and entered a single cavern. It was vast, though not as large as the main cavern, and had a relatively low ceiling hanging only a few feet above their heads. Tostig could tell it was not natural; the walls and ceiling were very smooth, without a single errant rock formation.

Long wooden tables stretched from end to end, bordered by benches rather than chairs. The wood had been smoothed by lifetimes of use. Like everything else Tostig had seen in the caves, the tables spoke of age and longevity.

Crowds of people, most wearing various colors of magicians' robes, lined up along the wall on the left side to pick up food from a serving space cut into the rock, connecting with a smaller room serving as a kitchen. Tostig was surprised by how many people there were and was even more surprised when he saw human, dwarf, and tselq children.

"There are children here?" he asked. He had thought magical ability did not manifest until young adulthood.

"Naturally," Maxwell said, surprised by the question. "Our magicians and other adherents partner with others just as in the outside world. Some find their partners within the caves, while others bring non-adherents here to live with them. Of course, children are a natural result of those pairings. Why would they not be?"

Tostig shook his head. What Maxwell said made perfect sense, but he realized that until this moment he had not understood the Sashu caves encapsulated a complete culture. His mind racing and his robes brushing against his skin, he joined the line.

MAGIC AND GODS

"*Tarra sarun,*" Tostig said, trying hard to imitate the sounds of the Sashu language from Yodmola Frostheart, an elderly dwarf woman who was teaching him earth magic. Imitating her was difficult; not only did he have to contend with the new language, but with her thick dwarven accent. He had trouble differentiating between that and the incantations.

The small pile of dirt in front of him on the floor of Yodmola's teaching room didn't move, much to his frustration. He was supposed to be lifting it into the air, but no matter how hard he tried to focus while he said the words, it wanted to stay on the ground.

"*Oskünr,*" the dwarf swore, seeming as frustrated as Tostig with his lack of progress. Only four days into his training, he was finding his lessons more difficult than he had been expecting. "You are not focused, and you are not saying the words correctly. Try again: *tarra sarun.*"

Tostig sat still as he located the spark of magic in his chest, then extended his right hand toward the small pile of soil and focused on moving it into the air. "*Tarra sarun,*" he said, the words rolling more smoothly off his tongue, though they still sounded foreign to his ears.

To his delight, the dirt lifted cleanly into the air a few inches, forming a small dust cloud. Feeling suddenly playful, Tostig inhaled and blew a small puff of air at the cloud. To his great surprise, the cloud disappeared instead of scattering as he had expected.

"But this is unexpected," Yodmola said, her voice booming in the small room. "This is advanced magic, and you achieved it without using your vocabulary. Do you know how to vanish objects?"

"Is that what I did?" Tostig asked with interest. "I was just playing."

"I have never seen a magician accomplish that at any level lower than master," she replied. "I am impressed. Now, let us do it again." She reached into the small clay pot full of soil and placed another small pile in front of Tostig. "This time, do not vanish the earth but use the ending word to drop it back onto the ground."

Tostig thought for a moment, trying to remember what the ending word was. As it came to him, he realized he could already feel the magic, though he had not yet looked for it. He took this as an encouraging sign, once again raising his right hand toward the dirt. "*Tarra sarum*," he said again, his voice deep and commanding.

The small pile of dirt again rose into a small cloud. Instead of blowing on it as he had before, he tried the ending word. "*Desena*," he intoned, hoping he didn't need to add "tarra".

The small cloud of dirt fell to the ground like tiny raindrops, lying scattered instead of in a neat pile as it had been. Tostig looked at Yodmola to see if she approved.

Yodmola smiled widely. "This is very good," she said. "Few in your position have managed as much in as little time. You progress well, young human."

Tostig smiled in return with a hint of amusement at her epithet. Though the dwarf woman in no way looked young with her craggy features, long braided hair, and embroidered master's robes, she still only stood as tall as he was when he was sitting on the ground. To essentially be called a child by one who only reached his waist seemed funny to him, though he knew better than to share his observations. She would not appreciate his amusement. "Thank you, Master," he said respectfully, inclining his head at her.

"Now, see if you can vanish the soil while it lies on the ground," she instructed. "I want to know the extent of this ability."

Not knowing what else to do, Tostig once again blew in the direction of the scattered dirt. Almost all of it disappeared when the air touched it, though some along the edges had remained. Before Yodmola could say anything, he asked, "What's the incantation for vanishing objects?" He wanted to hone this new skill.

Yodmola frowned. "I do not teach this skill before apprenticeship," she told him. "You must not only know how to vanish things, but what happens to them when you do, and how to use the spell with discretion. Though I am impressed by your spellweaving, I am afraid you are learning too much, too fast. We must not take you past what you can handle."

"I already know how to do this," Tostig protested. "What difference does teaching me the word make?"

"Blow your puff of air at the floor," Yodmola instructed.

Tostig wasn't sure what she was getting at, but he did so. The floor remained unchanged.

"That is the difference," the dwarf told him. "With enough power and the correct word, you could vanish the very rock beneath us. You must not learn this skill until you are properly prepared to use it."

Tostig was frustrated, but he understood her reticence. He finally nodded his acceptance.

"Go," Yodmola commanded. "That is all for today. I will report your progress to your other masters and to Cecy herself. You should be proud."

Tostig thanked her for the lesson and signaled to Ziva, who had already become accustomed to and even uninterested in his magical tutelage. She came to his side immediately.

His lesson with Yodmola had been his last, so Tostig went to the entrance of the caves to let Ziva play. He was finding it hard to make enough time for this, and it grated on him because he knew she needed activity to stay happy and healthy.

Tostig brooded over his lesson as he tossed sticks for Ziva to catch. He felt his progress was agonizingly slow, especially after seeing what some of the masters could do even without using the Sashu words, but his instructors apparently felt differently. Yodmola was not the only one who had told him he was progressing quickly.

As Ziva fetched the stick he had thrown, he tried again. Focusing on the packed earth in front of his feet, he raised his arm and intoned *"tarra sarum"* with as much strength and authority as he could muster. The ground rumbled slightly before a quantity of soil detached itself and formed a cloud, leaving a divot where it had once been. Tostig blew at it, and most of it disappeared.

He wondered what the use of such a minor spell could be, but reflecting on what his masters had told him over and over, he realized that what he was doing was simply building toward something greater. He'd just have to be patient.

BY THE END of Tostig's second week, he no longer had to consciously search for the spark of magic within himself before he wove spells. This, he was told, usually took much more time to achieve. He was not nearly as impressed with himself as they seemed to be, and he worked on mastering larger and more difficult spells.

"Concentrate," one of his masters, an old human woman named Maera, encouraged him one afternoon about four weeks after he had come to the caves. They were outdoors in the fall sunlight, surrounded by the brilliant colors of the trees, sitting cross-legged in front of a bubbling stream close to the cave system. "Call the water."

Tostig stared at the stream, frustrated. He had already learned to heat water using the energy around him, to cool water by taking energy away, and to direct steam, heat, and smoke in various directions. What Maera was asking for now was direct manipulation of the water: she wanted him to call the water itself up from the stream and shape it. He extended his right hand toward the stream for the fifth time.

"Laigui maura," he said smoothly, the sounds rolling over his tongue as though he had spoken the language for years.

Nothing happened.

Tostig grunted, balling his hand up into a fist and bringing it back down to his side. He couldn't figure out what he was doing wrong. He knew the words, he could feel the magic coursing through him, and his intent was clear, so why wasn't it working?

Maera chuckled, surprising him. She, like most of the masters, was usually quite solemn in her duty to teach the new generation of magicians.

"What's funny?" Tostig growled, forgetting to use a respectful tone of voice in his irritation.

"Look at Ziva," she said, her chuckle developing into a full-throated laugh.

Tostig glanced to his right, where Ziva was supposed to be lying down. Instead of lying down, she was sitting, one paw extended toward the stream. Despite his frustration, Tostig had to join Maera in her laughter.

"You want to be a magician, girl?" he asked fondly, ruffling the fur on her back. She looked at him, her eyes betraying nothing. Tostig turned back to Maera. "I need some time off today or tomorrow at the latest. Ziva needs exercise and activity. She's bored."

To his surprise, Maera agreed. "You may leave as soon as you call the water," she said calmly. "We will end our lesson there, and you and Ziva may have the rest of the afternoon."

Tostig felt his frustration begin again at her words. *As soon as I call the water*, he thought. *What if I never manage it, or at least not today? Is Ziva to laze around like a common house cat?*

Instead of complaining, he again extended his right hand toward the maddening stream of water. Just the way it cheerfully gurgled while he was failing made him angry. He struggled to master himself before again intoning the incantation.

"*Laigui maura*," he said, willing the magic to pass from his body through his hand and into the water. Somewhat to his surprise, a small fountain of water erupted from the stream, piercing the air above it like an arrow before falling back among the pebbles and rock of the creek bed.

"Good, very good," Maera said approvingly. "You've nearly grasped it. Try to bring the water completely out of the stream, even if you do not shape it."

It took Tostig eight more tries before he called the water to Maera's satisfaction. She dismissed him with an admonition to practice until he could not only call but manipulate the water. "Remember, there is power in your hands if your intent is clear," she said. "You may channel your power through your right hand, but use both of your hands to shape the water as you would a piece of clay."

Tostig leapt to his feet when she had finished speaking and helped her stand, handing her the polished wood walking stick she used. Hobbling away with a speed belying her age, Maera disappeared behind a copse of trees. Soon, the only sign of her passage was an increased falling of the autumn leaves disturbed in her wake.

"Heel, Ziva," Tostig said. "Let's get out of here."

Ziva jumped to her feet and took her place at his left side, nearly quivering in excitement to be going somewhere. He realized he really needed to advocate taking her out more. He knew his lessons were important, vital even, but so was Ziva's well-being, and she was his responsibility.

When they returned to the caves for the evening meal, Tostig joined the now-familiar line for food. He knew many of the others by name now, and several greeted him as a friend, including Maxwell, who was near the front. He smiled, exchanging pleasantries and allowing the children to flock around Ziva. He had discovered that Ziva was the only dog in the caves; the other animals consisted of three house cats, horses used by the traveling Chosen, and various livestock.

The meal was delicious: roasted chicken with herbed potatoes and preserved fruit spread over fresh brown bread. Tostig was always hungry at the evening meal, and he ate everything on his plate with enjoyment.

After the meal, Tostig reported to his poetry instructor, Paalavi. A tselq of middle age with five curls to his horns and healthy green skin, Paalavi dressed differently than the other masters. Most masters wore heavy robes with embroidery at the hems and neck, but his were lighter and unadorned, not much different from those worn by the apprentices. His thin, gray hair was tied back with a black fabric thong, and he didn't seem as muscular as other tselqs, though he was still more muscular than the average human. Altogether, his presence exuded peace and tranquility, though he was an exacting master of his art and expected the best from his students.

Tostig had not expected to enjoy poetry, but had surprised himself by developing a knack for the art. He enjoyed pushing his vocabulary to its limits while trying to find rhymes or rhythmic words to fit his verse. He thought this would be the talent he would pursue, though he also enjoyed painting.

Tostig's mind turned to Alanda, as it often did when he was composing. He thought of her unusual hair and pale complexion, of her icy blue but still warm eyes, and of her melodic voice. He missed her adventurous spirit and the way she seemed to attract interesting events and people, and he worried about her future as an orphaned young woman, alone in the world.

It was hard to put his feelings into verse, and even harder to think about sharing such a verse. So, after his instruction had ended and it was time for him to apply what he had learned, he dipped his pen into the ink pot and attempted a poem about the waterfall he had told Alanda about, the one with the rainbow within its falls.

> *Falling waters rushing down*
> *Crashing over rock and tree*
> *Violent are your raging sounds*
> *Unyielding, yes, entombing me.*

> *But yet I see within your waves*
> *Hope brought to a hopeless man*
> *Bright color, dancing pixie rays*
> *A rainbow from Annuah's hand.*

· · ·

PAALAVI STUDIED Tostig's attempt with a furrowed brow. "This is better," he said contemplatively, but it was obvious he was still not pleased. "Your imagery has developed, as has your sense of time within your verses, though both have room for improvement. You still struggle with your vocabulary."

Tostig nodded, accepting the criticism. Though he had come to the caves already literate, he had not been exposed to any of the great literature of the land. As a village boy, he only had access to the holy books of the sanctum, glyph chips, and the few secular books and scrolls the High Priest was willing to allow him to peruse; his family owned no books. None of it had prepared him for the demands he now faced from his literary masters, demands to create verses about beautiful things or momentous events, to write fictional accounts from his own imagination, or to write personal narratives with depth and understanding.

"I don't know how to change that, Master," Tostig finally said.

"I do," Paalavi told him. "I have been considering this for some time, and I believe you can be trusted." After rummaging in a cabinet that had always remained closed during their lessons, the poet straightened and handed Tostig a large tome bound in green leather with a gold inscription on the front in the common tongue.

"A dictionary?" Tostig asked, sounding out the new word. "What sort of book is this?"

"It is a book of words and their meanings," Paalavi explained patiently. "You may take it to your sleeping quarters and study it. It is not the only copy of the book we possess here, but there are few, and I expect you to handle it with special care."

It awed Tostig to be entrusted with something so valuable. Even in Lakeland, where he had known the High Priest, the deacons, and the acolytes all his life, he had never been allowed to remove any reading material from the small study of the sanctum. "Are you certain?" he asked Paalavi, feeling the weight of the tome as though it was made of gold and encrusted with the most valuable gemstones.

"I am certain," the master replied. He suddenly looked stern, the features on his broad face hardening. "Tostig, you must understand that as a magician, you will be entrusted with the well-being and aid of all the people of all the races of Ilbeor, from the meanest peasant to the highest of authorities. Compared to that, a book, even a rare one, is but a small responsibility. Learn the honor of your station, young one."

Tostig nodded gravely, taking Paalavi's words seriously. They had been drilled into him since the beginning of his training and he was only just starting to understand. That he, a messenger from the small valley village of Lakeland, was to be considered a person of power throughout the land, overwhelmed him.

"Go and study. See what new words you can use before our next lesson," Paalavi instructed. "You will use them when writing prose, as well."

Tostig nodded and thanked the poet before taking his leave with Ziva. He carefully placed the dictionary on the table in his quarters before taking her out for the last time that evening.

He returned to his room and left the globes lit for several hours, surprising himself by devouring the unfamiliar words. He had always enjoyed reading, but learning to write made the new words light up his senses and fuel his imagination.

He went to sleep exhausted but satisfied.

LITTLE CHANGED in the caves as autumn became a harsh winter cold. The only concessions the Sashu made to the chill were woolen under-garments and thick socks. Extra blankets could be requested, but most found the additional clothing sufficient. The thick rock walls, devoid of windows, provided insulation against the swirling snow and cold air, and no additional fires were lit.

Tostig progressed so quickly in his studies that he became known as something of a prodigy. What took most months to master, he mastered in weeks. Maera once remarked that he must have an unusual passion driving him, allowing him to tap into greater powers than most novitiates.

Privately, Tostig thought his determination to find and be with Alanda drove him; he was anxious to progress to the point at which they would help him find her. He only hoped she was not beyond his reach, matched, or married. Still, he told no one of her. He let them wonder.

As winter bore on, Tostig noticed something that had not occurred during his early lessons: Cecy herself often came to watch as he learned and practiced. She viewed the results of his efforts with an impassive face, often only nodding at him and whichever master he was working with before she left. He wondered about this; surely, as the religious and cultural leader of the Sashu, she had many demands on her time. He was not given much time to dwell on it; his masters kept him busy with ever more arduous tasks.

Once the snow melted, Tostig was promoted to apprentice magician. With this came certain responsibilities and certain privileges. He was allowed to choose the color of his robes and accessorize them if he saw fit. When presented with options, he was immediately attracted to the bright red he had worn as a messenger, remembering fondly how his mother had traded extra baked goods and coin to purchase the unusual fabric for him. He chose poetry as the art he wished to master, to no one's surprise, and they charged him with aiding the masters in some lessons for novitiates. The Watchers had returned three times over the winter, once with a human, and twice with tselqs.

After an intense conversation with Cecy and two of his masters, he had been granted an hour each afternoon for Ziva's exercise and activity, though during winter he confined many of their activities to the empty dining hall because of the depth of the snow outside. She learned a new version of her favorite game; instead of throwing a ball to her, he used magic to bounce the ball in random directions. After half an hour of this, she was usually exhausted, but he knew she loved it by the way her tail wagged when he brought out the ball.

One afternoon in early spring, Tostig and Ziva ventured out into the forest, despite mud from the recent snow melt. Tostig figured he would use the last few minutes of their time to bathe her before he returned to his other responsibilities. As Ziva romped around the clearing in front of the cave entrance, chasing birds and leaves and examining every stick, Tostig felt a tap on his shoulder. He turned and found Cecy.

Not having had many individual conversations with the Sashu leader since his first night, Tostig was not sure what to say. He greeted her politely and waited.

"You have impressed me, Tostig," she began. "As I have alluded, I am older than I seem, and I have seen many young magicians progress through their training here. Your skills and power are all but unmatched among them."

"Thank you," Tostig replied, uncertain what else to say.

"But I sense something else in you, something I feel it is important to address before you continue."

"And that is?" he asked, somewhat uncomfortably.

"You are searching for something," she said contemplatively. "Searching so hard it drives you to extremes, drives you to question your masters, and even to question my own decisions."

Tostig nodded but said nothing. It was true he questioned authority more often than was strictly accepted. Because of his unparalleled dedication to his lessons and his excellence at them, he had been allowed a certain latitude, which he knew he sometimes was guilty of exploiting.

"I do not fault you for your questions," Cecy continued, unperturbed. "In fact, I believe they show a mind open to learning new things about the world and the beings within it, and a certain reluctance to accept that which is given to you without knowing first the cost of the gift."

"Yes," Tostig said simply. He knew what she said was true, and he was grateful for her insight.

"I wish to ask you to do something," she said, turning to look at him directly for the first time. "Something not usually asked of anyone before they have reached mastery."

"What is it?" Tostig asked warily.

She placed a warm hand on his arm, and he could feel her touch even through the fabric of his bright red robes. He felt the hairs on the back of his neck stand up, though he was not sure what danger he was sensing. "I wish you to come to the next ceremony with the Sashu."

Tostig withdrew from her touch, not upset but still put off by her request. "The Watchers told me adherence to the Sashu religion is not required for magicians," he protested. "I prefer to remain faithful to the Covenant."

"I understand, and what they told you was true. No one is ever inducted into the Sashu religion without their free consent. We do, however, ask our masters to attend ceremonies of worship to the Nine, particularly Sado, for it is through him that your gifts were bestowed. After you have completed these rituals with us three times, we will trouble you no more. The choice will always be yours."

"Why do you ask me before I attain mastery?" Tostig inquired.

"Because I sense you may find what you are looking for, but do not yet know where to seek. I am offering you a glimpse into the world you have inhabited only at the edge for months, a choice you might make, nothing more."

Tostig thought it over for several long moments, turning away from Cecy and watching Ziva romp through the mud. He knew what she proposed was reasonable, and she had given him a straightforward way out if he did not choose to join the Sashu faith.

Three ceremonies. How bad can that be? At least then I'll understand their beliefs, even if I don't share them.

He turned back to Cecy and nodded tersely.

"Excellent," she said evenly. "We perform our rituals at the full moon and the new moon, so the next is still several days away. I suggest you refresh your knowledge of the Nine prior to attending." Without saying another word or waiting for his response, she turned toward the cave entrance and disappeared inside.

For the next several days, Tostig completed his lessons and his duties with a sense of anticipation he did not completely understand.

He was not exactly looking forward to taking part in the Sashu rituals, but he had to admit he was curious.

He knew they took place in the main cavern with the statues, though non-adherents were barred from entering without invitation. *Do they worship the statues? Or is there something else?*

When the full moon arrived, Tostig found himself inattentive, and he received rare chastisements from the master magicians who tutored him. He felt remorse, but also thought they might have been more understanding.

As instructed, he left Ziva in his quarters when night fell and the bell tolled nine times. She was so used to the caves she didn't protest, but settled on her mattress, circling and tugging at her blanket until it felt just right.

Extinguishing the lights, Tostig silently followed the mass of people toward the main cavern.

When he got there, he immediately noticed the globes had been extinguished, leaving the room lit only by the fires in the braziers in front of each statue. They cast an eerie, flickering orange glow, and no light came into the cave from the entrance despite the full moon. He stood near the back of the crowd as everyone gathered around the statue of Sado.

Cecy stepped in front of the adherents, wearing robes of deepest black with a hood drawn over her forehead. Tostig was forcibly reminded of Alanda's black cloak and the way it had draped almost to her eyes, protecting her from the sun.

I wonder what that cloak is protecting Cecy from.

"Friends," Cecy greeted the crowd, smiling more widely than he had ever seen her smile. Her teeth, as perfect and white as his own, gleamed weirdly in the firelight. "Today we gather for the full-moon celebration of the Nine, those to whom we owe our world, our gifts, our bodies, and our souls."

Tostig shifted uncomfortably. He did not like the idea that these deities owned any part of him or even of his world.

Cecy turned and bowed deeply toward the statue of Sado. The crowd followed suit, and, after a beat, so did Tostig. He knew he was supposed to participate, but if this was to be all it contained, he felt it to be no more than a charade, like children playing at being kings.

"Sado," Cecy intoned, her voice resonant and smooth. "We pay you homage for our lives, our gifts, and our world. We thank you for the gifts of your eight sons and daughters, and we thank you for the magic you have placed within our reach."

She bowed again, and again, the crowd followed suit.

The ritual proceeded almost identically from one statue to the next, Cecy naming the gifts of each of the gods or goddesses, beginning and ending with deep bows of homage. By the fourth statue, the one of Ybus, Tostig found himself bored. He wished he could discreetly return to his quarters, but he knew he had to see the ceremony through.

After they finished Xatra's ritual, Tostig was relieved. Surely, it was over. To his displeasure, the adherents formed a wide circle, expanding to the very edges of the cavern. They stood so close together they touched shoulders with the people to either side.

With an inward sigh, Tostig joined the circle between Maxwell and Kaira, a young female tselq with whom he was barely acquainted. He reasoned this must be the end, that it was similar to the final song of a fifth-day ceremony.

When everyone was in place, Cecy began to chant words Tostig did not immediately understand. They seemed to be in the language he used for magic, but he only recognized a few words. *Iluma*, of course, was the first word he had learned. He also recognized variations of *tarra*, which represented land and soil, and *cili*, which called upon the sky. With only those, he could not divine much meaning, and it disconcerted him when the people around him joined Cecy, chanting at an increasing pace. Tostig remained silent, listening and trying to understand, but also impatient.

A faint white glow appeared in the center of the circle. At the sight of it, the adherents became so excited and frenzied Tostig wondered if this was normal or something rare. Measure by measure, the white glow became brighter and took shape.

Tostig blinked, hardly believing what he was seeing. *Is this magic?*

Some kind of complex spell I haven't learned yet? If it were, he understood why Cecy wanted as many magicians as possible to take part.

The white light formed into a tall, bald, and portly human male. Tostig knew exactly who it was supposed to be, though he did not believe it was anything but an impressive bit of performative magic. The ghostly form of Sado turned slowly around the circle, seeming to look each of the awestruck adherents in the eye. When the apparition reached Tostig, its movement stopped.

Tostig froze, caught in the gaze of fathomless eyes, formless and transparent, yet somehow more alive than anything he'd ever seen. The spirit, if that's what it was, advanced toward him.

"No," Tostig choked out, suddenly more afraid than he'd ever been. The light got brighter the closer it came, until he was nearly blinded by it.

"Do not be afraid," Maxwell whispered, but as he spoke, Maxwell and Kaira stepped away. Blinded by the light enveloping him, Tostig felt utterly alone in an unknown place.

A voice deeper than he'd ever heard resonated inside of him, outside of him, everywhere and in everything, as Tostig dropped to his knees, his strength gone.

"I choose you," the voice said. The light faded and Tostig fell to the ground, insensible to the tumult surrounding him.

MISSIVE OF MAGIC

He sat upright in his bed, the early spring fur coverings falling around his naked body as he breathed ragged breaths in and out. It had happened again; a rent in the magical fabric of Ilbeor that he had not felt in more than fifty years.

There is a new Blessed.

The Blessed of the Sashu were always harbingers of substantial change, always powerfully magical, and he always tried to win them over to his cause. Thus far, he had failed, though he felt he had come close with the last one, a sorcerer named Crios. For the most part, their devotion to the Sashu faith, particularly in their father god Sado, always took precedence to their interest in earthly matters.

Perhaps it is time to take a new tack, he thought. *Perhaps it is time to simply take the Blessed, rather than try to meet with him clandestinely.*

He thought about the possible consequences. The way magicians were sent on missions was hard to predict; urgent messages came to Cecy, and she sent whomever she thought fit. The Sashu caves would be the best place to capture the Blessed, but the magicians of the Sashu were certain to put up a fight.

He didn't know the exact number of magicians in the caves: try as he might, he had never secured a spy among the Sashu. They were all too devoted to their strange religion. He knew they numbered in the hundreds, but that at any given time, many of them were out among the non-magical people of Ilbeor, providing magical aid. He knew there were also non-magical family members and Sashu adherents among their numbers, but he didn't worry about them overmuch. They would be no match for his fighters, and it was unlikely Cecy would even involve them in any sort of conflict.

Cecy herself was another problem; Cecy and the other non-elf immortals among the Sashu. Altoneir had never heard an explanation for their existence that satisfied him. Certainly, he did not believe they were favored by any sort of supernatural beings. However, their long life stymied him. Cecy had been the leader of the Sashu for almost a millennium, but by all accounts, she was human. Likewise, Grayson and the pair of freakish twins who summoned new magicians seemed to be human, and yet they, too, endured.

Altoneir shook off those thoughts; he was not going to solve that conundrum tonight, and there were more important matters to consider.

He threw off his bedclothes and dressed in his usual black water-cloth robes. A glance out the window told him the moon had not yet reached its zenith, but he knew awakening his council was necessary. He needed to send his magical fighters out into the world. Exceptionally powerful and at the apex of his larger army, the magical fighters should prove more than a match for the Sashu.

He had decided: rather than trying to convince this Blessed using persuasion, he was simply going to capture him and bring him to Sundersar Island. Here, in the luxurious confines of his castle, he could take his time and really talk to the Blessed, tell him how things in the world really stood, and find out just what the Blessed's capabilities were and how they could aid his cause.

Using a bellpull, he summoned one of the lesser-ranking hand-maidens. She arrived a few minutes later, slightly out of breath and tousled from hurrying across the castle.

"How may I serve you, my lord?" she asked, dipping into a deep curtsy. Her tone was perfectly deferent to his authority and status, but he detected a question in it beyond what she had asked directly. It was strange for him to summon servants at this time of night.

"Awaken the council and have them meet me in the council chambers as soon as it can be done," he commanded, not about to give her any more information. He knew even his servants were proud to be part of his cause, but it would never do to trust a mere handmaiden with too much information.

Noting the urgency, she hurried away with a breathy "yes, my lord," and disappeared around a corner.

He watched her go with a pensive expression on his handsome, stern face. He was not certain how his council and its military leaders would react to his new plan. It didn't matter because they would do as he commanded, but all the same, things would go much more smoothly if there was not a lot of debate.

Shaking his head a bit, he retreated into his chambers to prepare for the upcoming meeting.

NOT EVEN AN HOUR after he had sent the summons, he was pleased to find his council convened, dressed and as alert as if the summons had come in the middle of the day. When he entered the room, they were all seated in the eight chairs around the long oak table at the center of the room, the fire and chandelier lit.

That handmaiden did her job well, he thought as he surveyed the scene. She had not only summoned the council but had seen that the room was readied. Still, it was really no more than he expected from all his followers, from the meanest servant to the highest-ranking council member.

"There is a new Blessed," he announced from the door before moving down the table to his place at the head. "A human male, I believe, among the Sashu."

This pronouncement, the first the non-elven members of his council had ever heard, produced no audible reaction, but he noticed many glances between the assembled humans, dwarves, elves, and tselqs before they returned their attention to him.

Unperturbed, he continued. "My previous efforts to convince a Blessed to join our ranks have failed. Sending the travelers to talk with him has proven ineffective. This time, I propose to take the new Blessed by force and bring him here so that I, myself, may speak to him."

"What is his name?" asked Leilatha, a flaxen-haired elven maid and one of his closest advisors.

"I do not know," he answered, unworried. "We will know who he is when we go take him."

"If you know nothing about him, how do you propose to convince him?" Hugon, the youngest of the council and one who often spoke without thinking, asked boldly. "It seems as though, if he is human and Sashu, and a Blessed, he would be hard to convince."

Altoneir glared. Hugon had been chosen for the council for a proven strategic brilliance, but most of the council found his insistence at speaking on every issue, invited or not, irritating. He was little more than a child by elven reckoning: forty years old and having spent more than half his life on Sundersar Island, he was not as well-acquainted with the world as he thought.

"Do you not believe our cause is just and right?" Bryant, one of the leaders of the elite fighters, asked. He had more tolerance for the young man than the others; they often spent hours practicing swordsmanship together.

Hugon shifted uncomfortably. "Of course, I do," he said. "It's just that, strategically, taking an unknown person, especially a powerful magician, against his will and bringing him here seems a dangerous prospect."

Bryant was one of the few non-elven magicians on the island; since the Sashu found them so easily with the help of the mysterious, immortal Watchers, most magicians fell out of Altoneir's grasp. Having been taught by the elves and even Altoneir himself on two occasions, Bryant was as proficient at combative magic as anyone, with the bonus of being a born swordsman. He was also, Altoneir thought, exceedingly arrogant. Still, Altoneir let the interaction play out, knowing Bryant was the most likely person to bring Hugon to heel.

"A personal conversation with Altoneir will more than convince this Blessed, whoever he is, that our cause is just and right," Bryant said, stroking his gray mustache with one hand.

"How will they know who he is?" Leilatha asked, already thinking about how the thing could be done. Leilatha, though magically powerful in her own right, was not part of the fighting contingent.

"It is quite simple," Altoneir said. "The Blessed will be the one they all try to protect."

"You propose fighting the Sashu to gain access to him," Bryant said, sitting up straighter. The prospect excited him; he had done little fighting outside his daily training for most of his life.

"That is my plan, yes."

"When do we leave?" Bryant asked, already planning on marshaling his forces that very night.

"Immediately."

ANNEAU'S FIELD

The next morning, Alanda and Rinayai woke at *uht* and, even before they had broken camp, Alanda went back to the edge of Anneau's Field. Nothing but the sheet of ice was visible in all directions: vast, unchanging, unbroken ice. Alanda shivered. There would be no protection from the elements as they crossed; not so much as a rise in elevation broke the expanse. If there was a storm…

Alanda decided it was best not to think about it. The tselqs in Chinnua had told her that storms, though possible, were rare this early in the season. Despite the frigid appearance of the ice sheet itself, the season was only early autumn, and real winter had not yet set in, even this far up the mountains.

Trying to mask her uncertainty, Alanda returned to their small camp. After a hurried breakfast, they broke camp and packed. Alanda donned the multicolored coat, putting her cloak on over it, and put the ridiculous-looking boots on Alis's feet. Alis pawed the ground uncertainly; she had never worn anything but her own coat before.

"Those will keep your feet from getting too cold," Alanda told her, grinning despite herself.

Together, Alanda, Alis, and Rinayai somberly approached the edge of the field. The vast expanse seemed alien, so different from the mountain paths she was used to treading, so different from the hilly valley in which she lived.

Alanda would never forget her first step onto the ice. Crossing the threshold from the familiar to the alien landscape of the glacier marked a change, and she immediately knew the change could kill her.

The cold seeped through her leather boot, the two pairs of thick socks, and her very skin even as she stepped down on it. She looked at Rinayai, genuine fear in her eyes as she finally realized just how cold the journey would be. She no longer cared about the ridiculous look of her heavy patchwork coat; now she worried whether it would be enough to protect her.

"We do not have to do this," Rinayai told her, concern crinkling his eyes. "We could turn back and journey down the mountain and north to Ferncombe, as you said the elves advised you."

For the first time, Alanda truly considered it. She had - arrogantly, she now knew - rejected the plan as something that would keep her away from Blackwell and Kitz too long. What if the ice proved too much for her? What if she died on Anneau's Field? What would become of Kitz? Again, she wondered if he would even notice, and, pulling her foot off the ice, she stopped to consider everything she knew.

After several moments, she realized something. *It matters to me. Kitz may or may not notice my absence, but I know he needs me, and he needs me as soon as I can get back to him.*

Courage filled her, and she nodded at Rinayai. "Give me a moment, please," she requested. Taking off her pack and sitting down right where she was, on the ground at the edge of Anneau's Field, she pulled off her leather boots. Rummaging in her pack, she found the third pair of warm socks the tselqs had given her and pulled them on over the other two. Struggling, she pulled her tight boots back over the layers of wool. She stood again stepped onto the ice, this time with both feet.

Nodding to herself, she thought the third pair of socks might just make all the difference in the world.

"Alis, heel," she commanded, wanting to see how the cold would affect her companion.

Despite her discomfort, she couldn't help but giggle as Alis trotted nonchalantly onto the ice, her paws seeming larger than usual in the puffy tselq boots. Alanda thought she looked silly but hoped the boots would protect Alis's feet.

"Seven days?" she confirmed with Rinayai.

"Seven days," the tselq assured her, his horns tracing patterns in the cold air as he nodded.

"All right," she said, taking a deep breath. *This is for Kitz.* She took a few steps onto the ice, finding if she were moving rather than standing for any length of time, it wasn't as bad.

"Let's go," she told Rinayai, who was still hanging back, looking doubtful.

"You are certain?" he asked.

"My will is as stone," she replied, using a tselq phrase she had always liked.

Without another word, Rinayai joined her on the ice and strode forward, looking different in his winter clothing than Alanda was accustomed to. Tselqs on the mountain usually made few concessions to the weather. They only wore shoes when there was snow on the ground, and she had never seen one wear boots or a coat as Rinayai now did. She noticed, however, that his boots were not made of leather. Instead, they seemed to be constructed of thick gray cloth with hard soles.

Rinayai had been right about the light on the glacier. They hadn't traveled half a day before Alanda realized she needed more sun salve. She smoothed salve onto her forehead as well, worried the reflection from the glacier might get past her cloak. After she finished, she glanced back the way she had come and gasped in spite of herself. All sight of familiar land had vanished: whichever way she looked, the only thing she could see was ice. She suddenly felt insignificant.

Rinayai noticed her reaction and reassured her. "Tselqs feel the same way on their first venture here," he said. "It is disconcerting to lose contact with the land. Do not worry, young one, you will see land again in just a few days."

Alanda tried to shake off the unease and began trudging forward again. It just seemed so strange to be traveling in a place without trees, hills, or other features of the land. She realized, also, that she was unlikely to see any wildlife. Even with Rinayai and Alis for company, she felt alone.

The first day passed, and as Alanda was preparing to camp, Rinayai stopped her. "Wait," he said. "I have provisions to make the night more comfortable."

Alanda watched him pull an unusually large blanket from his over-sized pack. One side of the blanket was oddly shiny. Rinayai explained it had been woven specifically to be a barrier against the cold. "It is not often we have cause to cross, but in the case of one being called to become a guardian or a visit being necessary, the weavers created this material." He spread the large blanket directly on the ground, and she noticed it was filled with material, like her coat.

Next, Rinayai assembled a tent unlike any she'd ever seen. She'd noticed the smooth, thin wood poles attached to his pack but had assumed they were walking sticks or to test the ice. The sides of the tent were made of the same shiny material and extended to the ground on three sides. He attached the fabric directly to the ice using stout metal spikes and a hammer. Alanda knew she would never have been strong enough to hammer in the spikes; even the powerful tselq seemed to have some difficulty.

"Have you ever been to Dachilon?" Alanda asked, spreading her blankets inside the tent.

"Once," he told her. "It is common for a new shaman to make the journey before becoming fully qualified. Sincha, I am certain, will make the journey before the end of her apprenticeship, abbreviated though it may be. The scale of the buildings there and the amount of knowledge collected by the guardians will awe you. It is a sacred place."

As he spoke, he spread his own blankets inside the tent, and

Alanda noticed he placed them next to hers, so close they overlapped at the edge.

Rinayai noticed her gaze and said, "Do not worry, young one, for I think you know I mean you no harm. It will be important we stay close together in order to share warmth."

Nodding her acceptance, Alanda called Alis into the tent. She was surprised how little of the chill from the ice reached her. Getting out Alis's comb, she began their nightly ritual.

Their dinner was cold: there was no way to light a fire and no wood to burn. They quietly ate preserved fruits and vegetables, chilled but not frozen, and shared a piece of hardtack between them.

"How will we get more water?" Alanda asked, suddenly alarmed. Her waterskin, which she had filled in the morning, was already half empty. She had not thought of the problem prior to crossing, and she mentally berated herself for the oversight. She and Alis could not survive without ample water.

"Ah," Rinayai told her with some satisfaction in his deep voice. "We shall use magic. Let me show you." He went a few feet onto the bare ice, his boots making almost no sound. Bending down, he said a few words Alanda didn't understand, and beneath his large, gloved hands, the ice melted, forming a small pool of water.

Alanda leapt up and filled their waterskins with some of the clearest, coldest water she had ever seen.

"We will sleep with them next to our bodies, lest they freeze," Rinayai explained, screwing the top back onto his own waterskin and returning to the tent.

It took Alanda some time to fall asleep. She was warmer than she had expected, but save the one night with Tostig under the crumbling tower in the forest, she had never slept so close to anyone other than Kitz. She, Rinayai, and Alis huddled together for warmth, the cold waterskins nestled between them.

THOUGH ALIS and Rinayai both seemed to acclimate to the frigid, unchanging conditions on the ice sheet with relative ease, each day of travel grew harder for Alanda. She was colder than she had ever been, colder even than she had been when she had traveled with Alicia, delivering messages in the dead of winter. Then, at least, there had been trees and landscape to shield them from the wind. On Anneau's Field, the wind bit at the exposed skin of her face, chapping her lips, turning even her pale cheeks pink, and seemed to travel directly through the layers of clothing, chilling her to the bone.

On the second day, she was able to hide her growing apprehension as she grew colder and lost her breath more quickly, but by the third day, her struggles had become apparent. She could no longer keep up with Rinayai's long strides, and she fell further back until he was forced to slow down so they could stay together.

Rinayai stopped her at midday, before they would have normally stopped for food, and insisted they unpack their blankets and the tent. "We rest for a while," he decreed. "If we can get in more distance before night falls, we will do so, but for now, we rest."

Alanda opened her mouth to argue but changed her mind. She was exhausted, cold to her very bones, and the journey had become so difficult that even her traveler's spirit was abandoning her. Without questioning Rinayai, she unpacked her blankets and applied sun salve. As soon as he had spread the special blanket, she sat, wrapping herself in her blankets and shivering uncontrollably.

Rinayai looked at her in concern as he set up the tent, and Alis surprised Alanda by nosing her way under the blankets and right into Alanda's lap. She welcomed the shared warmth. She petted Alis with gloved hands as her shivers slowly subsided. When the tent was up and the wind off her back, Alanda relaxed as much as she could. She didn't like the delay, but she appreciated being warmer.

After a couple hours of rest and their midday meal, Rinayai gave her the choice of continuing until dark or staying put until morning. Feeling rejuvenated, Alanda decided to continue. He quickly dismantled the tent, pulling up the spikes with magic, and packed for the journey ahead.

After her rest, the next couple of hours did not seem as daunting, and she continued with little trouble. Cheerful and once again confident she could make the crossing, even if it was more difficult than she had ever imagined, Alanda helped Rinayai set up for the night.

The next day started much the same, Alanda feeling fairly well as they started, but matters quickly turned for the worse. Rinayai stopped so suddenly that Alanda and Alis actually took several steps before they realized it. Alanda backtracked to him quickly.

"What is it?" she asked. "The journey is not so difficult today; we don't need to stop."

"That." Rinayai pointed to their left. A great, dark storm cloud had come over the icy horizon and was moving quickly in their direction.

Alanda swore loudly and then called Alis to her, touching the dog for comfort. "What do we do?" she asked urgently. Out of habit, she scanned the landscape for some natural protection, but found none.

"There is nothing to be done but to prepare as best we can. The winds will be too high for the tent, but we must settle into our blankets and weather the storm. There is no outrunning it. You must be brave, young one. This will try us all."

Alanda nodded, trying not to show fear. Fumbling with the ties on her pack, she got out every blanket she had, and Rinayai did the same.

Instead of spreading the bottom blanket on the ice as he had done in the past, Rinayai bade Alanda and Alis sit on it. Joining them, he huddled close to Alanda and wrapped his blankets, her blankets, and the larger blanket around them as tightly as he could. "It will pass quickly," he said, trying to reassure her, "but it could be deadly. We must retain as much warmth as we can. Cover your faces with the blankets and get as close to me as you can."

A few minutes after they had arranged themselves, the storm hit with the force of a hundred horses, throwing icy snow and wind at them as though trying to force them off the mountain. Rinayai put his arms around Alanda and helped her keep the blankets drawn close, but after a few minutes, it was apparent even this would not be enough. Alanda began to shiver violently, her body unable to handle the cold wind, the ice below them, and the snow making its way into their cocoon.

Rinayai did not feel any actual fear until Alanda stopped shivering well before the storm had ended. She became limp in his arms, her breathing steady and shallow. Lifting a corner of the blanket to see her face, he saw her eyes had closed.

"Alanda!" he shouted over the noise of the storm, shaking her. "Open your eyes! You must not sleep!" He drew her right up into his lap, willing every ounce of his body heat to pass to her. He adjusted the blankets to cover them more completely and was relieved when Alanda spoke, though only for a moment.

"So warm," she murmured.

Rinayai became terrified at her words. Even under the blankets, even huddled together as they were, the conditions were far from warm. She should have been shivering; she should have been miserable. She should not have been warm.

The storm raged for another half hour, and he alternately shook her, forced her to open her eyes, and talked to her. Near the end of the storm, Alis began to howl even in the close confines of their huddle underneath the blankets. Rinayai knew the situation was dire, and besides his genuine affection for the young human, he knew she could not be allowed to die for the sake of Ilbeor.

When the storm finally ended, Rinayai packed pell-mell, not caring that the strings would barely tie, while trying to keep Alanda on his lap and off the ice. He heaved the pack onto his back, picked Alanda and her pack up, and ran across the ice as fast as his legs would carry him, Alis streaming behind.

THE WARMTH she felt was different when she woke up. It wasn't as complete as the warmth she had felt during the ice storm, not as pervasive, not as all-encompassing. There were edges of chill in this warmth, reminders that she was not at home on a warm summer's day, but out in the wilderness, surrounded not by walls but by the wilds of the Ilbeoran mountains.

Her eyes fluttered.

"Alanda, young one, wake yourself. It is time to wake." Rinayai's voice sounded as though it was coming from some distance away, though she somehow knew he was close.

Alanda slowly opened her eyes, but she was immediately confused. Above her, she saw the blurred outlines of trees, their leaves bursts of oranges and yellows against a backdrop of bright, clear light. She knew that was not what she should have seen.

"Trees?" she asked Rinayai before a more important question entered her mind. "Alis?" Her voice became stronger, and she struggled to sit up. Rinayai applied gentle pressure to her shoulders, keeping her down.

"All in good time," the tselq told her soothingly. "Alis is here, right next to you, though you may not be able to feel her through your blankets. We have come off the ice and into the forest on the other side; I carried you and ran the last miles. I was afraid you had left this world."

"We're…off the ice? Already? How long have I been asleep? What's happened?" She moved her eyes about, searching for Rinayai in the blurred landscape, and found him sitting cross-legged next to her, on the opposite side of Alis.

"Do not panic. I called upon the ancestors for strength and ran with you as I have never run before. Day and night we ran, and we did not stop but for brief moments to relieve and refuel our bodies. I also reapplied the sun salve you had in your pack, for I knew a burn could prove fatal." Rinayai's words were calm, measured, and reassuring. "You have slept for three days, and I believe it was only my body heat and the blankets I wrapped around you that kept you alive. I am grateful to whatever spirits inhabit your body; they are strong. You are strong."

Her vision cleared, and Rinayai's face came into focus. Its broad features were crinkled in concern, and his eyes were kinder than she had ever seen them. "It seems," she said, shivering slightly as she felt the chill of the air on her face, "your debt has been repaid. You have now saved my life."

Rinayai didn't respond to her words, but instead said, "Let us sit you up and put your hands to the fire. I believe the warmth will cheer you."

As he helped her up, Alanda realized she had been lying as close to a large campfire as was safe. Looking around as she got her bearings, she saw small patches of snow outside the clearing, though nothing like what they had seen right before they had gone onto the glacier; these were just light patches in shaded places, fairly typical of the high mountain passes in the fall.

She protested at first when Rinayai gently removed her gloves, but as she held her hands out to the fire and felt the warmth of the flames kiss her fingertips, she was thankful. Her fingers were red and somewhat swollen but were not, to her relief, white or blackened. Somehow, she had escaped frostbite. She flexed her fingers experimentally. They were stiff and achy, but fully functional.

Rinayai watched as she went through the movements. "I kept your hands between your body and mine as I ran," he explained. "I have hopes that your toes will have escaped the bite of the cold as well because of the layers of protection they had. I dared not look while you slept. Would you like to check?"

Alanda nodded and was about to tell Rinayai there was no way her fingers were going to manage removing her boots and socks. She did not have to, however, for the tselq leaned forward and began removing them, his large hands gentle.

Miraculously, Alanda's toes had also escaped frostbite. She could not believe her luck; she had worried about frostbite in her feet even before the storm. As she had with her hands, she flexed her feet experimentally. They still worked, though they, too, were stiff and painful. "Can you put some of the socks back on?" she asked. "And then I will put my feet close to the fire."

Rinayai agreed, and Alanda reached down with one of her bare hands and began petting Alis. She could only imagine the amount of distress her illness had caused her dog; they were trained to react when their masters were ill or injured, though the only other time that had occurred had been when Alis had led her to Kilynelle. Running along with Rinayai without having any contact with Alanda, especially in the silly boots Alanda noticed were absent from Alis's paws, must have been difficult for her.

"It's okay, girl," she said, noticing her shivers were subsiding. "I'm all right now. Rinayai took care of us, didn't he?" She hummed for a few moments, trying to soothe Alis, before she knew she needed to put her hands closer to the fire again.

"I brought you further down the mountain than perhaps you realize," Rinayai told her. "It might take some time for your body to adjust, but it's not nearly as cold here. We shall wait two days, possibly three, while you eat and regain strength, and then we will complete our journey to Dachilon."

Alanda realized she was hungry, and when she admitted as much, Rinayai surprised her by bringing her not only preserved fruits, vegetables, and hardtack, but a piece of meat he had obviously cooked over the fire at some point. "Meat?" she asked him doubtfully. "But I thought…"

"Yes, we tselqs are vegetarian, and yes, it hurt me to kill the animal, but I learned enough from the dog breeders to understand your Alis cannot survive on fruits and vegetables, and she was out of the food mixture Sincha packed. Please, eat. You will not offend me; I feel you probably need the extra proteins."

Alanda was uncertain what he meant by "proteins", but she was grateful for the meat. Lacking a more polite way to do it, she took it in her hands and took a bite out of it. It was still warm. *Rabbit, but unseasoned and overcooked.* She did not complain, knowing Rinayai would not understand how to cook meat. When she finished it, she moved on to the fruits, vegetables, and hardtack.

Rinayai watched her devour the food with undisguised satisfaction. "I was able to get you plentiful water while you slept," he said, "and once we reached the forest, I added what few herbs I could find. But I knew you needed food, and it pleases me to see you eat so well."

"Thank you, Rinayai, for everything," Alanda said sincerely after swallowing a portion of hardtack she had softened in the warmed water in her tin mug. She noticed a slightly bitter taste to the water, and she figured Rinayai had added either herbs or needles from the coniferous trees to make a kind of tea. As a shaman, Rinayai would have been trained in many herbal healing methods, and the warm tea felt good as she sipped it and soaked her hardtack in it. More quickly than she was expecting, Alanda felt a measure of strength return to her.

"Is there any sun salve left?" she asked, concerned about her hands and face even in the shade of the trees.

"Yes, there are still three jars. Your elf friend stocked you better than you realize," Rinayai replied.

"Could you…"

"Of course." Rinayai reached into Alanda's pack and pulled out a nearly full jar of sun salve. Alanda rubbed it generously over her hands, her face, and the part in her hair.

"You should rest now that you have eaten," Rinayai said. "It would be a pleasure to see you sleep peacefully after the dangers of the past three days, and I need some rest as well. I have not slept since the storm."

"You haven't slept in three days?" Alanda asked, astonished. "How did you even manage that?"

"It was what I had to do to keep you alive," Rinayai answered simply, no hint of a boast in his voice. "I knew I must run, so I ran day and night. Fortunately, there were no more storms." As he spoke, Rinayai got up from his sitting position and began arranging his blankets as close to hers as they had been on Anneau's Field. "It is important that you are as warm as possible," he explained, "so with your permission, we will share body heat again this night."

Alanda nodded, and they lay down by the fire, her body cupped into his, and Alis's warming her other side. Rinayai fell into a deep sleep almost immediately. After the cold, unyielding ice, the forest floor seemed soft to him.

Alanda was not as tired as she had led Rinayai to believe, but as her body continued to warm between the tselq and Alis and being bundled in the blankets, it surprised her how quickly she became sleepy. Though it was but late afternoon, both of them slept through to the next morning.

~

WHEN ALANDA WOKE the next morning to Alis's whine at *uht,* she was almost too warm, having been sandwiched between Rinayai and Alis all night. Her fingers and toes no longer ached, and she felt her strength returning. The warmth felt good as she sat up and stretched, putting her arms above her head, and felt ready to move. She told Rinayai so as they prepared to break their fast.

"You need three proper meals today," he replied when she expressed her readiness to continue to Dachilon. "And to rest. Though we do not have to journey through any more extreme conditions, I would prefer you to travel as easily as possible."

Alanda nodded, conceding to the wisdom of his words, though she was reluctant to delay any longer. *I must get back to Kitz.* Besides, she would not know the way to Dachilon without Rinayai.

"I'll hunt after we break our fast," she said. "Alis needs the meat. If you do not object, I would like some as well."

Rinayai looked at her very seriously for a few moments, not touching the portion of fruit and tea laid in front of him. "I do not object," he said finally. "It burdens my heart to know you are committing violence against the wildlife in the forest, but I also know it is the way of your people. You are not a tselq."

Alanda felt a pang of guilt, but she knew that even if she didn't eat meat, Alis would have to. She wasn't certain what was in the mixture the tselqs fed their dogs, but she wondered if some of the dog breeders might also have been hunters. She didn't know how they could raise such healthy dogs otherwise, and they obviously knew that if Rinayai had been told as much. She resolved to ask Sincha. She didn't think the new shaman would be offended by her question.

After they had eaten and drunk the nettle tea Rinayai made, Alanda strung her short bow, careful to avoid Rinayai's eyes.

"Alis, heel." They ventured into the forest. In the colder weather, game was scarce; most animals had gone to their dens and were not as active. After several hours, however, she was able to find a lone rabbit, replete with winter fat. Remembering the lessons of her apprenticeship, she dropped it immediately without undue pain; her arrow pierced its heart.

Taking her kill back to the clearing, she was somewhat relieved to find Rinayai gone. She skinned and cleaned her kill quickly, feeding Alis some of the raw meat immediately. She spitted and cooked the rest over the large fire, and by the time Rinayai returned, evidence of her kill was all but gone. She had wrapped and stowed the extra meat, disposed of the offal, and disassembled the spit. While she didn't feel eating meat was morally wrong, neither did she want to cause her traveling companion more discomfort than necessary.

Rinayai returned, bearing a pouch full of nettle leaves and a handful of other herbs. "I had to travel down the mountain for some distance to find this," he said, "but these herbs will make a tea to aid you in returning to your full strength." He heated water in a metal pan, cast the herbs in, and chanted a few tselq words over the mixture.

"Was that magic?" Alanda asked as he dipped her tin cup into the brew, filling it nearly to the top.

"No," he answered. "That was a request for a blessing from the ancestors for your strength and healing."

Alanda was touched. "How do your ancestors grant blessings?" she asked curiously. "Humans believe blessings come only from Annuah, the one god of all."

"Our ancestors go to live in the spirit world after the burial rites. They watch over us, and shamans are taught the words needed to call upon their blessings."

"Where is the spirit world?" Alanda asked, trying to reconcile this with her belief in Annuah's Great Mountain in the skies above Ilbeor.

"It is all around us, unseen but still here," Rinayai told her gently. "The spirits of our ancestors never leave Ilbeor; it is their station to watch over their descendants, their crops, and every part of their lives, that the tselqs may be fruitful, healthy, and multiply as we should."

Alanda looked around her, almost as though she might see this spirit world Rinayai spoke of if she just tried hard enough. She had to admit it would be comforting to know her mother and father were watching over her and that they could have an actual effect on her life and Kitz's life from their place in the otherworld.

Still, she thought, remembering her fifth-day lessons, *we must not base our faith on that which is most comfortable, but that which is right.* She knew her belief in Annuah was right; it was something she had felt deeply since childhood. It did not stop her interest in the tselq religion, however, and after a beat, she asked Rinayai how he thought the two faiths reconciled with one another.

"The different races of Ilbeor have many different beliefs," he said, his voice fairly rumbling with wisdom and consideration. "I think the wisest would tell you that no one knows what is right, or if what is right is even one system in the land. I think it is most likely the gods and spirits of the world manifest themselves in different ways at different times."

Their conversation turned to lighter things as the day progressed, and Rinayai did not object or even look askance at her portion of cold rabbit with the evening meal. By the time they had eaten, drunk another cup each of the hot herbal tea, and she had combed Alis, Alanda felt warm enough to whittle for the first time in several days.

Rinayai examined the figure slowly emerging under Alanda's skilled hands. He noted wingtips and the top of a triangular-shaped head. "A dragon?" he asked in surprise. "Have you ever seen one?"

"No," she answered, not slowing her whittling even as she looked at him. "I've seen pictures in the village hall, and the rest comes from what I imagine them to be. I'd like to meet a dragon someday," she added wistfully.

Rinayai said nothing. He had not met a dragon, but he had heard stories and he thought it unlikely they would be enjoyable or even safe companions. They seemed to be dangerous creatures, caring only about themselves and their hoards of riches. They were rumored to live in the caves along the western cliffs facing the sea. They stole from any they came in contact with, killing them more often than not.

When Alanda's hands got too cold to continue, she put away her project and brushed shavings from herself before pulling on gloves for the night. "We will travel tomorrow?" she asked Rinayai hopefully.

"We will travel tomorrow," he confirmed. "Your strength has returned, and we have supped well. Be prepared, however, for if I find you flagging, I will require us to stop."

Alanda nodded her head in acquiescence but made a vow to herself that she would do everything in her power to travel normally the next day.

ALANDA AND RINAYAI smelled Dachilon long before they saw it. A sulfurous, unhealthy smell permeated the forest for miles, and Alis whined uncomfortably when they first encountered it. Alanda, remembering the small lake Alicia had shown her, asked Rinayai if there were poisonous waterways around the place.

Rinayai looked surprised, for he had never encountered the smell outside of Dachilon. He wondered where else in the mountains such ponds existed. "Yes, young one," he told her. "There are many dangerous ponds and springs around Dachilon. Do not touch or taste any water until it has been approved by one of the guardians, for only they know what is safe."

Alanda nodded, unconsciously touching her full waterskin to reassure herself that she and Alis would not go thirsty before they reached Dachilon.

Rinayai chuckled. "Do not worry," he said. "Once you can smell the city, it is less than a half day's walk to its center. They will provide for you in a fine fashion once they have ascertained your purpose there. I caution you, however: speak little until I explain your place and your purpose. The guardians rarely allow visitors outside our own race to Dachilon and will be suspicious of you at first. Answer questions posed to you respectfully and quietly, nothing more."

"I will," Alanda replied. "And Alis? Will she be welcome there?" She had not considered this before, for the tselqs were known animal lovers, but these guardians were unknown to her.

"Very much so," Rinayai replied. "Though the guardians do not take part in the breeding of dogs, they are great lovers of animals. They will trust Alis long before they trust you."

Alanda laughed nervously. "Well, at least there's that."

As Rinayai promised, it took less than half a day to reach the main building of Dachilon, and they arrived in the bright sunlight of midafternoon. Alanda gazed at it in absolute awe; she had never seen a building so large and so beautiful. Built of light wood varnished to somehow make it sparkle in the sun, the magnificently carved towers and spires rose over the surrounding trees. To Alanda's eyes, the building seemed to go on forever in both directions.

You could house the whole of the human race in here, she thought in wonder. The building seemed larger than the entire village of Blackwell, including the outskirts.

"Welcome, young human, to the Library of the Guardians," Rinayai told her, smiling at her awe. He had felt similarly when he had first visited.

"This whole thing is the library?" Alanda asked, breathless.

"Not exactly, though that is what the building is called. It houses the guardians and has everything they need to live a peaceful life within its walls."

Alanda was silent as Rinayai led her to what seemed to be the front door. Though she saw no one in the clearing in front of it, she felt eyes on her and was certain there were watchmen in the glass windows. She kept Alis close, suddenly feeling very nervous.

When they reached the door, an imposing, heavy structure twice as tall as the tallest tselq, they were greeted by a tselq nearly a foot shorter than Rinayai. His skin was a paler green than Alanda had ever seen in a tselq. She noted that, though the tselq had the weathered face of the old, his horns only curled three times, with a hint at the beginning of a fourth. She surmised he was still rather young. In Chinnua, the old shaman Pallin's horns had eight curls.

"I am Tsetsic," the tselq announced, his voice less accented in the common tongue than many others of his race. He fingered a long, gray ponytail as he spoke. "I greet you in the name of the Order of the Guardians. I would welcome you to Dachilon, but first I must know the reason you have brought a human into our midst, young Rinayai."

Rinayai did not seem surprised that Tsetsic remembered his name. "This is Alanda, from the human village of Blackwell. She comes seeking answers about her mother's heritage and her rightful path forward. I have seen many things regarding her, and I would share them with you in a more private setting. Her dog is Alis."

Alanda's eyes flicked sideways to Rinayai as he introduced her. She didn't like the idea that he had seen visions of her he was not willing to share in front of her; she had suspected as much in Chinnua, but to have it confirmed was disconcerting. She remembered her feeling of dread when Rinayai had told her she would never return to Blackwell, and she wondered what else he had seen. Remembering his earlier admonition, however, she said nothing.

Tsetsic studied Alanda, not bothering to hide his scrutiny. Alanda stood proudly but did not meet his eyes; she felt it would not be right to do so, though Rinayai had not warned her against it. She wondered what the correct way to show respect to a guardian was.

Finally, Tsetsic said, "And what do you seek here, young human? You look unlike any human I have ever seen, and your garb raises questions as well."

Alanda bristled inwardly. At Rinayai's insistence, she was still garbed in the multicolor coat, her leathers and the elven cloak. Under Tsetsic's unwavering gaze, she felt ridiculous.

"I am a messenger," she finally answered. "My leathers are the last gift I received from my father, my cloak was given to me by the elves of Kilynelle, and my coat was given to me by the kind tselqs of Chinnua for crossing Anneau's Field. I have come here, enduring much danger and nearly the loss of my life, with questions of my mother's heritage I was told your order could answer."

"You wear the clothing of three races," Tsetsic mused, "and you have an occupation which puts you in the path of many peoples. Your eyes are as ice, your skin as snow. You are unique in many ways, young human. What vouchsafe would you offer?"

"I have no vouchsafe but my word of honor," Alanda replied defiantly. "The order has nothing to fear from me. I come only seeking answers and a time of safety before returning to my village."

Tsetsic's eyes strayed to Alis, alert at Alanda's side. Alanda saw the movement and became immediately defensive. "Alis is not a tool with which to parley," she said, her voice stronger and more confident than it had been since reaching Dachilon. "Though my words are true, I would not put her in jeopardy in order to prove that."

Tsetsic smiled suddenly, softening his weathered face. "You answer rightly," he told Alanda, "and your words hearten me. One must care unconditionally for the animal companions given them by the ancestors, and that you refuse to use Alis as a vouchsafe for your word proves more to me of your character than any assurances."

His smile faded as he strode forward and ran his fingers over the material of Alanda's tselq coat. He turned to Rinayai accusingly. "She crossed the glacier in nothing but this?" he asked, his voice laced with disapproval.

Rinayai quickly recounted their crossing, the storm, and Alanda's brush with death. "She is also wearing two sets of woolen undergarments and three pairs of woolen socks," he finally said, trying to defend himself.

"You are a fool to bring a human, especially one your claim is of some importance, across the ice thus garbed. You are lucky she survived; even without the storm, the protections you provided would not have been sufficient."

Rinayai bowed his head, seemingly in shame. Alanda wondered what else the tselqs could have done to protect her. They did not wear or use leathers or fur. What else could they have offered?

Tsetsic softened as Rinayai raised his head, and both Rinayai and Alanda looked at him for what was going to happen next.

"Come," he said, his voice conciliatory. "You have had a hard journey, and I will provisionally allow Alanda into our home. Provided she remains true to her word, she will achieve a more permanent welcome. Let us find you food and hot baths."

Behind him, the great doors finally opened. At first, Alanda thought they opened by magic. When she saw the tselq behind each door, she felt strangely relieved. There was already so much to take in; she was uncertain she could deal with an overabundance of magic. She expected such from the elves, but never of the tselqs.

Tsetsic wordlessly led them into a large foyer and up a polished wooden staircase. Here, he chose the left of three passages, much narrower than the foyer but still wider than the hallways Alanda had seen in human buildings, even sanctums.

"You will room next to one another," Tsetsic decreed. "I will have food and hot water brought to each of you. Would you like a separate tub for your dog?" he asked Alanda.

Alanda thought about what the right answer might be. Truth be told, she and Alis were both so dirty from their long journey that the idea of separate tubs of clean water was appealing. After a beat, knowing Tsetsic was a lover of animals, she told him so.

"Then it shall be done," he said. "The evening falls soon. For tonight, rest and keep one another's counsel. In the morning, I will return at dawn to offer a tour and find out more about how the guardians may help you." With that, he turned and strode quickly down the hall, leaving Alanda, Rinayai, and Alis standing in front of the doors to their new chambers.

DACHILON

Alanda had never felt anything better than the hot bath she took on the evening of her arrival at the Library of the Guardians. Soon after she, Alis, and Rinayai reached their rooms, a knock sounded. When she opened her door, she found three tselq women, all dressed alike in unbleached linen dresses without tuck or frill, holding large buckets of steaming water. They returned to her room four times, and the large tub in the washroom of her new quarters was filled to the brim with water hotter than she had ever bathed in. Steam rose above the tub in gentle wisps, and something smelled so enticing about it that Alanda could hardly wait to get in.

She relaxed into the steaming water and felt the remaining chill and stiffness evaporate. She realized the bath had some sort of sweet-smelling oil in it, accounting for the enticing smell; Alanda could see droplets of it widening as they broke the surface tension of the water. It was a full five minutes before she even remembered she was supposed to be cleaning herself. With a start, she took the small bathing cloth and a rectangular piece of light-yellow soap and went to work.

Somehow, the same female tselqs who had brought the hot water realized Alis would not like the same consideration. As Alanda bathed, they streamed back into the room, first with a smaller washtub for Alis, and then with buckets of water that were warm but not hot and did not contain any oil. Alis seemed to enjoy her bath more than she usually did, standing still in it and allowing Alanda to scrub her down with a soft-bristled brush and the same yellow soap. By the time she was combed and dry, she looked more pristine than she had in a very long time, her fluffy white fur standing in a cloudy halo around her face and body.

After her bath, Alanda changed into the simple tunic and pants she had worn while in Chinnua and explored her rooms. On first glance, they had overwhelmed her. The suite held three rooms: a large bedroom, a smaller sitting room, and the washroom. The bedroom was appointed with a large bed with four carved posts and bleached white linens softer and thicker than what she was used to; when she felt the covering, she discovered it was filled with the soft fabric scraps typical of tselq mattresses. Opposite the bed was a good-sized fireplace laid with glittering granite. Someone had come in to light the fire while she had been bathing.

The opulence of the room did not lay in the large four-poster bed or the stone fireplace, however, but in the rich dark wood of the walls, the huge windows of bubbled glass allowing plenty of natural light in, and the heavy draperies and canopies at the windows and over the tops of the bed. Surveying it all, Alanda wondered why the tselqs, who valued simplicity, would have such rooms as these.

Another knock sounded on her door and, opening it, she found yet another female tselq in a simple dress holding a large wooden tray that seemed like it should have been creaking with the amount of food atop it. The tselq didn't speak as she carried the tray into the sitting room and set it down on a small, varnished writing table with a chair. She bobbed a quick nod at Alanda before leaving, a question in her eyes that Alanda guessed had to do with the presence of a human in Dachilon. Alanda didn't explain herself and the tselq woman didn't directly ask.

Alanda examined the tray. There was no meat, and she hadn't expected any. Even in the absence of meat, though, the food looked filling and appetizing, especially the large clay bowl full of thick vegetable stew that looked similar to what she had been served in Karuk's house. None of the fruits or vegetables were preserved, though Alanda thought it late in the season for fresh food. Alis had not been forgotten, either: there was a bowl of what Alanda recognized as the same food Sincha had given her.

After laying Alis's bowl on the floor, Alanda sat on the upholstered chair and sampled the stew. It was delicious, as were the green salad, assorted fruits, and grainy bread. Alanda realized she was quite hungry and set into the food with relish and drank from the goblet of cold, clear water, though she avoided the silver tankard of yellow ale.

Though Tsetsic had told Alanda and Rinayai to hold counsel with one another that evening, they didn't. After their hot baths and meals, the exhausted travelers chose to don the simple white nightclothes left for them and fall into the comfortable beds. Alanda, not seeing a mattress for Alis, did something she had never done before: she allowed Alis to come onto the bed and sleep with her. She was loath to be parted with her after spending so many nights cuddled close to her, and she was not exactly comfortable in the large suite of rooms.

Alis woke her at *uht*, and Alanda immediately realized something new had been left for her. Wondering why Alis hadn't woken when someone came into the room, she reasoned to herself that the dog had been just as tired as she was, but it still discomfited her to know someone had visited the room while she slept.

Instead of her leathers or the tunic and pants she had worn in Chinnua, a clean woolen tunic was laid out on the large wooden chest of drawers near the door to her room. It was an earthy green similar to the tselqs' skin and plain but well-made. A clean set of undergarments, a pair of woolen pants, a belt, and a pair of cloth shoes with hard soles completed the outfit. Though glad to wear something other than her filthy traveling clothes, she panicked when she realized her leathers were nowhere to be found. Knowing how the tselqs felt about animal products, she worried that they may have disposed of or destroyed her father's last gift to her.

The clothing fit well enough, leaving Alanda to wonder where it had come from. If the tselqs rarely entertained guests from other races, how had they had clothing on hand to fit her? She suddenly wondered if someone had been set to make clothes for her upon her arrival. Frowning, she pictured one of the female tselqs laboring long into the night to complete the clothing, and her appreciation for all they had done to make her comfortable only grew.

She dressed and braided her hair quickly and went to the next door on her right to rouse Rinayai. Not having a dog to rouse him at *uht*, he was worried his extreme exhaustion and comfortable surroundings would cause him to sleep later than he should. When he came to the door, Alanda almost grinned at his tousled appearance; he had apparently slept quite soundly.

As Rinayai greeted her, she glanced at his nightclothes and suddenly remembered her earlier concern. "They took my clothes," she said without preamble, her amusement evaporating. "All of them."

Rinayai blinked at her, not realizing the import of her words. "They will have taken mine, too, of course. It is the way of the Dachilon tselqs to offer travelers clean clothes upon arrival," he told her. "They'll clean them and return them to us."

"Are you certain?" Alanda asked. "My clothing is made of animal hide. What if they decide to dispose of it?"

"They would never dishonor the lives of the animals sacrificed for your clothing by disposing of it wantonly," he assured her. "You will have it back once it has been cleaned, I am sure of it."

Alanda felt somewhat better but resolved to ask Tsetsic about it. She could not risk losing her leathers; she would feel as though her last tie with her father had been broken.

At dawn, Tsetsic arrived. When Alanda immediately asked him about her traveling clothes, he assured her they were simply taken for cleaning and repair. Satisfied, Alanda, Alis, and Rinayai followed him to a small dining room not far from their quarters. It, too, was elegantly appointed with the same wood-paneled walls, the rich brown varnish broken by two great tapestries depicting the peaceful lives of the tselq race. In the middle stood a round table, large enough for eight tselqs to be seated comfortably, but only set with three places.

"It's so beautiful here," Alanda commented to Tsetsic as they took their seats.

"What you see is but a fraction of the whole," Tsetsic told her, gesturing to three young, male tselqs who stood ready at a doorway on the other side of the room. At his signal, they filed silently out, leaving Alanda wondering who they were and where they were going. "The rooms reserved for guests are richly appointed, for we often entertain people of very high status here. The library is likewise beautiful, but the quarters for guardians and their apprentices are quite simple and feature only necessities."

The young tselqs entered the room, each bearing a tray with a large, white clay bowl and a clear goblet of an orange liquid Alanda had never seen before. Along with this, Alanda was thrilled to see a steaming mug of what she hoped to be coffee on each tray.

When her breakfast had been set in front of her, Alanda confirmed the mug contained coffee and the bowl hot porridge laced with honey. After taking an appreciative sip of her coffee, which was rich and hot, Alanda gestured at the goblet of orange liquid. "What is this?" she asked Tsetsic directly. "Does it contain liquor?"

Rinayai kicked her lightly under the table, a reminder not to be rude. She knew he meant well, but she was very serious in her decision to let no kind of spirit pass her lips after what it had done to her father.

Tsetsic didn't seem to mind the question. "There is no liquor," he assured her. "Though we do consume ales and wines here, we rarely do so when we break our fast. This is a mixture of fruit nectar, honey, and some particular herbs we grow on the grounds. It will not alter your mind, but I believe you will find it quite pleasant. It is called *tuteoa*."

Alanda took a cautious sip, but after that it was all she could do to keep herself from gulping the rest of the goblet like an unmannered child. The first thing she wondered was how they kept it so very cold without placing ice or snow in it, but soon, even those thoughts were drowned out by the sweetness of the explosion on her taste buds. "It's wonderful!" she exclaimed. "I've never tasted anything like it!"

Tsetsic and Rinayai smiled at her enthusiasm, each sipping his own goblet. "Alis's food will be here shortly," Tsetsic told Alanda. "I apologize it was initially overlooked. I have sent one of my apprentices out to the dogs' quarters to retrieve some for her."

Alanda smiled. "Don't worry," she said. "Alis will be fine, and I am sure you will spoil her with whatever you give her, just as you are spoiling me."

Alis's food came in due time, and the four occupants of the room set to their breakfast, making little conversation. Almost the moment they were done, the young tselqs bustled back in and removed their dirty dishes, including Alis's bowl, leaving them with a clean table.

Alanda, remembering that Tsetsic had referred to the young tselqs as his apprentices, asked, "Are apprentices always treated like servants?" She earned herself another kick from Rinayai for the question, but she was genuinely curious.

Tsetsic smiled tolerantly, his broad face kind and welcoming, understanding her question. Apprentices were not usually considered servants in other professions; she was simply curious about the lives of the guardians. "Only for a short time," he said. "It imbues them with an attitude of humility and, yes, servitude, that will serve them well as they advance here. We are, after all, servants, even if not in the traditional sense. We serve the knowledge we protect for the betterment of all."

Alanda nodded, satisfied, though she wondered if the tselq women who had attended to her the night before were also apprentices. The knowledge of it gave her more insight than she had gleaned from Rinayai's instruction and her own observation, and she found it a curious way to live.

"Now," Tsetsic said, "let us discuss your purposes here, Alanda. Rinayai, am I correct in assuming you have come merely as her companion and protector, as well as to ensure she was granted entrance here?"

Rinayai nodded. "I initially owed her a life debt, a story for another time, but that debt was paid on the way here. However, I and my community have decided my time is best spent as her traveling companion for the foreseeable future."

Tsetsic did not seem to find this odd. "All right," he replied. "So, you have questions, young human."

"I do," Alanda told him. "I was told if there were answers available, I might find them here." Wasting few words, she told him of The Hunger taking her parents, of Kitz's transformation from boy to prophet, and of the mysterious origins of her mother's inflammable blue scarf. It was clear on Rinayai's face that she had revealed more to the guardian than she ever had to him or the leaders of his community, but he didn't mind overmuch. Something about the guardians prompted confidences; he supposed they were trained for just that.

Tsetsic listened without comment. When she was finished, he observed quietly, "You have been through much, young one."

Alanda nodded, not disagreeing.

"Hearing your tale in full and with the confidence of a known shaman in Rinayai, I now grant you a permanent welcome here. This is not something granted to many outside our race. Take care you receive the privilege for what it is and do not abuse it."

"I am nothing but grateful for your hospitality and for any answers your order may give me," Alanda said formally. In her mind, however, she imagined Tostig's reaction to the idea that she had been let into the confidence of yet another secretive race. Would he consider this as much an accomplishment as becoming an elf-friend?

"Come. I will give you a tour, and then - " Tsetsic broke off as a gong sounded somewhere in the distance. "Ah," he said. "Our daily ritual comes early. I apologize; we never know quite what hour to expect it. Rinayai, you may accompany me if you choose. Alanda, I am afraid I will have to lead you back to your rooms. Welcome you may be, but our rituals are not for human eyes."

Rinayai looked at Alanda questioningly, and she nodded an assurance that she and Alis would be fine. It was clear Rinayai was curious about the ritual.

Bustling down the halls more quickly than she had seen him move thus far, Tsetsic led Alanda to her rooms. She had barely entered when he and Rinayai left her. Closing the door, she turned to Alis.

"Well, girl," she said, ruffling the dog's head, "it seems the mysteries about this place never cease."

ALANDA AND ALIS spent their time further exploring their rooms. She discovered the drawers of the massive dresser were mostly empty but for an additional set of nightclothes and an additional tunic and pants. She slowly unpacked her traveling pack, putting her belongings in the drawers and the empty frame against the wall next to the fireplace with her short bow and quiver.

Next, she ran her fingers over the intricate carvings on the headboard of her bed. Interweaving vines and flowers created a beautiful pattern that wove in and out of itself and was hard to follow. Noting that the curtains at the windows had been fastened open by being drawn in on themselves, she found the ties to them were actually sewn into a little passage in the middle of the fabric, causing them to bunch when the tie was drawn, and she thought that an ingenious solution.

As she and Alis explored the sitting room next to the bedroom, she wondered what the function of the room's many mirrors were. The walls were almost completely paneled in them; accustomed only to the small, scratched mirror on the wall in the sleeping room of her house in Blackwell, it was disconcerting to see herself reflected on every side.

Does anyone need to look at themselves that much?

It occurred to her that the mirrors were not placed for the room's occupants to view themselves, but to discourage secrecy. Every corner of the small room was reflected in at least one mirror; there could be no deception of either movement or expression in that room.

It took a remarkably short time for Rinayai to knock at her door after the ritual, and when she opened the door for him, she was surprised to find a churlish, if not downright disgusted, expression on his face. "What - " she began.

"They are fools," he said harshly, passing through the bedroom and into the sitting room and plopping down in a chair in a way that was most unlike him. "Fools, all of them. And they wonder why they don't live as long as most tselqs. Bah!"

Alanda was shocked to hear him talk disparagingly about their hosts. On the way to Dachilon, he had spoken nothing but good about the guardians and their lives at the Library. "What are you talking about?" she asked him, frankly curious and a little disturbed.

"The ritual Tsetsic spoke of is something I did not witness the last time I was here. Since I was not yet qualified as a shaman, it was determined I was not yet ready for the experience."

Alanda motioned her hand for him to continue.

Rinayai grumbled in gravelly tselq for a moment before switching back to the common tongue. "Cut into the mountain like a bowl, there is a set of seats encircling what seems to be a simple spring - most of the time. Approximately once a day, however, the spring erupts into a massive fountain, shooting some sixty feet into the air and gushing for several minutes before gradually settling down again."

"How amazing!" Alanda could not help exclaiming. She had never seen or even heard of anything like that in any of her travels, nor had her trainer Alicia mentioned it.

"Yes, but what is not amazing are the noxious fumes produced by the fountain," Rinayai said grimly. "The tselqs around me made a show of breathing it in, some even using fans to waft the steam into their own faces. I could barely hold in my breakfast. The air surrounding that fountain is poisonous, and any shaman worthy of his name could tell you that."

"Does it have a bad effect on them?" Alanda asked. "Will it make you ill after one exposure?"

"I breathed as little as I could, so I should not be greatly affected," Rinayai admitted. "But yes, I am certain that this ritual, as they call it, is the reason the guardians only live half as long as the average tselq. They consider it the price they must pay for their service and their position, and they even have elaborate rituals surrounding the final months of a guardian's life. It could all be avoided if they did not visit that fountain every day!"

"There must be a reason they do it," Alanda cajoled. "Is it connected to the spirit world somehow?"

"That is at the heart of the issue," Rinayai answered. "They believe the fountain is a connection to the spirit world, and some claim visions among the fumes. I saw nothing, and I have traveled the spirit world many times."

Alanda said nothing, trying to process all Rinayai had told her. She had not known the guardians only lived half the lifespan of average tselqs, though it explained why tselqs like Tsetsic with only a few curls to their horns looked almost as old as the old shaman in Chinnua. She considered the price they must be willing to pay to join the order; it was a steep price, especially in addition to their vows of celibacy.

Not only are they denied families, but they die young. It seemed tragic, and she wondered if all the knowledge and lore they collected was really worth such a sacrifice.

Rinayai left the room to bathe his face and prepare for the tour Tsetsic had promised. Though he had seen the public areas of the Library of the Guardians once, he felt honor-bound to accompany Alanda. With his new knowledge of the reality of their daily ritual, he no longer fully trusted the guardians with Alanda's life.

Tsetsic arrived at Alanda's room just after Rinayai left. She did not mention what Rinayai had told her; she suspected she was not meant to know did not want to cause any difficulty.

Rinayai joined them a few moments later, his face freshly washed and his manner settled back into its usual calm complacency.

Tsetsic led them through many rooms of the compound, pointing out works of art in the form of woodworking, metalworking, painting, and tapestry created by the guardians of the past. Each piece had historical significance, and most told stories of times long forgotten. Alanda gaped at an ornate ball room, a dining room large enough to seat the whole village of Blackwell, and a room that seemed only to exist for the purpose of getting lost in intricate tapestries depicting war between the tselqs and a short, blue-skinned race she did not recognize. When she asked about the tapestries, Tsetsic only told her there were many secrets within the halls of the Library of the Guardians and refused to answer any further questions on the matter.

He saved the actual library as the grand finale, bringing Rinayai, Alanda, and Alis to double doors every bit as heavy and ornate as those at the entrance to the vast building. Pushing on them was apparently a signal, for as soon as he nudged them, two tselqs behind them opened the doors noiselessly.

Alanda felt herself choke up as the vastness of the library came into view, though she could not quite understand why it caused such an emotional reaction. Wiping away errant tears, she controlled herself with difficulty and gazed at the true Library of the Guardians in a beatific state of wonder that delighted Tsetsic. It reminded her of the sanctum in Blackwell, though it was many times larger. The ornate woodwork and bubbled glass windows forced memories of her home and her family into her mind, and for a moment, she was over-whelmed.

She thought the whole village square could have fit inside the library at least twice. Its ceilings extended higher than any she had ever seen, and wooden shelves reached all the way to the top with broad staircases on metal wheels attached to allow anyone to reach any of the works stored on them. Shelf after shelf covered in books and scrolls greeted Alanda's awestruck eyes, and she couldn't keep her gaze on any one place. She wanted to see all of it, to experience all of it.

"You like it?" Tsetsic asked unnecessarily.

"It's breathtaking," Alanda admitted, not taking her roaming eyes off the cavernous room. "Have you read everything here?"

Tsetsic laughed as heartily as if she had told a very funny joke. "Hardly," he told her. "No one mortal could ever live long enough to read everything here. The guardians specialize in various areas of study, become experts, and both preserve and add to the lore within that specialization."

"What is your specialization?" Alanda asked.

"Elves," Tsetsic replied simply. "More specifically, their origin stories on Ilbeor. They came long before humans, you know. Two millennia at the very least, though a precise date of their arrival is hard to pin down. They arrived from the Pasling Sea and will not reveal their origins before they came here. It's been the dearest aspiration of many guardians to find that information, but alas, if any elf alive knows, they are not willing to tell us." His voice took on a far-away quality, and he gazed over Alanda's head and into the stacks of books and scrolls as though thinking about matters far beyond the tour of the Library.

"May I read something from here?" Alanda asked, breaking into his reverie.

"My dear, during your stay here, all you have to do is tell a guardian in the Library what you would like to study and they will bring you more than you could read in a year. For today, however, other issues press us. I have notified a specialist in human language that you require help to translate old runes. That is correct, is it not?"

"As far as I know," Alanda replied, feeling excitement rush into her with the idea that she might finally have the answers she had been seeking since she left Blackwell.

"Let us adjourn for our midday meal. After, we will retrieve your mother's scarf and bring it to Waidah."

ALANDA'S STOMACH felt full of butterflies as she carried her mother's precious blue scarf down a hall near the library, Alis trotting obediently at her side. She wasn't worried about the scarf being mistreated; just the state of the library and the preservation of the artwork around the massive compound was proof the guardians took special care of the belongings entrusted to them. She was, however, nervous about what they might tell her. Would she finally find out where her mother had come from? How would it affect her future, or would it have any effect at all?

Waidah greeted them outside a nondescript doorway set in the wall of the hallway. Alanda noticed immediately that she, too, looked older than the three curls to her horns suggested, and her skin was a paler green than even the other tselqs at Dachilon. Alanda actually wondered if she was healthy, but she knew it would be rude to ask.

As she was ushered through the doorway, Alanda was relieved to find a simple room with wood-paneled walls and a rectangular table surrounded by normal, straight-backed wooden chairs meant for tselq proportions rather than human. She didn't know if she could have coped with another extravagant room while they studied her mother's origins and found the simplicity of the room comforting.

On the table, Waidah had gathered several tomes that looked very old to Alanda's eyes, their pages thick and yellowed, their covers cracked and the gold letters fading. Her eyes roamed over the books, wondering if they held answers and what those answers might be.

"Here," Waidah explained, her voice serious and low, "are reliquaries of ancient runes gathered from humans in centuries past. If there is a translation for the runes on your artifact, we shall find it in one of these." Her voice was businesslike, but not unkind, as she gestured for Alanda and her companions to sit. "Does your dog require a cushion?" she asked courteously as Alis settled herself by Alanda's side.

"No," Alanda answered, laughing in spite of her nervousness. "Alis is used to outdoor conditions and will sit or lie quite comfortably on the floor."

"Then let us get to work. Tsetsic, you may go about your own research. I will send a message to you when it is time to rejoin our guests."

Tsetsic, who had not taken a seat, bade them farewell, leaving Alanda, Rinayai, and Waidah to make sense of the scarf and the tomes that might translate it.

"Now, let me see what you have here," Waidah said brusquely. Alanda silently handed the scarf over and waited for several minutes while Waidah examined it, trying to be patient even as she counted every moment. Finally, Waidah looked up from the scarf, her earthy green face shining with anticipation. For the first time since she had greeted them, she seemed eager to proceed with the work.

"I know just what we need," she said, excitement lacing her voice as she selected a tome with a cracked, dark red cover and a single, dusty blue jewel attached to the spine. "Though the artifact is quite recent, probably made within your mother's lifetime, the language is as ancient as they come."

Alanda and Rinayai both leaned forward to view the etching on the cover of the book, but it was runic and neither of them could discern its meaning.

"The language is called *Igethi*," Waidah explained. "It was the original written language of humans. You may not realize it, child, but your language has evolved rather quickly over the centuries since your race arrived in Ilbeor. Your people have adopted the elvish alphabet from which the common tongue is derived. That is what you are literate in now." As she explained, her face took on the same faraway look Tsetsic's had when he had been discussing the origins of the elves; it was easily apparent that her interest in human languages was the passion that drove her.

Alanda nodded. She knew the alphabet she could read was elvish, but the history of human language was not something that interested her, and she was impatient for more details about her mother's scarf. "What can you tell me about my mother?" she pressed.

Waidah pursed her lips and looked at Alanda severely. "You will have to learn patience, young one," she said with an edge to her voice. "Just because I know which runic language was used does not mean I can read it like a common scroll. It will take me some time to discern the meaning behind the runes, their sounds, and the words they represent in the common tongue."

"Forgive me, Waidah," Alanda said, backtracking. She realized she had gone too far. "It is only that my brother awaits me and I have traveled a long and difficult road to get here. I apologize for my impatience."

"You are forgiven," the tselq woman told her, flashing a reassuring smile. "I assure you I will move with what speed I can, and in the meantime, there are those who might tell you more about your brother, so you may better care for him when you return."

"The guardians know about prophets, human prophets?" Alanda asked in some surprise. Was there anything these tselqs *didn't* know?

"Prophets are not my specialty, but I do know one thing from my conversations with one who knows about them: no matter their race, prophets derive their power from the same source, being, spirit, or whatever you would like to refer to it as. Not even the most learned know from whence the power comes, but they all agree the power of the prophets comes from the same place. That is all I can tell you. You will have to speak to those who specialize in prophecy, and I am certain Tsetsic has already arranged for you to do so."

Alanda nodded, hoping she could speak to the specialist in prophecy before the day was out. She knew Deena's knowledge, though impressive compared with others in Blackwell, was incomplete when it came to Kitz's transformation. The old herbalist had already told her everything she knew, and any additional information Alanda could get on the subject would only help Kitz.

Waidah rapped the table with her large knuckles three times, and a young apprentice entered the room. "Please inform Tsetsic that his guests await him," she ordered.

Though the interview had taken less than a half an hour, Rinayai and Alanda understood themselves to be dismissed. Calling softly to Alis, Alanda led the way out. When they were out of earshot of the small room, she turned to Rinayai.

"How long do you think it will take her?" she asked directly. "I need to get home." She felt uncomfortable with her own impatience, but she was also feeling an urgency she had never felt before. Though she found the Library of the Guardians and the city of Dachilon beautiful and welcoming, it was not where she belonged.

"It will take her as long as it takes her," Rinayai told her. "As she said, you must be patient. I know you want to return home, but events move apace, and we must move with the current rather than against it. Leaving here without information about your mother's heritage or your brother's condition will render your entire journey pointless.

Aside from that, I am reluctant to cross the glacier again until winter has passed, and the weather taken a turn. You must not be lost, young one. Much depends on you."

Alanda huffed in frustration. "What depends on me?" she asked, determined to finally get some answers about what the tselq had seen back in the shaman's tent in Chinnua. "You refer to my importance, but you give me no answers about why my decisions and actions have anything to do with anyone outside of my own family. What have you seen of me?"

Rinayai did not immediately answer but gazed at her seriously. After several long moments, he finally spoke. "What I saw was uncertain and ambiguous. What I know is that much centers on you and that your journeys are far from over. I hesitated to tell you only because I can give you no straightforward answers about your future. Much depends on your actions as you move forward, and on the information we will find here."

They reached the front of the building, and Alanda stared moodily out the heavy, bubbled glass windows next to the massive front doors. The tselqs attending the doors stood impassively, not meeting her eyes, and seeming to withdraw into themselves in the presence of their sudden company. Outside, it was snowing more heavily than Alanda would have expected. The snow appeared distorted through the glass, warped into fantastic shapes as though from a dream or perhaps a nightmare. She wondered what specters haunted the wilderness: the spirits Rinayai claimed were everywhere, the hand of Annuah, the mysterious gods of the Sashu, or something else, some invisible power no one had named.

She gazed in silence for several long minutes, trying to regain her patience and control herself by listening to the muted sounds around her and concentrating on nothing else. The method was met with only limited success, however. Alanda thought over what Rinayai had told her and somehow knew he was still keeping things from her. He had seen something, something definite, that had caused him to abandon his community and travel with her. Why would he not tell her what it was?

Her reverie was interrupted a short time later when Tsetsic rejoined them. "I understand you are impatient for answers," he said without preamble. "I do not blame you in the slightest. I also understand you wish to speak to a guardian who specializes in prophets and prophecy. That can certainly be done, and I have already set the wheels in motion, but it cannot be done on this day. Instead, I have some things I would like to show you in the outdoors. Will you require coats?"

"I have a coat," Alanda answered, thinking of the multicolored coat she had worn on the glacier and not wanting to inconvenience the tselqs any further. "I will need my cloak, however, or a similar head covering. I will also need gloves and stockings and to return to my room for my sun salve."

Tsetsic looked at her in astonishment while Rinayai briefly outlined what she had told him about her difficulties with the sun. "Certainly, we will get you everything you need, Alanda," Tsetsic said respectfully. "Though of course I have taken notice of your paleness, I'm afraid I had not deduced the dangers such skin might face in the sun. Tselq skin does not react to it."

"Thank you," Alanda said simply. She was glad Rinayai had explained her sun sensitivity; she grew tired of repeating the information.

They briefly returned to Alanda's rooms, where she was brought a pale yellow linen scarf, soft woolen gloves, and woolen stockings to protect her ankles. After she had smeared sun salve on her exposed skin and donned the additional clothing and her tselq coat, she was ready. With a bemused expression, Tsetsic led them out a back door and into a very large clearing, loud with the noises of various animals.

Alanda clapped her gloved hands together in genuine delight, catching several large snowflakes between them as she did so. For a moment, she almost felt as though she were home and among the herds of her village. She had always loved animals, even before she had received Alis.

"The animals provide us with food and drink in the form of eggs and milk," Tsetsic explained. "We do not slaughter them for meat, of course. They also provide us with wool for our winter clothing and other necessities. What I wanted to show you, however, are our traveling crows."

"Traveling crows?" Alanda wondered aloud. She had never heard of such a thing.

Tsetsic led them to a corner of the clearing in which a small wooden building stood on high stilts about twenty feet off the ground. "You are not afraid of heights, are you?" he asked, a teasing glint in his eye.

"Of course not!" Alanda protested, affronted. How could she effectively travel through the mountains if she had a fear of heights?

"Good, for we must climb the ladder to reach the crows' nest." He indicated a rickety-looking ladder secured to the ground with stakes and extending all the way up into a trap door on the floor of the building. "I will go first, Alanda will follow me, and Rinayai will bring up the rear. I fear Alis will have to stay at the bottom. Even if dogs could climb ladders, she would scare the crows."

"Alis, stay," Alanda commanded, readying herself to climb the ladder. Even though it was true she wasn't afraid of heights, she found the tall ladder a bit daunting. It looked as though it would collapse under the slightest weight. Shaking herself slightly, she reminded herself that tselqs regularly climbed up and down this ladder and that they weighed considerably more than she did.

Following Tsetsic, she climbed hand-over-hand up the ladder, becoming more confident with each rung. By the time she had reached the top, her uncertainty had vanished, and she felt quite at ease as she poked her head through the trapdoor into the crows' nest.

"Ah, Callum and Vritri, well met indeed." Tsetsic greeted the two tselqs who were already in the building in the common tongue. The building consisted of only one room, larger than it had seemed from the ground. The two tselqs turned, surprised, as Alanda's head popped through the trapdoor.

"This is Alanda from the village of Blackwell in the valley," Tsetsic continued by way of introduction as Alanda pulled herself into the room. "She has been made welcome here and is to be shown the courtesy of any esteemed guest."

"Well met," said Alanda, placing her palm out, face up, toward the two tselqs.

Callum, the taller of the two, did not return her greeting, but Vritri seemed to be fascinated by her and lay his own warm palm atop hers. "Well met," he replied, his eyes alight with interest.

Callum said something in tselq to Tsetsic. Though Alanda could not understand his words, his tone was harsh, and she felt chagrined.

After Rinayai had been introduced, Alanda walked around the walls of the room, all of which were lined with stacks of wooden cages holding several crows apiece. Though she did not like the captivity of the animals, she noticed there were brightly colored wooden toys in each cage, and the crows certainly seemed well fed. On each cage was a label carved into a piece of wood. The captive crows had gnawed at the edges of most of them, but all remained legible, though the inscriptions were in tselq.

"They simply tell us where each set of crows is trained to go," Vritri explained when Callum wasn't forthcoming. "A group of crows is called a 'murder', if you can believe it."

"Why?" Alanda asked, startled.

"It started with the elves," Vritri explained. "When they first came to Ilbeor, they noted that crows often feast on the dead. Somewhere along the way, someone began calling a group of crows a murder because they signified death. The elves find great meaning in it. These particular murders are trained to go to specific places throughout Ilbeor. These, for example, travel to the humans' Sanctum of Oaos." He pointed to one of the cages, waggling his thick finger at the cawing birds. Alanda noticed his use of the common tongue was nearly perfect, his accent light. She wondered how often he found occasion to use it, living strictly among tselqs.

"Would I be able to send a crow to Blackwell to ask about my brother?" Alanda asked interestedly. She had resigned herself to not communicating with her village on the journey; perhaps now there was a way she could.

"No," Callum said brusquely in the common tongue. "They are trained to be sent to specific places and your *village* is not on the list of important places they are trained to go." He spat the word as if it were a curse instead of a simple designation of one place among many.

"These," Vritri broke in, obviously trying to distract her from her disappointment, "are trained for Emelle."

Callum seemed to feel Vritri was giving Alanda too much information and again spoke harshly in tselq. Alanda, feeling awkward, asked about the group of crows apparently content to wander about the floor, plucking bits of food and insects that had fallen from the cages.

"Oh, these?" Vritri laughed. "These are simply my friends, not trained to go anywhere. They stay near me because I feed them. Most crows are very self-sufficient, making them excellent messengers. They go on long journeys at speed and find their own food. They will eat nearly anything and are loyal to those who are kind to them."

Alanda knelt to examine the black, pecking birds. They did not look special to her; crows were simply a part of life. She had never imagined they had any special skills. She idly wondered if any of the crows she'd seen throughout her life had actually been messengers from the Library of the Guardians. She somehow found the idea to be disconcerting, though she couldn't fathom why.

Callum spoke again in the common tongue, though he didn't address Alanda directly. "Tsetsic, it is time for her to go. She should not be here. She is aggravating the birds with her strange look and scent."

"The well-being of the birds is Callum's responsibility," Vritri explained apologetically to Alanda.

Tsetsic took this in stride, not surprised by Callum's belligerence. He indicated Rinayai should descend first. Alanda, not knowing what she had done to offend Callum, felt she should offer some kind of apology, but what was she supposed to apologize for? Existing? Wordlessly, she followed Rinayai down the ladder to the snowy ground.

To her surprise, Vritri followed them, his personal murder of crows flying out the slotted windows of the tall building and joining him on the ground. "I have never met a human before," he said frankly.

Alanda smiled. "Well, now you have."

"Would you like to join us as I show Alanda our fields and herb gardens?" Tsetsic offered.

Alanda could see that Rinayai was not pleased, but he didn't interfere as Vritri and his birds joined them.

Time passed strangely in the Library of the Guardians.

Alanda often felt as though the wait for information she needed would never end, but then she would realize three or four days had passed without her noticing it. While they waited on Waidah to translate her mother's scarf and Acala, a guardian who specialized in prophecy, to find out what he could about Kitz's situation, Alanda and Alis were given leave to access all the public parts of the Library and the grounds of Dachilon.

On the first day after talking to Waidah, Alanda wandered into the library, again marveling at all the books and scrolls available in the immense room. Feeling shy, she approached one of the tselqs bustling about among the shelves and asked if she might read something.

"Certainly," the tselq said quietly; hushed voices seemed to be appropriate in the library. "What would you like to examine, young human?"

Alanda thought about it for a moment. Though she was literate, she had not been exposed to much text as a messenger beyond the instructions and maps she had been entrusted with. Her family only owned one book, a collection of stories given to them by Theldan one Winter Celebration, and she had enjoyed reading that. Thinking of it, she said, "I like stories, especially old ones. Do you have anything like that?"

The tselq chuckled. "Do you want to read of elves, tselqs, humans, dwarves, or Twanai?" she asked. "We have stories of all the races within these walls, and many are in the common tongue. I presume you are not literate in the other languages of the land?" She asked the question kindly, but Alanda suddenly felt ashamed and unworldly as she shook her head.

"I'd like to read about the elves," Alanda said finally, after considering the matter for a few moments. She thought that, given her status as an elf-friend, it might do her good to understand some of their literature.

"Certainly," the tselq said, leading her through the shelves to another area of the library. "I am Kwandah," the tselq told her as they walked. "Since I have been raised from my apprenticeship, the library has been my place. I will study here until I find a specialty that ignites my passion. Such is the way of the guardians."

Alanda noticed that Kwandah only had two curls to her horns and that her skin had not yet taken on the lighter green color she had begun to associate with the guardians. She surmised the tselq hadn't been here terribly long and, if Rinayai was correct about the poisonous nature of the geyser, hadn't been exposed to it for many years, either.

Kwandah's long, black ponytail swayed as she walked, tracing invisible patterns along the back of her yellow woolen dress. She finally reached the section she was looking for and pointed upward. "The scrolls of elven stories are up there," she said. "You will find many written in elvish script and some in tselq, but many are also written in the common tongue."

Alanda felt overwhelmed as she gazed up at the many scrolls on the shelf Kwandah had indicated. How could she choose only one?

Noticing her gaze, the tselq's broad face took on an understanding expression. "Would you like me to select one for you?" she asked kindly.

"Please," said Alanda, relieved. Perhaps after she had gotten her bearings, she would feel comfortable ascending the rolling staircases up to the upper levels and selecting things herself, but for now she was much more comfortable allowing Kwandah to do it.

Kwandah ascended a staircase close to the shelves of elven scrolls and picked through them. She rejected several, muttering to herself in tselq, before selecting one, a thick scroll tied closed with a red fabric thong. "This will be just the thing for you," she said. "I read it in my apprenticeship and found it gripping."

Alanda wasn't sure what Kwandah meant by calling a piece of literature gripping, but the recommendation suited her.

As the tselq came down the steps, she held out the scroll to Alanda. "I am sure I don't have to tell you to be careful," she said. "The parchment is not particularly fragile, but this is an illustrated tome and we would not want anything to happen to it. We would not want it to tear or have candle wax dripped on it, for example."

"I'll treat it with care," Alanda said. She looked to her left and saw a small alcove next to a window, a small table and chairs situated within it. "May I sit there?" She indicated the table.

"Of course," Kwandah said. "I will go back to my own studies, but should you need anything at all, please call on me or any other in the library. It is our pleasure to assist guests."

Alanda thanked her again and took the scroll to the alcove. She untied the thong and unrolled the scroll. The top of it was inscribed with a beautifully embellished title, "The Ballad of Ilvisar and His Ill-Fated Love".

Alanda was intrigued. She had never read anything particularly romantic; the stories in the books at home had been mostly tales of adventure and heroism. By the light coming through the bubbled glass window next to her, she began to read.

It did not take her long to become completely absorbed in the story, though she read slowly and often had to sound out some of the longer words. Ilvisar, a young elf from Caalenor, the great and ancient elven city in the Chilpar Mountains to the north, had fallen in love with a human princess, Amelyn, on his journey to the royal city of Emelle. The scroll detailed the many adventures he had trying to win her hand, and Alanda was enthralled by the rhythm of the words and the rich details that made her feel that she, herself, was witnessing Ilvisar's adventures firsthand. This was nothing like anything she had ever read; this was a work of art as well as the telling of a story.

Alanda read for hours, the task becoming easier as she sat in the alcove, the words flowing more smoothly the longer she read. She only stopped when Alis, who had been lying patiently next to her on the floor, whined softly.

Alanda looked up. The light in the window had changed; it must be close to midafternoon, and Alis likely needed a trip outside. Reluctantly, Alanda re-rolled the scroll and tied the red fabric thong back around it, being exceedingly gentle in her movements. Taking the scroll in her hand, she set off to find Kwandah to return it to its shelf.

She found the tselq at a larger table near the center of the library, several books in front of her as she ran her fingers along the page of an open one. Glancing at it, Alanda could not read the script and inferred it must have been in tselq. She cleared her throat softly, not wanting to startle Kwandah.

Kwandah looked up and smiled at Alanda. "Did you enjoy the story?" she asked, seeming completely unperturbed by being interrupted.

"Very much, though I didn't get to finish it," Alanda said. "My dog needs to go outside for some activity, I think."

"We shall set aside a small shelf for you to store it so you may finish it at your convenience." Kwandah got up and led Alanda to the back of the library and a series of smaller slots in a bookshelf, most of which held varied articles of literature and history. "Here, we keep that which we wish to examine again," she explained. She indicated one of the empty slots. "You may place the scroll here and return to it whenever you wish. As you find other things to read, you may use this space for them as well."

Alanda gently placed "The Ballad of Ilvisar and His Ill-Fated Love" into the slot, taking care not to crinkle the edges against the wooden sides of the compartment. "Thank you for everything, Kwandah," she said sincerely as she followed the tselq back towards the front of the library. "I think I shall spend a lot of time in here," she added frankly, again gazing up at the thousands of tomes the library held.

Kwandah smiled, indicating to the two apprentices behind the heavy double doors that Alanda wished to leave. As they pulled them open, she said, "You are welcome anytime, young human. We shall keep your scroll safe for you in the meantime."

ALIS SOON TOOK up with the Dachilon dogs, who worked as companions for certain guardians and herders for their flocks of live-stock and sheep. Alanda gleefully watched as Alis mimicked the herding dogs, following as they rounded up sheep and herded them into their enclosures. It was the perfect activity for Alis who, Alanda suspected, might be getting bored with her long sojourns in the library, compared to the active lifestyle she had been raised in.

Four days after Alanda had been shown the crows' nest, she stood in the yard watching Alis cavort with three other dogs in a snowy patch of the clearing, knowing she'd have to give Alis a bath before their evening meal. Lost in thought, she started a bit when she heard an unfamiliar voice from just behind her.

"Am I interrupting?" Vritri asked, smiling kindly at her, the skin around his wide eyes crinkling.

"What?" Alanda asked, startled out of good manners and polite greetings. She mastered herself, however, and continued, "No, of course not. I'm just watching Alis play. It's good to see her with other dogs. I think she misses the companionship of her kind." She indicated the snowy wrestling match.

Vritri laughed. "It looks like four dogs will need baths this afternoon. The apprentices will be so pleased."

"I'll take care of Alis." Alanda didn't want Vritri to think she would burden the apprentices with Alis's care.

The two stood in companionable silence for a few moments, watching the dogs play. "What brought you to this place?" Alanda asked suddenly. Of all the guardians she had met, she found Vritri the least intimidating and felt reasonably comfortable asking. It was a subject she had been curious about since first coming to Dachilon.

"Ah, my journey differed from that of most of the guardians," Vritri said. "Would you like to hear about it?"

"I would," Alanda answered sincerely.

"I did not come here directly from my community. Usually, guardians feel the call between the first and second curl of their horns and travel to Dachilon at that time. My path, however, began in rebellion."

"Tselqs rebel?" Alanda asked in surprise. They seemed like such a peaceful, orderly race. It did not seem in character to think of them as rebels.

"Not many do," Vritri answered honestly, "but there are outliers in every race. Before the first curl of my horns was complete, I found the farming life of tselq children was not to my liking, and I begged my parents to withdraw me from the gardens and allow me to work with my father, who was a horse trainer. Of course, they did not do any such thing; I am not sure if it would have been allowed even if they had wanted to. Instead of being obedient, I ran from my community and resolved to live on my own terms."

"How many years old were you when this happened?" Alanda asked. She knew the curls on the horns showed tselqs' age, but she had never known exactly how they correlated.

Vritri thought for a moment. "It is hard to say, for we do not count time in the same way as humans. As I said, I had not even grown into my first curl, though it was fast approaching. Perhaps nine or ten years?"

Alanda thought about Kitz and herself at that age. Neither of them would have had the skills to survive in the wild that young, but tselqs were raised differently. "How did you survive?" she asked curiously.

"My community was in the Chilpar Mountains, close to the shore of the Unresting Sea. I will not lie: there were times I thought I would not survive the first year, but I knew my community would not take me back without repercussion. Also, I did not want to return to the stringent life laid out for me there."

"Yet you came here," Alanda pondered, "where life seems even more inflexible."

"I learned to hunt and fish, to make small tools and gather the fruits of the forest. I was young enough at the time the transition to eating meat was not difficult, as I needed to for survival. I found a small cave, a crawlspace, really, where I was protected from the elements. I shared the cliff face with the Western Dragons."

"Dragons!" Alanda was thrown off her original questions. "What were they like?"

"Large," Vritri answered simply. "Dangerous and mean, but beautiful in their own way. Their scales are as hard as rock and vary in all the shades of the rainbow, their wings leathery like a bat's, and their caves nearly always emitted steam or even fire. I took care not to get too close, but I often saw them fly over the sea or the forest to hunt."

Alanda wondered how close to a real dragon her wooden figures came. She had whittled some over the past few days, but never where she could be seen. She thought she might show Vritri her creation when it was finished and let him judge its realism.

"So, you wanted to know why I came here?" Vritri asked after a pause.

"Yes," said Alanda, refocusing.

"That part was quite similar to the experiences of others," he told her. "Though I waited a while before I answered the call. My second curl had fully formed before I came to Dachilon."

"What do you mean by 'the call?'" Alanda asked.

"It is hard to explain, though I hear a similar phenomenon happens to acolytes in your religion. It is a feeling within you, but outside of you, pulling you. The call is what brings most guardians to Dachilon, though a few simply come because they envy our life here. We live in relative comfort, with less manual labor and easier winters."

"But you pay for it," said Alanda, thinking of the vows of celibacy and shortened lifespans of the guardians.

"We do," Vritri admitted. "But most of us consider it worth the price. To seek knowledge is a noble thing, and to preserve it guides the five races into the future."

"So why did you ignore the call when you first felt it?"

"For the same reason I left my community: I rebelled. I did not want to leave the freedom I had. Over time, however, the call became impossible to ignore. I suppose it was fated I come here, demanded by the spirits watching over me."

Alanda sympathized with some of what Vritri said. Though she had never rebelled against anything, she found solace in the isolation of the wilderness with only Alis by her side. She enjoyed providing for herself and having few demands on her behavior. She could hum, sing, or whistle without anyone looking askance at her. If she wanted to run, she ran. If she wanted to amble, she ambled. She had greatly enjoyed her life as a messenger, but she was acutely aware it was coming to an end.

"What is your specialty?" she finally inquired, realizing she didn't know even this most basic of information about her new friend.

"Animals, of course," Vritri chuckled, indicating the clearing and the snow-covered grazing fields beyond. "I study animal husbandry and the history of the interactions between various animals and the five races. Did you know tselqs have been breeding dogs for millennia? Our origin stories mention the first domesticated dogs in Ilbeor came when the tselqs arrived from the Unresting Sea."

"I had no idea," Alanda said. "No wonder you are so good at it. The messenger dogs are always so hearty and healthy; it is truly a marvel how well they are bred."

"No one knows where domesticated cats came from," Vritri continued, nodding acknowledgement at her praise of tselq dog-breeding methods, "though some opine that their origins trace back to the elves' arrival here. We tselqs breed cats as well, as you probably know, but even we do not know their origins."

"I knew that," Alanda said a bit wistfully. "I always wanted a cat as a child. My friend Maryah had one, and it was the sweetest thing. But my family was poor and couldn't afford to buy a cat, much less feed and care for one."

"Perhaps someday you shall have a cat." Unknown to Alanda, Vritri was already making plans for how he might gift her one after she returned to her village.

"Perhaps," Alanda said, but laughed as she turned her attention back to the dogs playing. "For now, though, I have my hands full with Alis."

Over the next weeks, Vritri seemed to turn up often wherever Alanda happened to be, whether in the clearing watching Alis play, in the library devouring elvish stories and the human poetry for which she had discovered a love, or even in the private dining room she shared with Tsetsic and Rinayai. Alanda didn't mind the intrusions. Vritri was interesting, knowledgeable, and kind, but most of all, he helped pass the seemingly interminable time on Alanda's hands as she waited, especially since Rinayai had become absorbed in studies of his own, spending most of his hours in the library among the books and scrolls.

Over a month after her initial meeting with Waidah, Tsetsic found Alanda and Vritri teasing Vritri's murder of crows with bits of stale bread they had cajoled from the cooks. "Waidah awaits you," he told her. "I believe she has found the answers you seek."

ALANDA ONLY TOOK time for the briefest of washes and to remove her outdoor clothing before rushing to meet Waidah in the same small room in which they had first met. Vritri accompanied her after asking if she minded if he came along, and she was glad for the company.

When they reached the room, she found it already fairly cramped around the rectangular wooden table: Rinayai, Tsetsic, and Waidah were already there waiting. She took a seat in the lone remaining chair, leaving Vritri to stand behind her and Alis to sit next to her on the floor. The room was crowded, but to Alanda it felt warm and inviting. Whatever she was about to find out about her mother, she would find out surrounded by friends.

Her mind was already racing with the possibilities. Was her mother a witch, raised in Ferncombe? Was she a member of the nobility of Emelle, as the High Priest and Deena had suggested? Was it something else entirely? She already knew her mother had come to Blackwell when she was no older than Alanda herself, and that she had come alone, but Dandelion had never shared her origins with anyone in the village. Somehow, a mysterious past did not seem odd when it came to her mother. She had skills no one in the village had taught her; she knew how to do things no one else in the village could.

"These runes are astonishing," Waidah said, spreading the scarf over the table with a small flourish. "As I suspected, they are written in Igethi, and I would wager the person who embroidered this for your mother was a witch or warlock from Ferncombe. That is the only place where they might still know the language. It is said they study and use ancient languages to add to their secret communications and in an attempt to weave spells, though they are not usually magicians. Of course, none of that can be proven; Ferncombe is unusually secretive, especially for humans." Waidah looked ready to give them all a full lesson on what little she knew about the witches and wizards in the far north, but Alanda forestalled her.

"Was my mother a witch, then?" As she asked, Alanda thought suddenly that it really was the most likely answer. Though not magicians, those raised in Ferncombe were said to be expert herbalists, skilled far beyond those who inhabited the other human villages in the valley. Dandelion's ability to create the perfumes and soaps might speak to that; it did seem miraculous she was able to extract such potent scents from the flowers in her fields.

"No," Waidah replied gently, looking at Alanda with an indescribable expression. She seemed almost nervous about revealing what she had found. Finally, she asked, "Does the name Alianor mean anything to you?"

"Not at all," Alanda answered, nonplussed. "Who is Alianor?" She wondered if that might be the name of the seamstress who had made the scarf.

"Your mother," Waidah told her. "You told me her name was Dandelion, and I am not sure from where she took that name, but she was born Alianor of Sovaria. It was for her this artifact was made, possibly at or near the time of her birth."

"Sovaria…" Alanda said, her voice trailing off as she realized the implications. Sovaria was the name of the royal family of Ilbeor, the human rulers from the city of Emelle, isolated on a lone mountain far to the northwest. "My mother was royalty?"

"More than that," Waidah pressed. "Your mother was a princess, sister to King Florian, who currently sits on the human throne."

Alanda suddenly felt dizzy. She had accepted that her mother might have been nobility. But royalty? The sister to the king? It was beyond Alanda's understanding how such a person could have ended up in Blackwell, married to a leatherworker and living on the outskirts. It defied logic.

No one spoke for several minutes, all waiting for Alanda to recover herself as she absorbed the news. When she found her voice, she asked, "Can you be certain the person the scarf was given to was actually my mother? Maybe it belonged to someone else originally. Maybe…" she trailed off, knowing she was grasping at straws.

"The only way to know for certain would be to ask your mother herself," Tsetsic offered. "But what you might not be aware of is that, approximately eighteen years ago, Alianor of Sovaria disappeared, having run away from her family with a member of the palace staff. The search was vast and far-reaching, and I was only an apprentice here when the news of her disappearance was brought by crow. The young man's name was, I believe, Gideon. Does that sound familiar to you?"

"No," Alanda said. "My father's name was Jondolan, and he had lived in Blackwell his entire life before meeting my mother. The one thing I know for certain is that she came to Blackwell alone and nearly starved to death. The blacksmith took her in, and she married my father not even a year later."

Tsetsic and Waidah both nodded. "Alianor was never found," Tsetsic continued, "but if your mother arrived in Blackwell alone and changed her name, it is likely no one in such a remote village made the connection. In fact, it is possible no one in Blackwell even knew of the princess's disappearance."

Alanda thought this over for a few moments. The story fit: the timeline, her mother's possession of the scarf, and the remote location of Blackwell all made sense. Somehow, however, the idea of her mother running away from her life and duties in Emelle for the sake of a forbidden love seemed out of character. Dandelion, though devoted to her husband and family, had never been demonstrative with Jondolan, instead treating him with a friendly partnership that didn't suggest any kind of deep romantic connection. Alanda had never found this odd. Marriages in Blackwell were often arranged by the couple's parents for reasons that rarely included romantic love. She knew the blacksmith had helped broker Dandelion's match with Jondolan, and now, thinking about it, Alanda supposed it would have been one of the first concerns. A young, unwed woman without a family would have to be married as quickly as possible.

Above all these considerations, however, Alanda somehow felt certain that what Waidah said was true. Though it had seemed unbelievable at first, she knew her mother had indeed been Alianor of Sovaria, which meant she was the daughter of a princess of the highest nobility in the land.

Her mind immediately went to Kitz, living a quiet life with Maryah, Serill, and Isaac, and she knew what she had to do to protect him. "No one can know," she said, her voice stern and strong in the silence. She was suddenly implacable, and everyone at the table looked surprised. "No one outside this room."

"Why?" Vritri finally had the courage to ask what no one else would.

"For Kitz. He is the nephew of the king and would be taken away from all he knows and forced to live among strangers and serve an unknown purpose in Emelle. No."

"Nephew of the king," Vritri muttered, seemingly to himself. Then, louder, he said, "There is more you ought to consider."

"Oh?" Alanda said, arching one pale eyebrow at him. "And what is that?"

"King Florian does not have a blood heir," Tsetsic supplied. "He has adopted an heir from one of the greater noble houses, a young human now known as Prince Gildan. Were blood relatives found who could succeed the throne, that adoption would be in question. Blood is everything in the royal house."

Alanda felt dizzy again. She knew of Prince Gildan, of course; it was impossible to live anywhere in Ilbeor without knowing the names of the members of the house of Sovaria, but the idea that she or Kitz could challenge the succession was preposterous. She would not allow it. "My mother left her family for a reason," she said. "Obviously, the scarf charts her lineage and royal history, but not the events of her lifetime. Am I correct?"

"Yes," Waidah replied. "The scarf's runes form a celebratory song of sorts, proclaiming Alianor's birth to Royal Mother Alesia. As first-born, she would have claimed the succession had she been male, but as a woman she was placed behind her younger brother. The song waxes poetic of Alianor's beauty and status and claims for her a rich future. It was a fitting gift for a princess. I should very much like to know who made it." Waidah looked wistful at the lack of this information.

Alanda laughed bitterly, thinking of her beautiful, serene mother eking out a bare existence by the work of her hands, often without the help of her drunken husband. Surely that was not the life for which she had left her royal family behind.

"I will not take Kitz to Emelle, much less to the palace. I will not claim my status as a member of the royal family, nor do so on behalf of my brother. This news shall not leave this room. Are we agreed?" Her tone brokered no argument.

One by own, Waidah, Rinayai, Tsetsic, and Vritri swore to her that her mother's lineage would not pass from their lips to anyone outside the room. She nodded, satisfied. When she returned to Blackwell, she would simply tell them the origins of her mother's scarf could not be identified, and she and Kitz would resume their normal lives in the village, or as normal as they could manage. "Now," she said, "as soon as I learn what there is to know about my brother, I will make my way back to Blackwell, where we belong."

"I have news to that end, Alanda," Tsetsic said, and Alanda detected a note of reverence in his voice that had certainly not been there before. She didn't like it.

"What is it?" she asked brusquely. Truthfully, she wanted nothing more than to return to her rooms and take one of the guardians' famous hot baths. She needed to think in solitude.

"I was told just before we met today that Acala has information for you regarding your brother and what might be known about his future."

"Where is he?" she asked before looking at Waidah. "Are we through here? May I have my mother's scarf?"

Waidah nodded silently. She had not known how Alanda would react to the news, but she was surprised at the vehemence of the girl's refusal to claim her royal status. In her limited experience, humans were power- and status-hungry. Alanda seemed to be an exception.

Without another word, Alanda gathered the scarf, folding it carefully before looking expectantly at Tsetsic. "Lead the way," she commanded.

ALANDA WAS unsurprised when the entire group, including Waidah, followed her from the small room into the main library to find Acala. Alanda didn't feel the awe she usually felt when entering the library; her mind was spinning with the information she had been given and anticipation for what she might learn, and she hardly noticed the shelves of books and scrolls.

She reminded herself to focus as Tsetsic expertly wound his way through the stacks to an alcove where Acala waited, sitting alone, a single scroll in front of him rather than the stacks of books Alanda had expected. Though she had never actually met the tselq who specialized in prophecy, she had compared him to Waidah in her mind and had expected to find him sitting amongst the evidence of his research.

Only one other chair was available at the small, circular table. Alanda took it without hesitation, motioning for Alis to settle next to her and leaving the others to arrange themselves behind her.

"What have you found?" she asked Acala bluntly. She was too tired and too overwhelmed to bother with the niceties of polite greetings and introductions.

Acala did not seem troubled by her mood. He calmly offered her the single scroll, which was sealed with dark blue wax embellished by the guardians' symbol: a tree, which, upon close examination, grew with scrolls instead of leaves.

"This is for you," he said, his voice heavily accented. It was clear he was not accustomed to the common tongue. "I took the liberty of writing all I know about your brother's condition, in the common tongue, of course. You should have no trouble reading it." Though Alanda had not been aware of him, he had often observed her reading for hours in her little alcove in the library.

"Thank you." Alanda accepted the scroll, placing it on the table in front of her without opening it. "But I would still like to hear what you have to say about Kitz." She used his name on purpose, reminding everyone they were speaking of a real person, a child, not an abstract.

"As you know, I was unable to send messengers to your village to learn anything specific about Kitz," Acala began, and Alanda was grateful he took her cue and referred to her brother by name. "The season is not amenable to travel over the glacier. That does not mean, however, that I was unable to come to any conclusions about him."

Alanda nodded, gesturing for him to continue.

"Most of what Tsetsic told me about Kitz aligns with what I know of prophets and prophecies, particularly among humans, though the transformation and condition is similar among all the races. Kitz experienced death, purification through fire, and rebirth. This is what your herbalist told you. Am I correct?"

"Yes," Alanda said. "Kitz was infected by The Hunger along with my parents, and one of my village leaders confirmed his death before they burned the house. No one can explain how he yet lives."

"What your herbalist might not have grasped was that the death he experienced was a true death, one in which his spirit left his body."

"Has his spirit joined Annuah?" Alanda asked. This was not something she had considered. Was the boy she had left behind with Maryah and Serill actually her brother, or was he truly just a shell?

"Annuah, if you like, or the spirits of the ancestors as the tselqs believe, or the great nothingness as the elves believe," Acala continued, not perturbed by her question. "He retains few memories of his life before The Hunger."

Alanda's eyes filled with tears. Kitz was really dead. Her brother was gone. A small sob escaped her, and she felt Alis snuggle up against her leg. Rinayai put his hand on her shoulder, but she shook it off.

"What does this mean for him?" She stifled her unhappiness in the face of the decisions she had to make.

"It is not for him you must make your decisions, but for yourself," Acala said, seeming to understand what she was struggling with. "The only vital thing for Kitz is that he must not be separated from the child who shares his thoughts. It is extraordinary he found one attuned to him so quickly and so close to home. Many prophets go years before they meet the one who can speak for them."

"Isaac is the only person in all of Ilbeor who can hear Kitz's thoughts?" Alanda asked sharply. The coincidence was too much. "He's only a child, barely more than a baby."

"There is only ever one."

Pushing the sheer unlikeliness aside, Alanda felt a stirring of pity for Isaac, Maryah, and Serill. They would be forever tied to Kitz, who could not even offer them gratitude or affection in return. *There may be some honor in being a prophet's mouthpiece,* she thought, *but that seems a poor repayment for the normalcy Isaac will never know.* With a pang, she remembered the normalcy she had fought the nobles for on Kitz's behalf and wondered if it even mattered.

"There may be outside forces at work," Acala continued, his voice still calm and measured. "Annuah, if you will, may have placed Isaac and Kitz in one another's lives for this very purpose. You may take some comfort from that."

"Comfort?" Alanda's eyes went as cold as her voice. "You tell me my brother is dead and his only solace will come from a small child who will never have a chance at a normal life, and you *dare* to tell me to take comfort?"

"Alanda," Rinayai murmured, "Acala is simply relaying what he knows of your brother's condition."

Alanda turned her eyes on him, and for the first time he realized how icy blue her irises actually were. They held no contrition and no mercy as she looked at them, but he read a deep desolation hiding behind her anger. She turned back to Acala, unflinching. "What more can you tell me?"

Acala met her gaze, addressing her without an ounce of sympathy. "For the rest of his life, Kitz will do nothing more than follow simple commands in his own tongue and speak prophecy as it is given to him. He will learn no skills not mastered prior to his death, and he will have forgotten all but the simplest of matters: dressing, eating, drinking, relieving himself, and the like. Preferences from before his death are but shadows of memories; even as his channeler relates them, Kitz understands little of his own thoughts. He will never again speak unless it is to relay prophecy."

Alanda nodded, swallowing hard and working to keep her stern facade, though both Rinayai and Vritri noticed a slight sagging of her shoulders, previously held rigid.

"These...prophecies." She stumbled over the word. "Will they always be riddles?"

"Kitz says what he is given to say, though we know not what power directs him. It is not uncommon for prophets to speak in rhyme or riddle. Again, we do not know why. What do you remember of the prophecy he gave before you left your village?" Acala's eyes gleamed, eager for more information to add to what he already knew. This was his first chance to speak to someone who had actually witnessed a prophet fulfilling his purpose, and he was very curious about what she would tell him.

Alanda shook her head. "I don't remember it word for word," she said. "Something about legacy and white, a spire of lies…we couldn't understand what he meant."

Acala nodded, disappointed in her answer, and stood, abruptly ending the meeting. "I have told you all I can. You will find the information I have given you within the scroll, as well as some other small details."

Alanda sat on the carved wooden chair as though she was made of ice. One by one, her companions left, save for Alis and Rinayai. Finally, Rinayai spoke.

"You should return to your rooms. You have discovered much today, and your world has changed whether or not you yet admit to it. You need time alone to think."

Alanda nodded woodenly, got up, and wove her way through the shelves without a word. Alis followed without being asked, but Rinayai stayed back. Alanda knew the way to her rooms, and he felt she would not benefit from his companionship in her current state.

When Alanda reached her rooms, she pulled the light metal chain next to her door, summoning one of the female apprentices. She had only done this a handful of times; she preferred to be as self-sufficient as possible and rather disliked the practice of forcing the apprentices into servitude.

Minutes later, a tselq Alanda didn't recognize knocked at her door.

"What do you need?" the tselq asked Alanda, dipping her head quickly as though not accustomed to the gesture. Alanda noticed her horns had only just reached their second curl; she had probably only recently arrived in Dachilon.

"Could I have a hot bath, please?" Alanda asked politely, tempering her mood to speak to the apprentice as an equal.

"Of course," the young tselq replied. She turned to leave.

"Wait," Alanda said, stopping the tselq in her tracks. She had a request, though she felt she was taking advantage of her status by asking. Even so, she wanted it so badly she eschewed her usual reluctance to ask too much of the apprentices.

"Yes?"

"Could I please have lavender bath things? Oils, soaps, anything you have available?" Lavender had been Dandelion's favorite scent. *Alianor,* she corrected herself. *Not Dandelion.*

"I will see what I can do." The young tselq actually smiled before she once again took her leave, seeming to understand that the request was important to this strange, pale guest.

A mere half hour later, Alanda sat in the hot, scented water, the smell of lavender surrounding her, the steam seeming to enter her very soul as she breathed.

"Mama," she whispered into the empty room. "Mama, what do I do?"

Alanda broke into sobs when no answer came, and those sobs became wails as she wallowed in the hot water and her own misery. She grieved for her parents, gone in body and spirit. She grieved for her brother, knowing now he was forever lost to her. She grieved for the life she had once had. She even grieved for the flickering hope of the life she had dreamed of making with Tostig. At that moment, everything she had loved seemed lost.

Sitting on the stone floor next to the tub, Alis pointed her nose toward the ceiling and howled, echoing Alanda's heartbroken cries.

When Rinayai heard Alis's howls, he sprang to his feet and rushed from his rooms, worried Alanda had done something desperate in her grief or that some other danger had befallen her. When he reached her door and heard her echoing cries underneath Alis's howls, he understood. Dipping his head, he took his hand from the silver doorknob and returned to his rooms. His heart ached for her, and it ached even more knowing he couldn't help.

VRITRI WAS NOT PRESENT to hear Alanda's cries; he was not permitted to accompany her to her rooms. After he had heard all there was to hear from Waidah and Acala, he returned to his evening duties, feeding and caring for the animals and ensuring the apprentices cleaned and refreshed kennels and stalls correctly.

As he worked, he thought hard. He had developed a genuine affection for the girl called Alanda, and he knew that affection would only grow as she spent the rest of the winter there. They shared a love of animals, and their conversations were easy and pleasant. He already dreaded her departure, knowing he would not be free to leave Dachilon for years, if ever.

Still, there were other matters to consider, matters of much more import than his new friendship. He wrestled with his options while he worked, and by the time his work was completed and the apprentices had gone inside, he had made his decision.

Crunching through the packed snow while avoiding mud puddles created by the animals, Vritri made sure he was alone before pulling out a tiny scroll, an unadorned feather quill, and a bottle of black ink he always carried. Quickly scratching a message using one of his knees as a makeshift table, he blew on the ink to dry it, waiting impatiently until he could safely roll the parchment and tie it closed with a thin linen band. He wanted to be done with this business, which he suddenly found unpleasant, although he never had before.

Still kneeling in the middle of the yard, he pursed his lips and made a soft, chirruping whistle. Immediately, his murder of crows flocked to him.

"I have work for one of you today," he said grimly, selecting one crow.

Tying the tiny scroll to its leg, Vritri carried the crow in one hand and climbed the ladder to the crows' nest, empty but for the crows waiting in their cages. Releasing the crow into the clear evening, he watched it fly off, beginning its journey over land and sea.

Before the crow was even out of sight, Vritri regretted sending it.

BLESSED

*T*ostig's surroundings surprised him. He was not in his quarters, but in a much larger cave with more furniture. Sitting up and automatically reaching to his right for Ziva, he realized he was not on a pallet on the floor, but on a raised platform. He opened his eyes fully, searching for his dog.

He found Ziva curled on a mattress on the floor, her familiar blanket arranged around her. He pulled his hand back, smiling. He didn't want to disturb her.

It took him a moment before another oddity presented itself: he had not awoken in the dark. The room was dimly lit by a single globe fastened to the opposite wall. He frowned. Ziva was fast asleep, meaning it must be night. She unfailingly awoke at *uht* each morning, despite the lack of natural light. This didn't bother him; whatever new situation was presenting itself to him, he felt at peace with it. His mind fairly radiated tranquility, and this in and of itself was new.

As his eyes and mind cleared, he took stock of his surroundings. Situated against a relatively flat wall opposite him was the expected table and chair, but the table was much larger. Near it, a small, round table separated two chairs with curved rockers, reminiscent of the chair his mother had rocked his younger sisters in. Looking straight ahead, he found another table, a half-circle carved with depictions of a small, bunched fruit, holding a metal ewer and bowl. The room was otherwise unadorned, but compared to the space he was used to, he found it rich and even frivolously appointed.

"*Iluma.*" He wiped the sleep from his eyes as he said the familiar incantation. Several more globe lights blinked into being, bathing the room in their soft yellow glow. Ziva raised her head and looked around. Finding Tostig, she went to him, nuzzling and licking his hand. He beamed at her.

"Tostig," a voice said, startling him. "You're awake. You have slept for quite some time."

Cecy stood at the entrance, bearing a wooden tray laden with large portions of meat, bread, cheese, and ale. "You do not have to eat if you are not hungry, but you have missed many meals."

Tostig took a moment to evaluate his own body. He hadn't noticed it before, but now he realized his stomach felt hollow.

"Thank you." He stood, moving toward the table in his woolen nightclothes.

Cecy took no notice of his state of undress. "You must have questions," she began after he had eaten most of his meal in silence. She rocked idly in one of the chairs, as though their meeting was a simple conversation between friends on a winter's night.

"Not many," he said, surprising himself. "For the first time since I came to this place, I can see clearly."

It was true. So many things he had wondered about since becoming a magician had become apparent to him in that one blinding moment of contact with Sado.

The father god of the Sashu.

The father god of everything.

Tostig now knew that Annuah, the god he had been raised to worship, was but a rough shadow of Sado. The Nine were real, so real they could be seen by those with the right eyes and felt by any who reached out. Their blessings and protections permeated the land, the animals, and all five of the races, whether or not they were acknowledged. Tostig was more certain of this than he had been about anything else in his entire life.

He looked at Cecy, gazing at her as though it was the first time he had seen her. A strange feeling ran through him as he looked at her, a feeling as though he had known her for a very long time.

"Who are you?"

She gazed back at him. "You may ask me any question, ask any member of the Sashu any question, and expect to receive honesty in return. However, you should not ask unless you are truly prepared to be answered."

"I feel a kinship with you I cannot explain. I would understand the source of it. Who are you?"

"I am the daughter of Sado." She met his eyes, and he saw she was as serious as she had ever been. He didn't doubt her, but he wondered exactly what she meant. She continued, "Long ago, many centuries past, my father put on a form of flesh as you might don your robes. He courted my mother, the witch queen Hedvig of Ilbeor, and I am their daughter. My mother raised me on an island off the Western Shore, an island now called Sundersar Island. When I was deemed ready, my father revealed himself to me."

"You are a queen and a goddess, both human and divine." Surprisingly, Tostig felt neither awe nor reverence, though he knew he should have felt both. He simply felt kinship.

"That is not entirely accurate. I am neither fully human nor fully divine. I served as Ilbeor's queen for a short time after my mother's demise, but as it became apparent I had stopped aging, I ordered a servant to stage my apparent death and abdicated the throne by default. The throne passed to my younger half-brother, who established the practice of male succession. Radulf never did like women." She looked contemplative as she thought of times long past.

"What did you do then?"

"I came here and helped my kin establish the Sashu. Our outreach to the elves was, and still is, repelled, but my older half-brothers identify human, dwarf, and tselq magicians."

"The Watchers," Tostig breathed.

"Yes. They are older even than I."

"Sons of Sado?"

"Born of the first human queen of Ilbeor. Even I do not know their names. I am not certain whether they know themselves."

Tostig nodded. Somehow, he was not overwhelmed or alarmed. The information fit his new understanding of the world and of gods who walked about in the flesh at their pleasure.

"Are there others like you?" he asked.

"Perhaps, though I have only ever known my half-brothers."

Tostig finally asked the question that had been echoing in his mind. "Who am I in all of this?"

"You are the Blessed."

TOSTIG SOON FOUND BEING the Blessed afforded him many privileges but did not excuse him from training. In addition to his existing lessons, Cecy began teaching him to lead the Sashu rituals at the full and new moons.

"The adherents saw the manifestation of Sado, saw him touch you, and heard his words. Such a blessing has not occurred in most of their lifetimes. They will look to you for leadership, whether you would take the mantle or not."

"I will take the mantle willingly," Tostig assured her. "It is my duty."

Though Tostig's personality had not changed, nor had his fleshly desires, Cecy was glad to see the solemnity with which he treated his new status. It would serve him well, for she sensed great change coming to Ilbeor and felt he would be a key part of it.

Cecy had seen a dozen or so Blessed in her centuries leading the Sashu, and each served a specific purpose, always the same, yet always somehow different. By his actions, inactions, decisions, and passions, this young magician would shape the world in ways even beyond his core purpose, but she didn't see any reason to burden him with this knowledge. She answered his questions about past Blesseds truthfully but simply, giving only general information about their leadership.

Tostig threw himself into his lessons with renewed energy, now able to direct his purpose and passion. The magic came so easily to him now; very few of the tasks set for him were overly challenging. He still had to learn how to direct magic for particular spells, but the power within him had grown so much that it no longer resided in his chest but burned throughout his entire body. Instead of using his right hand to direct the magic as he had done before, Tostig was now able to simply gaze toward whatever he was trying to manipulate.

One afternoon, just before they dismissed for the evening meal, Maera and Tostig had finished their work. She instructed him to call the water from the stream and manipulate it, and he suspected she had made this request for her own entertainment. He grinned at her, his youthful mischief on full display as he decided to give her a real show.

"Laigui maura," he intoned, gazing at the water bubbling by in the stream. He enjoyed channeling magic this way.

The water obediently rose and formed a sphere, and he could see tiny particles of forest detritus in it. He had never noticed the particles before, and he wondered whether Sado had granted him enhanced eyesight or if he was simply seeing the world around him more clearly now.

"Well?" Maera asked impatiently, snapping him out of his reverie.

Tostig raised his hands to chest height and manipulated the water. Enjoying how easily he could focus his magic, he morphed the sphere into the perfect representation of an apple, including a delicately veined leaf and a stubby stem.

"Bah!" Maera exclaimed, surprising him, but not enough to make him lose his concentration. "A novice with three weeks' practice could do that. You are the Blessed; stop using your hands and show me something that will make me proud to be your teacher."

Tostig immediately accepted the challenge but wondered what he could possibly form to impress the old magician. Complex objects were out of the question; he could make those before his transformation. He also wondered how to shape the water without his hands.

If I just imagine what I want the water to form, can I use the magic to shape it instantly?

He decided to try, imagining the old tower where he had trysted with Alanda so many months before. He remembered every detail, from the crumbling stone to the leafy vines encasing it, and he focused all his attention before casting his thoughts into that water. His thoughts, though, drifted from the tower itself to his last visit there, distracting him from his original purpose. He remembered everything, but even after purposefully remembering the details of the tower, his mind refocused on the girl he had taken there.

The water took shape. By the time the water sculpture had fully formed, Tostig's and Maera's eyes had become utterly transfixed upon it.

A foot over the bubbling surface of the water floated the head and shoulders of a cloaked girl, perfectly detailed down to the individual hairs on the tail of her braid. The water moved within the figure, undulating in soft ripples, making the bust seem a living thing.

Tostig did not see the small particles he had noticed before. As he stared at what he had created, he didn't even see the subtle rippling of the water, nor the distorted reflections of the trees in the clear liquid. He saw her white-blonde braid, her unfathomable ice-blue eyes, her face almost entirely devoid of color, her cloak black as the darkest night. He never wanted to stop looking.

"Who is she?" Maera asked sharply. There was a note in her voice Tostig couldn't immediately identify and didn't understand, but he understood Maera was not exactly pleased.

Tostig tried to shrug it off. He had not spoken of Alanda to anyone at the caves, and he was not eager to do so. "A girl I met on the trails when I was still a messenger," he said. "She was unusual, so I remembered her well."

Maera peered at him, her aged and cloudy brown eyes sharpening as she tried to discern the hidden meaning behind his casual words.

Tostig turned his gaze back to the floating apparition of the girl he loved and reluctantly let it go, knowing he would create it again. The water became formless, crashing back into the stream with a splash.

"I have only seen a magician create so perfect an image once before," Maera said slowly. "It was not of a person, but of the home she missed intensely. Because of her longing, she could remember every detail and shape the water so realistically I would have recognized the place were I ever to see it again. Such it is with this girl."

"She's no one," Tostig argued, trying to keep his voice flippant even as he hated himself for the lie. "Just a girl. I'll probably never see her again."

"She is not just a girl to you," Maera said simply. "That much is quite clear."

Tostig remained quiet. He couldn't argue with Maera; claiming Alanda was nothing to him was a lie he was not willing to repeat.

"I caution you, Blessed, not to let your attraction to this girl interfere with your training and, eventually, your duty. Though you may form attachments, marry, and have children, such is a life that must be pushed aside in the face of your new station, at least for the time being."

Not giving him an opportunity to reply, Maera took up her walking stick, stood without assistance, and made her way back to the caves.

AFTER THE EVENING MEAL, Tostig did something he had never done before: he begged to be excused from one of his lessons. After the disturbing and titillating vision of Alanda that afternoon, Tostig needed time to himself.

To his great surprise, Paalavi neither questioned nor protested the missed lesson. "It is natural you should want some time to ponder what has happened to you," he said, smiling kindly. "I often find a pleasant evening walk followed by a small repast of wine and cheese brings great clarity of mind."

Tostig smiled and thanked him, called Ziva to him, and left the caves.

After months with the Sashu, the forest surrounding the caves was as familiar to Tostig as the lower trails near the valley had been. He and Ziva set off south to the muddy banks of the Nairam River. He knew from his old messenger maps that following the river would lead him all the way to the Pasling Sea, but he was not interested in walking along the bank of the snowmelt-swollen waterway.

Tostig didn't bother trying to keep the hem of his red apprentice's robes out of the mud. It would have been an exercise in futility, and he knew from experience that the novitiates and non-magician adherents attending to the laundry would have no problem cleaning the robes. He squatted on the bank of the water.

The Nairam River, unlike the bubbling brook near the caves, was not clear and clean. Snowmelt from the top of the mountains and the soil of the wide riverbed stained the water a deep reddish brown. Tostig wondered if the stain of the water would detract from what he was about to do, but he decided he didn't care.

He had to see her again.

He closed his eyes, bringing to mind how Alanda had looked when they first met: her tight black leathers and boots, the pack that seemed too large for her small, thin body, the white-blonde braid casually worn over her left shoulder...he left nothing out, putting all the longing he felt into the mental picture.

When the picture was clear and exact, Tostig opened his eyes, gazed at the river, and pushed his magic and thoughts towards the deepest water. At his command, a column of water rose from the river, not nearly as stained as he had expected, and almost instantly formed into a rippling sculpture of Alanda as she had been on the day he had met her.

Ziva barked at the watery apparition, not sure what to make of it. While she was used to Tostig's magic, he had never created something so lifelike before. Tostig reached out to pet her without taking his eyes off what he had wrought.

His heart ached. After all this time, he still could not account for his intense feelings; he and Alanda had spent so little time together, but somehow he *knew* she was the one he was meant to be with. With the blessing of Sado coursing through him, he found his longing had only intensified. *Does that signify that Sado means for us to be together, or is everything just more potent now?*

He stared at Alanda's watery form, holding onto the magic in the back of his mind while his consciousness remained absorbed in what he had wrought. He stared until it was too dark to see, and even then, he considered calling light so he could stay longer. The spell was on the tip of his tongue when he remembered Maera's warning. What good would it do him to sit and moon over an image of Alanda when he had genuine work to do, real lessons to learn?

As Tostig and Ziva strode back to the caves, Tostig made a decision. As gut-wrenching as it was, he had to let Alanda go until he had completed his training and learned more about his duty and responsibilities.

When he returned to the caves, he asked the first adherent he encountered to find Cecy and ask her if she would meet him in his quarters. Answering no questions and avoiding attempts at conversation, he returned to his chambers and, as Paalavi had suggested, requested a portion of cheese and wine. Before that fateful Sashu ritual, he would never have dared to make such a request, nor did he think it would have been granted. Now, the non-magician adherent, a young human woman named Galiena, hurried to the kitchens to get him what he had asked for.

Cecy would not be hurried, even for the Blessed. Tostig had finished his cheese and wine and was reading a scroll of elvish poetry when she entered his quarters over an hour later. He didn't mind; she had many demands on her time and his request was not an urgent one.

"What do you need, Tostig?" she asked, her voice calm and friendly as she took her usual place in one of the rocking chairs. "Paalavi informed me you had asked for an evening free of tutelage. While I do not object to this as long as it is done sparingly, I wonder what might be on your mind."

Tostig set his scroll aside and sat in the second rocking chair, the small table between the two chairs the only thing separating him from Cecy. Without preamble, he told her everything he had withheld since coming to the Sashu caves. He told her about Alanda, about their meeting and their tryst. He told her about Alanda's family's deaths and his desperate wish to find her and request a match. He told her how hard it had been to follow the Watchers' summons and how it had only been possible because of their promise that, when he was ready, the Sashu would help him find her. Finally, he told her about unintentionally summoning Alanda's form when he called the water and how he had gone to the river to do it again.

Cecy listened in silence, her expression unchanging. Only when she was sure he had finished did she speak, and her words were as kind as they had ever been. "Child," she began, addressing him as such for the first time, "the Watchers came last night with a new magician while you slept. Given your new status, I asked them about your manifestation, and they told me of the girl you seek, as well as of the circumstances in which they found you. From that, I surmised much of what you have told me.

"To be the Blessed or even a magician is to make sacrifices for the good of the Sashu and of the world. There is no denying that. However, there is no reason you cannot pursue this girl when you have finished your training. To find a partner is to fulfill a calling within yourself that, left unheeded, will make you feel incomplete and alone. I have always encouraged the people of the Sashu to find a partner if that is their wish, and I would offer you the same advice. You are still a man, made of flesh, with earthly desires and needs. You must fulfill those needs if you are to be whole."

Tostig felt relief wash over him; from Maera's statements, he had wondered if he was expected to wait until he was an old man before finding love.

"When it is time, I will help you find her myself. I only ask that you complete your training and that you try your hardest not to let thoughts of her distract you. Calling manifestations of her when you are alone will only leave you wanting; try to resist, for no elemental manifestation will ever fulfill the needs of the heart."

"I know you're right," Tostig admitted. "It's just that seeing her, even only an image of her, gave me hope I will find her again. I even wondered if Cherasil himself had a hand in our meeting and the intensity of my feelings."

"Time will tell," was all Cecy would say.

They talked of other, less consequential things until it was time for Tostig to go to his bed. His days were so full now that adequate sleep was a necessity. Cecy wished him a good night and did something she had never done: she kissed him lightly on the forehead. "May the graces of the Nine follow you, Blessed, in your earthly life."

TOSTIG TOOK Cecy's advice and made no more trips to the river. She was right; it would only cause unnecessary heartache.

After he spoke with Cecy, his lessons in elemental magic took an unexpected and unwelcome turn: the Sashu wanted to prepare him for battle.

"Battle magic?" he asked uncertainly when one of his masters, an older dwarf named Thrandthrin, brought the idea up in his early morning lesson. "I am a man of peace, and Ilbeor is in harmony. Why do I need to be a battle mage?"

"Ilbeor's peace rests on the blade of an axe," Thrandthrin told him, his guttural voice cracking over the syllables of the common tongue. "Only simpletons and the ignorant truly believe peace means only the lack of war. Even now, there are several factions within the land who threaten the peace with demands for more than what they have.

"Because of this, the Sashu teach basic combat magic to every magician. For you, it is especially important because other magicians and even non-magicians will look to you for leadership. Were you to find yourself in a conflict, it is essential for you to prevail with the least bloodshed possible. The methods you will begin learning today will aid in that. If it helps, lessons in healing with Lomasi will begin soon as well."

Tostig knew he didn't have a choice. Blessed or not, the course of his lessons was determined by his masters and, due to his status, Cecy herself. Promising himself he would never use combative magic except in the sorest of need, he nodded his acceptance.

"Good," the dwarf grunted. "The first spell is one of the most basic, though some find it difficult at first. It is an elemental spell designed to create a deep chasm in the ground between two combatants or sets of combatants. This is essential, for if you can prevent fighting in the first place, bloodshed may not be necessary. The incantation is *avenci creari.*"

"*Avenci creari,*" Tostig repeated, careful to avoid casting the spell inadvertently.

"Yes," Thrandthrin replied. "Most magicians find it useful to place a hand on the ground. This helps direct the magic and prevent unintentional casualties, but it also carries some danger, for the magician must be between the opposing factions."

"What if I could cast it without that step?"

Thrandthrin studied him for a moment. "You have always shown abilities beyond those of a normal magician and have even more so since you received the touch of Sado. If anyone could do that, it would be you, but I caution you. Making a mistake in intent or thought could cause death, perhaps even your own. Today, we will practice using touch." He indicated a large stone, a foot or so across and irregularly shaped, sitting innocuously on the scarred wooden table of his teaching room. "Place your finger at the edge of the stone."

Tostig did; the stone felt as familiar as his own skin after his months spent in the caves.

"Speak the incantation and focus on creating a small chasm across the surface of the stone," Thrandthrin coached. "It may be only a scratch on your first try, but this will give you a feel for the spell."

Tostig knew intention and clarity were the keys to a successful cast. After a pause, he murmured, "*Avenci creari,*" and his magic coursed through his finger and into the rock.

The rock disintegrated; barely more than dust remained. He looked at Thrandthrin, wondering how the old dwarf would respond to his mistake.

Thrandthrin looked startled and swore under his breath but

collected himself and looked at Tostig more sternly than he ever had. "Congratulations," he said dryly, tugging his braided gray beard in agitation. "If you had lost control in that manner on a battlefield or dueling ground, you would have killed everyone, yourself included. Master yourself, Tostig. Too much power is far more dangerous than too little."

Tostig accepted the rebuke; Thrandthrin was absolutely correct. Though he had mastered spells quickly and easily since being touched by Sado, he struggled with the magnitude of the power he now had.

"Go get another rock," Thrandthrin commanded. "A bigger one."

Tostig called Ziva to follow him and left the small cave, easily following the winding passages to the main entrance. He felt like a small child, chastised and sent to the fields as punishment. The feeling chafed, though he knew Thrandthrin had been unerring in his remonstrance.

Knowing exactly where to go, Tostig ventured east to a small area in the forest he knew to be littered with red rocks similar to the one he had destroyed, perhaps the site of a long-ago rockfall or earthquake. He thought Thrandthrin had probably found the original rock there in the first place; it was well known to the carvers of the Sashu.

While Ziva sniffed around for interesting scents, Tostig examined the rocks. He wanted to show Thrandthrin he was sorry for his mistake. After a few minutes, he found what he was looking for: a large rock, nearly the size of a small boulder. He cleared the surrounding rubble with a wordless wave of his hand.

The rock was larger than he had originally thought, and he knew it might be too heavy. Nothing in his life as a messenger or a magician had prepared him for lifting and carrying exceptionally heavy weights. He had been told not to use magic for trivial purposes until he was a master, but he was tempted to bewitch the air underneath the stone to carry some of the weight.

That Thrandthrin would not be pleased with the use of magic simply to make an assigned task easier was not the least of his concerns. Finally, however, he decided he would rather not use all of his strength to carry the rock. "*Aeuri censa*," he mumbled, his gaze riveted on the ground underneath the rock.

The rock lifted almost imperceptibly, and Tostig knew the spell had worked. He bent and lifted it effortlessly, the cushion of air beneath it taking on much of the weight.

"Ziva, heel," he commanded, and she immediately came to his side. Together, they headed back, Tostig carrying his unwieldy load.

When he reached Thrandthrin's teaching room, he considered ending the spell and not letting the older magician know he had used magic to ease the work of carrying the stone. He stopped, however, reflecting on Cecy's lecture about honesty as the Blessed of Sado.

"The Sashu will trust you even with their very lives," she had told him. "And you must never abuse that trust with dishonest words or actions. The consequences could cause them to question their very faith itself. Promise me, Tostig."

He had promised.

Tostig entered the room with his lightened load, but the displeasure he had imagined never came. Thrandthrin took no notice of the spell, nodding as Tostig set the rock on the floor and muttered "*desena*" to release the cushion of air. The rock hit the ground with a muted thud.

"Try again," Thrandthrin ordered without so much as a greeting. "And if you destroy this rock, you will bring me yet a larger one, but without the use of magic."

TOSTIG FELL into his bed each night completely exhausted. His whole body ached constantly, even after he had bathed in the warm underground spring. Thrandthrin had made it his personal mission to train Tostig in the proper focus of his power, and for days Tostig had been carrying rocks of increasing size from the forest to Thrandthrin's teaching room.

When the dwarf finally realized they had reached the point at which Tostig was physically incapable of carrying larger rocks without magic, he resorted to requiring him to clean the prodigious rubble from the teaching room floor by hand, using only a small brush and pan. This required Tostig to work on his hands and knees for hours on end, and he wasn't pleased when he found out Cecy had suspended his other lessons while he worked on mastering the magic coursing through him.

While Tostig cleaned the floor, Thrandthrin stood over him and tutored him in matters on which he'd never been educated. Thrandthrin explained that Ilbeor, while seemingly one large landmass, was actually a series of smaller ones connected by grating edges called *faults*. He told Tostig how to find the faults by reaching out with his magic, which would allow him to use them in battle and to be wary of earthquakes. He tutored Tostig in many other features of the land and how they might be magically manipulated, and when he tired of instructing, he talked endlessly about the brewing of beers and ales that had been his profession before he had manifested magic.

It took nearly a week before Tostig finally succeeded and created a deep chasm in a large rock without destroying it. He looked up for the first time in days, a hint of his characteristic grin gracing his face for the first time in days, only to see Thrandthrin scowling up at him darkly.

"That took far too long," he said roughly. "You are the Blessed. You are the highest-ranking Sashu magician, positioned only under Cecy herself. Your skill is unmatched, your power greater than even that of the elves, and yet if you cannot learn to control it, to control yourself, you are no better than the youngest of novices." He turned on his heel and strode out of the teaching room, his grizzled gray hair fanning out behind him.

The next day, Tostig was allowed to resume his regular lessons, and it was with great relief that he joined the healing master, Lomasi, in her strangely appointed hut, which she called a greenhouse, above the cave system.

Lomasi, a tselq woman with seven curls to her horns and fine, snow-white hair falling to her waist, lectured Tostig the moment he stepped into her greenhouse. Surrounded by the herbs and plants she cared for with religious zeal, she made a formidable figure as she stood to her full seven-foot height, her muscular arms crossed over her chest. Despite her age, her skin was still a hearty, healthy green and her musculature had not declined.

"Healing magic is not like your rocks. Your rock breaks, you get another rock. You break a living being, they pass into the spirit world and no magic will bring them back. Are you prepared to have that on your conscience?"

Tostig immediately understood why Cecy had not allowed him to come to Lomasi's lessons until he had mastered the exercise with the rock, but he wondered how he would ever control his power well enough to attend to fragile, living bodies. Lomasi had spoken one of the inviolable truths of magic, a truth he had learned at his very first lesson: that which is devoid of life cannot be given life. If he took a life from the world, he could not call it back.

Seeing the gravity on Tostig's face, Lomasi knew she had said enough. "Come," she encouraged, seeming to shrink back to a more reasonable size as she uncrossed her arms and relaxed. "I have something I want you to do, and then we will take the first steps in learning true healing magic."

She led him to the back of her slatted wooden building, kept warm by a stone fire pit during the cold months and protected from the elements with slats of clear glass that covered the space in the wood with the pull of a string.

In the very back corner of her greenhouse sat a large stone pot filled with rich, brown soil Tostig knew she had fertilized and cared for using her own secret methods. He longed to put his hands into it; the first time he had felt it, the loamy softness of the soil had reminded him of his mother's vegetable garden. Lomasi placed a small linen pouch into his hand. He glanced at it and then at her, nonplussed.

"Open it," she urged, "and see the beauty of what lies within."

Tostig carefully unwound the complicated knots of string holding it closed. When he opened the bag, however, he was decidedly unimpressed by what he saw: *seeds*, just three plain, white seeds. He looked at Lomasi, and she clicked her tongue at him as she noted his lack of appreciation.

"Seeds?" he asked.

"Seeds," she confirmed, "but not just any seeds. You are lucky, young one, to come to me at just this season. Cared for properly, they will bloom into some of the most beautiful flowers in Ilbeor. Called *aiyonia* by my race, the red blooms will reach the size of your hand." She glanced at his red robes. "I think you will appreciate their vibrant color."

Under her instruction, Tostig planted the three precious seeds in the soil, sprinkled a small amount of water over the pot, and repeated a Sashu entreaty to Iarae, goddess of flowers, to guide their growth. Once completed to her satisfaction, Lomasi told him they would do well until the next morning, when they would need another sprinkling of water.

"And tonight," she instructed as she led him out of her greenhouse and into the spring sunshine, "and every night hereafter, you will pay homage to Iarae at her shrine and ask her to aid the growth of the *aiyonia*."

Tostig agreed readily; he was still growing accustomed to the practice of asking specific gods or goddesses of the Nine for help or guidance, but with the certainty that had come with his transformation, he knew his words to them held weight.

Upon a table a short distance from her greenhouse, Lomasi had placed a bunched fruit Tostig immediately recognized as the fruit decorating the table in his sleeping quarters.

"What are those?"

She smiled, her full, pale-green lips parting to show a mouth without many teeth left. "These, young one, are some of the sweetest-tasting fruits you will ever find. They are called grapes and are grown in some tselq communities in the lower elevations bordering the southern valley, where the soil is naturally rich and the weather temperate. They are delicate; their skin will pierce at the slightest touch of a sharp object to reveal the flesh and seeds within, but they are also susceptible to the most nuanced of magic. They can be healed."

Tostig frowned. "If they are dead, I cannot bring them back to life."

"Correct," Lomasi affirmed, "but you forget that once a fruit has been cut from its vine or tree, it has already begun the process of dying for want of sustenance. From that time until its decay, it exists to sustain others."

Tostig nodded, wondering how he could heal fruit already in the process of dying.

"In the case of the grape and certain other rare fruits, the skin and flesh are susceptible to our healing magic. You will practice spells to knit flesh and heal wounds on the delicate surface of the grape without presenting a danger to living beings, and they can still sustain us if we consume them while they are fresh even if you are unable to repair the damage done to them."

Tostig felt a slow smile creep across his face as he understood her meaning. "So, you'll be able to teach me to cast healing spells without risk to life and health."

"Yes," Lomasi confirmed. "And the first spell you must learn is *feuro hiesa*."

FEURO HIESA WAS the simplest of healing spells and would only work on flesh wounds. As Tostig labored over the grapes, struggling to knit the makeshift wounds she inflicted with her small knife, he was relieved to find he had mastered his magic to the extent that he could work on the small fruits without destroying them. Those hours were still difficult, as he was often forced to accept that he had caused irregular swellings, deeper injuries, and internal damage to the grapes he was trying to heal.

After each lesson, Tostig and Lomasi would split the grapes between themselves and enjoy the sweet explosions on their taste buds. No matter what deformity or damage Tostig caused, none of the grapes had been rendered inedible, and he looked forward to the small repast with Lomasi before continuing his day.

Lomasi lent him the most difficult scrolls he had been asked to read: detailed descriptions and diagrams of the anatomy of each of the races, along with some dedicated to the more common animals. She expected him not only to read but to memorize them, and he spent many late nights trying to force his tired and reluctant mind to accept the new information. As he worked over the grapes, improving each day, Lomasi peppered him with questions and became most displeased if he got too many incorrect.

"How can I teach you advanced spells of healing if you do not know human quadriceps from tselq livers?" she would ask irritably, inevitably plying him with more scrolls to study each night.

One early morning, several weeks into his advanced training, Tostig woke with a clearer mind and more focus. This was evident in all his lessons: within three days, he could fully heal several types of wounds, remember the anatomy he had studied in the night, manipulate the earth, air, and fire for battle, and was told by Paalavi he could begin working on his final poem as a student: a piece meant to show the old master the very essence of Tostig's inner being.

Tostig could never pinpoint what had changed; it just seemed as though all the instruction, information, and methods fell into place for him, and instinctually knew how to use his power appropriately.

His *aiyonia* blossomed into buds, hinting at the bright red yet to be revealed. He delighted in caring for the plant, praying to Iarae in hopes his petition for a vibrant life for it would be heard, and watching it grow unnaturally quickly under his attentions. It seemed to Tostig the opening of the blossoms on the *aiyonia* coincided almost exactly with his increased acuity. He gained confidence as a magician and as an adherent of the Sashu religion, feeling his faith had been well-placed.

After breaking his fast on a particularly lovely morning, he approached Lomasi's greenhouse to find her waiting outside for him, a broad grin on her face. "Come and see what you have done!" she crowed.

Five *aiyonia* blossoms had burst into full bloom overnight, and the profusion of the brightest, richest red Tostig had ever seen stunned him into silence. He examined the flowers, his fingers hovering a hair's breadth from the petals, as close as he could get without risking bruising them. He thought he had never seen anything more beautiful.

Lomasi pulled his hand back from the plant. "Watch," she said. She raised her knife and drove it into the very heart of the plant, where the mass of stems and leaves connected with the roots under the soil.

"No!" Tostig exclaimed, but it was too late.

Lomasi issued one command in a dispassionate voice that chilled him to the bone. "Heal it."

Looking at the gaping wound where Lomasi's knife had been, Tostig began to frantically review all the words of healing she had taught him and all the various parts of the plant he had learned. Time was short; she had cut the sustaining supply of nutrients and water from the roots to the beautiful, vibrant parts of the plant.

Tostig decided to rely upon the simplest spell, but to use his power and knowledge of the plant to push it further and to heal the rents in the roots and their connections to the stem and the leaves. Frantically willing his magic into his fingertip, he placed his index finger atop the wound and uttered, "*Feuro hiesa.*"

The spell came out much louder than he had intended, and as he felt the magic course wildly from his finger into the plant, he knew immediately what he had done. He felt it before he saw it, but the evidence came quickly enough. Before his eyes, the beautiful red blooms faded, wilted, and dropped onto the soil. The vibrant leaves withered and browned; the stems became dry twigs. Within seconds of his spell, the *aiyonia* he had cared for, prayed for, and nurtured had withered into death under his hands. He wasn't aware of the tears flowing down his cheeks as he gazed at it, still touching the wound in the center he had tried so desperately to heal.

"Now you know," Lomasi said sadly from somewhere behind him. She quietly departed the greenhouse, leaving Tostig alone with his loss.

SACRIFICE

After the loss of his carefully cultivated *aiyonia*, Tostig finally internalized exactly how much power he contained within himself and how deadly it could be if not controlled. Working closely with his masters over the following weeks, he gained command of his magic in a way he had never even realized was possible, and he progressed through his lessons with a focus and purpose greater than he had ever had.

One evening, after he had presented his final work of poetry to Paalavi, Cecy came to his sleeping quarters, her arms full of his favorite bright red cloth.

"Good evening." Tostig stood from his table, where he had been studying a scroll on Twanai anatomy. "What's this?"

Cecy smiled, and he thought he detected a hint of pride in her eyes. She held out the bundle. "See for yourself."

Tostig was confused; he already had two sets of red robes and one set of black hanging on pegs; he hardly needed more. What he had was already more clothing than he had ever owned. He took the bundle from her and set it on his bed. Shaking out one of the garments, he suddenly grinned, boyish delight showing on his face for the first time in a long time. The robes, while similarly cut and the same red, were made of a heavier fabric and embroidered along their edges with gold runic symbols.

"Congratulations, Blessed," Cecy said. "Paalavi informed me he released you from his tutelage this evening when you presented your final work to him, and the other masters agree there is little else they can teach you. You are now a master. You have accomplished in months what usually takes years, and Sado's blessing is only to be partly credited for this triumph. Your hard work, dedication, and talent had already set you above the other apprentices."

"You believe I'm ready to teach?" Tostig asked, laying each of the three sets of embroidered red robes neatly across the bed.

"Yes, but you will not teach until you are considerably older, other than perhaps some odd lessons for younger magicians. Tostig, it is time for you to be sent back into Ilbeor, armed with your new knowledge and power, for the betterment of all the races."

Tostig nodded, knowing Cecy would not have designated him a master unless she and his own masters felt he was ready, but still feeling somewhat intimidated by the idea of being sent out on his own.

"When will I leave?" He crossed his quarters to the pegs where his apprentice robes hung, taking down all but the black, which he would need for Sashu ceremonies. He hung the new robes in their place, carefully folding his old ones so they could be repurposed for the next apprentice who chose the color. He set them on his table and turned to Cecy expectantly.

Instead of telling him where his first assignment would be, she sat in one of the rocking chairs, looking at him seriously until he joined her in the other one. Apparently, this was not to be a brief meeting.

"There is something we must discuss. I had a visit from Grayson last night."

"Grayson was here?" Tostig asked. He remembered that the traveler Grayson was the bodily form of the god of knowledge, Annukai, but he had understood that he rarely came to the Sashu caves.

"Yes. He has seen something in your immediate future, in our immediate future, that he felt bound to notify me of. This does not happen often."

"Is it Alanda?"

Cecy allowed herself the briefest of small smiles. "No, it is not about the girl," she said, "though I intend to keep my promise and allow you to find her now that you have achieved mastery. Unfortunately, the news Grayson brought is of much greater immediate importance than your affections."

"I don't understand. I know it's time for me to go out into the world, as you have said, but why would Grayson find that to be of such import?"

"I am certain you have heard of the elf Altoneir," she said, changing the subject.

"Of course," Tostig replied. "Altoneir has set himself up to oppose the human king, Florian. He lives on an island somewhere in the Unresting Sea. From everything I understand, he's gathered quite a force, but not enough to oppose King Florian's army or the might of the other races, if it came down to that. What's he got to do with me?"

"Altoneir lives on Sundersar Island, not far off the coastline, north of here. He actually lives in the very castle from which my mother and I ruled Ilbeor for a time, though that is not of consequence. For the last three hundred years, he has sequestered himself there, amassing his forces and making his plans for power. What is important for you to know, however, is that in those three hundred years, he has never failed to try to recruit the Blessed to his cause."

Tostig nearly laughed with relief. "Is that all?" he asked. "You have nothing to worry about. My loyalty is first to the Sashu, and second to the greater population of Ilbeor itself. I would have thought you already knew that."

Cecy remained serious. "I do," she said, "but this issue has unfortunately passed the antics he has used on past Blesseds. Grayson did not come here to tell me of another recruitment attempt."

"Then why did he come?"

Cecy took a deep breath and leaned forward, gazing at him with more solemnity than he had ever seen. "There is a magical force on its way here on Altoneir's behalf. They're coming for you, but we will fight as one, nonetheless."

"A magical force? Coming here? For me?" Tostig was flabbergasted. Even though he had known of Altoneir even before coming to the caves, he had never realized the elf had a force of magicians under his control. Another question entered his mind. "How does he even know about me?" Tostig asked. "I've not left the caves since Sado's blessing."

Cecy pursed her lips. "We have never been certain about that, but he has always known when a Blessed walked the land. While we do not think there are any spies among the Sashu, he is certainly getting the information somehow." Cecy relaxed back into her chair and began to rock again, looking for all the world as though they were discussing nothing more serious than the weather.

Tostig tried to mimic her rocking and calm demeanor; she and the other masters had taught him to moderate his emotions, even in difficult situations. "What does he want with me?"

"Our last Blessed, as I believe I told you, was chosen over fifty years ago, though he chose not to take on the responsibility and went his own way. Altoneir contrived a meeting with that Blessed after he left the caves and attempted to convince him, as he had the one a century before him, to join his cause and fight for him. The last Blessed was human, as you are, but the one before that was a tselq. Neither joined him. Grayson believes he has sent his fighters to capture you rather than to convince you to serve him."

Placing his hands on his knees, Tostig leaned forward. "What do we know about who and what is coming?"

"Our information indicates that Altoneir's force is about a hundred strong and mostly composed of elven magicians. In order to remain undetected over the weeks it would have taken them to reach us, they likely traveled in groups of no more than two or three, and only recently convened near the coast of the Pasling Sea."

"We have more than that in the caves," Tostig pointed out.

"Yes, but you would be unwise to underestimate the talent and abilities of those he sent. Though we are confident he has no spies within the Sashu, Altoneir is aware of our numbers and the extent of our magical prowess. Though we do not believe he will involve himself in this skirmish, he has many magicians that rival even our masters in power. Not you, of course, and certainly not me, but most of our magicians are only comparable to his at best."

"And his purpose for all this is to capture me and bring me back to his island? What would he do with me then?"

"Use you to his own ends," Cecy replied. "I know no more than that."

"I will never go willingly with someone who sets himself against the Sashu or, if it came down to it, my own race."

"Neither would any of the Sashu fail to defend you with their lives if need be. Do not underestimate their devotion to you and to what you represent." Cecy rose suddenly from her chair. "Come. We have much to prepare. Grayson believes Altoneir's forces will be here in a matter of days."

"Where is Grayson now? If there is a conflict coming, why did he not stay? Why did he not warn me?"

"He warned me because it is I who will assemble the forces necessary to repel the attack. As to why he is not here, I can only tell you that the gods, in fleshly form or otherwise, rarely interfere. This is the place of mortal beings and the elves, not the gods. Come now, let us go to our planning."

TOSTIG FELT out-of-place standing next to Cecy as she issued instructions to the magicians. Though he had grown accustomed to helping her with the new and full moon ceremonies and to the respect and admiration of the others, it felt strange to be in a place of leadership when the stakes were so high. He stood at her side as she explained what was coming and why, and he tried not to look awkward while she explained that the job of the Sashu forces was to protect Tostig from capture.

"We must be ready within the next two days," Cecy said to the group of rapt magicians, most of whom had never performed battle magic other than for practice. "We must draw the battle away from our home to protect the young and the non-magicians, but also to protect our relics and our heritage." She indicated the statues lining the main cavern where they were meeting.

"Where will we go?" Paalavi asked reasonably.

Tostig shifted uncomfortably. Paalavi had always seemed to be the most peaceful, beauty-loving magician among the Sashu. The idea of him fighting was not one Tostig found palatable.

Cecy did not seem to have any of the same misgivings and answered him directly. "We will meet their fighters south along the Nairam River to create a boundary to their ability to retreat. Make no mistake; I expect to annihilate these forces, and we will offer quarter only upon complete surrender."

"Are we to accept quarter if they offer it?" a young dwarf magician named Reikuni asked. Tostig recognized her as one of the more advanced apprentices who had reached the caves shortly before he had. He wished he had gotten to know her better before this, but he only had a cordial relationship with the dwarf, greeting one another as they passed in the hallways.

Cecy turned to Tostig. "What do you think?"

Tostig was alarmed at being asked his opinion, especially in front of the entirety of the Sashu, but as he had been trained, he kept the surprise from his face. Finally, he said, "I believe it would be more worthy to accept quarter and preserve your life, and I know we would spare no effort to return any captured Sashu to our home." He looked at Cecy, hoping he had answered correctly.

"I agree," she said simply. "We can afford to spend no more lives than absolutely necessary, which brings me to another point." She looked over the convened magicians seriously. "It is unlikely we will escape this conflict unscathed; therefore, we will conduct a Ceremony of Leaving prior to proceeding to the battlefield."

A murmur ran through the crowd, and Tostig felt his own brow furrow despite trying to remain as calm and neutral as Cecy herself. A Ceremony of Leaving was generally reserved for a dying adherent to the Sashu religion. He had never been taught about performing the ceremony for a larger group, particularly when the odds seemed stacked in their favor. He looked at Cecy quizzically.

"Later," she whispered.

Tostig nodded almost imperceptibly.

"The Ceremony of Leaving will take place tomorrow at full dark," Cecy announced. "Until then, arm and armor yourselves as you see fit."

Tostig once again had to make a concerted effort to keep his face calm as the murmuring crowd of magicians dispersed. Almost every magician in the caves was fighting if they had even some of the necessary skills; the only ones staying behind were the novices and some of the older masters.

"Will we allow non-magicians who are proficient in the bow or blade to fight?" He walked alongside Cecy as she strode down one of the many passages leading off the main cavern.

"No," she said. "They would stand no chance in a conflict of this nature. The only reason I am encouraging the use of physical weaponry at all is that it may be necessary if the battle becomes close enough to call for hand-to-hand combat. In all our long history, the Sashu have never waged a battle against a force such as this, and I would like to be ready for any eventuality."

"I am proficient in the bow," Tostig began.

"You will carry no weapon, and nor will I," Cecy stated. "We will, of course, don clothing appropriate for the task we find ourselves about to perform."

"And what would that be?" Tostig wasn't certain any armor he had ever seen would be effective against a magical attack. King Florian's conscripts had stained and stiff leather jerkins or sometimes mail shirts. Though those might work against physical attack, he couldn't help but think of the many ways he could get around it magically.

Cecy seemed to understand. "The armor worn by the armies who fight physically differs greatly from what you or I will don for this battle. We will hardly look any different from we do now, but our robes will be enchanted to ward off some attacks, and we will wear headpieces to protect us from physical blows and manipulated elements."

"Helms?"

"Helms, yes, and pauldrons, though we will don no chest pieces or gloves in order to allow full range of movement and direction of our magic. You will find, I believe, that in the stress of battle with many demands accosting you at once, the use of your hands will again become necessary."

Tostig nodded as she led them into the small armory he had noticed but never entered.

"Fit him as befitting any master," Cecy instructed Maxwell, who was manning the table with various helms displayed for the use of the magicians. "Do not offer him anything that would distinguish him as Blessed. We do not want him easily identified, though it is my suspicion they will notice him quickly enough."

"Of course, Cecy," Maxwell replied, and busied himself with a simple but undamaged helm of a dull silver color. "I believe this will do, and pauldrons to match."

Cecy nodded her approval. "I leave him in your capable hands, Maxwell. I, of course, have my own supplies."

"Thank you," Maxwell said simply as she left.

In a matter of minutes, Tostig was fitted with a leather skullcap and the dull, silver helm. To his surprise, it was not as uncomfortable as he had feared, but still resented any constraints on his body. This was simply not something anyone had planned for; the Sashu hadn't been part of any major battles or wars for centuries.

Pauldrons followed, and Tostig did not like the way they felt on his body. He informed the non-magician that he would participate in the battle without them.

"Blessed!" Maxwell exclaimed. "I wouldn't hear of - "

"It is not for you to say what you would and would not hear of," Tostig replied, his voice sterner than usual. "I need the full measure of movement of my upper body, and these would restrict that."

Maxwell looked as though he would like to argue but lowered his eyes to his work cleaning the padded skullcap to go under Tostig's helm. "Yes, Blessed," he muttered. It was clear he was not happy.

Tostig returned to his quarters with Ziva, his new helm and skullcap in his hands. Setting them on the table, he called Ziva to him and combed her. Though it was not her usual combing time, she acquiesced without complaint, seeming to realize something was happening and routines were changing.

Just as Tostig had made himself ready to join the rest of the Sashu for the evening meal, Cecy appeared at his door with a large armful of garments in different colors, though none, he noticed, of the red he preferred. He watched silently as she laid them out, one by one. It reminded him of receiving his master's robes the previous night.

Other than color, they were identical to his other robes: heavy cloth embroidered in gold. Before he could ask, Cecy told him, "I am sure you have noticed your favored color is absent. I assure you I have not ignored your preference; as the only magician who wears that bright red, the color is too distinctive. We do not want you easily identified, and we do not know how much Altoneir knows about you."

Tostig nodded and surveyed the choices. "I may choose any of these?"

Cecy nodded. "Any or all of them, if you would like to add variety to your wardrobe. But you must choose one to wear when we fight. I will ensure enough of the color among the Sashu that you might blend in."

Tostig pointed to a forest green set matching the color he remembered lining Alanda's water-cloth cloak. If he couldn't wear red, he thought he would like to match the girl who still haunted his dreams.

"Very well," Cecy said. "All of these are imbued with wards for your protection. Are there any of the other sets you would like to add?"

"The black, I think, and the gold," Tostig aid. "And if it is not too much trouble, I would like to ward a set of my red robes as well. Not for the upcoming conflict," he added, seeing Cecy's look, "but if this elf is truly out to capture me, I aim to be ready for a fight wherever I might be."

She nodded. "I will have it done, and before you leave the caves, I will have Thrandthrin teach you the words we use to create such wards. I know you learned many of them in your training, but our particular combination may escape you. After your evening meal, please come to the large masters' meeting room for additional planning."

"Of course," Tostig replied, carefully concealing his excitement at being part of the Sashu masters' planning. He hung up the robes and headed to the dining hall, Ziva at his heels.

THE MEETING of the masters did not offer many surprises. From what he had learned of battle maneuvers and strategies, his placement on the left flank rather than at the center was expected. Altoneir's fighters would look for someone in a more protected position; he would be more anonymous in the flank. Tostig was surprised, however, that it was Thrandthrin rather than Cecy who took the lead: though Thrandthrin had never seen a battle bigger than a skirmish, he was apparently considered a master planner and strategist and was well-read on the subject. Tostig left the meeting with a new appreciation for the dwarf and all the masters, feeling confident their plans would be fruitful when they faced Altoneir's forces.

As Tostig prepared for the Ceremony of Leaving the next night, he donned the new warded black robes; Cecy had insisted he remain garbed in such until the immediate danger had passed, even while in the caves.

As he had been tutored, he led the Sashu to the statue of Xatra, the goddess of death. In this ceremony, she would be the only deity paid homage. Side by side with Cecy, Tostig faced the Sashu, his hood covering his head and most of his forehead. "Tonight, we pay homage to Xatra, goddess of death, and ask for peaceful passage to the otherworld should our fleshly lives end on the morrow." Tostig's powerful baritone rang with authority as he spoke.

He turned alongside Cecy and bowed deeply to Xatra's statue, feeling rather than seeing those behind him follow suit.

"Xatra," Cecy intoned. "It is you who passes judgment on our lives and deeds as we leave this life to enter the next. We plead for your mercy and beg of you to understand we have strived to live our best lives, as the gods have commanded, instructed, and expected of us."

"We ask you, Xatra," Tostig continued, rising out of his bow, "not only to judge us with mercy, but to beg of your brothers and sisters to comfort those left behind should we depart this land."

"We ask you, Xatra. We beg you, Xatra," the adherents intoned behind him.

"We stand ready to cross the threshold from our fleshly lives to all that comes after," Cecy stated.

"We stand ready! We are ready!"

The crowd behind him grew frenzied as they repeated the phrase with greater and greater volume and fervor. When Cecy and Tostig turned to face the adherents, Tostig was shocked to find many of them on their knees, their hands raised in supplication. This was outside his experience; of all the Sashu ceremonies and rituals he had taken part in, never had he seen such a loss of decorum. Even the masters in the crowd behaved such, their usual reserve and calm demeanors nowhere in evidence as they shouted.

He turned to ask Cecy, but she simply shook her head and took his left hand in her right, raising them above their heads in a kind of tribute. "We stand ready! We are ready!" she cried with the assembled Sashu.

After a beat, Tostig joined in. He felt his heart beating fast and hard in his chest, along with a kind of excitement and anticipation, and he thought he knew why Cecy had allowed such a loss of restraint.

By the time the ceremony had concluded, Tostig was emotionally exhausted. Never, whether in the sanctum of Annuah or in the Sashu celebrations, had he witnessed or taken part in such a display. *At least,* he thought, *the Sashu are ready.*

~

THE SASHU MAGICIANS, save the novices and a few elders left behind to watch over the non-magicians and children, headed south to the Nairam River to intercept Altoneir's fighters the morning after the Ceremony of Leaving. There was a palpable sense of anticipation as they, over two hundred fifty strong, trod to the river in twos and threes.

When they reached the empty field along the river, they saw that no one from Altoneir's forces was yet in sight, and they fanned out to their assigned positions. Tostig took his place in the middle of the left flank, close to the river's bank, and gave no orders or did anything to distinguish himself. His forest green robes, warded by Cecy herself, were not distinguishable other than the embroidery designating him as a master magician.

"Fine day for a fight," a dwarf next to him, a younger master named Dromuth, said in a heavily accented voice. Tostig did not know Dromuth well because he was a traveling magician who just happened to be in the caves at the time of the upcoming battle.

Dromuth was right, in his way. The early-morning sky was clear, the weather cool and breezy. It was a fine day, though to Tostig, the fine weather seemed to mock their purpose. Shouldn't the sky be as threatening and dangerous as their mission? Shouldn't Aaldir have sent rain and thunder?

Tostig grunted an acknowledgement while noticing that next to him, the tselq woman Agisa did not seem nearly as eager. She stood calmly, her eyes closed and her palms slightly raised at her sides, chanting words in tselq. Tostig, knowing Agisa had not chosen to join the Sashu religion, wondered if she was entreating her ancestors for victory, or perhaps for a lack of violence at all. Agisa, like most tselq magicians, loved peace and tranquility and disliked disruptions to her routines.

He searched the center of the assembled magicians for Cecy, and found her on the front line, waiting calmly for their adversaries to appear. Her appearance was as it always was but for the silver and gold helm and the gleaming silver pauldrons. Despite her calm expression, she looked fierce, and Tostig wondered how many battles she had taken part in.

"They come," Cecy said, just loudly enough for Tostig to hear.

Tostig gazed across the field to the stand of trees on the other side. For a few moments, he saw nothing and wondered what Cecy had seen. Then he saw a single emissary. It did not surprise Tostig to see that the emissary was an elf, but his appearance belied the fact he was likely the commander of Altoneir's forces. He was tall but slightly built and thin, his hair white and flowing over blue water-cloth robes. He didn't look like any of the fighters Tostig had ever seen or imagined, and he exuded a sense of peace and tranquility rather than violence or conflict.

"We have no fight with the Sashu. We seek only the Blessed. Our leader requests an audience with him at his home on the Unresting Sea, and if that audience is granted, we will trouble you no more." The speaker had a smooth, honeyed voice that did not seem to match his passively disinterested expression.

"The one you seek is not among us, herald," Cecy said from her position at the front of the Sashu magicians. Power seemed to radiate from her as she held her hands palm up, spread wide and at waist height. "The Blessed is hidden from he who would be master of all."

"He is part of your fighting contingent," the herald stated flatly, seeming to have no particular argument to make against Cecy, but rather as though he was stating the obvious. "The Blessed would not be left unprotected in the face of the might you know we can wage against your people, Cecy of the Sashu. And make no mistake, we will fight if it is necessary to achieve our master's aim."

Cecy laughed, a single, mirthless note. "The might? I know we outnumber you at least twice, if not thrice. It would be wiser for you to turn back, though I know your master will not allow you to make such a concession. We were forewarned by the gods of your intent, and we stand ready."

"We will find the Blessed," the herald continued, still seeming unperturbed. "His identity will become obvious."

"Perhaps," Cecy said. "Or perhaps you will find the combined strength of myself, the Blessed, and the magicians of the Sashu will easily overwhelm you, and your master will be left with nothing."

The herald said no more, but raised his hand, two fingers pointing upward and the rest fisted close to his palm. He twisted his wrist sharply, and at that, perhaps a hundred blue-robed fighters assembled behind him.

Tostig studied the fighters carefully, looking for any advantages or weaknesses. They were, as Cecy had said, mostly elves - most magicians of the other races were found and brought to the Sashu before Altoneir could ensnare them. None of them wore an expression Tostig would have expected when a battle was imminent: they looked calm and cool without a hint of ferocity or battle lust. They wore no armor, but somehow this didn't make them seem any less deadly. Their very uniformity spoke of a fighting unit that would work seamlessly together.

"Blessed!" called the herald. "Will you not show yourself and avoid the bloodshed sure to occur if you do not? Many will die while you hide yourself, and my master wishes only to speak to you."

Tostig remained silent, keeping his face carefully impassive. Cecy and the other masters had prepared him for such a call, and he knew Altoneir's aim was capture rather than willing discussion. If he went with the herald and the fighters, he would be hard-pressed to escape when negotiations were found to be impossible. Tostig was not sure exactly why, but the exiled elf seemed to think Tostig was a particular danger to him, even over the danger Cecy herself presented.

Tostig's eyes flicked to Thrandthrin, the commander of the contingent he was a part of, waiting for the signal to begin. Thrandthrin, too, was standing stock-still in the flank's rear, but even as Tostig looked at him, he jerked his head upward.

As they had planned, Tostig and several of the magicians on the left flank turned toward the river in unison. Together, they raised their hands, and Tostig shouted the word along with the others, though he knew his magic would provide most of the power. *"Laigua puida!"*

As Tostig felt the magic flow through him, strong and sure, he was certain this would be his greatest water manipulation spell yet. The Nairam River to their left rose in the center and on the side of the enemy, the water forming a towering cliff over the opposing forces. As one, Tostig and the other magicians swept their hands in a downward motion, and the wave of water crashed over the herald and his fighters, knocking most of them off their feet even as they were summoning their first spells. Many of them struggled for air as the water flowed swiftly through their ranks. Even elves were not immune to the fury of rushing water.

As they regained their feet, their mouths already forming the spells they would send toward the Sashu, Cecy used their distraction to mount a full-scale attack.

"Archers!" she shouted, surprising the few magicians who had regained their footing and focus. They had clearly not been expecting a physical attack, and even as balls of blue light rushed from Altoneir's forces to the Sashu, the front ranks of the Sashu magicians knelt. A small row of archers from each flank aimed. Before they could shoot, Tostig heard the dull thud of two bodies hitting the ground, the first casualties of the battle.

"Loose!" Cecy called, and as soon as the archers had shot, the front row of each flank produced a fireball between their hands and flung it at their drenched opponents.

A kind of organized pandemonium the likes of which Tostig had never seen or imagined broke out. As several elves on the far side fell from bow shots, the rest redoubled their attacks on the Sashu, countering their fireballs with more streaks of light. Tostig knew the light was intended to incapacitate rather than kill; Altoneir's forces would have been warned against killing him outright unless no other options were available.

Spells clashed in the center of the battlefield, creating large flashes of light and fire as they collided and neutralized each other. Tostig saw several of the elves on the other side fall, their numbers decreasing quickly, but that did not stop them. For a moment, Tostig stood fascinated by their eyes. They never stopped looking for him, even as they cast their spells, their eyes flicking across the rows of Sashu fighters for one who stood out with greater power than the rest.

"Tostig, move!" Thrandthrin shouted from behind him, breaking him out of his momentary trance. He immediately redoubled his efforts at offensive magic, throwing orange fireballs with his hands even as he uprooted several trees at the edge of the battle and sent them hurtling into the enemy masses. He was careful not to vocalize the spells, as they would recognize his superior power if they knew he was the one wreaking so much destruction, but he could not stop his eyes from flicking to the trees and then the boulders that were the targets of his magic.

Cecy stood in the center of the fray as her fighting magicians wrought their spells around her. A wind seemed to surround her, whipping her long, dark hair and black robes as she formed her hands as though she were drawing a circle in the air, blue light spanning between them into a great, crackling ball. Casting her hands outward, she struck down several of the enemy fighters at once, including their commander.

They showed no sign of confusion at the sight of their fallen leader or their dwindling numbers, and Tostig heard more bodies hit the ground behind him amid the battle cries of the Sashu. The contingent would not stop hunting him, even as they realized the Sashu sorely outmatched them.

"Wind!" he shouted from Cecy's left, and as Cecy prepared another one of her singular strikes, the left flank caused a gust of wind to newly unbalance the shot, burned, and electrified opponents.

The spell was unsuccessful, the rush of wind passing harmlessly through their opponents, barely seeming to unsettle them. Altoneir's forces regained their focus, and those who were able redoubled their offensive, firing spells at the Sashu with a ferocity Tostig would never have guessed possible.

As he fought, he watched them use elemental magic as he had, hurling boulders, uprooted trees, and raw fire into the Sashu ranks. They were no longer aiming to incapacitate, but to kill. He understood now why Cecy had refused to underestimate the small force: even though less than half of them were left standing, their skill was proving deadly.

He saw a group of them take aim at the front line of Sashu surrounding Cecy, and he knew if he didn't act fast, she could be taken down. It was that realization that caused him to make the very move Cecy had warned him against. Separating himself from the protective ranks of the left flank, Tostig ran pell-mell between the two forces, dodging some spells and catching others on his warded robes. He felt the impacts, but they did not harm him as he continued to run, seeking the no-man's-land between the two forces.

Reaching the very center of the battling forces, Tostig knelt and struck his fist into the ground with all of his might. "*Avenci creari!*" He roared the incantation, putting all his magical power into it, and he not only opened a chasm between the two forces, but caused the ground to crumble under the entire front line of Altoneir's forces. He watched with satisfaction, panting from effort, as several fighters were swallowed by the earth, distracting those remaining from their focus on Cecy.

He realized his mistake as soon as a fierce elf woman on the opposing side shouted, "That's him! Seize him!"

The entirety of Altoneir's forces rushed him, using wordless magic to effortlessly leap over the chasm. No longer were they fighting the Sashu, but rather, their entire focus was on capturing him. Even as he sprang back from the onslaught, the entire Sashu force abandoned their positions to surround him, as planned for his inevitable identification.

Several broadswords were drawn by Sashu fighters as the forces collided, Tostig was aghast at the danger he had placed his people in. Magic flew in all directions, and it became hard to recognize which spells came from whom.

Tostig found himself alongside Cecy, who had rushed to his aid. While she cast her blue rays of lightning, felling several soldiers at once, Tostig cast hot blasts of air, cooking them from the inside out.

The smell sickened him, as did the thought of the lives he was ending, but his focus was on decimating the opposing force.

Tostig realized the exact moment the wards on his robes were exhausted; a fireball thrown at him caught on his robes and they began to burn. Clearly, those left no longer cared about taking him alive but had decided to eliminate the threat of the Blessed in the most final way possible. Quickly, Tostig summoned water from the river to put out the flames, but as he glanced down, several spells sped toward him at once.

"No!" Paalavi shouted, and before Tostig could stop him or even cast a spell to defend himself, he threw himself in the way of the rushing spells.

The spells met him with a quiet finality, striking his body in midair even as he dove in front of the Blessed. His motion stopped as though he had hit a wall, and his lifeless body thudded to the ground right in front of Tostig and Cecy.

Tostig's grief and rage were indescribable, and he no longer felt a twinge of regret at the lives he was ending as he and Cecy led the rest of the Sashu in completely devastating Altoneir's forces. Though their focus and intent had been on capturing or killing Tostig, they were quickly forced to go on the defensive: though the Sashu had suffered losses, barely a quarter of their fighters remained standing.

Within minutes of Paalavi's death, the Sashu fighters buried the remainder of Altoneir's fighters in sheer numbers, using both magic and broadswords to take them down. When the fighting finally stopped, none were left standing, and the remaining Sashu stood among the destruction, breathless with battle lust.

At Cecy's command, strong and sure even in the aftermath, the Sashu broke ranks and began the work of tending their wounded and counting their dead.

～

Tostig had never felt such crushing sadness: not when his childhood friend had died of a mysterious illness, not when he had found Alanda's family devastated by The Hunger, not even when his own infant brother had died in the night before he was a month old. The once-smooth clearing had been rent by the chasm he had created, and the river flowed into the open space as though a dam had been breached. He gazed across the clearing, once one of the most peaceful places he knew, and saw the bodies from both sides, his heart breaking with the desolation of it all.

He could not escape one fact: they had all died because of him.

Cecy joined him as he bent to check the body of a young tselq woman named Libet, one of the newer Sashu who had been promoted to apprentice only days before. Instead of staying sheltered in the caves with the novitiates, her change of status meant joining the fighting force. As he gazed at her body, her startlingly green eyes stared into the heavens as though looking for an answer to why her life had so abruptly been ended.

"She should have been in the caves learning her chosen art," Tostig choked to Cecy when she arrived, his voice catching on his immense grief. "This is - "

"Blessed, you must listen to me right now. Look into my eyes," Cecy insisted, her voice calm, but laced with a concern he had never heard from her. He lifted his eyes unwillingly from Libet's body. "This is not your fault. You did not ask to become the Blessed, and you invited no one to attack our home. This is not your fault."

He nodded, a terse movement. Cecy knew she would have to counsel him further, but there was no time to coddle him in that moment. All around them, the injured lay waiting for aid, and the dead for dignified interment. She, Tostig, and the other remaining magicians labored into the night, clearing the battlefield of all but the stains left behind by the blood of the fallen.

They buried the bodies of the enemy with as much dignity as those of their own. Cecy and Maera, who had joined them from the caves, reminded the Sashu that the enemy were all sentient beings who had been on opposing sides of a battle they had not initiated. The other survivors did not protest their reasoning: all life was given by Sado and deserved respect.

Upon returning to the caves, Cecy addressed the surviving group, still over two hundred strong, in the main cavern. "We will perform the Ceremony of Dedication tomorrow at nightfall," she told them, naming the ceremony to relinquish the dead into Xatra's care. "Until then, all normal lessons and activities are to cease, and only essential functions must be performed. I would like all of you, fighters and non-fighters alike, to rest, recover, and find solace in whatever way seems best to you."

Tostig, who had stood in the front row for her speech, nodded and traded condolences with those around him before seeking the solitude of his quarters and Ziva's company. Not being trained for the chaos of battle, Ziva had stayed behind.

Ziva, knowing only that something unusual had occurred, greeted Tostig enthusiastically, breaking her training briefly and jumping to put her front paws on his chest. He ruffled the long, black fur on her head and allowed her to lick his face.

"How about a bath, girl?"

She wagged her tail, recognizing the word. She enjoyed the warm water of the bathing cavern just as much as he did.

Gathering a fresh set of his red master's robes, Tostig led Ziva to the bathing rooms, only exchanging pleasantries with those he passed. No one tried to engage him in longer conversation; they were all as exhausted as he was.

The warm water of the bathing pool, more crowded than usual, soothed Tostig's tired muscles, and it felt good to wash the grime of the day from himself. Ziva, too, enjoyed being washed and toweled as dry as possible, and Tostig felt better in the embroidered red robes.

He slept fitfully, dreams of battle haunting him until he woke, panting, several times, only able to go back to sleep after reminding himself where he was and that the battle was over. After several of these awakenings, he finally dressed for the day, though Cecy's proclamation the night before meant that if he had wanted to stay in bed past *uht*, it would have been allowed. Tostig rose and donned his black robes, the only ones left from his apprenticeship; he wanted no special adornments. He decided that instead of waiting to break his fast with the rest of the Sashu, he would take Ziva for a predawn walk.

"Heel, Ziva," he said, and they left the caves before most of the Sashu had stirred.

Though he did not have a particular destination in mind, Tostig wound through the dimly lit woods until he found himself back in the clearing where the battle had been fought. It did not look as it had before, and Tostig halted before the new vista, breathless for a moment.

Where the chasm he had wrought met the Nairam River, a waterfall had formed, flowing into what seemed to be a small but deep lake in the center of the clearing. The falling water caught the light of the impending sunrise with sparkles of pink and orange as it poured into the larger body of water. From the chaos of the battle, something of true beauty had been wrought; it was as though it was always meant to be.

Tostig looked around, ensuring he was alone. Though he had been certain all of Altoneir's fighters had been killed, Cecy and Thrandthrin both had warned him there had certainly been those who held back from the battle in order to deliver news of its outcome. He drew his black hood over his head in much the same way he did during Sashu ceremonies, but this time, his goal was anonymity. He hoped if there were any observers, they might not recognize him.

No one accosted him as he walked to the banks of the new lake, just out of the tumult at the base of the small waterfall. All was silent and still but for the rushing of the water, and he allowed Ziva to explore the area as he knelt by the side of the water.

After some time staring out into the reflective hues of the small lake, his thoughts wandered to Paalavi, who had given his life for Tostig. The old poetry master had been a being of such preternatural calm and artistry that Tostig could not reconcile himself to the martyr the tselq had become. "I'm sorry, Master," he whispered into the stillness. "I'm so sorry." A single tear escaped his eye, and he did not bother to wipe it away.

He thought of Paalavi, of the pale, gray-green skin of the aged tselq, of the many curls of his horns, of his gentle voice and persistent insistence upon excellence from a barely literate novice. He thought of the gift of the dictionary when he had become an apprentice and chosen poetry as his art, and the worlds it had opened up for him. He thought of Paalavi's pride in his accomplishment when he had presented his final work only three days before.

"*Laigui maura*," he whispered without even realizing beforehand that he was going to call upon his magic.

From the rippling surface of the small lake, a figure arose and began forming itself in front of Tostig's eyes: the head and shoulders of his old master. The likeness was excellent, but the expression on the water sculpture's face was one of immeasurable grief, the grief Tostig knew Paalavi would have felt if he had survived and witnessed the devastation left behind. Tostig even imagined a tear running down the old tselq's cheek, though that level of detail was not actually present on the water sculpture. Tostig stared at it for several minutes, unconsciously supplying the trickle of magic needed to sustain the image.

"It is a good likeness." The statement, coming from just behind him, startled him out of his reverie but did not alarm him. Cecy's voice had become almost as familiar to him as his own mother's. He turned to her.

"Good morning," he said, his voice flat. He let the magic go, and Paalavi's likeness splashed back into the water.

"Good morning, Blessed." Cecy sat down next to him, folding her legs demurely under her embroidered azure robes. "When you were not present at the morning meal, I thought I might find you here."

"I hadn't realized it had grown so late."

"That is of no consequence. I gave the Sashu the day for reflection, and you are no exception. I wished to talk to you, however. I can feel the weight of guilt emanating from you as though it were a physical force."

Tostig did not reply, instead reverting his gaze to the water. He wasn't sure exactly what he was feeling, but guilt was certainly part of it.

"I will only repeat once what I told you yesterday: neither the battle nor any of the resulting injuries or deaths were your fault. You are the Blessed, young man, and throughout your entire life, things will happen around you, sometimes even because of you. That does not make all those things your sole responsibility. There are forces at work greater than you and I." She paused, waiting for him to respond. When he didn't, she continued, "That is not what I came to discuss, however. You will deal with your feelings over time, and I know you are wise enough to come to a sense of peace within yourself."

"What did you want to discuss, then?" Tostig attempted to put more inflection in his voice, to sound more like himself, but what came out sounded foreign, as though it had come from a completely different person.

"What you will do next," Cecy answered simply. "There are several options open to you, and we must decide how best to proceed. You understand, of course, that Altoneir will not stop pursuing you."

Tostig nodded. "Am I to stay in the caves and teach?" He thought that was the strongest possibility since Cecy had told him Altoneir had no spies among the Sashu.

Cecy shook her head. "As a young master, and even more so as the Blessed, your place is not here, sequestered from the world. Your place is out in the land, lending aid and counsel. I have an assignment for you, and after you have completed it, you will have the freedom you once sought to roam the land. As a magician, your advice and aid will be sought in any place you visit, and of course you and I would stay in touch so I might know where your travels have taken you."

Tostig tried not to show his surprise. "What's the assignment?" His voice sounded more like his own.

"A messenger on horseback, one of our network, arrived just this morning. The village of Hardfelden has been devastated by fire - nearly all of their buildings have been destroyed, many of the villagers have been sorely injured, and they have requested our aid. Will you go?"

Tostig stood and dusted off his robes. "Of course, I will go. Ziva!" He looked around and saw Ziva streaking towards them.

"Your horse and provisions are being readied," Cecy told him as they began the walk back to the caves. "It will take you three days to get down the mountain and into the valley, and another three to cross to Hardfelden. Do you know its location?"

"Yes, of course," Tostig said. Hardfelden was north of his own village, but not so far away he was unfamiliar with its location. "But it will take me more than six days to reach it."

"You underestimate the abilities of your horse," Cecy answered calmly. "Use the commands we taught you and allow your horse the freedom to reach the speeds she yearns for in the open spaces of the valley."

Tostig nodded and increased his pace.

"Tostig?" Cecy called from behind him. She continued her slow amble, oblivious to any urgency.

"Yes?"

"Remember what you did in the battle yesterday. Remember your own power, which exceeds even what I expected from the Blessed. Altoneir's forces will report it to him, but you will not find yourself in constant danger. It is my suspicion he will find another way to seek you out."

Tostig nodded tersely and turned back to resume his quick walk back to the caves to prepare for the journey.

EHNJA

*T*ostig frowned at the nearly full saddlebags laid across his bed. Never before had he packed for a journey as long as this one would be - after all, Cecy had said that after he was done with his assignment, he was free to traverse Ilbeor, using his magical ability to assist and advise wherever he was needed.

In the bags was food enough for his journey to Hardfelden, blankets and supplies for sleeping in the wilds, his small container of salt and seasonings, his wineskin and waterskin, and his cooking supplies. What he had to consider now was clothing: should he attempt to take all three sets of his robes along with his nightclothes, that he might be prepared? Or should he pack as he had when he had been a messenger and only take one additional set of clothing?

Tostig took his last set of red robes from their peg and rolled it as tightly as he could, placing it beside the others in the saddlebag. Thinking he would not be sleeping out-of-doors every night, he also added a set of nightclothes, the soft tunic and pants worn by all the Sashu.

He knew after he had finished his work at Hardfelden, he would journey south to Lakeland to see his family and then to Blackwell, but the road after that was unclear. If he was, as Cecy had promised, truly free to go where he would, he knew he would stop at nothing to find Alanda, but he had no way of knowing what kind of journey that would lead him on.

"Tostig," a voice from the door said just as he was tying up the saddlebags after concluding his packing.

He looked up to find Cecy, a worried expression on her face and a light gray stone tablet clutched in her hands. He frowned; it was not like Cecy to look worried. "Cecy," he said, "I was just ready to be on my way."

"There is something I must discuss with you first. We have had additional news from the messenger that brought us tidings from Hardfelden, and there are things you need to know in light of that news." She crossed the room and sat in her customary rocking chair, still clutching the stone tablet to her breast so he could not see what was on the other side.

His frown deepened as he joined her in the small sitting area. She knew the urgency of his mission; was it not she, herself, who had decided to send him? If she was willing to delay his departure with whatever her news was, he knew it must be serious. "What is it?" he asked, leaning calmly back in his chair, his posture belying both his curiosity and his impatience.

Her azure robes swished slightly as she rocked, looking pensive. Whatever this news was, it had her greatly concerned. "There is news of an Urothu attack on a village in the southern valley," she said. "Are you familiar with Basendale?"

"Of course," Tostig said, his heart beginning to pound. He never heard of Urothu attacking an entire village, and he feared what the result might have been.

"The village was decimated. Every person within Basendale was killed, every dwelling and structure burned. An attack of this nature has not occurred in many years, possibly even in your lifetime. Usually, the Urothu content themselves with destroying travelers and hunting parties unfortunate enough to cross their paths. An attack like this suggests premeditation and malice, though we are not certain what brought them so far from the Gray Hills."

"Were any other villages attacked?" he demanded urgently. Basendale was only a two-day journey from Blackwell, and his fear for Alanda spiked his pulse.

"No," Cecy said, and he felt himself relax slightly. "Only Basendale. The citizens of Blackwell attended to the burial of their neighbors. No other Urothu attacks have been reported, at least as far as the messenger was aware, and that in and of itself is a concern."

"I would consider that news to be good tidings," Tostig protested. Surely, Cecy was not suggesting it was unfortunate that no other humans or other civilized beings had been killed.

"Of course, we are glad no one else has been killed," Cecy said, an edge to her voice as though Tostig's insinuation offended her. "But it is not in character for these creatures to travel without leaving a trail of death in their wake. Considering the news about Basendale, we would have expected other villages to be attacked or, at the very least, news of travelers or hunting parties being murdered. That they acted in such a focused manner, killing only those in that particular village, suggests a level of planning and intent we would not normally think the Urothu capable of."

Tostig understood; if the Urothu were acting in a manner inconsistent with what was known of them, it suggested they were banding together for an unknown purpose. That was indeed concerning, but the selection of Basendale stymied his attempts at finding the reason for the massacre.

"As far as I am aware," he said finally, trying to work through his thoughts with the reason and logic instilled by his training, "Basendale is of little importance to the greater population of Ilbeor. It is part of no major trade networks, houses only minor nobles, and does not have a population large enough to present a threat. Why was it targeted, if indeed it was?"

"I do not know," Cecy said, her voice thoughtful. "It is just as you say - Basendale was insignificant to all but those who lived there. It was just a village, one among many, inhabited by a relatively small number of humans, most of whom were simple farmers. I cannot think of a reason for it to be targeted, but another salient point is that

Urothu do not work together well enough to target anyone for any reason. They are a wild race, ruled by their passions, and are all the more fearsome because of it, but it has been many years since even one of them has been seen that far south. In order to wreak the destruction the messenger described, there had to have been many of them working together."

Tostig sat in silence, rocking softly in his chair. He didn't know exactly why she was giving him this news in particular. It certainly didn't sound like he could render any aid to the doomed village if everyone there had been killed and all the buildings and farms destroyed.

After several moments, Cecy broke the silence. "It is because of this unprecedented attack that I have felt led to tell you one of the greatest secrets of the Sashu, a secret that even most masters have not been told."

Tostig stopped rocking, now wondering more intensely what was carved onto the hidden side of the stone tablet. To be entrusted with secrets not shared even with the masters of the Sashu took his breath away.

"You have not, of course, heard the name Ehnja in any of your studies," she said, pronouncing the name in a strange accent he did not recognize.

"No," he said. "I've never heard that name."

"The name is rarely uttered, because to be known would give her power greater than she can be trusted with," Cecy continued. "Ehnja is a goddess, matched in power only by Sado, her brother. But her purposes are not for life, peace, and the good of the races. Rather, Ehnja promotes lawlessness, war, and chaos. She is darkness personified, and those who know her name often fear to speak or hear it."

"A tenth goddess?" Tostig breathed, struck nearly dumb. In all his studies of magic and the Sashu religion, he had only ever learned of the Nine.

"Yes," Cecy said, "but not a child of Sado. Ehnja works against that which Sado and his children have created. She holds nothing but malice for our gods and the peoples of Ilbeor."

"Have you met her?" Tostig asked.

"No," Cecy answered. "She does not walk the land in flesh and rarely deigns to manifest. Ehnja works in shadow. But the reason I tell you of her now, Blessed, is that I fear you must be on the watch for her machinations. This attack may be but a beginning to a larger plan laid by her, for we can think of no other being who might have the power to control them, to entice them to move in large groups, and to target specific populations. We may never know the reason Basendale was targeted, but I fear her hand may be behind it."

She finally turned the stone tablet over. On it was a carving of a being Tostig could only describe as portraying abject misery and horror. It had four faces lined in a row, but they were not of the known races, like the other gods and goddesses. One face was that of a fearsome predator, fangs protruding from thin lips, whiskers coming out of its cheeks. Another was of a bird-like creature with a sharp beak and beady eyes. Yet another was a serpent, again with fangs protruding. The final face, however, was what made the carving truly frightening, for Tostig could not put a name to what he saw. The chisel had gone deep, giving the suggestion that the last face was dark, and the cuts made it broad and square, with pointed horns protruding from its forehead. The eyes were mere slits, and Tostig thought he would always imagine them as fiery red. It was a face of something unworldly and evil, the face of a monster from his childhood nightmares.

The row of frightening faces was situated atop a body roughly in the shape of a thin human female wearing a dress of the most scandalous cut Tostig had ever seen. Tostig's breath caught. "Did the person who carved this actually see her? Is this what she looks like?" he asked.

"We do not know, for the carving is even more ancient than I am. It was found in the ruins of an old stronghold in the Gray Hills long ago and brought here. Only with my father's help was I able to discern who it represented, and I have kept it among my most secret belongings ever since."

"Why are more people not warned about her?" Tostig asked

reasonably. "It seems as though, with the threat she poses, it would be wise for the Sashu masters, at least, to be aware of her presence."

"You speak truly, but you fail to realize the power the knowledge of her conveys. With but a few discontented beings, a whole religion could be set up surrounding her, paying homage to her and giving her power. We cannot take that risk, and I ask you to hold this knowledge close to your heart, asking questions only of myself or Grayson."

Tostig nodded, though he still didn't wholly agree with her reasoning. "You have my word."

"There is one other thing you must know," Cecy continued, her voice determined as though she were bound to get the worst over. "She is aware of the Blesseds of Sado as soon as they are touched, and more than one has come into contact with her. Almost without fail, the Blesseds were killed. Such was the fate of not the most recent Blessed, but the one who came before him. I do not want it to be your fate."

"What must I do?" asked Tostig, wondering how he could be expected to prevail against a deity.

"At present, there is nothing to be done but to be on your guard. You have a purpose in Ilbeor, Blessed, and that purpose will not be fulfilled if you live your life in fear of what might be. Keep a watchful eye, and report anything you see to myself or to Grayson, who will attend to your steps more closely now that you are leaving."

She placed the stone tablet face down on the small table, handling it gently so it would not crack or crumble. Placing her palms on her knees, she sat still as she surveyed Tostig somberly, waiting. As he looked at her, he was struck for the first time in a long time by how beautiful she was, with her cinnamon skin gleaming healthily in the glow of the yellow light from his globes. She seemed not much older than himself, though he knew she had lived for centuries. Her azure robes, brighter than most colors worn by the Sashu, set off the color of her long, dark hair, and her serious expression did nothing to mar the beauty of her face. Tostig realized he would miss her when he left the caves.

After a few moments, he finally spoke. "And what of Basendale? Is there anything we can do?"

"There is not." A look of sadness crossed her face. "There is no helping Basendale, and there will be no rebuilding since all of its citizens are gone."

Tostig nodded, and her words felt like a physical weight pressing on his shoulders. He thought, given all the powers of the Nine and the magical prowess Sado had blessed the Sashu magicians with, there should have been some aid they could render. But he remembered that no magic could bring life to that which had none. He could not bring the villagers of Basendale back; not even the gods could do that.

"Do not despair, Blessed," Cecy said. "I know what I have told you has given you much to consider, but all is not lost. We are here, and we stand ready to better the lives of the peoples of Ilbeor. We stand ready to fight against the evil of Ehnja, if this is indeed her doing. And you, yourself, stand ready to fulfill your duty. Never before has a Blessed had your potential, Tostig. I want you to remember that and remember it well. If there is anyone who can stand against the evils of this land, it is you."

She stood abruptly, picking up the stone tablet and turning it against her chest. "Now," she said, even as Tostig stood, "you must go to Hardfelden and begin serving your purpose."

Tostig watched her leave, not knowing what else to say. Reminding himself of his original purpose, he slung his saddlebags over his shoulder, took up his bow and quiver, and prepared to leave the caves.

PART III

FROM THE PROPHECY OF
BEIANARIAN AND THE MAGUS

Trusting blindly, walking into traps set
By foes yet unknown and numbered as friends,
Beianarian treads alone, betrayed
By the goodness of her unguarded heart.
Clinging to those she holds dearest in life,
Threatened by plots of undiminished malice
That which she loves most is lost to her sight
And that which she fears becomes stronger still.

The Magus, strong and pure of heart and mind
Stands, set to fight the terrors of the land
Love of his people and the one he seeks
Holding him still in the face of darkness.
Against him flows the black heart of evil
In the land rages the sea of chaos
Well hidden from all but those who would see,
Entombing the wise in ruins of good.

Peace is but an idea bereft of war
Eluding powers of the land, striving

On many sides for ill-begotten gain
Marching toward the end of all they hold true.

from The Prophecy of Beianarian and the Magus
set forth by Algernon of House Agelon
Second Age, 246

NIGHT TERROR

Altoneir laid back on his pillows, somehow not as sated as he usually felt when Iantris lay beside him, her delicate breathing barely affected by their lovemaking. Usually, he felt a sense of peace in her presence he felt nowhere else, but today, his mind was feverish with conflict and indecision.

"You must take this Blessed," Iantris whispered to him, her lips so close to his ear that he could feel the slight wisps of air tickle him as she spoke. "Though the fighting contingent failed, this Blessed cannot compete with your power. You must take him, and soon."

"I have lost the razor edge of my fighting force," he said, his voice low but still somehow dripping with stress. "They were overwhelmed by the power of the Blessed and Cecy the Undying. More than a hundred fighters, centuries and millennia of experience, wiped out by untested magicians on a field far from our goal."

Iantris stroked his hair soothingly. "Peace, my love," she purred. "This loss is not the end of all. You must not lose hope. The situation can still be righted." She moved her hand to his bare chest, tickling his skin with her fingernails.

Altoneir drew a ragged breath, already feeling his want for her rekindle. He tried to focus, but it was difficult with her so close, her naked body cupped against his, her hand trailing fingers of fire across his chest. "I must change tactics," he said finally, his voice hoarse with need. "This Blessed cannot be taken by force; that much has become clear. The Sashu are more of a threat than I originally believed, especially when Cecy and the Blessed work together."

"This Blessed does seem to be more powerful than Blesseds previous," Iantris conceded, still stroking his chest. "But you, my love, are yet more powerful. You must find a way to take him. Imagine the power he would bring to your cause and the upset it would create among the Sashu and even Cecy herself."

Altoneir imagined it and smiled softly at the image of the Sashu, broken without their cornerstone, and Cecy, powerless against the might of himself and of her own Blessed. To remove the Blessed from their ranks would be a devastating blow, revenge for the losses he had suffered. "How could we bring him to our side? Our past recruitment efforts were unsuccessful. The Blessed is always loyal to the Sashu."

Iantris smiled as she spoke her next words. "If we are to take the Blessed, we must first break the Blessed." Taking his hand, she told him her plan.

Just as Altoneir was beginning to understand how they might persuade this Blessed to join them, a knock sounded on the door, fast and urgent. Altoneir scowled. "Enter," he called, vowing that he would address the interruption after whatever news was to be had was said.

His scowl deepened as a middle-aged human burst into the room, a small scroll clutched in his pudgy, dark-skinned hand. Altoneir had never really liked Wilmot, but the man had proven himself useful as his Master of Messages.

"What is it, Wilmot? More news from Emelle?" His voice oozed condescension and irritation. Wilmot had brought little enough news of import for years, but the Master of Messages often felt even the most trivial of matters required Altoneir's immediate attention.

"From Dachilon, my lord," Wilmot answered, out of breath from his rushed journey. He hardly seemed to notice the fact that he had rushed in on his master when Altoneir was in bed in a state of undress; early hours and other considerations rarely stopped him from doing what he perceived to be his duty.

Altoneir perked up slightly at the news, his pointed ears rising as he took his hand from Iantris and sat up in bed, the bedclothes only covering the lower half of his naked body. He had not had news from Dachilon for quite some time; Vritri had always been quite circumspect with communication. He motioned for Wilmot to hand him the message, and he quickly scanned it.

Without dismissing Wilmot or seeming to care about his state of undress, Altoneir threw back the bedclothes and stood, motioning for Iantris to do the same. As he took his black, water-cloth robes from where they had been left hanging across an armchair and began dressing, he finally spoke, his voice clipped as he issued his orders. "Convene the council," he commanded.

Wilmot departed the room with haste, seeming like he would nearly explode with importance as he realized this message had been received well; this message might lead to action.

"Deena!" Isaac exclaimed one afternoon when winter had blossomed into a fine early spring. Having just had his fifth birth celebration, Isaac was hard at work learning the universal glyphs. He seemed glad for the distraction as he hopped quickly to his feet and bounded to the front door. "May I go to your house and see your birds?"

Maryah was about to reprimand Isaac for his presumption, but Deena shook her head, showing she didn't mind the child's cheerful question. "Yes," Deena told him. "But not today. There's a storm coming, and we don't want to get caught in the rain, do we? I'll come and take you to the birds tomorrow, and that's a promise."

"If you are a good child and learn the fourth glyph," Maryah interjected, shooing Isaac back to his task. "The fourth glyph tells you someone needs help, so it's very important to learn. I want you to tell me what it is when I hold it up to you, and tomorrow you shall draw it in the dirt before Deena comes."

"Kitz wants to go. He likes birds," Isaac commented nonchalantly as he returned to the fourth glyph chip, seeming bored as he traced the symbol with his small forefinger.

Maryah simply nodded and asked Deena if she would like to take a seat and have a cup of tea. Most of the attention from the village leaders had ceased in the months following Alanda's departure, but Deena still visited frequently. Asking Deena if she wanted tea was a formality; the old herbalist enjoyed Maryah's particular brew and always accepted. Maryah enjoyed her company; though Serill was a kind and generous husband, men could not truly understand the household realm of their wives and most, including Serill, did not make much attempt to do so.

Once Deena had seated herself in Maryah's rocking chair with her tea, she asked her customary first question, as pointed as it always was. "How are *you*, Maryah?"

Maryah always appreciated the question. As a middie wife, mother, and the guardian of a prophet, few enough people ever inquired about her personal wellbeing. "I am...reasonably well," she replied, taking a sip of her own tea as she sat in Alanda's chair. "Isaac seems to have found a new energy and defiance since his birth celebration and has been more difficult to manage than usual."

Deena nodded in understanding. She did not have any children herself, but as the village's herbalist and healer, she was well-acquainted with the challenges of child rearing. "That is often the case," she told Maryah reassuringly. "Rest assured, Isaac is not becoming anything but what he should be. It is normal for children, especially boys, to begin asserting their independence at this age, and the time is ripe for him to be given more responsibility. Respond to defiance firmly so he learns he must not disobey you or his father, but also allow him to explore his own sense of being an individual. Isaac, especially, needs this latitude."

Maryah was a bit surprised by this advice. Most of the mothers and fathers of Blackwell didn't concern themselves with their children's explorations of independence, but instead responded harshly to displays of defiance, expecting complete obedience and subservience until their children reached the age of apprenticeship. Even then, children were expected to obey their parents, but they were given more freedom and allowed more of a chance to speak their own opinions.

"Isaac is essentially an apprentice," Deena said reflectively, mirroring Maryah's thoughts, "though he is still but a small child. This is difficult for him because he is not yet old enough to understand the importance of his position, and I am not surprised he is acting out. I also know that makes things difficult for you, Maryah, because to respond to Isaac in the way most mothers would respond to defiance would be inappropriate. You are dwelling in uncharted territory."

"I'm grateful for your understanding," Maryah said. "I have felt much the same about Isaac, though I couldn't put it into words."

Deena nodded and changed the subject. "What of Kitz?" she asked. "Has there been any change? I know he has spoken no prophecy, but has his behavior changed in any way?"

Maryah shook her head. "Kitz is as he has been since the fire. He is obedient to simple commands but shows no interest in anything, even Isaac. The 'thinks' Isaac tells us are usually related to food or drink. The comment about Kitz wanting to see the birds surprised me, and I have to wonder whether it came from Kitz or whether Isaac was simply stating his own desire for Kitz to come with him tomorrow. Isaac doesn't like being separated from Kitz for any length of time; it seems to make him anxious."

"Kitz loved my birds as a child, much as your Isaac does," Deena mused. "I often wonder how many of his former preferences have remained within him. Isaac's request that he come see my birds makes me think perhaps something of Kitz's former mind remains. That would be a hopeful sign indeed."

"I have him go outside every afternoon for a couple of hours on nice days, as you suggested. Serill built a chair for him, so he doesn't have to sit in the dirt. He goes out when I tell him to, but he doesn't seem to have any preference for it. He just sits there, staring."

Outside, rain began to fall, softly at first but quickly becoming a downpour as the storm arrived. Maryah glanced out the window, noting the valley grasses blowing sideways in the wind like waves on the sea. She looked back at Deena. "You must stay for the evening meal," she insisted. "Serill will be home soon, and I have a nice stew cooking. There is plenty for one more, and then you can observe Kitz yourself."

Deena glanced to the chair Kitz sat in, his back ramrod straight, his eyes focused on something neither woman could see. She shook her head. "There doesn't seem to be much for me to observe, dear," she said with some regret, "but I would enjoy supping with your family."

Deena and Maryah made inconsequential small talk as Maryah finished the evening meal and quizzed Isaac on the first four glyphs. Deena noticed the boy did well but seemed frustrated by the exercise. "I *know* the glyphs, Mama," he protested angrily before Maryah began her third iteration of questioning. "I won't do the glyphs anymore, not ever!" He stamped his small foot in consternation.

The way Maryah dealt with this defiance raised her in Deena's esteem. In most households, such a display would have resulted in a beating along with many harsh, angry words. Instead, Maryah knelt and looked Isaac in the eye. She told him firmly, but without raising her voice, "You may not *ever* talk to Mama that way or tell Mama what you will or will not do. Is that understood, Isaac?"

Isaac fidgeted under her stern gaze but replied dutifully, "Yes, Mama."

Deena was already impressed with the minor scolding and Maryah's lack of temper, but what happened next differed greatly from what she had experienced in the more traditional households. The chastisement over, Maryah hugged her son. "Now," she said, "tell Mama why you don't like the glyph chips without using naughty words or tone."

"Kitz already told me the glyphs," Isaac said, his small voice trembling with the effort not to take a defiant tone. "I can do all the glyphs and it's boring to sit down and do them every single day. I want to play with my wooden horse!"

Maryah glanced at Deena, clearly at a loss.

"Kitz told you the glyphs?" Deena asked him. "How did he tell you? He didn't say words to you, did he?"

"No!" Isaac shouted, clearly frustrated. "He can't say words!"

Deena noticed Maryah was about to reprove him again and held a hand up, stopping her. "It's okay, Isaac," Deena said. "Try to explain it to me. I just want to understand, that's all. Can you help me understand?" Having never spoken to a child so small about a matter of such importance, she tried to find the right combination of solemnity and simple language.

Isaac seemed calmer once he realized Deena was going to listen. "Kitz told me with his thinks," he said. "He told me all the glyphs and showed me with his thinks and then I knew them, too."

Maryah took a seat at the kitchen table, letting Deena handle the situation and carefully observing how the wise older woman dealt with her emotional child. *This situation really is bigger than he is*, she thought. *I can see why he might be frustrated that the adults around him don't understand how he communicates with Kitz.*

Deena held her hand out to Maryah, silently requesting the set of glyph chips. Maryah quickly handed them to the herbalist, who picked one at random and held it up to Isaac. It turned out to be the sixteenth glyph, one which offered directions to lost travelers and was often used at waypoints. Having only been instructing Isaac in the glyphs for about a week, Maryah hadn't taught him the sixteenth glyph yet, or any glyph beyond the fourth.

Isaac easily identified the symbol and explained its use in his small, singsong voice, sounding slightly bored. One after another, he correctly recognized each glyph, not making a single mistake. When he had finished, he didn't seem proud of himself but asked his mother slightly impatiently whether he could go play. Not knowing what to say, Maryah jerked her head toward the corner where Isaac kept his few wooden toys, silently giving him permission.

Deena sighed. "Well," she said, "it seems you don't need to teach him the glyphs." Thinking over the implications of how Isaac had learned the glyphs, the herbalist remained silent while Maryah completed the evening meal, and Isaac played imaginary games with his figurines. Kitz, as always, remained silent and still in his chair, neither saying anything nor seeming to notice anything around him.

When Serill returned home, his beard dripping from the steady rain, Deena rejoined the conversation, listening as Serill described a new tool he had been working on and as Maryah proudly relayed Isaac's accomplishment with the glyphs. Reaching across the supper table, Serill ruffled Isaac's curly hair and praised him. "Now you must learn the duties of a man of the house," he told him seriously before taking another bite of stew. "Mama will teach you, but so will I. We shall go hunting on the sixth day."

Isaac's face lit up, and he turned to Kitz, who had finished his stew. "Papa's taking us hunting, Kitz!" he exclaimed.

"Not Kitz," Serill said gruffly. "Just you and Papa."

Isaac's small face fell. He had not been separated from Kitz for any length of time since Kitz had come to live at their house, and though he could not name them, it seemed he felt his responsibilities keenly. "I have to stay with Kitz," he told his father sadly, his voice somehow seeming older than his age.

"No," Deena interjected. "Your mama will take care of Kitz while you are gone. She knows what he likes to eat and what he likes to do. You must learn to hunt, Isaac. It's very important."

The relief on the small boy's face was so palpable that the hearts of every adult at the table ached for him. Not noticing their expressions, Isaac grinned and asked his father, "Do I get to have a bow and arrows now, like you?"

ALTONEIR RESTLESSLY PACED the council chambers, not looking at any of his gathered advisors or even at Iantris, who stood in her white robes in a corner of the room, observing. Many of them had been serving him for nearly the entirety of his self-imposed exile. "The children are of royal blood but do not yet have royal protection," he pointed out. "The girl will reach Emelle eventually, whether or not she plans to. Once she and her brother are there, it will be nigh-on impossible to reach them. We must act quickly."

A tselq named Calian, young by elven standards but quite aged for his race, studied his large hands as he rested them on the long table. He idly noticed that his former healthy green color was fading; the tips of his fingers were graying, as was normal in aged tselqs, but he did not welcome the change. He fervently believed in the cause he had served his entire life and wished to live to see Altoneir's plans come to fruition.

When Altoneir had not spoken for several moments, he raised his head. "Vritri writes that the young girl travels with a tselq. We do not know their exact route or when they will arrive at any particular destination. Searching Ilbeor for them would be a lengthy and possibly fruitless proposition. We know the boy's position; why do we not pursue him?"

"He is second born," Altoneir stated. "The girl is more valuable."

"Perhaps," Leilatha interjected, "but perhaps not. As you know, the human line of succession is male dominated. The younger boy would have a more direct claim to the throne. I would say his arrival would even displace Gildan's claim. As the adopted heir, Gildan has no hereditary claim to the throne. A male blood relative would supersede even the king's preference. We all know how important blood relations are to the Sovaria dynasty."

"Leilatha speaks truly," Iantris said softly from her corner. "Though reason would suggest the girl is of greater importance, the humans' preference for male monarchs plays reason false."

Leilatha did not respond, but neither did she look appreciative of the support from the mysterious elven lady. Iantris was not part of the council, yet Altoneir insisted on including her when she was present in the castle. She wondered if Iantris held any sway over their lord other than that of a bedfellow; it was something she had wondered often over the centuries.

Altoneir stopped pacing. "So, we take the boy," he stated, making his decision clear and unarguable. "Once we have him, we will parley with Emelle for some, if not all, of the things we desire."

"If the girl goes to the palace, the king may decide that since the bloodline is not broken, the boy is not worth concessions," Hugon pointed out.

Altoneir glared at the young man and regretted the absence of Bryant, who had been killed by the Sashu, on the council to bring him to heel. Of the five races, humans were his least favorite, but he had conceded early on that he needed cooperation from all to achieve his aims. "The king will decide no such thing," he declared with certainty. "The boy is a prophet. Even without his pedigree, such a person is valuable. With it, getting the boy back from us and into the clutches of the royal court will be the king's highest priority."

"You really believe the king will grant you a position at court and on his council?" Leilatha asked, her genteel voice rising slightly. "To make such a concession to any elf would be unheard of, but to do so for an elf who has been in open rebellion for three centuries seems highly unlikely."

Iantris stepped forward and whispered in Altoneir's ear for a moment before regaining her place in the corner of the room. After listening, Altoneir studied Leilatha carefully. The slightly built elven lady had been one of his first recruits and was his most trusted advisor besides Iantris herself.

"Leilatha," he said, his voice much gentler than the one he had used when addressing Hugon, "I truly believe if we hold a blood relative of the king's, one who would qualify by heredity to take the throne and a prophet, Florian will grant nearly any demand in order to bring him back to Emelle." His voice rose at the end, his excitement at finally having an actionable idea obvious to everyone. He had been waiting centuries for this opportunity, this hole in the kingdom's defenses. Their army, while powerful, was too small, even with half the dwarven race having joined their ranks, to compete with the conscripted human army of King Florian, much less the forces of the other races, should they decide to ally with the humans.

Leilatha met his dark eyes, wide and sparkling with excitement and agitation. His looks were a perfect foil to his own; slight and flaxen-haired, Leilatha contrasted almost perfectly with Altoneir's tall, dark form. She felt her love for him swell as she saw hope, so long absent, alight in his eyes. Concealing her feelings perfectly and painfully aware that it was Iantris, not herself, who Altoneir loved, she finally responded. "We take the boy, then," she said with finality.

A murmur of assent ran along the table as the convened elves, humans, tselqs, and dwarves, seven in number after the loss of Bryant, agreed. Bringing the boy to the island was a certain way to bring Florian down and make him accede to their demands. It was an opportunity that had not presented itself in all their time plotting, planning, hoping, and discussing the future of their land.

Altoneir waited until they had all talked themselves out and silence reigned. When he was certain their discussion had concluded, he issued a single, abrupt command.

"Assemble the travelers."

ISAAC'S BEHAVIOR improved as he adjusted to his role and Maryah, bucking tradition and custom, allowed him many of the same freedoms of expression afforded to twelve-year-old apprentices. Though she scolded him for defiance or disrespect, she allowed him to share his thoughts and observations outside of speaking Kitz's thoughts, and under her careful care, her son flourished into a boy much more mature in his thoughts than his tender age suggested.

One night after dark, Maryah and Serill were enjoying the quiet time between the children's bedtime and their own. "I will take Isaac out tomorrow for sixth-day hunting," Serill commented, smoking his pipe as Maryah repaired one of Kitz's tunics.

"He will enjoy that," Maryah replied absently, rocking gently and not taking her eyes off her sewing. She wondered briefly why Serill had even mentioned it; he always took Isaac for sixth-day hunting now. She faintly registered Serill rising from his chair and crossing to his pack by the front door, but she did not look up from her work until he came to her chair and awkwardly knelt beside her.

"What is it, dear?" she asked, concerned. She wondered if he was upset about something. He rarely paid her any attention in the evenings, preferring quiet after the clamor of the blacksmith's shop by day.

"I have something for our son," Serill announced, his voice containing a hint of glee that was most unlike him.

Maryah smiled. She knew what he had and could not wait to experience Isaac's excitement when he saw it in the morning.

With a small flourish, Serill brought his hand from behind his back. In it was a small bow, tiny really, but of exquisite craftsmanship.

Maryah put down her sewing and reached out to touch the dark wood. She knew little of weapons, but she knew childhood versions of them were usually made simply and passed around the village due to the necessary frequency of replacement as children grew. This bow was no rough, used practice instrument, though. The wood contained tiny, beautiful carvings depicting the forests of the mountains edging their valley, polished to a high shine, and she felt it was more a work of art than a weapon. She looked at Serill wonderingly.

"I wanted his first bow to be something he could keep," Serill explained. "Perhaps even something he could pass on to his own son. He may not appreciate it now, but he will as he grows."

Maryah reached out a hand and touched Serill's cheek, the roughness of his beard scratching her soft skin. "It's beautiful," she told him. "What a wonderful thing for you to have done for him."

"I won't get all his bows made like this as he grows," Serill continued. "The expense would be too great. But Isaac is a child who has taken on the responsibilities of one much older, and I wanted him to have something special."

Maryah was startled, though she kept her face calm and her smile in place. Serill never spoke about Isaac's role. She knew he loved his son, but the raising of children was the realm of women, and fathers rarely interfered. She hadn't realized Serill had given much thought to Isaac's unique life.

"You are a good father to think of such a thing. You're right that he may not appreciate the beauty of this gift now, but as he grows, he will realize what you have given to him."

Serill leaned forward and gently kissed his wife on the lips. "I want to offer you a measure of praise as well," he said. "You may not think I notice, but I see how carefully you are rearing Isaac and how well you care for Kitz. You are a good wife and mother, and I am happy we are together."

Maryah fairly glowed. Serill was not a demonstrative man, and she didn't know where this outpouring of thoughtfulness had come from, but she appreciated it. "Thank you for saying that," she told him with a soft smile.

Serill rose in an abrupt return to his usual bearing. "Come," he said. "It grows late, and we must rise early before Isaac and I leave." He placed Isaac's new bow and a small quiver of tiny arrows carefully on the table where the boy would see them first thing in the morning.

Maryah set her sewing aside, placing Kitz's half-repaired tunic on the small round table next to her chair. Together, they quietly entered the first sleeping room, careful not to wake Isaac on his small cot next to their large bed. They didn't speak as they changed into their nightclothes and got into bed, but Serill kissed Maryah's forehead before he rolled away to go to sleep. She smiled as she, too, drifted off, tired from the duties of the day.

Isaac woke when it was still fully dark outside, sitting straight up in bed and looking wildly around. Maryah, a light sleeper, opened her eyes and saw him dimly in the moonlight filtering through the open window. She was surprised, for he always slept the night through. She wondered if he had experienced a nightmare.

Isaac finally found his mother in the darkness, though he couldn't see her clearly enough to look into her eyes. "They're coming," he said, his voice flat at first but then rising to a frantic shout as he repeated the phrase. "They're coming. They're coming!"

"Isaac, what - " Maryah began, rising from the bed to comfort her small son. She heard Serill sit up beside her and knew he would not be pleased with the interruption to his sleep, but she didn't worry about it in the light of Isaac's distress.

"They're coming!" the boy screamed.

She had just reached him and moved to take him into her arms when she heard the front door open with a crash.

MISSION

Tostig's horse, a chestnut mare named Nellie, trod the trails with an able step. She and Tostig had trained together for his final four weeks at the Sashu caves. It was often necessary for magicians to travel with speed and as little exhaustion as possible, so when the masters had found out Tostig was not trained in riding, they had immediately paired him with the mare and had the stable master teach him to ride.

Tostig enjoyed riding, though he was far from an expert horseman. Even when cautiously using the trails surrounding the caves, he found he could move more quickly on Nellie than on foot, and Ziva had grown accustomed to traveling beside the mare. They could travel farther distances between camps, and Tostig found himself in the valley only three days after leaving what had become his home.

Though he had grown accustomed to the caves, Tostig found the solitude of travel a refreshing change. He would never again be a messenger, but at least he was able to travel as he once had. The solace and beauty of the forest offered no fewer charms on horseback than it had on foot; Tostig breathed it in, reveling in the fresh smells, the sounds of birds, and the sight of fresh growth on the forest trees.

Upon reaching the edge of the forest and seeing the vastness of the valley spread before him, Tostig drew in a sharp breath. To the south, Blackwell was but a short distance away from the entrance to the Guilnora trails, but Hardfelden was to the north, and he veered in that direction with nothing but a longing thought. His mission was urgent.

He urged Nellie into a gallop, wanting to see what she could do on the open land and knowing Ziva would be close behind. Nellie fairly flew through the tall grasses, as though the open valley was the land she had been born to traverse. Cecy had told him it would take three days to reach the village by horseback; Tostig now wondered if they could cover it in two.

"*Iprass!*" he urged Nellie, wanting to put space between himself and Blackwell. He felt his magic flow through his hands and into the reins, the command signaling Nellie to push herself, but also containing a minor spell that imbued her with magical energy and stamina. He wasn't sure if it was possible for the horse to increase her speed, but she did, and Tostig felt his robes and his hair whipping in the wind of her acceleration.

I might visit my parents after this mission, Tostig thought as they raced through the grasses. He tried hard not to think of paying Blackwell a visit but knew he probably would. If Alanda was there, he had to see her.

Tostig glanced back and saw Ziva streaking through the grasses behind them, unable to keep up with Nellie's speed. He was comfortable as long as she was in sight, but he knew at this pace he would have to rest both dog and horse.

They took several short breaks throughout the first day in the valley, stopping at streams and lakes to drink and rest. Tostig deplored the need to stop, eager to use his new skills, but he knew no matter how much magical energy he passed to Nellie, the horse could not gallop all day.

Ziva ran up to them about twenty minutes after they had stopped for the night. Panting, she approached Tostig for approval and instructions, and he praised her enthusiastically before telling her to go drink.

The weather stayed fine, and though Tostig was thankful for a lack of storms, he thought a nice, cooling rain would be welcome. Spring in the valley was much warmer than it was in the mountains.

Tostig could tell by the smell at the end of the second day's ride that they were nearing Hardfelden; the acrid stench of burnt wood and grass irritated his nostrils. He slowed Nellie and pressed on past their usual camping time.

When they reached the village, night had fallen. He stopped and dismounted, leading Ziva and Nellie slowly into Harfelden, looking for someone who could tell him what they needed. He felt very out of place. Looking about, he saw several soot-stained, tired men picking through the rubble by lantern light, but no one took notice of him, and he wasn't sure how he was supposed to announce himself. At the caves, his status meant all recognized and respected him, but alone in the world, he wasn't sure how to behave.

"Well," a pleasant, unhurried voice said from behind him, startling him out of his uncertainty. "If it isn't the Blessed. It's about time you arrived."

Tostig whirled around, his red robes flaring, to face the stranger who somehow knew his title. He found himself looking at a young man with light brown hair, wearing black magician's robes lined with red. The most unusual thing about him was the fact that he was perfectly clean: not a spot of soot, dirt, or sweat was present.

"Who are you?" Tostig demanded.

"Me?" The stranger laughed melodically. "No one of any great import. My name is Grayson, and you are sorely needed here."

TOSTIG HAD no time for a long, drawn-out conversation with Grayson. He had made the connection instantly, knowing Grayson was the fleshly form of Annukai, god of knowledge, but that did not change their circumstances. Tostig was anxious to do what he could to help the villagers.

"You will find the injured in the sanctum," Grayson had told him, pointing. "It was not fully burned, and the main room is being used as a hospital of sorts. I would begin there if I was in your shoes, Blessed. I am not in your shoes, however, and you may begin where you see fit, of course." He had laughed then, a light, cheerful sound that in no way belonged in the grim setting.

Tostig had simply nodded and set off toward the sanctum, leading Nellie by her reins and calling Ziva to follow him. Grayson had not come with him but had walked toward one of the burned houses and the men who labored there. Tostig had briefly wondered what Grayson was planning to do but dismissed the thought.

He's a literal god. He will do as he wishes, whether or not it's to the apparent benefit of anyone.

When he reached the sanctum, an older woman with a distinct look of fatigue rose swiftly from her place near the back of the room. Clad in a dirty woolen dress of drab gray, she introduced himself as Claudia, the village herbalist and healer. She quickly outlined what she had done for the villagers in the near two weeks since the fire, and Tostig was impressed she was able to accomplish so much without magic. Remembering Lakeland's healer, he quickly reprimanded himself for forgetting just how adept they were at using herbs and salves to heal, and asked Claudia to show him where he could best assist.

One patient stood out to Tostig; a small child, barely more than a baby, who had severe burns over most of his body. Claudia led Tostig straight to him, and the baby lay motionless in his mother's arms, not even crying, but seeming to be inches from death.

"I've been giving him sleeping potions," Claudia told him as they hurried over. "And I've applied salves to some of his body, but his burns are beyond what I can manage. He will certainly die without your help, magician."

Tostig flinched when he saw the child because it was clear he had been in the middle of the fire. Most of his skin was blackened and charred, his face red with bubbling burn blisters. Privately, he thought it was a miracle Claudia had kept the child alive at all, given the severity of his injuries.

"Hand him over to Claudia," he instructed the baby's mother, and then he set to work. It took nearly half an hour, but between the herbal remedies Claudia had already applied and carefully invoked spells to heal much of the baby's skin and underlying tissue, Tostig and Claudia stopped the pain and ensured there would be minimal scarring.

While the baby's mother thanked him profusely, offering him everything from food to all the coin in the family's coffers, Tostig was mesmerized by the baby's eyes. Though not pale or white-haired like Alanda, the eyes were a nearly identical icy blue, and they stared at Tostig as he worked, the pain in them fading into relief and then childish glee as the burns were healed. As Tostig got up to move to the next patient, the baby clapped his small hands in excitement and babbled at him.

Tostig's labor at the sanctum took all night and most of the next day; it seemed most of the village had suffered injuries or burns, some quite grievous, and while Claudia had kept most of them alive, her skills were not equal to the task of returning their bodies to their previous states. Claudia assisted him as he moved from person to person. She applied more healing salves and administered herbal remedies while he invoked magic.

He didn't feel his exhaustion until sundown the day after he had arrived. He had healed most of the serious injuries, leaving many of the minor ones to heal with herbal remedies to save his strength. Ziva had taken the role of comforter, much to Tostig's relief. Independently of him, she had wandered around the room, lightly laying her head on people's laps, offering comforting licks to their hands or faces, and whining to alert Tostig when she sensed someone in great pain. Tostig thought she had been born for a life as a magician's pet rather than a messenger dog and wondered if her fate had been tied up in his before they had even been paired.

After sunset, Tostig rose and left the sanctum, knowing he had done all he could for the time being. He inquired of Claudia, who looked more exhausted than he felt, where he might spend the night and where he could quarter Nellie.

"The inn's burnt," Claudia told him, her voice rough with labor and lack of sleep, "but there's an empty hut in the community of the old on the outskirts. Fire didn't make it there. I'll see food is brought to you. Public stables were burnt, too, but seeing as how it's spring, your horse should find plenty of grass to eat if you picket her near the hut, and the lake's not far."

Tostig led an exhausted Nellie and Ziva to the hut she had indicated. He took the animals to the lake to drink and then picketed Nellie a few yards away from the hut; there was plenty of unburnt grass for her. He was pleased to find the hut clean and well-ordered, though there was a thin layer of soot over everything.

"*Natiga*," Tostig muttered, sweeping his hand tiredly over the raised bed platform. He would clean the rest in the morning; he was too weary to do it before he ate and slept.

"Now *that* is a good use of your magic," a voice said from the doorway.

Tostig turned to find Grayson entering the hut, balancing a large tray laden with more food than Tostig thought he could eat. There was even a bowl of raw meat for Ziva.

Grayson set the tray on the table after he had nodded at it, causing the layer of soot to disappear. He placed the bowl of raw meat on the floor and chirruped at Ziva. To Tostig's surprise, Ziva immediately came to Grayson and began eating. It was the first time she had ever taken a command from anyone but him.

"Eat, Blessed," Grayson urged him, indicating one of the two wooden chairs at the table. As Tostig sat, Grayson took the chair opposite.

"The name's Tostig," Tostig grunted after he took a long draught of water and then cut into a slab of salted pork. He found that, though he had grown used to the title in the caves, he didn't like being addressed such outside of them.

"Right you are," Grayson said cheerfully. As Tostig ate his meal, Grayson took a small, stringed instrument from his bag and began idly playing. The tune was not familiar to Tostig, though he found it soothing.

"What are you doing here?" Tostig asked Grayson when he

finished eating what he could and drinking the tankard of ale that had come with it. The liquid was welcome to his parched, irritated throat.

"Well, I came to offer what help I could, of course," Grayson answered, affecting surprise in his voice. "And to meet the Blessed, for I knew you would be attending this village." He did not stop playing his instrument as he spoke.

"How did you know?"

"Why, Cecy told me, not two days past. I called upon the caves to speak to her about other matters."

Tostig was taken aback. "How did you get here so fast, then?" he asked, curious. It had taken him nearly six days on horseback to reach Hardfelden from the caves.

Grayson smiled at him. "I flew, of course," he answered easily. He offered no further explanation. "I suppose you need your rest. We shall talk on the morrow as we labor for the sake of this village." He carefully placed his stringed instrument back into his bag and stood gracefully, unfolding like a swan opening its wings.

"You - " Tostig began.

"Flew," Grayson confirmed. "Good night, Tostig." He strode across the small room and left, closing the door softly behind him.

Tostig shook his head at the closed door and looked at the remains of the evening's meal. He wondered if someone would come to collect the dishes or if he should take them to the lake and scour them; there seemed to be no resources for cleaning dishes in the small hut. Deciding he would take care of it in the morning, he rummaged in his pack for his nightclothes and fell into bed, even eschewing Ziva's usual combing. The prickly comfort of the straw-tick mattress and feather pillows enveloped him, and he soon drifted into sleep.

TOSTIG AWOKE WITH A START, having dreamed of Alanda riding through the valley on a horse. As he rubbed the sleep from his eyes, he desperately tried to hang on to the wisps of the dream, wanting to remember everything, but as dreams often do, it drifted away.

He went straight to his pack, ignoring the early-morning chill and Ziva's protesting whine. Rummaging around, Tostig found a small, cylindrical leather case with a lid on one end. Popping the lid off, he withdrew a scroll of parchment for the first time since he had left the caves. On it were the verses that had released him from Paalavi's tutelage, the old poet having told him all he needed from that point on was practice and continued critique. He felt a pang of remembrance and grief as he felt the smooth, slight weight of the parchment in his hands.

Unfurling the scroll, Tostig read the words he had written and thought of his longing for the girl he had met so long ago on a never-to-be-forgotten day in the woods.

Whispering trees and babbling brooks
Trails unending in the mountain passes
Searching the land, my home forsook
Far behind me in the verdant grasses
Searching, searching for life's true purpose.

A glance and a smile, an ice blue gaze
Holding me rooted in the passing of time
Promises made in the fleeting days
A longed-for life might soon be mine.
Traveling, traveling, but not alone.

Lightning flashes in a clear blue sky
Signaling change in life and direction
Earth breaks beneath me with a creak and a sigh
Changing my path with deep reflection
Moving, moving to a place unknown.

. . .

Powers of water, powers of gale
Powers of bright and destructive fire
A gift given me from beyond the veil
The gods from above my duty require
Reaching, reaching toward my destiny.

A voice from on high calls for me
The father god touches me with his hand
Towering mountain to deep blue sea
I am called alone to wander the land
Trying, trying to be all that I should.

Through my hands are great deeds wrought
My power to break but also to heal
The magic flows through me and I am sought
To vie with the powers that others wield
Fighting, fighting for the peoples of the land.

Though my hands command the forces of land
The surges of sea and rainbow rays of light
The birds will not come to rest on my hand
And the wild beasts before me take flight
Standing, standing apart from the world.

I have in my grasp the power to aid

The gasping echoes of powerful change
But the one thing I long for, for which I have prayed
The remnants of a love and vows exchanged
Departing, departing like a dying flame.

Love comes to me only in dreams
Nightly phantasms of misty surreality
My power divides me like a rock in a stream
Sapping from me a lover's vitality
Wanting, wanting the touch of her lips.

When daylight breaks, dreams do fade
But the memory of her stays with me always
The warmth of her touch, the fire of her gaze
Haunts me as I attend to my duty
Grasping, grasping at the old promises.

Forth into the land I am sent
To use my gift across land and sea
Power in my hand and in my pen
Forces of the world bow to me
Longing, longing for what is not mine.

To stop battles and wars before they are fought
To end strife and turmoil between the peoples
Not mine are the miracles that I have wrought
Mandated to fight alone against the land's evils

Wielding, wielding the gift of the mage.

Wandering, wandering the world alone.

TOSTIG SIGHED and rolled the scroll back up, replacing it in its protective tube. It seemed as though, in this instance alone, he had captured his feelings about everything that had happened since the Watchers had taken him to the Sashu caves - learning magic, becoming the Blessed, having all the power he had never imagined having, but still not having the one thing he longed for most.

Was he selfish for continuing to want her? Would she really want to be married to a magician, to live in the caves while he was sent out on missions? For Tostig knew that, freedom or not, his duty would call him back to the caves, teaching when he was not working in the land, and taking part in the Sashu rituals.

The life wouldn't be so different from that of being married to a messenger, he thought reflectively. *She would live with the Sashu instead of in Lakeland or Blackwell, that's all.*

Except he knew that wasn't all. If Alanda came to the caves, she'd have to give up her religion; though she would not be required to adhere to the Sashu beliefs, neither would she be able to attend fifth-day services at a sanctum. She would have to leave all the people she had known behind, and this after losing her parents to The Hunger. *No*, he decided, *it wouldn't be fair to her.*

Tostig turned when he heard the door open without a knock. It did not surprise him to see Grayson, again holding a tray of food for him and for Ziva.

"You are up early this morning," Grayson said, crossing the room to set the tray on the table.

Tostig frowned. How had Grayson known he would be up? It wasn't even *uht* yet, and Ziva had gone back to sleep on her pallet. It was on the tip of his tongue to ask, but he decided against it. He'd just get another non-answer.

"Dreaming of the girl?" Grayson asked.

"How did you know?" Tostig blurted out, unable to keep his question to himself.

"I know what I know," Grayson answered simply. "Of course, you dream of her. She is part of your fate, a piece of your destiny."

"Then the gods *do* intend for us to be together?"

"I did not say that, did I?" Grayson shook his head in disappointment. "You must learn to listen to that which is said rather than that which you want to hear."

"Then what do you mean?" Tostig was aggravated and didn't bother keeping it from his voice.

"Simply that your fate is entwined with that of the girl," Grayson explained. "How it will end is beyond even my knowledge. You should eat." He chirruped at Ziva as he had the previous night, and she immediately awoke and came to his side.

Tostig shook his head at Ziva's strange obedience to this man who should have been a stranger. "Why does she come when you call?" he asked curiously. "She's not supposed to do that for anyone but me."

"I have a way with animals," Grayson said casually. "Qhalina and I worked it out long ago. I got an accord with the animals of the land under her care, and she got a particular bit of knowledge she wanted from me."

Even knowing Grayson was the fleshly form of Annukai, it was strange to hear an apparent human speaking of conversing with a god, and of offering a trade even more so. "I see," Tostig said finally.

Grayson's laugh rang through the hut. "No, you do not," he chuckled. "Nevertheless, you must eat. We have much work to do today and for many days to come."

Tostig finally sat down and ate, surprised by the main dish in front of him: hot porridge laced with brown sugar and honey. He wondered where Grayson had gotten such a delicacy from a village decimated by fire, but again decided not to ask.

"You acquitted yourself well in battle, Cecy tells me," Grayson said conversationally as Tostig ate.

Tostig grunted, taking a gulp of watered ale. "I did what I had to do, but I called too much attention to myself."

"You did not," Grayson countered. "Had you not done what you did, you would still have been recognized, and the battle would have ended with you being taken captive and your powers restrained. You change the course of history with your whims, as have all the Blesseds before you."

Tostig gaped at him, a spoonful of porridge halfway to his mouth. "My powers can be restrained?"

"Not by many, but there are some who can limit the expression of a magician's powers with a carefully worded incantation. You yourself will be taught those words when Cecy deems you ready for the responsibility of knowing them. They are effective on all but the gods and their children."

"Do the gods use such spells?" Tostig asked.

"The gods don't need them," Grayson said gently. "We do not use spells to focus our powers, for doing such would limit us to the use of the languages of the land-dwelling beings."

"And...Ehnja?" Tostig asked, almost afraid to bring up the tenth goddess. "Does she use her powers over the land as the other gods do?"

Grayson surprised Tostig by scowling deeply, frown creases marring his otherwise young-looking face. "Ehnja uses her powers as all the gods do and has the same limits as well. We cannot interfere directly in the happenings of the land, as I am sure you have learned. We can only use our powers to supplement or, in Ehnja's case, destroy things in the world."

"If Ehnja is so vengeful and has the power to destroy, then why does she not? It seems as though that would be what she wants the most."

"Ehnja, regardless of what she may seem to be, does not seek the end of the world nor the end of the land-bound beings on it. Ehnja desires disorder and chaos and works in the shadows to achieve her ends so the rest of us might not interfere with what she does."

"And yet, she has caused the deaths of Blesseds before me," Tostig said flatly.

"Unfortunately, the Blesseds are a particular target for her, given that Sado chooses them specifically to work good within the land. You do not yet know how much power you hold, young one. That realization will only come with time, and it has more to do with your life force than it does with your magic."

Tostig didn't understand, and that frustrated him. He grunted and finished the last bite of his porridge.

"Let us talk of things we can control," Grayson pressed. "We can, for example, help this community recover from their losses. I suggest we shift our focus to that."

After Tostig changed into his robes, he and Grayson set out together. The sun was barely up, but people were already sifting through their burned belongings with the same hopeless, tired expressions.

"We will start at the sanctum," Grayson said.

"Are there more injured to be treated?" Tostig asked. He thought he had healed everyone to the best of his ability the day before.

"None with injuries that cannot be treated by Claudia," Grayson answered. "No, we need to get the sanctum repaired so the people may have their fifth-day services. Whatever Annuah may seem to us, to them he is a source of comfort, and they will rally when they return to worship and ritual."

Tostig felt Grayson was correct. If the people could attend fifth-day services while they rebuilt, their spirits would be higher and they would be more hopeful. The pair headed for the sanctum, red and black robes billowing around them, and set to work.

Two days later, while they worked on rebuilding the village's inn, Tostig asked Grayson why he could not simply wave a hand and see the village rebuilt.

"Alas," Grayson said with some regret, "I cannot. In the fleshly form I have taken, I cannot perform miracles, but only work similarly to you and aid the people through the use of my own magic. I am certain you noticed, though, that there was no shortage of wood and logs for the villagers. That was Iarae's doing, after I entreated her for her help. Though the villagers are made to toil, as are all the beings of this land, they did have help, and not just from me."

Tostig was not quite satisfied with this answer but reminded himself there was no way for him to know all the ways of the gods. Their system was not his, and Grayson himself was evidence that he could not completely understand them.

TOSTIG AND GRAYSON labored for two weeks and three days, and when they decided the work that could be done magically had been done, they prepared to leave Hardfelden and let the people pick up the pieces of their lives. They had helped rebuild, magically carrying and lifting heavy wooden logs and boards, healing injuries from the construction, and offering solace and advice to those who had lost everything.

As they turned their backs on Hardfelden, now mostly rebuilt, Tostig mounted Nellie, facing her southwards. "Where will you go next?" he asked Grayson.

"Oh, here and there," Grayson answered, laughing in that singularly carefree way he had. "I do love to travel. I have something for you as well." He rummaged in his bag and pulled out a tiny wooden dragon, intricately carved, with small red gemstones set for its eyes.

Tostig took it and marveled at the smoothness of the wood, absent many of the imperfections he would have expected in a carving of this size. Running his finger over the smooth belly, marked only by representations of the scales of the dragon, he had a sudden idea. "Alanda made this, didn't she?"

"Yes," Grayson said. "She gifted it to Myrine of the Kilynelle elves, but Myrine and I thought you might enjoy having it. We worked together to place the gemstones."

"Rubies," Tostig breathed, turning the dragon so the stones caught the light and made it seem a living thing. "It's beautiful. I knew she whittled, but I had no idea she had such skill."

"She has many skills, most of which she has yet to discover herself. Keep this as a remembrance until you meet again."

"I will. Farewell, Grayson, and thank you." Tostig inclined his head at the god-turned-man and nudged Nellie's sides with his heels. "Ziva, heel."

Setting his sights on Lakeland and his family, Tostig rode at an easy trot southeast through the valley, Ziva at his side. It was time to bring his life prior to the Sashu into accord with the life he was now living as the Blessed.

MUSIC

Julen let his last note fade into silence, feeling the same satisfaction he felt at the conclusion of every Kilynelle gathering. Though he rarely used words in his song, he found great meaning in preparing new music; he knew his orations were more than just simple, pleasant sounds to their ears. For a millennium and half over again, he had been singing for them, but somehow the music was always new.

Returning to the roundhouse he shared with Dmeter, Julen untied the thong holding back his long, chestnut-brown hair and ran his fingers through the smooth length, his mind elsewhere. Dmeter would be back from his latest assignment the next day, but this night was to be a lonely one.

Julen had grown used to it over the centuries of their partnership and didn't mind. He would use the time to indulge in his passions. Like Myrine, he spent little time resting, but rather in adding beauty to all that surrounded him. His particular passion, other than his music, was the addition and manipulation of the tiny, twinkling elf-lights lining most of the roundhouses and some of the common areas.

As the lights in his own home blinked on, he stared up in satisfaction: unlike most roundhouses, which had lights simply added to the juncture between the walls and roof, the roundhouse he shared with Dmeter contained lights running up each of the ceiling beams to the domed top.

Julen smiled and pursed his lips, whistling, his timbre low and somber but his intention anything but. At his whistled command, the lights in his roundhouse changed from a soft yellow to a soothing indigo, dimmer than the yellow lights had been, giving each of their belongings an otherworldly cast. He knew he was not the only elf with the ability to change the colors of the magical lights, but he was the one who used the ability most frequently. The change enchanted him.

Exchanging his deep purple robes for the lighter, simpler clothing he wore at night, Julen carefully examined his day garments for rents, tears, or signs of wear before carefully hanging them on the hook behind the curtain near his and Dmeter's large bed.

So it has been, so it is, and so it will be, Julen thought of his nightly routine, unchanged for centuries, but somehow soothing. His life was a tranquil one, and he knew he had much to be thankful for.

Crossing the large room, Julen stoked the day's fire back into a cheerful flickering and added a few logs. He bustled about, putting things into place under the blue light, until the fire again became hot enough for the tea he consumed each evening to strengthen and soothe his vocal cords. Casting herbs Myrine specifically set aside for him into the kettle, he followed her instructions and let the water heat with the herbs inside. As the mixture heated on a metal trivet over the fire, Julen set his honeypot on the table, turned back his blankets, and contentedly sat in a chair to think about the next day's song.

He began as he always, did by humming softly and tunelessly, soft enough that one would have to be right next to him in order to hear. At the beginning, none of the notes stood out, but as he continued to hum, a haunting melody began playing itself in his mind. His humming took on the tune of his mental melody, and he committed the notes to memory.

The tea boiled, and he removed the kettle from the trivet and set it on a woven pad on the table, immediately pouring some of the mixture into a ceramic mug made for him by one of the artisans. Adding a generous portion of honey, he allowed the mixture to cool, not humming, but contemplating the melody he had begun to create.

"There is something different about this one," he murmured to himself as he took his first sip of the healing tea.

He contemplated it while he drank his tea in silence, and the idea that this was one melody that meant more than it seemed kept nibbling at his consciousness until, by the time he had drunk two mugs of the herbal, honeyed tea, he was convinced.

Such a feeling did not come over him often. Over the centuries, Julen's songs had been about soothing and invigorating the emotions of his clan, giving them an experience at the end of each day that both calmed and brought them together. Though each of his songs was unique to the day it was created, most of them had similar qualities, and the effect on his listeners was rather predictable. Even the oldest elves in the clan, those who had listened to Julen sing nightly for centuries, looked forward to the music at the end of their gathering.

It was only once every century or so that a song took on a new meaning and brought about new emotions. Thinking over the melody, Julen thought this might be one of those. He would not be certain until the next day, however, when he would complete the song. The only thing he knew for sure was that he would sing what he was meant to sing: he did not know exactly how or whence his songs came to him, but he relayed them faithfully.

After his tea, Julen set about his usual evening occupation: modifying the elf-lights in strategic points around the settlement. Some of the lights had been there as long as he had been singing for the elves, or even longer, but Julen enjoyed moving them incrementally, so they complimented the flora and foliage and gave a sense of movement and vitality after the sun had set. As he manipulated them, he kept them at a soft, peach color that would not disturb the elves at their rest, and he knew his changes would bring a favorable glow to the nightly gathering the following evening.

The haunting melody never left him. For some reason, he connected the melody with Alanda, the strange human elf-friend who had captured his heart. He hadn't thought of her much since the Summer's End celebration.

What does she have to do with this music?

~

JULEN DID NOT WAKE at *uht*; both his profession and his hobbies took place in the evening and night hours. Though he rested less than many, he often slept well past sunup. Knowing his nightly activities and preparations, the other elves, even his parents, had long since accepted his strange schedule.

He was just putting on his purple robes when an elf woman, olive-skinned and chestnut-haired like he was, knocked on his door and walked gracefully into the roundhouse, her muted green robes flowing like water around her.

"*Ama*," Julen greeted his mother in Yrui. "What brings you here this morning?"

Appolina's brown eyes, ancient and fathomless, looked troubled. "I watched you at work last night, my little leaf, and it was clear something was heavy on your beautiful mind. I did not care to interrupt, but in my dreams I saw you alone with the pale elf-friend, the background one of fire and blood. It chilled me to my bones, and I have not found rest since."

Julen frowned. Though he had slept dreamlessly, as he often did, the news that Alanda had entered his mother's dreams disturbed him. Clearly, something important was being missed. "The elf-friend entered my mind as I was composing tonight's song," he confessed. "I do not know why, but the melody haunted me, and I thought of her for the first time since Summer's End."

"This carries significance," Appolina stated, her smooth voice portentous. She came to Julen and motioned him to turn to the side so she could knot his blue belt. "You finish your song in the late morning hours, unless I am much mistaken."

"I do," Julen confirmed.

Despite her worry, Appolina smiled. "You are well suited for your calling, though of course I have known and said as much for centuries. May I take your repast with you?"

"Of course." Julen turned to the pot of wheat mush he had placed over the fire and checked it. "Your timing, as always, is excellent, *Ama*," he said. "It will be pleasant to break my fast with you."

Taking the pot off the trivet, he carried it to the table and set it on a woven mat. Portioning it into two white bowls, he added dried fruit from the winter stores and a drizzle of honey. When he was finished, he placed an inedible pink bloom on the side of each bowl, adding beauty to the necessity of their meal.

"You do set a lovely table, though you sup simply," his mother commented as she seated herself in Dmeter's usual chair, settling her robes around her with practiced movements. They ate in companionable silence.

"Now, what of this young girl?" Appolina asked as she collected the plates from the table and went to the washing area to scrub them with sand.

"I cannot honestly tell you, *Ama*. I will have to complete the melody and see what comes to mind, though your dream makes me feel as though she is someone for whom I should keep a close watch."

"If you follow her, it will be to your ultimate doom."

"*Ama*, do you not think that is a little dramatic?" Julen asked. "I do not even know when she will next appear in Kilynelle, though I do have some idea of her destination. She was to cross the glacier to Dachilon, though of course you are aware of that."

"She survived the crossing and will return here."

"How do you know?"

"If she had not, my dreams would not have taken the shape they did. My little leaf, tread carefully with her. She is a small pebble who will create large waves. Take care you do not get caught in the current." Kissing his cheek, Appolina left the roundhouse.

Julen watched her leave, shaking his head. His mother had only had two prophetic dreams that he was aware of, but both had foretold true events in a way no one could discern until after those events had occurred. He did not know what to think about her dream about him and Alanda, but he knew he had to finish the song. Checking to make sure his space was in perfect order, he set off to wander the ancient woods surrounding Kilynelle.

~

JULEN MARVELED at the early spring growth in the deciduous forest surrounding Kilynelle. The ancient trees, first purple-leaved from the latent magic in the air, then gloriously colored at Summer's End, and finally bare in the winter, were budding. Some showed growth in the form of lightly colored leaf buds, and others flowered in a way that seemed magical to him. *How,* he wondered, *do their dormant branches know to bud at the beginning of spring? What power told them the time had come?* He had watched some of these trees grow to greatness from saplings, but the new life that budded every spring never failed to enchant him.

After he had walked for perhaps an hour, Julen stopped at a familiar stream and knelt, cupping his hands in the gurgling water. It was icy cold snowmelt from higher on the mountain, but he did not mind. He found it invigorating and was glad he could again taste the water straight from the stream without first having to melt the ice.

His thirst sated, he stood and released his first note, a deep "ah" that reverberated through the empty forest. Satisfied with the note, he sang the melody that had come to him the previous night, and he shivered as the last note died away, leaving him with only the sound of the bubbling stream. As he had sung, he had thought of nothing but *her,* the elf-friend, and her pale, pointed face so stark against her black leathers and cloak when she had come to Summer's End. The song, though it contained no discernible language, was about her, and he knew it. But what did it mean?

He began to walk, paying no particular attention to his direction. He had been walking the forest surrounding Kilynelle for centuries and knew it as well as he knew his own home. As he walked, he sang the melody again, adding inflection and deepening some notes while lifting others. In his mind's eye, he watched her react to the song: he watched her face brighten as he hit the highs and fall as the melody became melancholy.

Suddenly, Julen extended his voice as he'd never done before, sending a high falsetto peal of anguished sound into the forest. He hadn't planned it; it had just come. Such was the way of creation sometimes, but he had never uttered a sound like the one that had just escaped him. He cut it off abruptly.

What in fair nature was that?

JULEN SANG for the circle that night, as he always did. As always, he made eye contact with each elf and spoke to some over matters of little import. He had never understood what drove him to speak to some and not others, but he always followed the impulse.

The niceties complete, Julen began the evening's song. His simple "ah" enthralled the elves from the beginning, but as the haunting melody progressed, the elves around the circle grew restless. Instead of rising and falling with his melody as they usually did, they shifted in their places, shuffled their feet, and turned to one another to whisper in the common tongue rather than using Yrui that would interrupt the song. What Julen had wrought for that night's circle had made them uncomfortable and disrupted their routine.

Julen himself was uncomfortable, and every movement, every whisper from his audience threatened to divert his attention from the music. He focused his eyes on Dmeter, who had returned that afternoon and who was the only elf in the circle whose unswerving attention was still focused on Julen and his song. Even Appolina and Weidheri, Julen's parents, had averted their gazes from him and were looking at one another.

Dmeter nodded somberly, encouraging Julen to finish his work. Julen did, and when the final note, the falsetto that seemed to hold all the pain in the entire land, faded, the circle finally grew silent and still. All eyes focused on the singer as he stood, vulnerable to their judgement, wondering if he should have forced a change to the melody, something he never allowed himself to do.

"Julen," said a voice from the side of the circle, breaking the silence. "Thank you for the music."

The voice belonged to Myrine, the healer who had saved elf-friend Alanda's life so many months before. He wondered if she, too, saw the face of the girl in the music or if she was simply trying to heal the environment from the toxins his song had released. Truly, the air around the circle felt tainted with discord and pain, and that was not something the elves were accustomed to.

No one said another word. One by one, the elves stood and left, traversing the land in their silent way. The usual chatter was absent, and it seemed to Julen that even the animals and trees had gone quiet in the wake of his song. He looked for Myrine, hoping she might have stayed behind to talk to him, but all he saw of her was the long, blonde hair swaying in time to her steps as she followed Garratt and Kataryna back to their roundhouse.

"What was that?"

The voice startled Julen, though under normal circumstances it would not have. It belonged to Dmeter and was the most familiar voice in his world, but Dmeter had circled behind him and Julen had not heard him approach.

Julen turned to his partner, his eyes pools of what could only be described as desperation as he silently implored Dmeter to understand. "It was what I was given to sing, like every other night."

"It was not like every other night," Dmeter countered. "It was disconcerting, and the end note, beautiful as it was, brought pain and fear to my heart."

"That was not my intent."

"I know it was not, for a more peaceable, loving elf cannot be found in all of Ilbeor," Dmeter said soothingly. "Come, let us return home and you may muse upon the morrow's song. Perhaps what you will be given will be more soothing."

There was no hint of Dmeter's usual smile on his face as he led Julen back to their roundhouse and set about preparing Julen's evening tea, a service he loved to provide. Julen's haunting melody and the piercing falsetto at the end had broken something inside of him, and though he was not a prescient being, he feared it foretold great pain to come.

Julen, as was his habit, hummed tunelessly while his tea was heating, and Dmeter stood behind him, idly running his fingers through his partner's long hair and listening closely. To both of their relief, the humming soon broadened into a soothing song, one imbued with a sense of harmony and well-being.

"I do not understand what it means," Julen said, sipping his honeyed tea and surveying Dmeter across the table. "Was I to discomfit my friends one night only to soothe them the next? Why was I given something so chilling one night, and something so warm the next?"

"I have never pretended to understand the inspiration from whence your songs come," Dmeter murmured, reaching across to stroke Julen's cheek. "It has always seemed magical to me, otherworldly, and a gift greater than most can claim to have received. Perhaps tonight's song was a portent, a warning."

"Have you heard anything on your journeys to suggest that Kilynelle is in danger?" Julen asked. Dmeter often heard the news of the land before it came to Kilynelle. In the course of his duties as a messenger, he got a feel for the land outside their settlement.

Dmeter shook his head but then surprised Julen by answering, "I was going to speak to you of this in the morning, but there has been an attack on a human village that I wished to speak to the Council about."

"An attack on a human village?" Julen asked, surprised. "I thought the land was at peace. Who were the attackers?"

"Urothu," Dmeter said simply. "I did not see the village myself, but the elves of Isasari informed me of it when I brought their messages. The word is the entire village was killed, the buildings destroyed. It was beyond help long before anyone even knew what had happened, and the Urothu have disappeared."

Julen refilled his mug with hot tea. As he added the honey and stirred the amber liquid, he said, "Do you think this attack was connected to my song?"

"No, I do not," Dmeter replied gently. "The attack itself happened months ago, but this was the first occasion I have had since winter to travel to the valley. I only mention it because this level of Urothu activity suggests there might be something bigger at hand."

"The song brought to mind the elf-friend, Alanda," Julen said, pondering his words. "I cannot explain exactly how, but I saw her face clearly in my mind's eye as I composed it, and again as I sang it. I fear her story is not to be a happy one." He then told Dmeter about his mother's seemingly prophetic dream. "I do not know what my place in her story is," he concluded, "but I feel sure my fate is somehow intertwined with this young human."

Dmeter did not reply, but changed the subject to easier topics as Julen finished his tea. When he had, Dmeter stood up and held out his hand. "Come," he said, his voice honeyed with the love he felt for his partner. "Walk with me this night. We shall banish all fear and enjoy the chill of an early spring."

Julen rose and took his hand, leaving the mug to be scrubbed later, and together, they left the roundhouse and their worries behind.

JULEN AND DMETER woke earlier than usual the next morning. Dmeter was accustomed to rising at *uht*, though he had no assignments, and the compromise between their two schedules meant they rose at sunup. After they broke their fast together, Dmeter took his dog Gabi with him to speak to the leatherworker, and Julen spent the morning tending the flowers in the garden in front of their roundhouse.

None of the elves addressed the haunting melody, but all greeted him as courteously as always, stopping to talk to him as he attended his work. They shared tidbits about their own work and concerns, but to Julen, it felt as though the clan was trying to erase the memory of the song, and it did not weigh comfortably on his mind. Right or wrong, he had sung what he was given to sing, and he felt the night's song should not be brushed aside like ashes on a hearthstone.

His chores done, Julen was preparing for his daily forest walk when he heard the distinct clopping of hooves approaching Kilynelle. He stopped lacing his boots and listened, as did everyone in the settlement, for visitors on horseback were rare. This one seemed to be traveling at speed as well, rather than using the slow amble of the usual elven rider.

As he peered out the door of his roundhouse, he watched in astonishment as a human rider clad in green and brown galloped straight into the middle of the settlement's circle and halted his horse with a suddenness that caused the animal to rear back on its hind legs. The rider almost seemed to fly off the back of his horse as he dismounted, and in a loud, clear voice, he called, "I carry a message for Alanda of Blackwell on behalf of Maryah of Blackwell. Where might I find her?"

Julen was among the group of elves that approached the rider, but it was Garratt who spoke first. "Alanda is not here," he said, "though we have some idea of her destination. What news do you bring, rider?"

The messenger did not seem perturbed at Alanda's absence, almost as though he had expected it might be so. "I was instructed to give this message to the Council of Kilynelle if its intended recipient was not present," he said calmly, holding out a small scroll tied with twine.

Garratt took the missive and untied it immediately, reading over it quickly. "Thank you," he said to the messenger, reaching into his belt pouch for some coin to pay for the delivery. "We appreciate your speed in attending to this message and will see that Alanda receives it as soon as may be. Would you take some refreshment before you leave?"

"No," the messenger said curtly, taking the offered coin. "I have other matters to attend to today. Is there to be a return message?"

"No, thank you," Garratt replied calmly. "We shall send one of our own messengers with any information that is needed."

"Very well," the messenger said, mounting his horse with practiced ease. "Blessings be to you," he called as he turned his horse and rode away from the circle.

Garratt turned to the gathered elves. "We must act quickly," he said. "Julen, will you please send Dmeter to the Council's gathering place as soon as may be?"

Julen nodded his assent, his curiosity piqued by Garratt's sense of urgency. The elves, as a rule, did not move so quickly. When your life was measured in millennia, there was usually no cause to rush about. He wondered what the message contained to cause Garratt's obvious concern.

As the Council moved toward their gathering place, Julen hurried off toward the leatherworker to find his partner. He sorely hoped it was not the answer to the portentous song of the night before, but he feared Alanda's troubles were just beginning.

DOWN THE MOUNTAIN

Rinayai made a sound of disgust as he gazed at the garments Tsetsic had laid out for the second crossing of the glacier. "It is an abomination," he spat in tselq, turning away from it.

His reaction disturbed Alanda, though she couldn't understand his words, but Tsetsic mastered the situation. "No more an abomination than to allow this princess to die crossing the ice because of our ancient laws," he answered in the common tongue, and Alanda, hearing his answer, felt sure of what Rinayai had said before. "Besides," Tsetsic continued, "we harmed no animals to make these garments."

Rinayai turned back around and gestured at the thick, fur-lined clothing, gloves, boots, and hat laid out for Alanda's inspection on the dresser in her room. "Explain to me how no animals were harmed in the making of leather and fur," he said, his voice still harsh, but reverting to the common tongue.

"It is our practice in Dachilon to use the materials from any animal found deceased on our grounds to make warm clothing for our old to use during the winter," Tsetsic explained. "No animals were killed for these garments but were rather found dead. We performed the rites of burial before taking what we needed."

Rinayai looked slightly mollified. "You are certain?"

"Absolutely certain. You know no tselq would willingly kill another creature without reason, and certainly not to make clothing of its hide." He turned to Alanda. "You will wear both sets of underthings the tselqs of Chinnua provided for your first crossing and all three pairs of woolen socks. You will find your new boots have room to accommodate the bulk."

Alanda nodded. "This will make the crossing safer?"

"Yes," Rinayai assured her, thinking of her near-death on the ice during their first crossing and suddenly finding himself grateful for the extra protection. "You should cross with little difficulty if you do as Tsetsic has instructed. Additionally, since we waited out the winter here, there is less chance of storms."

"Very well," she said. "I will change and pack." She glanced to the bed, where the leathers her father had given her were laid out, clean and in as perfect a condition as when they had been given to her. "Thank you for everything you have done for me," she added.

"It has been our pleasure, princess," Tsetsic replied.

"Don't call me that," Alanda shot back at him. "My name is Alanda, and I am not a princess."

"You are what you are, whether or not you would have it be so," Tsetsic said. "But as you wish, Alanda." He and Rinayai left the room to allow Alanda to change.

Alanda and Rinayai, with Alis standing beside them, bid farewell to the tselqs who had helped them during their stay. Alanda thanked Vritri especially. "You made my stay here pleasant, and I am glad to call you a friend," she told him sincerely.

Vritri smiled easily. "As am I," he said, extending his hand, palm up, to Alanda.

Alanda placed her gloved hand atop his. "I hope we will see each other again."

"Come," Rinayai said, "we must go before the dawn advances further. We have a long march to Kilynelle."

They had decided to travel to Kilynelle to restock her supply of sun salve on the way to Blackwell. The Dachilon tselqs, despite their skill with herbs and plants, had been unable to duplicate it, and Alanda would run out before their journey's end.

Nodding a final farewell, Alanda, Rinayai, and Alis took their leave of Dachilon.

~

THEY REACHED the ice within a few days, and Alanda felt a deep sense of trepidation as she considered the seven-day journey ahead of them. *What if the fur clothing is not enough? Could I die on this crossing, as I almost did on the first?*

Rinayai seemed to read her thoughts. "Has the cold touched you thus far?"

Alanda shook her head. She had been quite warm, sometimes too warm, as they had traveled up to the glacier.

"My skin has been cold these past two days," Rinayai continued. "If you have not felt it, you will have no trouble crossing this time."

"All right," Alanda said uncertainly, and, as she had done before, she cautiously placed one foot atop the ice, noting the crack between the ice and the forest floor. To her surprise, her foot registered no more cold on the ice than on the forest floor. She felt a surge of relief and confidence. "Let's go," she stated firmly before she could grow frightened again. She and Rinayai stepped onto the ice, Alis to Alanda's left wearing her puffy, colorful boots from the first crossing.

The crossing was easy compared to the one before. The only part of Alanda that grew cold was her face, and she remedied this by taking one of the tunics the tselqs had gifted her and wrapping it around her face up to her eyes. Even camping was easy, for Rinayai still had his windshield tent and ice blanket.

They made the crossing in seven days without incident. Alanda gleefully changed back into her leathers after they had traveled a day down the mountain. She stowed the fur clothing in her pack. She might not need it again, but she would not disrespect the tselqs' gift by leaving it behind.

They angled northwest to Kilynelle, and as they hiked the rugged paths down the mountain, Rinayai tutored Alanda on tselq history.

"Do you remember Sincha, the tselq who has taken my place as shaman of Chinnua?" he asked.

"Of course," Alanda replied. "She is a remarkable woman."

"Her very name suggests her new station," Rinayai said. "She was named for a legendary shaman who made the first crossing of the Unresting Sea to Ilbeor. That Sincha brought peace to our race and was responsible for the building of Dachilon and the tranquil life we lead."

"Were the tselqs not always peaceful?" Alanda asked, curious. It sounded as though Rinayai was suggesting that this first Sincha had caused their peace, which would mean that they did not always have it.

Rinayai frowned. "Little is known of the life of the tselqs on Moacha, the land from whence we came, other than it was hard and full of enemies and fighting. The old stories tell of our crossing, but not of our lives before it."

"What was Ilbeor like when you came to it?"

"Beautiful," Rinayai said. "The songs all sing of the beauty of the land, a beauty which I do not believe is diminished even by the many peoples that populate it now. The valley is green and fertile, the mountains alive even though they were formed of rock. When we reached Ilbeor, it was said to be empty of all but a small population of dwarves, who either arrived long before the tselqs or originated here altogether. They were in what is now called the Gray Hills and did not object to us, so long as we did not disturb their strongholds."

"How did your people communicate with the dwarves? Surely your languages were not similar," Alanda pressed, curious about the origins of the land. She had never met anyone with such a long cultural memory.

"The exact method of communication was probably preserved at the Library of the Guardians," Rinayai answered, "but other than that, it has been lost to history. I would imagine much gesturing was used until the races found common words to share with one another, much as it was before the common tongue."

Alanda couldn't imagine a time before the common tongue. Communication was fairly easy in Ilbeor, since all the races knew that language. She thought it must have been very difficult to communicate intentions before it existed. "So, the first Sincha is responsible for your life as it is in Ilbeor, even all the centuries later?" she asked.

"Millennia," he corrected her. "But yes. There have been some changes to our lifestyle as the world grew and the races learned new things, but our peace, our love of animals, and the knowledge in the Library of the Guardians was all the doing of Sincha. She had a glorious vision, you see, of a peaceful land where tselqs could live fruitfully without the violence we faced in our old land. From it, she prescribed a way of life that would sanctify that peace. We have lived such ever since."

Alanda was in awe that the doings of one person, even a shaman, could have such a lasting effect on an entire race. She thought most of the doings of most of the peoples in Ilbeor were not significant in a larger sense, but only to the lives surrounding them. It was amazing to her that one vision from one shaman had wrought such change, such a desire for tranquil lives, and all the strictures that went along with those lives.

The subject changed as they continued to tread the mountain paths, often having to take special care when the slope became steep. In these instances, Alis proved the most adept, placing her paws carefully but never seeming bothered by the angle of their descent. When they could talk, Rinayai pointed out various trees and flora, giving her the tselq name for them and telling her of any healing properties they might have. Alanda was familiar with some of the herbs he pointed out, their new growth just beginning to show on the forest floor, but his knowledge was vast and deep, and she learned much from him.

THEIR ROUTINE BECAME familiar and comforting as the weather warmed as they descended the mountain. Alanda often saw small game on the trails, thin from winter. Though she longed for meat after their long stay in Dachilon, she didn't hunt, but contented herself with the ample provisions in Rinayai's enormous pack in addition to edible plants and berries found along the way. Alanda knew she could enjoy meat when they reached Kilynelle, and after seeing Rinayai's reaction to the fur and leather given to her for the crossing, she was loath to offend him by hunting for her food.

They stopped one night about halfway to Kilynelle, and as Rinayai started the fire with magic as he usually did, Alanda asked him to show her how.

"The word is *incenta*," he told her, and the small fire flared a bit in recognition of the spell. "However, saying it is not enough. You must have the spark of magic within you."

Alanda concentrated hard on the fire as though she were trying to force her will upon it as she said the word. As Rinayai had predicted, nothing happened, and she sighed. "Magic is beyond me, I'm afraid," she said wistfully. "Though I wish it wasn't. It seems so easy to do things like start fires when all you have to do is say a word. I might work over kindling with my flint and steel for ten minutes before I start a blaze, and you can do it in a second."

"Do not deplore your need for flint and steel," Rinayai said soothingly. "You accomplish the same thing with it as I do by invoking magic, and just as I carry the ability inside me, you carry the ability within your pack and intellect. I can accomplish nothing by magic that you cannot do yourself, using your experience and the inventions of the ages."

Alanda nodded, though in her heart of hearts she still wished she had that spark of magic. Regardless of her heritage, she was nothing but a normal traveler, and she wished she had something that set her apart, as Rinayai and the other magicians did.

Rinayai set to work over the fire and his cook pot, filling it with water and adding preserved vegetables, potatoes, and herbs he had found. Alanda marveled at how the stores in his pack seemed never-ending and wondered, not for the first time, how tselqs traveled long distances without hunting. In her own pack, she could only carry a week's worth of provisions, and even then, she had to put herself on a strict ration if she had not been able to hunt. Rinayai's pack was easily twice the size of hers, and much of the space seemed to be taken by the apparently endless array of preserved fruits, vegetables, and hardtack.

The resulting soup was delicious and filling, but Alanda again found herself thinking it would have been much improved by rabbit or even flying squirrel, not to mention venison. She kept her thoughts to herself, however, and enjoyed dipping her hardtack into the flavorful broth and drinking cool, clear water from the small forest spring near their campsite.

After they had cleaned up dinner, Alanda combed Alis and then sat near the warm fire to begin a new wooden figurine.

Rinayai smiled. "I enjoy watching you at your hobby," he told her. "You seem so peaceful and content, and the carved dragon you showed me in Dachilon was done with a skill I would not have thought possible from a human with only a knife and wood. You have a talent for this."

"Thank you," Alanda said, beginning to shave the bark off a piece of wood she had taken from the trail that day. It seemed strong and hardy, and she was ready to work on a new project, though she was not sure what yet.

As Alanda considered the wood in her hands, Rinayai got out his small metal teapot to make the tea he insisted they both drink each night. A nightly tea was a tradition he had begun as a young shaman, and it was his opinion that it was good for the health of any living being, though he could not get Alis to drink the slightly bitter, unsweetened brew. As he cast his various herbs into the boiling water, Alanda began to carve.

"What are you working on?" he asked her as the tea steeped in their tin cups.

"A flower," she said contemplatively. "A bloom like one my mother had in her field. Foxglove. It had the most beautiful purple blooms that drooped like little bells, and the scent was one of my favorites. I've never tried to capture it in wood before, so we'll see where this takes me."

Rinayai watched her hands as she deftly removed the portion of wood she was going to use and carved in a long, curving stroke. He did not have the talent of visualizing what might come of the medium, but he liked to think she was creating the general shape of the flower and its stem. The wood seemed to come alive under her strokes, forming a smooth curve that somehow suggested movement.

Rinayai maintained a respectful silence as he pulled a small book from his pack. Copied by one of the Guardians during their stay in Dachilon, the book spoke of human politics and history. Since he was going to travel with Alanda, he should know more about her people and their priorities. Though their course was set for Blackwell, his vision in Chinnua had suggested she would never return there, and he thought it best to be prepared to be embroiled in the human dynasty and politics of Emelle.

Rinayai read and Alanda carved until the sunlight was gone and all that was left was the flickering of their fire.

As usual, Alanda heard the elves of Kilynelle before she saw them. She turned to Rinayai, grinning. "I always thought they sounded like Deena's aviary," she said. "But I can understand some of it now." She took off her gloves, exposing Moonshield to the light. Quickly applying sun salve to her hands and wrists, she stowed the gloves in her pack.

Alanda led the way to the familiar entrance to Kilynelle. She had her flute out and ready, and when they reached the edge of the settlement, she put it to her lips and played the Yrui greeting loudly enough that anyone nearby could hear it.

As the elves noticed their presence, their Yrui conversations slowed and then halted as they all looked at her, expressions of amazement on their faces. Alanda played a questioning note, but no one answered either in Yrui or the common tongue. Finally, after what seemed to be an age to Alanda and Rinayai, Julen and Dmeter approached her. They held hands, and both were obviously concerned.

"Julen, Dmeter," Alanda said, "I'd like you to meet - "

"We have not the time," Julen interrupted her, and Alanda was astonished at the lack of the elves' customary courtesy. "You should come with us, Alanda. Your friend is welcome if you do not mind him hearing what we have to say."

"I don't mind," Alanda answered, shooting a confused and worried look at Rinayai. "Julen, what's going on?"

"You will see," Julen said. "By some miracle of circumstance, you have arrived on the same day as the messenger from Blackwell."

"A messenger from Blackwell?" Alanda became alarmed. "What message did they carry? Is Kitz all right? Maryah, Serill, Isaac?"

"Come," Dmeter said, not offering any further explanation as he and Julen turned, fingers still intertwined, to walk toward the huts bordering the settlement's circle.

Alanda and Rinayai followed, Alanda nearly frantic with worry. Rinayai could do nothing to stem her concern, for he knew if a messenger had come from Blackwell, the news was not likely to be good.

More elves joined Julen and Dmeter as they walked. Alanda recognized Myrine and Garratt, but most of the others were only hazy memories to her as members of the group of elders who had presented her with her ring and argued with her over her crossing of Anneau's Field.

She hurried to Myrine, hoping her friend would be less mysterious than Julen and Dmeter had been about the message and its contents. "Myrine, what - " Alanda began.

"It's your brother, Alanda. Kitz. He's been taken."

JOURNEY

*M*yrine ushered Alanda and Rinayai into the small roundhouse she shared with her parents. Julen, Dmeter, and as many of the elders as could fit inside joined them as Alanda was offered a seat at the table.

"Taken?" Alanda said sharply, shrugging off her pack and placing it haphazardly next to the door. "When, and by whom? Who sent the message?"

"Your friend Maryah sent the message, just as you told me she had promised to do at the beginning of your journey. The messenger would have taken several days to get here from Blackwell, even on horseback, and I would imagine she sent the message the very moment she could."

"Who took him?" Alanda's voice held the sharp, commanding note she had used in Dachilon upon finding out her birth status.

Myrine looked at Garratt and then at the rest of the elders before she answered. "Maryah did not know. She simply stated that a group of men, elves, tselqs, and dwarves broke into their home in the night and took Kitz. Both she and her husband attempted to protect your brother, but both were sorely injured and unsuccessful. The boy Isaac was unhurt."

Alanda would have been concerned about Maryah and Serill's injuries at any other time but given that Maryah had been well enough to send the message, in the present she only had ears for news of Kitz. "Men, tselqs, elves, and dwarves? How would a group of so many races collaborate to kidnap my brother, and why? Is it usual for prophets to be in such danger?"

"As to the why, we assume it was because news spread of your brother's transformation and status," Garratt said slowly. "News of these matters seems to spread with alarming quickness, and many powers within the land would crave having a prophet under their control."

"I do not believe that is the reason," Rinayai broke in. He looked at Alanda, a question in his eyes. She nodded, and he explained what they had found out in Dachilon. "The news of Alanda and Kitz's heritage must have spread past the boundaries of the Library of the Guardians," he concluded, "though I do not know who would have taken word outside the city. No one in the room with us when we found out was a traveler, and I do not believe they would have found it prudent to share the news with any messengers that came through, as few as they are. Still, however, the timing of this attack leads me to believe word has reached unfriendly ears about the present state of matters."

"Then we know the who, as well," Julen said. "We already suspected as much, but this news confirms why he would have done what he did."

Alanda slapped her hand on the table. "Who, then, by Annuah? And how do we get him back?"

Garratt spoke up again. "Altoneir," he said simply. No one else broke in to explain.

Alanda was confused as well as frustrated by the lack of information. She knew who Altoneir was, of course - everyone knew the rebel elf's name, though few knew his origins or true purposes. What she couldn't understand was why he would want her brother.

Rinayai put a hand on Alanda's shoulder, knowing her desperation for actionable information. "Altoneir is one of your kind." He stated the fact as though it were obvious, but the question in his words was still obvious to everyone in the room.

"Yes," answered one of the elders Alanda wasn't familiar with, "but he's been in exile for over three centuries. Self-imposed exile, I might add. His purpose is simple: to remove humans from the seats of power in Ilbeor and install elves, himself in particular, in their place."

"Why?" Rinayai asked. It seemed to him that, prophet or not, one boy would hold little interest to an exiled elf. Try as he might, he also couldn't see why Kitz's blood status would make him valuable to someone whose primary goal was to see humans off the throne in Emelle.

"Altoneir is one of the oldest of our race," Myrine said. "Some believe he was here for the first crossing more than three millennia ago, a claim which has never been substantiated. That he is ancient is certain, even compared to the elves of my clan. Most of those who remain from the crossing live in the city of Caalenor. He was partnered with an elf name Aenwyn for well over a millennium, but she died in an avalanche that devastated the mountain settlement where he lived, along with his parents and many of his friends. He blamed humans for this tragedy."

"Why did he blame us?" Alanda asked, beginning to feel more composed now that information was forthcoming.

"When humans came to this land, near fifteen hundred years ago now, they made treaties with the elves that claimed the valley for human habitation. At the time, most elves lived in the mountains already, and Caalenor had long since been established in the Chilpar Mountains, but some settlements still existed in the valley," Dmeter told her. "Altoneir's original settlement was one of those. By his reasoning, the humans' greed for the fertile land of the valley was the reason his partner and other loved ones were on the mountain when the avalanche came."

"I still do not understand how he intends to gain power over the land by replacing the human royalty with elves. Each race rules itself, and surely, control over a race he hates would bring nothing but sorrow to Ilbeor."

"Altoneir feels as though humans have the true rule of Ilbeor since, in his view, they forced the other races to move out of the Claresea Valley, and they take it upon themselves to treat with the ruling members of other races as though the whole of Ilbeor belongs to them."

"The tselqs rule by council," Alanda said, repeating something she had learned from Rinayai on the journey.

"Yes, that is true, and we elves have no real central leadership," Myrine responded. "The dwarves and Twanai likewise rule themselves in their own ways, but Altoneir still feels humans have too much authority."

"But what does this have to do with *Kitz*?" Alanda asked in frustration.

"You're forgetting your status," Garratt explained. "It is said Altoneir has spies throughout the land. It is probable that news of your status came from inside Dachilon's very boundaries. As a blood-heir to the Sovaria dynasty, Kitz would be a powerful bargaining chip. It is to that purpose, I suspect, that Altoneir expects to use your brother. No other explanation makes sense."

Rinayai felt Alanda sag under his hand as the full implications hit her. She was silent for a few moments while she processed the information. "So, we get him back," she said finally. "We confront this Altoneir, and we get my brother back, then we hide him away in one of the elven settlements with Isaac and his parents."

"It is not that easy," Julen told her gently. "Altoneir resides on Sundersar Island in the Unresting Sea. Even if we could amass a force strong enough to contend with Altoneir's army and his magic, which is greater than that of almost any living elf, we could not reach the place where Kitz will be held."

Alanda sagged yet more. "Then tell me what to do," she said dully, all the fight seeming to have gone out of her as she desperately reached for anything that might save her brother. "I'll do anything, anything in this world, to get him back."

Rinayai spoke before anyone else could. "Even claim your place as a princess of Ilbeor?"

THE NIGHT of Alanda's arrival in Kilynelle, she and Rinayai took places in the nightly circle after being entreated to do so by Dmeter, though neither of them really wanted anything more than to rest in the comfortable guest houses. No one had told Alanda of the jarring, foretelling music preceding her arrival, but Dmeter felt it was important for her and her companion to hear Julen's song that evening. Alanda sat impatiently while Garratt, on behalf of the elven council, formally welcomed them to Kilynelle, and Julen completed his usual routine of greeting the elves before he began his song. Given the news about Kitz, sitting still did not suit her.

When Julen reached her, he bent and took both her small, pale hands into his larger, olive-toned ones. "Elf-friend Alanda," he said gently. "You have endured much toil since we last met, and tonight's song was composed to set your mind at ease. I rarely know the meaning of that which I express in song, but I know that."

After speaking to her in the common tongue, he kept hold of her hands and whistled in a low, soothing tone. Alanda felt her muscles relax and her mind clear as he did so, and she knew he was employing his particular brand of magic. She did not appreciate the intrusion on her thoughts; she wanted to be ready for action. But she was powerless against Julen's spell, and by the time he had left her and moved on to speak to Rinayai, she was no longer restless.

She heard Julen thank Rinayai for her own life and the aid and companionship he was providing before he moved into the center of the circle, declining any more small talk. Alanda noticed the elves around her seemed tense as he began to sing, and she wondered why, but soon her thoughts ceased altogether as she was drawn into Julen's song.

None of the other circles she had attended had contained a song as warm and tranquil as the one Julen now sang; Alanda felt almost as she had the first time she had relaxed into one of the tselqs' hot baths in Dachilon. Though he used no words, Julen's simple monosyllabic intonation spoke to her of peace and gave her hope for the future of her family. The highs and lows that had thrilled her and set her heart both racing and melancholic on her first night in the elves' circle were not present; the whole song was one of calm and aspiration. Though the intonations were flawless, the song seemed designed not to imbue the beauty and expectation, love and loss that she had heard in previous songs.

Alanda's travel weariness ebbed away as the music continued, and after the song was over, she felt as calm as she had ever felt, certain her path was the right one, and hopeful the future would bring about her reunion with Kitz and a happy life for them both. Somewhere in her mind, she knew her hardships were far from over, but as Dmeter and Julen led them to the roundhouse she had stayed in on her previous visit and one next to it for Rinayai, the hardships of her path were far from her mind.

THE ELVES of Kilynelle required a full week to prepare Alanda and Rinayai for their long journey across the mountains and valleys of Ilbeor to the Royal Mountain, which lay in the far northwest. They had to gather and preserve as much food as possible, assemble fresh clothing for travel into the summer, and Myrine had to make enough sun salve to keep Alanda healthy.

"For," she told Alanda seriously when Alanda protested the time it would take to prepare, "if you burn in the long journey across the valley, you will die without aid, and none but the elves and your healer are familiar with the concoction you need or how to heal you if you fall ill."

Dmeter and two of his friends constructed larger packs for both Alanda and Rinayai in the elven fashion, using thin wooden poles for the frames and a waterproof linen for the holding areas. In them were placed food, personal effects, and new traveling clothes . Myrine, knowing how much Alanda liked the elven water-cloth, even included a new cloak of brilliant purple to show her royal status. Fresh blankets were traded for ragged, dirty ones, and Rinayai's wind shield was included to guard against spring and summer storms, but his ice blanket and the furs Alanda had worn across the glacier were left behind.

During the intervening time, both Rinayai and Alanda were tutored in human politics, the houses of the nobility, and seemingly trivial matters such as mealtime deportment and court manners by the blonde elf who had originally warned Alanda against crossing Anneau's Field. Her name was Trislee, and she had studied human ways and politics for almost the entirety of their habitation in Ilbeor. She was, Alanda thought, more knowledgeable than some of the nobles themselves were bound to be, and Alanda was overwhelmed with the amount of information she was being given. She knew she wouldn't remember it all.

"Remember, when you are brought to the royal court, effect a deep curtsy as you enter the room, and curtsy all the way to the ground when you are presented to King Florian and Queen Sokorri. Do not rise until bidden to do so and take care your skirts are arranged in a way that protects your modesty. Here, let us practice your movements."

"I will not have skirts," Alanda had objected, thinking of the traveling leathers and the lighter linen ensemble she would likely wear when the summer grew hot. "How am I to modestly lower myself to the floor in traveling clothes?"

"You will not wear your traveling clothes when you are presented to the king," Trislee answered gravely. "Due to the necessity of conserving space in your packs, we cannot provide you with appropriate clothing for court, but we will provide you with the coin to purchase or have made an appropriate dress. Alanda, you must not even consider meeting the king and queen in your traveling clothes. You must promise me this."

"She will not," Rinayai answered. "Alanda would never jeopardize her brother's situation by appearing anything less than a princess when she is brought to her uncle, the king."

Alanda agreed reluctantly. It seemed to her that matters of dress were unimportant given her business with the royal family, but from what Trislee was telling her, form and manners were of utmost importance to the nobility. As much as she felt her business overshadowed such customs, she also knew she would have to act the part of nobility to be taken seriously by the royal family.

Trislee went on to gently instruct her in the art of the proper human curtsy. Alanda, clumsy at first, soon mastered the movements required and curtsied to Trislee's satisfaction. After that, Trislee taught Rinayai the proper bow for the royal court, a flourishing thing Alanda thought looked ridiculous.

The days passed more quickly than Alanda had thought they would. Each night, she and Rinayai sat in the elven circle and listened to what news there was before letting Julen's soothing songs relax them into readiness for bed.

Alis woke Alanda at *uht* on the day their travels were to begin, and Alanda sprang from her bed, ready to move. She met Rinayai, Myrine, Garrett, and Julen outside the healer's hut in the pre-dawn light, still tying her braid with the thong her mother had given her. She looked much like she had the second time she had visited Kilynelle in her black leathers, her hair braided, and her black cloak fastened on, the hood ready for the sun.

Wordlessly, Julen assisted Alanda in hefting her larger pack onto her back. When it had been secured and balanced, he came around and took both her hands. "Safe travels, elf-friend," he said softly, then whistled a tune in Yrui Alanda didn't know the meaning of.

"He is wishing you farewell," Garratt told her. "I, too, wish you farewell, Alanda."

"I will see you sooner than you may think," Julen whispered to her in the common tongue, words only for her to hear. She looked at him, startled, but he would say no more.

Myrine gave her a hug, the gesture encompassing the genuine feeling of friendship that had arisen between the two women, elf and human. "Safe journeys. Remember to stop at a human village as soon as you can after reaching the valley and buy horses. We would give you some of our own, but our horse master..." She trailed off, referring to her mother, who detested humans and, to a lesser degree, those of any race that was not elven.

"I understand," Alanda said.

"There is coin enough in your pack to cover your needs," Garratt said.

Alanda would have usually protested; she preferred to be self-sufficient rather than indebted to those around her. In this case, however, she did not have time to work for the money she needed.

Rinayai surveyed Alanda critically. Her large pack seemed to dwarf her, but she carried it well. Both boots were firmly laced and knotted, and she was covered from neck to toe in leather. He knew she had sun salve on her face and neck; he could smell it. "Are you ready?" he asked, an oddly formal note to his gravelly voice.

Alanda squared her shoulders and turned her back on the hut and the elves who had come to send her off. "Yes," she answered simply.

Together, they strode to the edge of the settlement, and Alanda turned to wave goodbye. She could not be certain when she would see any of them, though Julen's final words stuck with her.

As one, the four elves waved back at her, and Alanda set her face toward the familiar trail. She led the way out of Kilynelle, Alis on her left and Rinayai just behind her on her right. She felt ready to face her future in order to get her brother back, ready to take her place as a member of the royal family, and ready for the long journey. As she trod the familiar path down the mountain, she set her sights on the royal city of Emelle.

I'm coming, Kitz, she thought. *No one is going to stop me from finding you and making you safe.*

FROM THE PROPHECY OF BEIANARIAN AND THE MAGUS

Foreign paths she has trod far from her home
A path winding through the annals of time
Seeking reunion with those left behind
Striving for a life she will never know
Walking close by the divine, ne'er knowing
The truths of those fated to walk with her.
Brushing the canvas of fate she knows not
Resisting the pull of destiny's hand.

The path thus far trod, he yet seeks anew
The marriage of old fate and new duty
Life once filled with the trills of tradition
Summoned to wanderings without a breath
Rife with danger and chanced meetings unknown.
A babe brings to him new knowledge of pain
Turning his course to more passionate ends
Thwarting divine decree to seek changed ways.

Paths diverged, the woman and the magus
Forth from their intertwined dooms, denied love

Forbidden the other, to steal sorrow
Guided by dark lies to bright clarity.

from The Prophecy of Beianarian and the Magus
set forth by Algernon of House Agelon
Second Age, 246

In Memoriam

Charles Thomas Smith, Jr.
February 24, 1959 – March 15, 2014

ACKNOWLEDGMENTS

My eternal gratitude goes to so many people who worked with me, encouraged me, helped me, and tolerated my various writing moods through not only this work, but through the journey that began for me about twenty years ago in a little wooden house in Sherman, Texas as I began to truly learn the art of storytelling.

My first acknowledgment can never be given to anyone other than my beloved partner, Jeffrey Klapprodt. From the moment he came into my life nearly ten years ago, he has not only supported my writing, but encouraged me and pushed me to always be better, always keep learning. From the onset of *Messengers of Ilbeor*, he has been my reader, my critic, my support...from the wiping of tears and the sharing of laughter, the tolerance for late nights and the patience for both writer's mania and writer's block, the compliments that boosted my confidence and the questions that helped me grow, Jeffrey has been my rock and my safe space. Thank you with all of my heart, my love.

To my children, Patrick and Cynthia Dupew, I owe the inspiration for some of my favorite characters, the sharing of the passion for storytelling and art across medium and genre, and the space and love they have always given me to pursue this dream. You two are my heart and soul, and my life was made whole by the very existence of yours.

To my editor, mentor, and best friend Alan Rogers, all I can say is thank you for so many things, but mostly for being there from the very beginning. For always demanding excellence from me, for always pushing me to my creative limits and then right past them, for editing my work with a keen eye and a wickedly sharp pen, for teaching me how to build rich worlds and complex characters, and for all the late-night conversations…thank you from the bottom of my heart. Here's to another two decades (and beyond) of friendship, work, and creative communion.

To my team of early readers, Cynthia Mendoza, Crystal Darks, Windy Desmond, and Kā Riley, thank you for your steadfast encouragement, the consistent catching of plot holes and other story snafus, and for always reminding me that you are looking forward to the next chapter of the story. This book could not have been written without the four of you, and I sure hope you're all ready to take up the mantle again as I write the second installment of the series!

A special thanks goes to the Penguins, those powerhouse writers who surround one another with laughter, encouragement, advice, and writing memes. I am privileged to call myself one of you. And to Moms Who Write, who understand the challenges and joys of motherhood and writing in a way that no one else can quite comprehend. The women and men in these two amazing communities are my tribe, my people, and I cannot fathom what the work would be like without that shared sense of purpose and love for our craft.

No writing journey starts with a complete novel, and no art is created in a vacuum. With that in mind, I would like to acknowledge not only the people above who made all the difference in the creation of the Ilbeor universe, but the people who have been there for the whole journey and given me the tools, time, and space I needed to become a writer in the first place.

To my dad, Gary Jost, who once said something to me in a Bookstop when I was a child that I never forgot and have passed on to my own children. He said to me, "I will always buy you books." And true to his word, almost every weekend I was with him, he took me to that bookstore and not only allowed me to pick what I wanted but encouraged me to push my limits in reading level and genre. I truly believe that gift, that tiny freedom, fostered a love for story and literature that lasted the rest of my life. Thank you, Dad, for teaching me from childhood to love and value the written word.

To my mom, Cynthia Mendoza, who bought me a gift that led to my first explorations of storytelling and the first realization that yes, I wanted to be an author: my first electric typewriter, as much paper as I could ever want or need, and sheets of carbon copy paper. I may be dating myself here, but that first gift of my writing career made me feel that writing was a valuable occupation that deserved my time and attention. I wrote my first attempt at a novel on that typewriter the summer after my freshman year in high school, spending my days off from school typing away on the floor in my mother's bedroom, spinning my first long story. Thank you, Mom, for teaching me that talents and arts deserve to be pursued with vigor and dedication, and for being my first and most steadfast supporter.

To my first partner and the father of my children, Clint Dupew, thank you for your steadfast support and encouragement as I began my adult foray into storytelling and writing. Thank you for placing importance on it, for being interested in my first story attempts, and for supporting me in so many ways as I strived to learn the craft.

And finally, to the group of people in my very first online writing group: the mighty and memorable WizardTales: it was with and in this group that my first real understanding of longform storytelling clicked into place. There were so many people in this group that shaped and encouraged me as a writer, but a few in particular who bear individual thanks. First, to the late Charles Smith, the first person not only to encourage my writing but to push me harder than I thought I wanted to be pushed to improve. His unwavering demand for excellence alongside his steadfast friendship and advice taught me more than any creative writing class ever did. To Hamza Rahim, my dear friend from the other side of the world, who has always and still is always up for good conversation and shared passion for storytelling. To Jayadev Calamur, Alan Rogers, Crystal and Matthew Darks, Sunil Koujalgi, Krystol and Jon Grayson, James Smith, Chuck "Jag" Smith, April Ceres, Locke Gaskill, and so many others: thank you for being part of my life. I wouldn't be the person or the writer I am today without each and every one of you.

For all the people, named and unnamed, who made this possible, I

will never, ever forget you, and I hope our friendships and partnerships continue to withstand the test of time.

ABOUT THE AUTHOR

T.J. Klapprodt lives and works in the vibrant city of Fort Worth, Texas, alongside her partner Jeffrey, her children Patrick and Cynthia, and her critters Finnick, Sophie, and Margie. A woman of many passions, T.J. is a dedicated teacher of newcomer emergent bilingual students, loves all things related to books and literature, and enjoys every iteration of Super Mario Brothers Nintendo has to offer.

When she is not building new fictional worlds, teaching, reading, or indulging in video games, you can find T.J. enjoying her favorite movies (usually old ones she has seen countless times), cuddling with her critters, or playing taxi driver for her children and their friends. Her family is her entire world, and she relishes nothing more than spending time at home with the ones she loves most.

T.J. graduated from Texas A&M University in 2001 with a Bachelor of Science in Psychology and from University of Texas at Arlington in 2012 with a Master of Arts in English Literature. She considers herself a lifelong learner, especially when it comes to the art of story-telling, and is always seeking to improve in her personal life, her career, and her writing.

T.J.'s greatest hope and lifelong dream is to share stories with the world, sending readers on literary adventures to ignite their imaginations, fuel their passions, and satisfy their human need for exploration, love, connection, and loss. She hopes you'll join her for this first of many forays into the world of Ilbeor!

ALSO BY T.J. KLAPPRODT

Continue the adventure in December 2024 with *Court of the Seven Dances*, the second installment of the *Legends of Ilbeor* saga

Explore the origins of a villain in June 2024 with *From the Sundering Snows*, an ancillary volume of the *Legends of Ilbeor* saga

To delve further into the world of Ilbeor, visit the author's website at www. tjklapprodt.com

Email the author at tj@tjklapprodt.com

For unique insights and literary perks, join the author's monthly newsletter, *News from Ilbeor*